I0671579

Veil of Destiny

A novel of the Seven Deadly Veils, Book Five

Diana Marik

Veil of Shadows
The Blue Veil, a novella
Veil of Mists
Veil of Darkness
Veil of Secrets
Veil of Destiny

Coming Soon:

Veil of Orion
Veil of Honor

Veil of Destiny ~ Seven Deadly Veils, Book Five
Copyright © 2019, Diana Marika Preston
Cover Art by Kris Norris

Published by Diana Marik
Released March 2019

This is a work of fiction. All characters, places and events are from the author's imagination and should not be confused with fact. Any resemblance to persons, living or dead, events or places is purely coincidental.

All rights reserved. No part of this publication may be reproduced in any material form, whether by printing, photocopying, scanning or otherwise without the written permission of the author.

Praise for Diana Marik's Veilverse

Veil of Secrets

"The characters are well-developed and fascinating. The series plot is growing and expanding; the action, suspense and romance are woven perfectly together!"
—LM Reigel Reviews

"Ms. Marik has created an interesting, intricate vampire world. All paranormal fans need to read this series filled with strong, sophisticated, fun, sexy characters."
—Amazon Reviewer

"A fantastic installment in this intriguing series. Superb! A delicious plot! Once again all her richly developed characters pop in the spotlight teasing with juicy clues behind the veil. When it's pulled back be prepared for some shocking revelations."
—Goodreads Reviewer

Veil of Darkness

"The chemistry between Miranda and Remare is extraordinary. Marik holds nothing back in this action-packed romance, which delivers all of the danger, darkness and sensuality that readers crave; this is one series not to be missed." TOP PICK!
—RT Book Reviews

"Smoking hot chemistry! A wonderful suspense and action novel complete with a sizzling romance. Very addicting!"
—L.M. Reigel Reviews

"Another fantastic read in this series. An amazing journey. The characters come to life on the pages pulling you into their world."
—PNR/UF Book Lover's Haven

Veil of Mists

"I am obsessed with this series. Diana Marik has created a high intensity series that grabs you and doesn't let go."
—Lisa Reigel Reviews

"Danger and deception know no bounds in this riveting second installment of the *Seven Deadly Veils* series. Complex liaisons deliver the action and suspense paranormal fans crave. The passion and sensuality exceed expectations."
—RT Book Reviews

"Completely captivating! I LOVE this series and can't get enough of RRRemare. So much happening in this book...deception at its finest! Just when you think you have it figured out, everything changes. Definitely couldn't put this book down and one hell of a ride."
—Paranormal/Urban Fantasy Book Lovers Haven

The Blue Veil

"Marik's compelling delivery commands readers' attention; the easy, seamless passion and intensity between characters is a welcome companion to a perfect balance of action and suspense."
—RT Book Reviews

"The characters are edgy and intriguing. The plot is suspenseful and sexy. I'm drawn into this series and fascinated by this world that Ms. Marik has created."
—Comfy Chair Books

"I am so Team Remare. This novella just keeps us hooked."
—Sik Reviews

"Just one word...Remare. Love that dark and dangerous vampire."
—Paranormal/Urban Fantasy Book Lover's Haven

Veil of Shadows

"The suspense is as dramatic and intense as the action, and paired with Marik's steamy sex scenes, will leave readers satisfied on many levels. Off-the-chart chemistry."
4 STARS HOT—RT Book Reviews

"I flipping LOVED this book. I was drawn immediately to the main characters of *Veil of Shadows*. The characters are edgy, sexy, and intriguing. Her writing style drew me in and kept me fascinated; the suspense kept me on the edge waiting to see what would happen next. *Veil of Shadows* is fast paced and action packed. I highly recommend this book to fans of paranormal romance and romantic urban fantasy."

—Comfy Chair Books

"Ms. Marik has made this new paranormal world come alive and leave me begging for more."

—Sik Reviews

"I absolutely LOVED it! With so many awesome characters, can't decide who I love the most! Refreshing story that completely captivated me. I simply couldn't put it down until the last page." —PNR/UF Book Lover's Haven

Dedication

For Ellie, Always Remember!

Acknowledgments

As always, I'm incredibly thankful to my readers who've sent me wonderful words of encouragement and affection. And to my fans in the Marik's Mortals Fan Club—you guys humble me and make me smile. Special acknowledgment to my editor, Jessica Bimberg—Lady Awesome, who continually inspires me to excel in creating memorable characters and stories that captivate and delight. And to my cover artist, Kris Norris for the wonderful book covers she designs for me. You guys rock!

Chapter One

"You don't look happy."

"I'm not," snapped Guy de Montglat. "I did not think Miranda's infatuation with Remare would last, let alone have her married to him." He shook his head, as if contemplating the alternatives. "She'd have been better off married to Valadon."

William "Ryder" Montglat didn't understand his father's perturbation as they traversed the catacombs in Sardinia on their way to question one of their prisoners. Both were deeply relieved that Felicity was nearly fully recovered from her attack, so Ryder thought there was little left for Guy's agitation. "Does it really matter who she marries? She seems happy."

"Of course, it matters. Valadon is a purebred, a full Blueblood. His blood is very powerful. Remare is only half-Blueblood. Miranda's blood won't be as strong as it could have been." His father gave him the once over. "I almost could fathom you as her husband if it weren't for your caprices."

Ryder laughed. *Not that I have that many.* "You're so sure Remare will turn her?"

"Wouldn't you?" Guy slanted him a look. "Of course, she'll be turned. Valadon and Remare know what she is, how valuable she will become to their house. It's just a matter of time. I'd hoped Valadon would have turned her before Savinien woke from his sleep. We'll need her when that happens. For now, I fear the Vampire Nation will suffer greatly if Caltrone is elected chancellor."

Try as he might, Ryder didn't have his father's interest in vampire politics. "Do you really think that, or is your animosity of Caltrone clouding your views?"

Guy stopped and narrowed his eyes. "You know damned well what he had done to Savinien, and you can ask me that?"

They continued walking to the dungeons. "I don't understand why you don't just run against him. You'd make a great chancellor."

"That day may yet come, but not now. In any case, I want you in London. Miranda is there now, and I need you to keep an eye on her. Her fool of a husband didn't accompany her. I don't know what he was thinking."

"London. Fine. I'll go. For how long?" Ryder asked.

"For as long as she's there. I should think a few days. Leave as soon as we're done here." Guy faced him. "And, this time, keep your distance."

Ryder smirked at his father's unspoken words. The last time Guy had assigned him to guard Miranda was in New Mexico while she was exploring petroglyphs; he hadn't known of their shared ancestry, and he'd discovered depths of her abilities even she was unaware of. Those memories were some of his most pleasant ones. "I wasn't planning on introducing myself. I'll stay to the shadows. I work best there, anyway."

"Good. Now, let's see what other information our prisoner has to share today."

Mind reaping was a talent the truly old ones possessed, and his father was a skilled navigator at mining what he needed with little to no injury to the person involved. Though, in this captive's case, whatever agonizing pain or damage Guy caused was welcomed. For what their prisoner had done, Ryder wanted to strangle him with his bare hands.

When they reached the cell with the reinforced walls and thick polyethylene front, his father's voice was deceptively pleasant. "Good morning, Brandon. I trust you slept well."

***

"It's a forgery, all right. Man, Jordan is going to be pissed. He sent me here to London because he had his heart set on this Vermeer."

"How can you tell? You've been staring at it for hours." Orion, who'd been busy texting, peered up from his phone.

"It hasn't been hours. Has it?" Miranda Crescent, art history professor and authenticator for the New York museum, glanced at her watch and was surprised to see how much time had passed. "You've seen me do authentications before."

"Yeah, but I never really understood everything you were saying." He ran a hand through his shorn locks, as if forgetting he'd had it cut. A burgeoning rock star, he didn't want to be recognized by any of his fans so he'd changed his appearance as much as he could.

Miranda smiled at Orion—her friend, sometime roommate, ex-fiancé, and current bodyguard, courtesy of her new and over-protective husband, Remare. "Sometimes, it's just instinct," she murmured. "But you can't put that in a report. I had a feeling something was off."

She had meticulously sharp eyes, often spotting tiny details others missed, but would not sign off on an authentication until she had the analytical results generated by her computer scan. "The human eye can detect only a limited amount of variation in color; a computer program can pick up almost ten times that." She stood back and scrutinized the painting. "In the last decade, forgers have gotten so damned good. But they're human, and sometimes, they make mistakes. However miniscule."

"What'd you catch?"

Miranda recalled her notes. "It passed the alcohol swab. The tacking and the stretchers are legit for Vermeer's time period. But forgers use a solution to wipe down a painting of lesser value of similar age, so when they paint the new version, it appears genuine for that particular era. Then, they start from scratch using the type of paints the artists were known for. Some of the compounds are no longer extant. Also, if I detect any of the polymers used in modern acrylics, I know it's a fake."

"Is that what you caught?"

"Not quite. This guy's too good." *You're so bright, my friend. But so am I.*

"It looks okay to me. It has all those cracks the old paintings have."

"The craquelure. Forgers use special ovens to heat the painting. Speeds up the aging process, makes those fine lines. In the natural process, you get fluctuations where the artist used thicker amounts of paint. Artists aren't machines. Not each and every brush stroke is the exact same thickness so the craquelure will have its variations. Not so much here."

"What else?"

She exhaled. "The odor. It has the musty scent of age, but also...you should be able to detect it, you're a Were."

"Well, I didn't think you brought me along for my good looks." Orion took a deep breath of the painting. "It does smell old, but something's off." He sniffed, again. "There's the remnants of mold, but I could swear there's a tiny trace of...bleach?"

"That's part of the solution forgers use. Thanks." She nodded. "Look here." She pointed her scanner at the painting. "See the subtle differentiation in the angle of a stroke."

"Damn. My eyes are pretty good, but I would never have spotted it unless you pointed that out."

"You have to know what to look for. Why do you think I spent hours on the plane going over Vermeer's history?"

"Remare's private jet was snazzy. I still can't believe you married him."

"At times, neither can I." She smiled. "But I did. I'm gonna call Jordan. Tell him the bad news. See how he wants me to qualify it."

"Just tell them it's a forgery."

"Ah, not quite. A certain amount of diplomacy is necessary. Museums don't like being informed they've got a forgery on their hands." No wonder they contacted Jordan when it was common knowledge he'd be away at his son's graduation from Yale. They knew he'd send her to authenticate. Miranda was two courses shy of a PhD; the administrators undoubtedly thought they could unload the forgery on the Americans. *Not so!* She'd studied under the world's best authenticators in Paris.

Basically, she knew her shit. Sooner or later, she'd go back for her doctorate degree, but not yet. Packing up her equipment, she asked, "Hey, you wanna stay a few days longer in London? Check out some sights?"

"Sure. If it's cool with Remare."

"It'll be okay." She wasn't quite certain how Remare was going to react, but it was only a few more days. He'd deal. She'd text him: *Miss you!*

She moved to the window to complete her call. "Hi, Jordan, it's me. Yeah, I've got some bad news." Cursing erupted on the other end of the phone. "Yes, I completed all the tests. This guy's good. Really good. Interpol is going to have a hard time catching him...or her." She paced in front of the window with the afternoon sun shining down on her. "How do you want me to word the document?"

More expletives on his end.

"Okay, okay. I'll state it as such, as *'undetermined'*. That should appease them." But, then again, maybe not. Anyone in the art world knew when a painting was stamped *'undetermined'*, it was a nice way of saying: *"We're pretty sure it's a forgery, but since we might be doing business with you in the future, we'll cover your ass, for now.*"

Miranda snorted. If the public knew just how many forgeries hung on the walls of the best museums in the world, attendance would drop dramatically. And, more importantly, so would sponsorship and patronage. Museums needed those funds to stay alive.

"Listen, Jordan. As long as there's no rush now to return to New York, I want to take a few more days off and do some research on a couple of artists. I saw a library specializing in old texts on the way to the museum I want to check out. Pretty please?"

"Well, since you're a newlywed, I can hardly refuse you, can I." Jordan's voice sang through. "I take it your husband will be joining you?"

Miranda hadn't exactly informed Remare of her plans. "I'd suspect so." She laughed. He was going to blow a gasket when she told him. Remare hadn't been keen on the idea of her going in the first place since they'd only been married less than a week.

"All right, then. I'll see you when you get back. Email me all your findings."

"Will do, boss. And thank you, again." Miranda exhaled as she ended her call. As far as bosses went, Jordan Knox was one of the best.

She strode to where Orion stood with his back to her. He'd just finished texting as she put her chin on his shoulder. "So, pal, you feel like doing some sightseeing while we're here, since we're in no rush to get back? See Buckingham Palace, Big Ben, Trafalgar Square and whatever else we want."

Turning his head toward her, he raised one brow. "Did you let Remare know you're gonna stay on longer?"

"I will." Since Orion hoped someday to become a full-time Torian, he wanted to impress Remare. "Did you tell Bas we'd be here a few days more?"

"He's still in Austria. I'm hoping when his mission's over he can join us here."

Orion's significant other was Bastien, an Elite Torian in Valadon's private guard. The leader of New York's vampires, Valadon was also Remare's boss and oldest friend. Together, the two powerful vampires ran ValCorp—Valadon's business empire. Bastien was one of the best when it came to covert ops, and whenever he went on assignment, Orion worried. She sympathized. Her anxiety meter rose significantly whenever Remare left on a mission.

"What say we grab one of those double-decker busses and do up this town?"

"Whatever my lady wishes."

***

Remare's leg was twitching. He never twitched, but having his wife across the pond in England vexed him. He knew it was a business trip; she'd be home in another day or two. They both had demanding jobs that required travel, but still, the feeling of unease nagged at him.

"Remare, you look like you're about to bust out of your skin," Valadon chided as they lounged in Valadon House's main living room.

"I have much on my mind."

"If you're that concerned, why don't you fly out and meet Miranda? Take a few days, enjoy the sights. Have a proper honeymoon. There's nothing crucial going on now that I can't spare my second a few days away."

"I just got back from being away for six months. I have no intention of leaving you, again. Even though it was *you* who assigned me the sojourn in Canada." Remare frowned at the punishment he'd received for dating Miranda behind the

High Lord's back. Something he should have been more forthcoming about in the first place. Hard call to make when he knew his oldest friend and liege had been enamored of her. In the end, it had all worked out, and Valadon had given Remare his blessing to wed.

Valadon chortled as he raised his drink to the vampire whose face was a younger version of his own sitting across from him. "For the next few weeks I'm going to enjoy the company of my son, Vincent. You should go to London."

"I volunteered to accompany her." Remare swept his hand through the empty air around him. "She doesn't want me there. Said I would be too much of a distraction." That only caused more laughter from the group of Torians around them. "She'll be back soon." When his foot started twitching, again, he immediately stilled it.

"I miss my better half, as well." Vincent offered, "I invited Olivia to join me here in New York; she said I should take the time to get to know my father, instead. Which I am doing. However, next weekend she'll be arriving."

Remare ground his molars. He didn't like coming under the scrutiny of others as he wallowed in silent misery. "I think you should spend time with your father." He was glad Vincent had fully recovered from his injuries—with Miranda's help. Her *Elemental* abilities had saved the life of the younger vampire. "And, since you two have much to talk about, I'm going to work out in the training room. If you'll excuse me."

In the locker room, Remare quickly changed into a pair of loose-fitting pants. He was glad none of the other Torians were present. Tonight, he wanted solitude. Once on the mats, he refined his sword-dancing technique. A skill he used to hone his reflexes and speed. He focused his concentration on turns and thrusts, going faster and faster with each set, but memories of practicing with Miranda surfaced, and he stilled as images of her smiling face haunted him. He could smell her scent of orange blossoms and remember the way she tasted. His hunger stirred to new heights.

Blocking her out took more determination than he thought it would, but he resumed his routine of movements, quickening his swiftness and extensions at an alarming pace, until he was coated in a fine layer of perspiration. He was an excellent warrior, but what made him truly exemplary was his speed, something he never neglected in his practices. Breathing heavily, he returned his sword to the wall mount and hung his head.

Still restless, he worked out with weights until his arms and legs ached and sweat ran down his limbs. The few Torians who entered the area must have sensed his mood and kept their distance. Not wanting conversation, he'd hit the pool for a few laps to unwind and call it a night.

As expected, the pool area was deserted. He discarded his sweat-soaked pants and dove in. The cool water was soothing as he glided across the pool's length.

He'd only completed a few laps when he heard the door opening. Katya.

She was still angry with him for sending her lover, Tristan, on a mission without her. He swam backwards a few strokes. She removed her clothes and joined him in the pool. Remare nearly hissed. He'd seen her nude body numerous times before. She and the other female Torian, Irina, had been his lovers for decades, but now he was married, and being naked in a pool with another female felt too much like disloyalty.

She swam toward him. "Have you heard any word from Tristan or Bastien?"

"Yes. Their mission is nearing completion, and he should be returning soon." He swam slowly away.

Katya kept pace with him. "You know I have several assets in Europe. I would have been a valuable resource on the mission."

It was rare any of the Elite Torians ever questioned his orders; if it had been anyone else, he would have chastised them. But he knew she was missing her lover. "We've been through this, Katya. I will try to assign you as many missions with Tristan as I can. However, you must understand there are going to be times when that is not possible."

She ducked her head under the water and sprang back up. "I know. I just feel so useless here. I lived in Europe for centuries, Tristan grew up in Montreal, and he doesn't know the region as well as I do."

"He's been prepped, and Bastien knows the area very well." He would have continued the conversation, but his phone started ringing.

Grabbing a towel as soon as he exited the pool, he quickly wrapped it around his hips. Miranda. "My darling, I've missed you. What time does your flight leave?"

"Hello, Remare. I've missed you, as well. Turns out the painting was a forgery. A very good forgery. Listen, as long as I'm here, I'm going to stay an extra few days and do some research. I discovered a library I want to check out."

"You're what?!" He pictured her cringing at his tone.

"Only for a few days more."

"That is not what we agreed on."

"I know. But, hey, your last business trip lasted six months. I'll be gone for less than a week."

Remare knew if he ground his molars any more, they might wind up as stumps. "You're still in the London area? And Orion is with you?" London was Lord Herbert's territory. Remare and the lord had been friends for centuries. There were few outside ValCorp that he trusted completely and without hesitation; Herbert was one of them. He exhaled. She was reasonably safe there.

But under no circumstances was she to travel to Northern England. Those lands belonged to Lord Acton, an unusually cruel and vicious vampire lord Remare detested. He didn't want to imagine what would befall Miranda if Acton ever got his hands on her. His body shuddered at the memory of his beatings, as if he still bore the scars of the sadistic lord's torture.

And Gideon, Acton's second. There was no other as cunning and lethal as his former adversary. The only one Remare considered a rival in swordsmanship. Gideon would follow Acton's many debauched plans without question to keep in favor with the ambitious lord, who, rumors suggested, wanted to challenge Caltrone for the title of chancellor.

"Yes and yes. Everything's fine. London is such a cool city, and I figured I'd show Orion a few of the sights as long as he's had to put up with me in the museum."

"That is his job. He's there to keep you safe."

"I already am, and I appreciate the concern, but don't you think you're overdoing it?"

"Not at all. You're my wife, and it's my responsibility to see to your safety."

"It's only a few days. Pfft. By the way, I love your home here. Much better than staying in a hotel. Bed's pretty comfy."

"No more nightmares?" He'd been worried. Miranda had woken screaming from the continued visions of a burning woman and the horrors she'd seen in her dreams.

"Nope, not a one. And thanks for the chauffeur and car. Way cool."

"You're very welcome."

"Remare, don't be angry. Be happy I'm able to do my research. It's important to me."

Her voice stirred something deep in his belly. "I know it is." He sighed. "It's just frustrating being away from you."

Katya leapt out of the pool, and he turned away as she wrapped a towel around herself.

"What's that sound? It sounded like splashing."

"Yes. I've been working out my frustrations in the training area and in the pool."

"Who's with you?"

He was tempted to say no one, but Miranda was incredibly intuitive, and he didn't like lying anyway. "Katya joined me a few moments ago. She's still upset with me because I sent Tristan on a mission without her."

"Tell her I say hi. And Remare? It's only a few days. I'll be home before you know it. And I'll make it up to you when I see you next."

He grinned, then growled deep in his throat. "Yes, you will."

"Love you. I'll call later today. Gonna take Orion shopping on King's Road and Kensington High Street. He should have a blast."

"Stay safe, Mir-randa." He glanced back at Katya and then whispered, "I love you, too."

Katya smirked as she passed him. "Now, you know how it feels."

Chapter Two

"It looks really great on you." Miranda eyed the gray suit Orion was trying on. Foregoing sightseeing Big Ben and Parliament, they decided to go shopping on Jermyn Street, instead. Bas had texted Orion some of his favorite boutiques in London, so naturally, Orion wanted to visit them all. She was a little shocked at the costs of some of the outfits, but since Orion's career as a rock star was taking off, he could afford to spend the dough or the quid as the Brits referred to it.

She gazed down at the groups of shopping bags and boxes containing shirts, ties, pants and other male apparel. "You know you're becoming a clothes whore."

He laughed. "I know. Isn't it great?" He studied himself in the mirror. "This works, but I think I like the blue one better."

"So do I. It makes the blue in your eyes stand out more."

"What the hell!" He shrugged. "I'll take them both."

"Good. Then we can get out of here. I'm starving." Miranda hated shopping for herself, but with Orion, it was fun. He had a wicked sense of humor about the shops and some of the people they met. So far, none of the salespeople seemed to recognize who he was. Only one shop employee, a young woman, raised an eyebrow when she saw the name on the credit card.

He rubbed his stomach. "Yeah, I could do with some food."

"You said that an hour ago, but then it was, 'just one more store, just one more'."

He smirked. "I was in the mood."

"So, it would seem." Orion wanted to carry all his purchases, but Miranda held onto a few. As they were making their way to the car and driver, she spotted another shop down one of the side streets. Not as large or eye-catching as the boutiques on the main strip, this one seemed older, the lettering on the sign suggesting it had been there for a long time. But what caught her eye was the assortment of canes she saw through the large windows. She handed Orion his bags. "Take these to the car. I'm gonna check out that shop there."

"I thought you were hungry."

"I am. I won't be long." She hurried down the street and smiled when she saw the assortment up close. Feeling only a little strange at shopping in a men's store, she swung open the door and was immediately greeted by an older salesman.

"Can I be of assistance?"

She loved his accent, slightly different from the ones she'd already heard—more cultured. "Maybe. Right now, I just want to browse."

"Ah, American. Are you here on holiday?"

Miranda was impressed with his warmth. So many of the salespeople they met were friendly toward them; only a few were a bit standoffish. Rather than explain her business, she nodded. "Yes, but only for a few days."

"All right. If you need me, just signal. My name's Hugo."

Miranda surveyed the store. Several leather goods lined one wall. Belts, vests, gloves, wallets, et cetera. The other wall had glass displays of rings and cuff links. This store seemed to specialize more in accessories than actual clothes. She made her way to the canes.

Orion joined her. But then went to where the vests were.

Miranda started examining the canes. Remare already had his favorite sword cane. Somehow, she didn't think any of these canes contained lethally sharp implements. When she found one with a wolf's head on the handle, she showed it to Orion. He snorted and went back to scrutinizing the vests.

She continued perusing the canes. Some had brass handles in various shapes, each was painted in dark colors. Finally, one seemed to jump out at her. It was black, but unlike the brass ones, it had a crystal on top. Miranda lifted it from the pile and held it in her grip, checking out its weight. She wasn't sure if Remare would like it, but she did. If he didn't use it, she would. She laughed. They'd be a matching couple walking down the streets together. She sighed when she saw the price, but then thought, why not?

"A splendid choice." Hugo moved toward her. "Not many customers favor the canes anymore, but we do get gentlemen who still prefer them."

"Yes, it's for my husband."

When Hugo peered up at Orion, Miranda simply said, "Friend."

"Hey, you getting that for Remare?" Orion, still wearing the black leather vest, picked the cane up and twirled it. "I like it."

"Not sure he'll like it, but I wanted to get him something unique."

"This particular one is old." Hugo sniffed the wood. "Alderwood. Some are made from hawthorn, oak. This one's very strong. It will last a lifetime."

Miranda wondered if he'd say that if he knew Remare was a vampire. Orion found a wallet and two rings he simply had to have and put them down on the counter. As they were paying for their purchases, she asked Hugo, "Is there a tavern or restaurant nearby? We've been shopping for hours and nearly missed lunch."

"There are several. But I think you might like Becks. It's two blocks south of here. Their shepherd's pie is particularly pleasing to the palate. Turn left at the corner. You can't miss it."

"Okay, thanks."

"Have a good day."

Miranda loved the charm of Beck's Tavern with its dark wood paneling and floors. And the stained-glass windows with the diamond-shaped panes only added to its appeal. She especially liked it since it was frequented by locals. This late in May, it would only be a couple of weeks before tourist season was in full swing, and no one looked forward to the crowds.

It was great to sit and enjoy the ambience. Unfortunately, she had trouble understanding their waitress. Her accent was different from most of the others they'd met—Cockney, Miranda thought. Apparently, British English and American English seemed to be two separate entities; either that or their server spoke way too fast.

Orion seemed to enjoy his sandwich, but she had to grin when he frowned after tasting his warm beer. "I told you some things are different here."

"Still tastes good. I'm gonna hit the men's room."

After he left, one of his bags nearly tumbled to the floor, but Miranda reached out with her power and caught it before it fell. Pushing it back into the empty seat, she scanned the crowd to see if anyone had noticed. Usually, she was more careful about using her *Elemental* powers in public. One raven-haired woman with a dark complexion sitting two tables away smiled knowingly. *Damn! Busted!* Miranda sipped her soda, hoping the woman thought she'd imagined it.

No such luck.

"May I join you for a moment?" Said woman was of Indian descent but spoke perfect English. She appeared to be late twenties, attractive and intelligent. "I'm Sarita."

Miranda gestured to the empty seat. "Hello, Sarita."

Sarita whispered, "Most of our kind are more prudent when using our powers. We don't use them in public."

Heart beginning to race, Miranda was shocked and wasn't sure she'd heard her right. She needed a moment to process what the woman was saying. *"We?"*

Sarita pointed to her hand. Then, she stealthily summoned a spoon a few inches away from her hand. "There are a few of us." She smiled. "Did you think you were the only one?"

Miranda blinked. "Ah, I didn't know." At Sarita's raised brow, she added, "I'm Miranda; I'm from..."

"Your accent—New England. I'd guess...New York?"

Miranda nodded. She was always chagrinned whenever anyone said she had an accent. Some New Yorkers tended to think everyone else had an accent. She'd learned that in Paris. And, again, when she traveled out west in New Mexico. "Is it that obvious?"

"For me, yes." Sarita smiled.

Miranda could detect no negative vibes. She was good at sensing others, and Sarita only exuded serenity and good will. "There are others?"

"Quite so. Don't you have friends in New York with similar gifts?"

Miranda was never comfortable with disclosing information about herself or her gifts. Especially to strangers. "Not really."

"You should come and have a drink with us tomorrow night. There are several of us who get together at The Wand, eh, The Wanderer. It's a bar." She rummaged through her purse for a card and slipped it across the table. "Most of us don't arrive until seven or eight. We'd love to get to know you better, and I'm sure you must have questions."

Miranda fingered the card and frowned.

As if reading her mind, Sarita added, "There's nothing to fear. We're a peaceful crew. And we respect everyone's right to privacy. If you do decide to come, don't bring the wolf. Certain members get uncomfortable discussing our abilities when *Others* are around."

Others as in people who had enhanced hearing like Weres and vampires. "I'll consider it, but I can't make any promises."

"Fair enough. But it would certainly be a pleasure having you with us. Agatha could probably answer more of your questions than me. She gets excited whenever she discovers another of our kind. There's so few of us, now. I hope you'll join us; if not, nice meeting you, Miranda." Sarita rose and left the pub.

"Who was that?" Orion joined her.

"You won't believe this," Miranda whispered, "but I think I just met another *Elemental*."

"You're kidding."

Miranda pushed the card in his direction. "She wants me to meet up for a drink tomorrow night. Says there's more of our kind."

Orion examined the card. "Are you gonna go?"

"Not sure." Miranda tapped her nails on the table. "She said to come alone."

"Oh, no. Wait a minute. Remare said I'm to keep an eye on you 'at all times'. He'd flip out if I let you go without me."

"I know. And I'm in no rush to go solo, either." She considered the possibilities. All her life, she'd wondered if there were others of her kind. Now that she'd finally met another, she was curious as all get out, but still, the thought of going alone was less than thrilling. "There may be a way around that."

***

In his castle's study in Northern England, Lord Acton ended his phone call and leaned back behind his ebony oak desk. "Well, that was enlightening. It appears Miranda Crescent is staying longer in England than anticipated."

"So, what? She's only human. Whatever would you find interesting about her?" Gideon was bored. His interests lay more in the political arena of the Vampire Nation. If there was even the chance Acton may become chancellor, Gideon could become Lord of Northern England, something he'd desired for centuries.

"According to Magritte and Vivienna, she's a touch more. They believe she's an *Elemental*. If she is, I think she would serve us well here in the north."

"An *Elemental*?"

Acton nodded as he leaned forward and tapped the tips of his fingers together, the way he usually did when he was contemplating something nefarious. "Remare was foolish to let her travel so close to my lands without a proper escort."

"I still can't believe he married a human. I didn't even think he liked them."

"The rumors suggest Remare was ordered to do so by Valadon when it appeared he'd be married to Vivienna. The High Lord didn't want to lose his favorite mistress and *Elemental* to another court. This way they could share the woman."

Gideon smirked. "She must be something else in bed or a powerful *Elemental* for him to order Remare to marry."

"Yes, I agree. Let's find out which one it is, shall we? Before one of the other courts learns of her abilities."

"I'll take care of it. I'll contact our agent in London. Go down there if necessary."

"Do so. And quickly."

Chapter Three

As they drove past Parliament, Miranda sighed. She'd wanted to ride the red double-decker busses that reminded her of the ones back in New York. The second level allowed tourists a better view to see the wonderful architecture of some of the older buildings. Still, she was grateful their driver, Alex, was patient enough to take them wherever they wanted to go.

London was a magnificent city. Like Paris, it had an old-world scent to it. New York was only a few centuries old, but the European cities had that timeworn feel to it her home city did not. She inhaled deeply, trying to get a sense for the city. It didn't feel as old as Paris, though she imagined both cities were probably close in age. Her skin prickled. It was as if the history whispered to her of long-ago events: the battles, deceased monarchs, the changes in culture—of fashion and music. Closing her eyes, it was as if she could go back in time and witness the proceedings as they were happening. *Odd.*

She shook herself of her reveries. "Have you got enough pictures, yet?"

Orion smiled. "Just one more."

All morning long, while they were on foot, Orion had been going crazy taking pictures of Parliament. He made her pose on the bridge so he could get Big Ben in the background. Miranda loved his youthful enthusiasm and had taken pictures of him hamming it up.

When she'd been a grad student in Paris, one of her classmates had invited her and a few other students to spend the weekend in London so she'd seen the sights before. Still, they held their grandeur. Watching the guards with their impeccable uniforms and focused concentration had been a thrill. So was visiting Parliament Square with Gillian Wearing's statues of the suffragettes. The inscription still stayed with her: *"Courage Calls to Courage Everywhere."* She'd posed for so many pictures her cheeks hurt.

After lunch, as they were driving, Miranda noticed the sign for the Herkimer Library, the place that specialized in books from the seventeenth century and older. Her pulse heightened, and she got excited at the prospect of possibly finding the Draxton and Courant books she'd long been searching for. "Stop! Stop the car." She instructed Alex to pick them up in a couple of hours.

Once inside the enchanting library, she felt something magical, as if she could just touch the old tomes, she'd be able to travel back in history and said, "You know, you don't have to stay with me. I just want to do some research."

"Nah, it's okay, I want to. Check out the architecture." Orion gestured to the high arched ceilings with the wooden beams and the colonnade beneath them. "This place is awesome."

"Suit yourself." After an hour, he'd start getting jumpy. Like Bastien, he couldn't sit still for a moment, some part of him was always in motion. Something he said about architecture was niggling at the back of her mind, but she wasn't sure what.

The Herkimer was more like a museum than an actual library, and she wondered if she'd be able to examine some of the books. When she'd approached one of the attendants, she was instructed to speak to their director, Henry Trembley, who was now examining her ID as she sat in his office. She hoped being an authenticator for one of New York's museums would allow her access to the old texts, but from the frown on the older man's face, she didn't think so.

Trembley, who was dressed in an impeccable gray suit and carried himself as if he were an aristocrat, cleared his throat. His tone was that of an erudite scholar who had little patience in dealing with others of lesser academic backgrounds. "You do realize our books are historical masterpieces and not to be mishandled by curious visitors."

Miranda had dealt with elitist snobs before in her profession, so his condescending attitude didn't offend her. Much. "I assure you I'm more than a curious tourist. I have graduate degrees in art history and certificates in authentication. I know how to handle rare and delicate books."

His frown returned as he continued to scrutinize her credentials.

Miranda remembered Remare was friends with Herbert, the ruling vampire of London, and wondered if he could pull some strings. She didn't like using him in such a manner, but snooty museum executives got under her skin. She texted Remare.

For you, anything, Remare texted her back. She smiled then sulked when Trembley handed back her ID.

"I'm afraid petitions are required several months in advance, and I can't possibly grant your request without sufficient notification."

"I see. All right, then, I thank you for your time. I'll peruse your masterpieces in the section on art history."

"Good day, Miss Crescent." He didn't bother rising or shaking her hand. Nor did he address her as professor as most academics in the field did.

"Bad break, Miranda." Orion rubbed her shoulder. "Sorry about that. I'm sure you had your heart set on studying, but hey, we can do more sightseeing."

Miranda smirked. "Let's have a seat in the art gallery." She led him to where the biographies on medieval artists were. "I'm not sure we're going to do more touristy things today, Orion. Where else did you want to go?"

"Bas gave me a list of things to see. I want to ride on 'The Eye', their Observation Wheel; we didn't get to ride the one in Paris. And, hey, those boat rides on the Thames look great."

She wasn't sure about the wheel. That was something she wanted to do with Remare. "You know New York is supposed to get one of those wheels in the next year or two. I guess they heard how chic they were and decided they needed another tourist attraction."

"Really?"

"Yup. That's the rumor. Actually, it's supposed to be happening soon." She held his hand. "Orion, there's something I want you to do for me. I'm gonna be here for at least a couple of hours. I want you to scout out that bar, The Wanderer. Get a feel for it."

"We're gonna go there tomorrow?"

"I am. You're going to be somewhere nearby. I can understand their need for privacy. But I'm not reckless, either."

"What makes you think you're going to be here that long? The director said you couldn't—"

"Professor Crescent, will you please come with me?" A middle-aged woman with salt and pepper hair approached. "I'm Mrs. Alice Gordon, Head of Reference." She smiled warmly. "Mr. Trembley has reconsidered your request and has arranged a private room for your use."

Miranda smiled. "Of course."

As they followed Mrs. Gordon, Orion snorted. "You knew he was going to change his mind, didn't you?"

"I had a feeling he might." She grinned as they hung back a short distance.

"I take it Remare has contacts here."

"True. Some in high places. Now, please go and check out that bar. You see I'll be perfectly safe. Nothing bad ever happens in libraries."

"Give me your phone."

"Why?"

"Just give it over."

She did. Orion examined it. "Okay, battery is three quarters full. You run into any trouble, any trouble at all, you call me."

"I love you, too." She reached up and kissed his cheek.

"Remare's going to kill me if anything happens to you."

"Nothing is going to happen. Now, scoot." He did.

Mrs. Gordon escorted her to one of the corner rooms with the large windows so the occupants could occasionally glance out at the rest of the library. Inside, there was oak paneling and a few portraits of former patrons. A burgundy couch and recliner were set against the back wall, and lining the front of the room was a wide desk and chair. "Some of the visiting scholars use this room. I'm sure you'll be comfortable. You've already been logged in on the computer and our databases so you can scan our collection. Type in your requests, and one of the attendants will bring them to you."

"Thank you. This is all very considerate. Please tell Mr. Trembley I appreciate his thoughtfulness."

"I will. May I bring you some tea while you wait?" She smiled warmly. "We have several different types."

"Jasmine Green?"

"Of course. It will take just a moment. Please make yourself comfortable." She closed the door behind her.

Miranda texted Remare, *Thanks. All's good.*

Her heart thumped when he texted back a purple heart.

Miranda sat at the desk and typed in Antoine Caron, a sixteenth century, French painter famous for his Mannerist style of figures in architectural settings. That's what had been niggling in the back of her mind. He was also the name Peralt had once recommended, known for his themes of magic and the occult. If Peralt wrote about *Elementals* and suggested this artist, she wondered if Caron would classify her kind under magic. She'd soon find out.

"Here you go, Professor." Smiling affably, Mrs. Gordon returned with a tray of tea and biscuits. "Our guidelines request you drink the tea while on the couch or the recliner." She pointed up at the list of rules posted on the wall every academic was familiar with. "No liquids or food of any kind are to be anywhere near the texts when they arrive. And no photography of any kind."

"Understood. I've worked with rare books. I'll treat them as if they're my very own." Miranda complied with Mrs. Gordon's requests then went to work.

Wearing the required gloves so no oils in her fingertips would damage the pages, Miranda spent the next few hours scrutinizing Caron's historical accounts for any mention of *Elementals*. She used her magnifying glass to study his paintings for any clues. Artists in this time period loved using hints of other works in their paintings. Nothing was completely as it was perceived to be, at least not to one who studied extensively.

She downloaded further elucidations by modern scholars who interpreted the allegories present in the paintings. Wishing she had her laptop, Miranda used her journal to take copious notes. She was about to start on another artist when she flipped the page, and something caught her eye. Caron's painting, *The Book of Origins*. In it, a scholar, who reminded her of Faust, was perusing the pages. His face of rapture at having discovered something in the old tome was astonishing. Using her magnifying glass, she meticulously examined the painting.

She wanted to discover the titles of the other books on the desk to the left of the scholar. She wondered if one of them could be Draxton or Courant, but Caron didn't include those details in his painting.

Odd, none of the other research contained any other information on this painting. She wrote down as much detail as she could then moved on to the other books on artists.

The books written in Latin were a lost cause, so were the ones written in Old English, but Middle English had potential. She'd taken courses in college in medieval literature, so she could do a thorough, if not an exact, interpretation. She wished Nick, her former assistant and Valadon's nephew, was there to help. He could read a dozen or so languages, including Latin. If she could scan the pages, she could easily run it through a translation program. But she wouldn't endanger the pages that way.

She concentrated on the books written in English. Miranda was lucky she'd trained herself to read remarkably fast. Disciplined and focused, she scrutinized paintings for the most minute of details. It's what made her a good authenticator. Or, as Jordan would say, "exceptional".

After hours spent perusing texts, Miranda sat back, cracked her neck and rubbed her eyes. Needing a break from the artists, she decided to focus on the two authors who also wrote about *Elementals*. She searched the library's databases for Robert Courant. Nothing came up. Same with Thomas Draxton. She sighed. If Montglat had searched for centuries and he couldn't find them, there was little chance she'd have better luck. She reluctantly agreed with her mentor; the books were most likely destroyed by fire.

After a while, Mrs. Gordon popped in. "Would you like another pot of tea?"

Miranda glanced at her watch and removed her gloves. She'd totally lost track of time. "No. I had no idea it was this late. Do you think it would be possible for me to return in another day or two to finish my research?" She had no idea how much sway Remare had, and she didn't want to push it.

"That would be proper. Many academics need more than one day to complete their research." She fished out a card and handed it to Miranda. "Please contact us when you are certain of the date and time, and we'll do all that we can to accommodate your request."

"Thank you, Mrs. Gordon. You've been wonderful, and I appreciate all that you've done already."

"My pleasure, Professor."

Chapter Four

Later that night, Miranda and Orion strolled along the banks of the Thames. Even though it was a warm night, the breezes off the water kept it cool. Orion had wanted to take a ride on one of the tourist cruise boats, but Miranda preferred to do that with Remare. Right now, she was content to just look out at the city and admire its beauty. She could sense the oldness of London here and inhaled the clean, briny scent of the river. So much history, so many events, so many centuries. Of all the cities in Europe, she thought London most resembled her hometown. Comparatively, New York was an infant timewise.

Seeing her rubbing her arms, Orion said, "Hey, are you cold? You want my jacket?" He started removing it when she stopped him.

"No, it was just a slight chill. I'm fine." Every now and then, she got the oddest feeling they weren't alone, but when she turned back to look, no one was there.

Orion hugged her and massaged her shoulders. As a Were, he radiated heat, and she quickly absorbed his warmth. "What were you thinking about a minute ago? You had your eyes closed and started smiling."

Miranda loved Orion. He was the closest thing she had to a brother and her best guy pal. But he wasn't Remare. "I was just thinking how romantic it would be if Remare was here. No offense, but there are just some things I'd rather do with him. Though, I'm not sure we'll ever get the chance to."

He made a mock hurt face. "Aw, gee, I guess I know where I rate."

She whacked his arm. "You know what I mean."

"Yeah, I do. I keep thinking, if Bas was here, I could ask him about certain suits and styles. You're cool, Miranda, but I don't think you know as much about fashions as he does."

She laughed. "You're right, I don't."

"I bet I could talk him into riding the wheel."

Every time Orion mentioned Bas' name, his face lit up. "I'm sure you could. You two look good together."

"Thanks. Sometimes, I feel like we're just two guys, best buds." He exhaled. "Like when we were kids and I got excited about going to the skating rink to play hockey, but it's more than that."

"I know." After taking one last look at the Thames and the way the currents reflected the moon, she hooked her arm around him, and they started walking back to Remare's town house. "Have you heard from him, recently?"

"Yeah, he texts. Says he can't talk much. He's doing surveillance."

They passed an old man on the street walking his dog. "He's got Tristan with him. Remare said he's the best shot in the Torian guard, and that the mission was a short one. You'll see him again, soon."

"I know." Orion sighed. "I still worry, though. I hate that I don't know what's going on."

She elbowed him. "How do you think I felt when you guys went after Peralt? At least you got to go with him. I had to stay behind. Remare's pretty powerful, but he's not invulnerable. I worry, too." Miranda checked their location as they neared the town house. Searching the shadows, she thought she sensed something strange for just a quick moment, but all was quiet, undisturbed.

When they were safely back in Remare's London home, Miranda gave him a call at their previously agreed upon time. She pictured him atop ValCorp's roof, looking out over the city. He wanted privacy, and the reception was clearer up there. Her heart yearned for him, his voice a soothing balm. "Yes, Orion's a great bodyguard. We're doing fine. Tomorrow, I'm gonna go back to the Herkimer Library I told you about, the one with all the ancient texts. Thanks, again, for getting your friend to pull some strings. They were very accommodating, but I feel like I've barely scratched the surface. I want to learn more about *Elementals*."

"As do I, Mir-randa. I know it's important to you. That's why I had Lord Herbert contact the library's director."

"Rem, I have other news. It's exciting, actually." She hesitated for a moment. "I met another *Elemental*. In a pub. Orion and I were having lunch, and she spotted me. She knew, right away, what I was." She wasn't going to tell him she'd accidentally used her powers in public. He'd go ballistic.

"Who is this person?"

"Her name is Sarita. Indian background, but she speaks flawless English." Miranda tried to contain her burgeoning enthusiasm. "Remare, she says there are others like me. She wants me to meet them tomorrow night."

"Are you going to?"

"Yes. Nothing ventured, nothing gained. I'm not all that comfortable meeting with strangers, but if I don't, I may never get the chance, again."

His tone turned authoritative. It annoyed her at times, but she knew he was just being concerned. "Where is this meeting supposed to take place?"

"Some tavern in SoHo, not far from where we were shopping. I have the card somewhere."

"You're taking Orion with you, yes?"

Miranda didn't like lying to Remare, so she sort of bent the truth. "Of course, he's already scoped out the pub. Nothing hinky registered."

"Listen to me, Mir-randa. Your talents are a marvel; many would desire to possess them. There are people who would use you for your abilities. Dangerous people. Promise me you'll be careful with whoever you meet. You don't know their histories, or with whom they might have a connection."

She scoffed. "I've taken all that into account. But, if I don't meet with them, I'll never know. Don't worry. I'm not gonna throw caution to the wind. I'll act prudently." She tried to alleviate his concerns. "Everyone is not a potential enemy."

He grunted. "But some are. I want you to text me the address of the tavern and promise to stay in touch. I don't want to have to worry overmuch about you, although I already do."

"Ye of little faith." She chortled. "Show some confidence in my abilities. My instincts are pretty sharp. If I have the slightest inkling something's off, I'll beat feet out of there."

"Orion will be with you. He's not to leave your side for one moment, agreed?"

Miranda exhaled. "Of course. I love you, too. I'll be home in a couple of days."

"Not soon enough. I've missed you." He growled. "Our bed is cold without you."

"Then, get an extra blanket." She laughed. "I've missed you, too. Orion and I went for a stroll near the Thames. I kinda wished you were there so we could walk arm in arm. London is really a beautiful town. I'd like to share it with you."

"We will have plenty of time for such strolls. And I promise you, we will visit some of London's more famous sites."

"Sounds good to me. I'll call you tomorrow."

"Good night, Mir-randa."

"Night, Remare."

***

Remare ended his call and stared eastward, imagining Miranda walking on the streets in London. He didn't like the idea of her meeting with strangers and wished he were there with her. It would have been wise to insist on full names; he sighed. But she'd asked him to trust her instincts. He did. To a point. She was safe as long as she stayed in London, but Lord Acton's territory was not far away. It worried him.

He scoffed. So, this was love. No wonder he'd avoided it for centuries. Like his sword, it cut deep. Part of him believed he'd have been better off never meeting her. He'd be resolute, steely focused on his work. But he'd also be empty inside. Like his scabbard without his sword. Hollow. He closed his eyes and let the cool air drift over him. His heart ached being so far from her. But something else was troubling him.

What if Miranda grew fond of the other *Elementals*? She'd told him the Weres were her family, but that she didn't really belong. He wondered if that was the reason she hadn't agreed to move in with him at Valadon House. Did she feel like an outsider because she wasn't a vampire? The thought should have occurred to him sooner, but it hadn't. He'd been too focused on other matters. What if she found the family she longed for with the *Elementals*? Would she forsake him to be with them?

No. Not his Mir-randa. They were committed to one another. He was polluting his head with doubts. This was what love did to fools like him.

Still, the thought lingered.

***

Tristan gazed up from the schematics of the installation they had under surveillance and eyed Bastien as he got ready for his date. He shook his head. "I don't know how you do it."

"Do what?"

Tristan wasn't quite sure how to phrase his next words. He wasn't a prude. He enjoyed sex as much as anyone. And he especially relished sex with Katya. But one thing he never did was cheat on his lovers and didn't like guys who did. "How you can sleep with someone for information. It makes my stomach rebel."

Bas snorted. "It's just sex. Like you haven't done it before."

"Yeah, sure, we all have, especially when we were younger. I just don't think I could do it now that I'm involved with someone."

Playfully, Bastien grabbed his shoulders and kissed his temple. "Good thing they've got someone like me to do the dirty work." He grinned. "Besides, I'm the pretty one."

"Sure, you are." Tristan shrugged. He was reluctant to ask what had been on his mind for some time, then decided to go for it. "But aren't you involved...with Orion?"

Bastien stopped tying his tie, closed his eyes and blew out a long breath. "We're just friends. Good friends. His star as a musician is just beginning to rise. I'm not going to do anything to jeopardize his career. The overwhelming majority of his fans are female. How do you think they'd react if they learned he had a male lover? His sales would plummet, and attendance at the concert halls would wane." He slapped on some cologne. "I won't be responsible for that."

"I didn't think... I mean, I didn't know..."

"What? That I fuck guys as well as females? All in the name of loyalty to House Valadon. You think I'm the only one?"

"No, but I remember you told me about some woman you loved back in Paris. Not to mention Persephone."

"Josette and I were never going to work out." His shoulders sagged. "She proved her devotion was to Vivienna, not me." He stopped combing his hair. "And Persephone was strictly business."

Tristan studied him. "You don't have an inclination for either..."

"Double your pleasure, double your fun. Nope, no preferences. I get as much satisfaction from one as I do the other. Always have, always will."

Tristan was still uncomfortable with the prospect of Bastien sleeping with one of the supervisors at the plant that manufactured the weapons like the one that nearly killed Valadon's son. "I've seen the way Orion stares at you and you at him, when you don't think anyone's watching. It looks real, man."

"It is. I care about him. Deeply." Bastien turned to him, his body tensed, taking on a defensive posture. "Has anyone said anything to you about it? Are they opposed?"

"No. Not at all. Didn't mean to rile you up. But everyone kind of knows. They're cool with it."

Bastien's voice lowered. "Even though he's a werewolf?"

"No one's said anything to me, and I haven't overheard anything." Tristan shrugged. "As far I know, he gets along with everyone. Orion's like one of the family, now."

"Not my family." Bastien grunted. "My dad's okay. I suspect he's had his share of male lovers in the past before he married my mother. However, *she* does have a problem with it." He rolled his eyes. "Wants me with an aristocratic female."

"And you?"

"I'll be with whoever the fuck I want to be with."

"And Orion?"

Bastien rose a brow. "What about him?"

"Does he fuck others, too?"

"We've shared females together. So, what? Who cares?"

Tristan's stomach began to roil. "I just thought you were exclusive."

"Are you and Katya? Man, that was unexpected. She was with Remare so long I didn't imagine her being with another Torian."

"That's long over with. He's married to Miranda, now."

"Now, *that* was a shock." Bas checked himself in the mirror as he finished dressing. "I didn't think he'd actually marry her."

"Have you seen them together? You can get a sunburn from all the heat they throw off."

"Yeah, I've seen them. So, how about it, are you and Katya exclusive, now?"

"Not sure." Tristan rubbed his head. "We started out just being friends. Then, it got physical. Now, I don't know what we are."

"Do you love her?"

Tristan sank deeper into the chair. "I keep asking myself that question. She was so pissed I was going on this mission without her." He smiled. "She really cares about me. She's beautiful and the best sparring partner I've had since…"

"Since Zoe."

"Yeah, since Zoe. I think I got so good at building walls since she got killed, hell, even before that. Back when we first split. I'm not sure I even remember what it felt like to be that intimate with someone."

"Oh, you'd know all right."

"It's like part of me wants to be able to get close, again, and part of me is hanging back. Hard to reconcile."

"Yeah, I get it. Listen, I gotta go. We'll finish this discussion another time." Bastien finished adjusting his tie, gave one last glance in the mirror, then reached for the door. He turned and flashed him the pearly whites. "Duty calls."

Tristan saluted him. They'd been friends for centuries, and he worried about him. He'd seen Bastien in a rare quiet moment after he returned from Europe. Bas wouldn't admit it, but being manipulated by Josette had affected him more than he wanted to admit. And being tortured by his sister must have been a punch in the nuts. No wonder he was so guarded.

Tristan hoped Bastien realized what a good thing he had with Orion and didn't do something stupid to blow it. He'd known guys who deliberately did that so they wouldn't get too involved with someone. Become vulnerable. Some men were just too damned proud for their own good.

He feared Bastien was one of them. Sure, Bas liked playing the party animal. But underneath? He was as vulnerable as any of them. Maybe even more so because he hid so well behind his shield of indifference. Bastien deserved some happiness. And, if Orion could provide that with him, so be it.

Tristan just hoped that someday, he, too, could learn to love again.

Chapter Five

"What's wrong, Remare? Your leg is twitching, again. You only do that when you're deep in thought or something is aggravating you. Which is it?"

He stilled his knee, uncomfortable that Valadon had noticed. "I spoke with Miranda. She's met another *Elemental*. They're going to have drinks tomorrow night." He shook his head. "I don't like it. Miranda is far too trusting." Remare rose and strode to the bar in Valadon's office and poured himself some wine.

Valadon peered up from his computer. "She has Orion with her. Have faith in Miranda. I'm sure she knows what she's doing."

"I have a great deal of faith in my wife." He narrowed his eyes as he pondered their last conversation. "There was something in her voice. A slight hesitation. I fear she's not being completely forthcoming with details."

"She obviously doesn't want to worry you. If you're that concerned, fly out to London. See for yourself."

"I'm considering that very thing. Even though she asked me to trust her judgment." He sighed. "If I go, it would seem like a lack of faith on my part."

Valadon smirked, obviously amused at Remare's discomfort. "Perhaps not. Just maybe she misses you as much as you're missing her."

Remare considered his options. "Bastien and Tristan are still away on their mission. You're already missing two of your Elite Torians."

"Yet, I have the others here with me. Gregori and Irina will accompany me if I choose to leave ValCorp, but as I don't have any set plans at the moment, I think you should see to Miranda."

Something in Remare's heart warmed at the thought of seeing his wife, again. He missed Miranda, but knowing Valadon approved of their relationship gave him a sense of satisfaction and contentment he hadn't known in some time. Valadon seemed happy to stay close to ValCorp, visiting with Vincent before his son and girlfriend left to spend some "alone" time together.

The Elite Torians were in peak shape, as were the mid-level Torians. Remare'd been supervising them while Tristan was away and was impressed with their progress. Especially Asanti's son, Jacob, who excelled not only in matters of finance, but also with the rigorous workouts all Torians completed. "Jacob has been progressing well with his training. More so than I'd expected."

"I know. I've read the reports and watched him. He's quite dedicated. Of course, he's also managed to find some down time." Valadon leaned back in his chair. "He's been socializing with your ward, Selena, who from all reports has also been performing well. They pair up as sparring partners whenever possible."

Remare smiled. "She may have a leg up there. Look who her grandmother is."

"Madame Lord Dione of Montreal told me she didn't want her granddaughter unable to defend herself, so she trained with the best, including Tristan's father."

"Good. I suspect Jacob and Selena will make excellent Torians. Given the information our agents were able to ascertain in Switzerland, what have you decided concerning Merlinder, since we now know he was behind the attempted assassination of Magritte that saw your son injured?"

"That's a bit of a conundrum. If I inform Magritte of our intel, she will have him executed."

"Another option is?"

"I'm considering keeping that information to ourselves. Merlinder is in severe financial distress. If I make suitable arrangements, he may prove to be a worthy ally. We can certainly use one in the High Council."

"He may, indeed. And if not?"

"He will have wished he had. I'm having my agent make a very lucrative offer to him. Let's see if he bites. I believe he will."

"He'd be a fool not to. Any other news from Europe?"

Valadon swiveled his chair. "Just a bit of curiosity. Vivienna has been in contact with an old friend of yours."

Remare sipped his wine. "Which one?"

"Gideon."

***

Royal Albert Hall hadn't been on Miranda's list of "Must Sees", but since Orion had been patient enough with her time in the library, she'd agreed to go with him. Ever since they discovered that music store in SoHo, he'd been excited about seeing RAH.

The concert venue was spectacular and reminded her of Carnegie Hall, where'd she'd seen Josh Groban play. One of Lizandra's favorite singers was Adele, and together, they had watched a video of Adele performing at RAH, so Miranda had some idea of its grandeur.

Orion was like a kid, gushing enthusiastically about the acoustics, peeking into rooms and giving wide-eyed glances at the photos of all the musicians who had played there. He seemed particularly pleased at finding a photo of a South African band who originated a song called, "The Lion Sleeps Tonight". He kept singing about something being a whim away until she started humming along with him. She was learning more about the history of music than she ever needed to know. It was only fair; Orion had had to listen to her accounts of artists over the years.

She was glad they'd come and enjoyed seeing how happy he was. "Maybe someday you'll play here."

"Maybe. With Valadon backing me and Bas managing my career, it's certainly a possibility."

Next, they headed for nearby Hyde Park. As it was getting close to the full moon, Orion was getting restless. His innate energy vibrating at such a high pitch, he needed to stretch his muscles and burn off some of the excess heat. Making sure she was comfortably situated on a bench under one of the trees, he donned his ball cap, sunglasses, and then ran miles around the park.

He must have gotten hot from his exertions and removed his T-shirt, baring a toned body that included a chiseled six-pack. After tucking his shirt in the back of his jeans, he got some whistles from some passing teens but kept on running.

Damn, he was one handsome male. And fast! Orion was one of the swiftest wolves in Black Star Clan; there was no way she could keep up with him and wouldn't even try. Besides, she'd gotten plenty of exercise from all the walking they'd done. She was sure she'd worked off the calories from the apricot scones they'd had for breakfast.

When he returned, she handed him a bottle of water, which he quickly gulped down, then sat beside her. "It's nice here. Reminds me of Central Park. While I was running, I saw some guy playing guitar and a couple of performance artists dressed up as statues. Man, how they can stand still like that for so long boggles the mind."

Miranda inhaled deeply and glanced around. "I suppose it does." But, in her heart, nothing compared to Central Park—her home away from home and Werehaven, the domicile of the Black Star Clan and her best friend, the Were

Queen. She'd remember to get something special for Liz before they left London.

"You still want to go to the library after lunch?"

"Yup. Orion, you don't have to accompany me there. If you want to see other places, please do. I know Remare overdoes it with his need to protect, but I'm telling you I'm plenty safe there.

"I know you are. I'll stay for a while. But you gotta promise to keep your phone charged and stay in contact." He frowned. "It's not the library I'm concerned about. It's your meet up at the tavern."

"What? You checked it out and said it was okay. Besides, you're going to stay in the area, so all's good."

He sighed. "I should be able to go inside with you." He swallowed more water. "Not sure I like the idea of you going in alone."

She rubbed his arm as he basked in the sunlight. Miranda had never been a sun worshiper, even before she learned she had vampire blood in her ancestry. She'd gone to Coney Island in Brooklyn with the Weres one time, preferring to stay under the umbrella at the beach. Lizandra had threatened to throw her in the water unless she got her ankles wet.

Miranda had complied but, later explained the sun gave her a headache, and she was perfectly happy reading a book in the shade. It had always been that way. She'd loved seeing Liz, Orion and the other Weres whooping it up in the waves. The water just wasn't her thing.

"Hey, don't you trust me? I'm not helpless." She raised her right arm. Her dominant side. "You've seen what I can do; I can take care of myself."

He chuckled. "I still can't believe you kicked Irina's ass. That vampire was out for blood."

"And don't forget Bastien's sister, Isabelle. When she threw you against the wall, I thought she broke your neck. I terrified the hell out of her with my fireballs." Actually, she'd scared herself with uttering a malevolent voice that had not been her own. The memory still haunted her and made her shudder.

"I was unconscious, but Bas told me what you did and how you broke his chains." He took her hand and kissed her wrist. "Sorceress."

She laughed. "Hey, only Remare is allowed to call me that."

He snorted. "Fine. You ready to head back? I wanna take a shower before we head out, again."

"Sure." She gazed around as she rose. Every now and then, she had the feeling they were being watched. But high up, only a couple of birds circled around and perched in the treetop.

Later that afternoon, after she finally talked Orion into visiting Trafalgar Square, she was back at the Herkimer Library, perusing her texts. She glanced up and out the window overlooking the library. No threats, nothing out of the ordinary. Mrs. Gordon, the head reference librarian, was helping others with their questions. Everyone was going about their business. Remare and Orion had spooked Miranda; still...something felt odd.

After examining the texts from yesterday, she moved on to another source. An anonymous book by a monk who had lived during the seventeenth century, Peralt's time. He didn't mention the word *Elementals* in his entries, but what he did write intrigued her. He'd been injured on the road from Southwark when his horse-drawn cart had broken a wheel. In his attempt to fix it, the cart had fallen and crushed one of his legs. Nearby villagers had brought him into their town, and a "*wizened woman*" attended him.

He swore he saw angels when she cared for him—angels who had the power to heal. The townsfolk told him he'd been delirious with fever. He went on to say, she used chants and placed "*crystals of sparkling intensity*" over his wounds. When his fever broke and they removed the bandages, the scarring had been minimal—far less than what had been expected. He was told it was his continual prayers that had helped heal him.

The monk, fascinated by his experience, began to investigate others who seemed to have miraculous cures. When he recounted his experiences at the monastery, they laughed and said he'd consumed too much wine. The following year, he returned to the village with a barrel of wine to thank them for caring for him. When he inquired about the healing woman, he was told she'd died, but that her daughter was also a gifted healer. When he beheld her, his eyes began to shed tears at her inner beauty. "*A child of the angels,*" he'd called her.

Miranda wondered if any others had written about such incidents. She remembered reading accounts of monarchs with remarkable abilities and began scanning members of the aristocracy during this time period and came across accounts of King James. There were recorded accounts he had the "healing benediction". Those that suffered from a multitude of maladies were healed by simply his touch. Miranda scoffed. History tended to favor those in power who had a great deal of wealth and influence.

But what if? What if there were those like her who had the power to heal? Of course, the kings would say it was a gift from God. Centuries later, they burned women who were "gifted, touched by supernatural forces". Powers that once were revered, people began to fear.

And what they feared, they killed.

She blew out a breath. She'd done the research on the Inquisition in Valadon's archives. Thousands had perished in the name of religion. Innocent women whose egregious crimes were having knowledge of medicinal herbs and healing powers. She snorted. Was it any wonder those of her kind stayed hidden? History had a nasty habit of repeating itself.

Mrs. Gordon knocked on the door and entered. "Would you like more tea?"

Miranda shook her head. The librarian had been helpful in recommending texts and even retrieved a few for her. Something the attendants usually did, so Miranda was grateful for all the older woman had done for her. "Thank you, but no."

"I see you've been studying ancient healers. I've found the histories extraordinary. So many stories of our kings and queens and their abilities. But I prefer the folktales of the villagers. Much more colorful."

"It's hard to separate fact from fiction. Some of the accounts border on the fantastic."

"Oh, I wholly agree. But, in the olden times, they had to make do with what they had and often relied on the beliefs of the elders to care for the infirmed. My sister has always been fascinated by stories of the ancient healers. She runs a bookstore, now." She handed Miranda a card. "Gemma prefers living in the country. A small town called Rye. It's in Sussex. I hope, if you have time, you take a trip there. The gardens are beautiful this time of year. There's also a poison garden up in Northumberland; it was believed some of the more dangerous plants held curative powers. It's quite the tourist attraction, now."

"Not sure how long I'll be in England, but I thank you. You've been very kind."

"Think nothing of it. I hope you discover what you've been searching for."

Miranda didn't think what she was looking for was in any of the books. "Research is an ongoing thing."

Mrs. Gordon sighed. "It is, indeed. Is there anything else I can help you with?"

Miranda hesitated then decided she had nothing to lose and asked, "Have you ever heard of a text called *The Book of Origins*?

One brow arched as Mrs. Gordon smiled. "I take it you don't mean Darwin's *On the Origin of Species?*"

"Not quite." Miranda had read Darwin's theories on natural selection and the evolvement of the races when she'd been an undergraduate. "Yesterday, while I was doing research on the artist, Antoine Caron, I came across a version of his painting called *The Book of Origins*, but I couldn't find any research on it. I know it's the title of the painting, but I wonder if Caron wasn't referring to an actual book in the painting."

Mrs. Gordon leaned against the doorframe and seemed to ponder the possibilities. "Caron is not one of the more popular artists, however, he did live during the fifteen hundreds. Some of the subjects in his Mannerist works were exaggerated to the point of offending some church members. It's quite possible his work was destroyed before any scholars could analyze it fully. But let me do some research and see what I come up with."

"That sounds great." Miranda suspected libraries were like museums. Each had works not seen by the public, either because of damage or they were in the process of restoration. She hoped Mrs. Gordon had access to those volumes.

Miranda glanced at her watch and shivered. Since Orion wanted a steak for dinner, she'd told him they'd go to The Flat Iron. Sure enough, when she looked up, he was striding toward her. "Thank you for your help, Mrs. Gordon. I've enjoyed our chats."

"So have I. Have a good evening, Professor." She left.

Orion approached. "Ready to go?"

Her stomach picked that moment to growl. "I'll say."

Chapter Six

Cautious at first, Miranda inhaled the air around the street she was about to enter, trying to get a bead on her surroundings. Older sections of cities have their own distinct scent. Not just the aromas of food, places or people, but of age and circumstance. Paris smelled older, New York was darker, but London had a complex scent all its own that reflected its unique history beneath the veil of brine from the Thames.

Exhaling, Miranda considered her options. She didn't usually walk down deserted alleys by herself. Especially in cities she was unfamiliar with. During the day, this SoHo section of London had looked harmless enough—bustling with people, alive and exhilarating. But, now, with the sun setting, the street was already dark, covered in layers of shadows. It felt creepy, eerie. Foreboding.

Why was it deserted? Shouldn't there be people up and about? She glanced at the card, again. Yup, The Wanderer should be up ahead. Miranda scanned the shadows, her empath skills on high alert for any danger. She couldn't perceive any bad vibes or deviations in the pitch of her senses. There was nothing threatening that she could detect. Still...something felt off.

She patted her pocket. Her phone was still there, and Orion was just around the corner, so she should feel reasonably safe. She moved into the shadows. With each step, it felt as if her way was getting darker. Another step. Silence, then something shifted in the darkness, and her hands quickly heated, her fingers tingling with power.

"Oh, put it away. Do you want everyone here to know what you are?"

Even though Miranda was confident in her abilities to defend herself, shivers ran down her spine. She strained to see the figure in the shadows. "Who are you?"

"No one you need to be concerned about." A stranger stepped out of the darkness. Male, tall, light brown hair that almost looked blond, leather jacket. Physically built. When he tipped his hat toward her, his wrist revealed a bracelet of beads and stones that were seemingly familiar. "I'm waiting for someone else."

"You always wait in the shadows?" Miranda pulled back her power and gestured to The Wanderer. "How come you're not in the bar?"

"Not really your concern, is it?"

"How'd you know what I was?"

"Your fingers were glowing." He smirked. "I once knew a girl; she had amazing powers. Just like yours, I suspect."

His voice had a slight English accent, but something about him suggested he was foreign. "You're not from around here."

"I'm from many places. London's just a flyover for me."

Miranda inched her way toward the lights of The Wanderer. "What are you doing here?"

He seemed amused with her and grinned. "Doing someone a favor." He gestured to the tavern. "Go on in. There's no danger here. At least not right now."

Miranda glanced at the bar and then back. By the time she turned toward him, he was already gone.

His voice echoed from the other end of the alley. "Be wary, flygirl."

Miranda shook her head at the strangeness of this meeting and the underlying feeling she'd met him before but couldn't remember where. Steeling herself, she made for the tavern's door and the welcoming voices of the people inside.

***

Ryder was impressed with Valadon's agent. She moved stealthily in the night, but he'd know her scent anywhere. He'd smelled it enough in Switzerland. He gazed down at her from his perch above. There was something about her that called to him. Like him, she preferred to work alone. "Go home, Carla. She's got her watchdog with her. She's in no danger."

"Who the hell are you?"

"A friend. We work for the same team, only our coaches are different."

"Why should I trust you?"

"You shouldn't. But, right about now, Valadon should be calling you home. I hear he's sweet on you." Without waiting for a reply, Ryder took off. He grinned when he heard her phone buzzing.

***

The Wanderer seemed typical of the many other taverns Miranda had seen in the city: The painted bar sign was clearly displayed above the black façade. The three diamond-paned windows revealed the warm, inviting glow inside. Still not sensing any bad vibes, she pushed the door open and scanned the bar for Sarita. Miranda spotted her sitting at one of the back tables with a few friends.

Sarita waved to her. "I'm so glad you decided to join us. You found the place okay? Some people get lost with the side streets. I should have warned you ahead of time."

Welcomed by a flurry of greetings from Sarita's mates, Miranda was delighted by all their accents; she'd miss their charm when she left for home. "Not at all. I Googled the place so I wouldn't get lost."

"Ah, she's a New Yorker, all right." A middle-aged black woman with hair so short she was nearly bald chuckled. "Your accent's telling."

Miranda grinned. "I suppose."

"You'll have to tell us all about New York later. I'm sure you have lots of questions for us." Sarita said, "Let me make proper introductions." She gestured to the red-headed girl on her left and went clockwise. "This is Isadora—eh, Izzy—Rose, Vicky, Loren, and Esme."

Silently, Miranda repeated their names, hoping to remember all of them. "Pleased to meet you."

"I'm sure you're as curious about us as we are about you. It's not every day we find a new *Elemental*." Sarita signaled the waitress. "What's your poison?"

"Cranberry juice and vodka. On the rocks."

Loren, who had long dark hair pulled back in a ponytail and appeared to be around Miranda's age, added, "And another round of pints for us."

Miranda felt strangely at ease with the group, who ranged from the college-aged Izzy to the more mature African-English Rose. "How on earth did you find each other?"

Sarita laughed. "We come from different backgrounds, but most of us met at the hospital. I'm a nurse; Rose is a pediatrician. Loren is a paralegal; Izzy is still at university and hasn't made up her mind yet what she wants to major in."

"Don't listen to her," Izzy interjected, as she twirled a strand of her red hair. "I'm leaning toward music; I just haven't finalized it as yet."

"You must hear her sing. She's a great soprano," Sarita said. "She had a part in one of the plays on Theater Row."

"A few parts." Izzy shrugged. "But nothing major, yet."

"What do you do, Miranda?" Vicky, who had a short crop of blond hair, asked.

"I authenticate rare works of art. I work for one of the museums back in New York."

Vicky's brow rose. "Sounds exciting. Do you like your work?"

Miranda nodded. "As a matter of fact, I do."

"I run a hair and nails salon, but we also do facials and full-body massages." Vicky said, "You must stop in the shop if you have time." She seemed to be studying Miranda's complexion then slid her card toward Miranda. "We have our own line of beauty supplies."

After the waitress returned with their drinks, Rose lifted her glass. "Here's to full moons and singing rocks."

Strange toast, Miranda thought, but raised her drink.

"Welcome to England, Miranda." Esme, whose dark hair was cut in a bob, warmly smiled. "I'm a yoga instructor. Health and wellness all the way."

Miranda was momentarily stunned by the beauty and grace Esme emanated. It was rare to meet someone with that much serenity. More reserved than the others, her mysterious dark eyes held a wealth of knowledge Miranda found intriguing. "Thank you. It's a pleasure being here."

Miranda scanned the group and decided she liked them. A strange sense of camaraderie started to set in. For the first time in a very long time, she didn't feel like a freak, alienated because of her gifts. Joy blossomed in her heart at meeting others of her kind with powers like hers. "Sarita said…"

"That we're rejects from Xavier's school for the gifted. Don't believe a word she says." Vicky laughed, and the others joined in.

"I think Miranda is curious about our talents." Checking to make sure no one was watching, Sarita sipped her drink and then puffed out a cloud of blue vapor which quickly dissipated. "Water is my element. With the overcast weather here in England, it's important to be able to tame the wild beast." She pointed to her dark hair.

Izzy called the wind currents to move her beer a few inches. "Air." She winked. "On a hot, humid day, when you need a breath of fresh air, I'm your girl."

Rose and Lauren placed their hands flat on the table, and Miranda felt it vibrating. "We're earth *Elementals*." Rose said. "Possibly one of the reasons why we're so fond of our gardens."

"And what's your specialty?" Vicky sipped her drink.

Miranda wasn't comfortable discussing, let alone displaying, her talents in public. Before she could respond, Sarita said, "Now, Vicky, Miranda is our guest and might not feel comfortable with us. Show her yours."

Vicky narrowed her eyes and sat back. Miranda wondered if there was some discord between the two. "As you wish." Vicky made the flame go out on the candle in the holder in front of them, and then it came back stronger and darker than it had been. The flames were blood red. Miranda could feel the heat of them on her face.

"Whoa. Are you trying to burn me knickers?" Sarita chastised. "Lower it, now."

Vicky exhaled then complied. A bit reluctantly, Miranda thought. This one liked using her power and letting others know her capacity for it.

All heads turned to Esme. "My talents are a bit different. I don't have the physical powers most *Elementals* have. Mine are more mental."

"Be careful around her," Rose warned. "She can mesmerize you with her eyes and her voice. It's no wonder she excels at yoga. Her voice sedates her clients."

Esme smiled whimsically at Rose. "As if you can't."

Miranda was still reluctant to show her hand, but since everyone else's cards were on the table and she knew they were curious about her, she held her hand over the flame and then closed her fist.

Sarita studied the candle. "The flame still burns in the jar."

Miranda opened her palm. Blue flames danced on her hand. The others stared in wonder. She made the sign of a happy face with the flames then extinguished them.

"Most impressive." Sarita smiled. "It looks like we found another fire *Elemental*."

The others seemed delighted, except for Vicky, who seemed to scrutinize her.

"So, are you like their leader or something?" Miranda asked.

"I wouldn't say that." Sarita shook her head. "We all have varying degrees of abilities. As I'm sure you're aware, we keep our particular skill sets confidential. That's why we asked you to keep your handsome companion away. We don't trust outsiders much. We've all sworn vows never to reveal ourselves to non-Elementals. We ask that you uphold our oath."

"I've never been one to advertise my talent. I assure you, I understand your need for privacy and confidentiality."

"We don't take our abilities for granted or use them unwisely." Rose met Miranda's eyes. "For centuries, our kind was persecuted and suffered at the hands of those who lack understanding."

"How do you know the history? I've searched volumes for information on us. There wasn't much out there. Some information on telepathy and telekinesis—research done by experts in the paranormal field." Miranda wasn't going to discuss Peralt's findings. If they asked about his books, she'd have to reveal Valadon's archives, and that simply was not happening.

"You won't find our history in any books." Sarita huffed. "Any references will have us classified as witches. And I'm sure you know what was done to them during the Dark Ages."

"Surely, there has to be some records somewhere of others like us?" Miranda wondered if they were communicating silently in the way of vampires. They had that same look Remare and Valadon shared when they spoke mentally, and she wondered how long the women had known each other.

"Most of the accounts of us don't refer to us as *Elementals,* but rather as wiccans or sorcerers." Loren said, "What little knowledge we have is passed down generation to generation."

Miranda's curiosity stirred. "So, our abilities are inherited?"

Loren looked surprised. "Of course, sometimes, our gifts skip a generation or two; didn't your parents instruct you?"

"My parents were killed when I was a child. I had no instruction." Again, they remained silent, and Miranda wondered about their non-verbal communication.

Sarita asked, "Surely, in a city as large as New York, you've run into others?"

Miranda shook her head and grimaced. "Not really. A few Weres, a couple of vampires. No *Elementals.*"

"Be careful of the vampires." Loren's voice was harsh. "They're not to be trusted. In times past, they tried to capture us. Use us for our abilities. They're vicious."

Miranda wasn't about to disclose she was married to one. "What about men? Are there male *Elementals*?"

Rose laughed. "Of course. But those chaps don't socialize the way we do. They prefer to keep their secrets to themselves."

Miranda asked, "Your parents or your grandparents never spoke about any books or historical accounts?"

Vicky sighed. "God, you're stuck on history."

Miranda sipped her drink. "It's in my nature. I'm an art historian. History has always fascinated me."

"There is one who might speak to you. An elder." Everyone looked at Izzy with admonishment. "Well, there is."

Sarita spoke. "That's her secret to tell. Not ours, sister."

"That's all right." Miranda slid her hand in an arc of peace. "I would never invade someone's privacy. That being said, if she wishes to meet with me, perhaps guide me in a certain direction, I would like to meet this person."

"That would be a discussion for another time. Chill, women." Sarita became jubilant and waved off any further questions. "Miranda came for a night out. Enough talk about us. Tell us about New York. Have you met anyone famous? Movie stars?"

Why does everyone think people who live in New York City know actors and actresses? "No one famous." Miranda thought of Max and Sasha who worked on a soap opera, but somehow, she didn't think that would impress this bunch. "Famous, huh? Not really. Sorry to disappoint." No way was she mentioning Orion or Valadon, let alone Remare.

And, so, the conversation went on and on, with them asking questions about her city and the people there. In some ways, she was surprised about the image and reputation her city had, and in other ways, she wasn't surprised at all. "All right then, it's late, and I really should be getting back. It was a pleasure meeting all of you. I hope we can meet, again, before I fly home."

A voice whispered in her mind, *"You are home, sister."* Miranda scrutinized the faces of the women to see if any of them had uttered the words. Nothing stirred.

"I'll walk you to the door." Sarita stood and accompanied her. "I can call you a taxi if you wish."

"No need. I can find my way. My car's not far from here."

"I'm glad you came tonight." Sarita smiled. "I should have told you about our oaths sooner. I wasn't sure you'd show. The few foreign *Elementals* we've met were somewhat skittish at meeting others. Closet cases. You were bold to come here tonight."

Miranda grinned. "Fortune favors the bold."

Sarita laughed. "Yes, sometimes, she does. If you want, I'll contact Agatha. See if she'll meet with you. I can't make any promises. She's a bit of a recluse since she retired. Lives out in the country mostly, now."

"Yes, I'd like that."

After exchanging phone numbers, Sarita gave her what looked like a quartz crystal necklace. "A gift. For good luck. The earth *Elementals* believe crystals have beneficial qualities. They also make beautiful jewelry."

"Thanks." Miranda held it up to the light; the milky white gem was translucent.

"I'll call you when I know something."

"It was a pleasure meeting you and the others. I hope we can get together one more time before I leave."

"I hope so, too. In fact, I'd count on it. We meet so few of our kind."

Miranda was about to turn right to go to Orion, but something on her left caught her eye. A flicker of light. The alleyway was completely dark, now, except for the glow radiating from the tavern out into the street. As she followed the flame farther down the alley, images appeared on the brick face. Swirls of color in intricate designs. Stunning. The more she followed the shadowy form, the more the sketches resembled detailed drawings. Landscapes. Seascapes. Each picture more beautiful than the previous one. "Wait! Who are you?"

Miranda followed the caped person into a dimly lit lot behind the building. The specter used its power to create a fire whip she arced into a circle of thin flame which she tossed against the far wall. Three smaller circles followed until a target was in place. Then, the cloaked stranger constructed a violet flamed bow and arrow. She pulled the fire string back and shot the arrow at the target, hitting the bull's eye. She then bowed and gestured for Miranda to do the same.

Wondering who this silent dark being was, she said, "All right, but I've never done this before." *How hard could it be?* Miranda stretched a thin cord of flame between her hands then pitched it against the wall. Amazed she could do that, she tossed three more blue circles of fire. Neither of their flames burned the buildings.

Constructing the bow and arrow was a bit more difficult. Miranda had to concentrate harder, but she did it. Pulling the arrow back against the flaming string, Miranda almost felt frost burn from her flames but aimed her arrow and let it fly. It hit just shy of the bull's eye; she turned to the robed entity.

"There you are. I thought you went the wrong way." Sarita appeared, and her face went livid at the enigmatic presence. "You don't belong here. This is ours."

Before Miranda could say anything, the mysterious figure disappeared into the night. "What was that about?"

"A *Dark Elemental*. Don't befriend any of them. They're dangerous."

Strange, Miranda didn't get that vibe. She would have liked to have spoken to the *Elemental*, but as Miranda scanned the area, there was no trace of her. No hint of who she was or that she'd ever been there. Only the echo of a memory.

Even the drawings had disappeared without leaving any residue behind.

Chapter Seven

"Remare!" Miranda was momentarily stunned and excited to see him standing in the living room; she almost thought she was hallucinating. She ran across the carpet and leapt into his arms, breathing his masculine, sylvan scent deep into her lungs. Not content at being close enough, she wrapped her legs around his hips. With no hint of modesty nor a spared thought for Orion looking on, she kissed Remare passionately. When she rubbed against him, he purred, loudly. She broke from the kiss. "I've missed you."

He chuckled. "I see that. I missed you, too."

She stroked his jawline where he used to have a thin line of beard; now, the goatee was only on his chin and upper lip. Her heart beating out a staccato, she asked, "Why didn't you tell me you were coming to London?"

"It would have ruined the surprise." His exuberant smile warmed her. "And, after your enticing welcome, I would say more surprises will be planned in the future."

She gradually slipped her ankles down his legs, but he kept his arm around her waist.

"It's good to see you, too, Orion. Thank you for keeping an eye on what's most precious to me." He kissed her temple.

Orion grinned. "A pleasure."

"Miranda and I are attending a dinner party tonight at the home of the lord of London. You're welcome to join us."

Miranda turned to him. "What dinner party?"

"It is customary for visiting vampires to greet their host lords. Herbert is expecting us. He's quite anxious to meet you."

"If it's okay with you, I think I'll stay in tonight." Orion reached for his guitar. "I want to work on some song lyrics. And you two look like you could use some alone time."

"As you wish. Mir-randa, your dress is hanging on the closet door. How long will it take you to get ready?"

"Are you sure about this? It's pretty late." Miranda knew it was a moot point as soon as she said it; vampires were nocturnal and required little sleep.

"Not at all. And there are a few matters I wish to discuss with him."

"Okay. Ten minutes, tops." She checked to make sure Orion had shut his door before asking, "Do we have time for a quickie?"

Remare grinned as his eyes hinted at delicious wickedness. "I don't do quickies, as you should know. I only do longies. Now, go and get dressed. We'll have alone time later."

She grumbled, "I'll be useless to you by the time we get back." In the bedroom, Miranda unzipped the garment bag and marveled at the black gown. Some dinner party, but then again, vampires liked to dress up for meals. Thank God, she and Orion had already eaten; vampires didn't dine until almost midnight. She snickered, wondering if that was the origin of midnight snacks. She dressed quickly and refreshed her makeup. As for her hair, she lifted half of it up into a ponytail and left the rest to glide down her back.

In the living room, Remare stood silently as she approached. The space between them condensed, became electric. His vibe rubbed seductively against hers, sending shivers through her. His appeal never more compelling than now. Miranda stopped ten feet away to regard him. He was dressed in a black tone on tone, elegant suit, custom tailored, of course. Sophisticated, but oh so deadly. Always, an air of danger hovered around him. It both excited and made her wary. She breathed deeply to steady her throbbing heart. Seductive, yet protective, he was certainly one of the handsomest vampires to walk the planet with his wavy black hair, high cheekbones and sensuous lips.

Yet, there was so much about him she didn't know. At this moment, with their connection so strong, so powerful between them, she sensed his otherworldliness more than usual. It was only during these fleeting moments when she got a glimpse into his true nature, whose depth she couldn't fathom but felt its presence. Within the darkness of his eyes was a world of knowledge humans would never be able to grasp. Without fear, she dove deeper into his darkness, forgetting the power of a vampire's allure.

History, journeys, so many years, centuries of existence. She was peering into his very soul, and what's more, he was letting her, inviting her to look deeper. Miranda had always wondered why vampires were the chosen ones. Why were they bestowed with long life when humans and Weres weren't? What was it about them that made them nearly invulnerable to life's ravages? Why did the powers that be bequeath them such startling speed and strength? And their mental abilities were almost terrifying in their capacities she wasn't sure she wanted to discover what that entailed. So many mysteries to ponder. Remare. Vampire. Hers.

"Mir-randa. You stand rapt as if you're looking at me for the first time."

"I want to tell you something."

He motioned for her to continue.

"I love you."

He grinned sexily, his dark eyes mesmerizing. "I think I already knew that."

"No. It's more than that. I don't just love you... I'm in love with you. Always have been. And, sometimes, it terrifies the hell out of me. You still scare me."

His eyes narrowed. "How can that be?" His voice held concern.

She moved closer to him and slid her hands up his lapels to wrap around his neck. "I don't think I've ever felt this way about another. I wasn't even sure I could or that it was even possible. You open doors inside the mansion of my mind I didn't know existed."

"We have time to discover whatever is behind both our doors. Possibilities grand and mischievous." He massaged her back to soothe her. "I think our lives together will be very interesting."

Of that, Miranda agreed. She kissed him to break her reveries. Whatever it was about him that enthralled her could wait for analysis at another time. "Thank you for providing the car and Alex to take us around."

"I didn't want you riding the underground or having to wait for taxis. Herbert assured me Alex was trustworthy. And an excellent chef."

"Oh, yes." Even though she and Orion had frequently eaten out, Alex had made them a fabulous chicken cordon bleu that was simply scrumptious. And the scones and assorted pastries in the morning were divine.

During the ride to Lord Herbert's home, Miranda appreciated the sights of London's toniest district, the homes reminding her of Manhattan's swankiest sections on the Upper East Side with the black cast iron fencing out front. "I'm glad you came to London." She enjoyed holding Remare's hand, feeling their connection, his strength in hers. She'd missed that one simple joy.

"I didn't want to abandon Valadon, again, so quickly after being away, but he assured me he'd be fine and encouraged me to leave. He knew I was missing you terribly."

"Good to know." It was almost scary how used to being around him she was becoming.

After parking, Alex opened their door. Remare exchanged a few words with him, and then they were met at the door by one of Herbert's servants. "This way, please."

Lord Herbert raised his drink in salute. "My old friend, Remare. At long last." Herbert was a robust vampire of average height with a slightly round physique. His dark blond hair was thinning on top but coifed in waves to the side of his face. The two vampires embraced and did the manly back slap.

Remare seemed happy at seeing his former colleague, and Miranda was glad he had friends in other courts.

"Herbert, this is my wife, Miranda."

"A pleasure to meet you, my dear." He kissed her knuckles. "I was surprised to hear Remare had married, but now, after meeting you, I can see how you would captivate him."

"I'm pleased to meet you. Remare has said many great things about you."

"Dear girl, you must have me mixed up with someone else." Herbert laughed. "Let's go into the drawing room. Harrington is in there with his daughter, Auriel."

As always, Miranda's eyes flew to the many bookcases and objects d'art around the room. Remare introduced her to another couple and then to Harrington, a white-haired man of impeccable taste who apparently was part of England's financial commission. When the discussion turned to business and politics, Miranda zoned out and, instead, focused on the portraits hanging on the walls, of which there were many.

A striking blonde, dressed in a stunning light blue gown, approached them. "Hello, Remare."

Remare's body straightened. The movement so slight Miranda hardly noticed it. "Auriel, this is my wife, Miranda."

"Welcome to London, Miranda. Your first time?" Auriel smiled graciously.

"Not really. I spent a weekend here when I was a grad student in Paris." Miranda shook her hand. The vampire was stronger than she looked, and Miranda thought she'd have half-moons imprinted on her skin from where Auriel's fingernails had dug in.

"We were so surprised when we heard Remare had married." She slanted him a look. "He gave us no clue of his impending marriage the last time he was here."

"Well, he does enjoy his surprises." *He gave me no friggin clue, either.*

After some small talk, the butler announced that dinner was served, and they moved to the dining room. Miranda never really understood why, at formal dinners, husbands and wives were separated. Remare was seated to Herbert's left, and Miranda was diagonally across from him. She supposed it was felt spouses had plenty of opportunity for conversation, and at these gatherings, each wished to speak to others. Since Miranda didn't know anyone else, she simply observed the others.

In particular, Auriel, who seemed to be giving Remare the eye or imagining him naked when she thought no one was looking. Miranda's Dark Angel wanted to stab Auriel's hand with her fork and shout, *"Mine!"* but refrained when her Light Angel reminded her, "She's only looking." Remare was a handsome male. She found him intensely desirable. Was it any wonder others did, as well?

"Ah, there you are, Winifred. I was afraid we'd have to start without you." Herbert nodded toward her. "My companion and my second."

"I tried to end the call sooner, but you know how he is. Remare, so nice to see you, again."

Remare rose and kissed her cheek. "You look wonderful. It's good to be back in London." He gestured in Miranda's direction. "My wife, Miranda."

"How do you do?" She wasn't sure she should rise, so she remained sitting.

"Nice to meet you." Winifred sat by Herbert's right.

The first course consisted of some sautéed vegetables of which Miranda nibbled a few. Then, soup. When the smoked salmon was served, Miranda's stomach tightened. Not a major fish eater, she actually hated the taste. It made her nauseous, even though she didn't have that problem with shrimp or lobster. Lizandra and Lawe had cooked wonderful meals with those crustaceans, and shrimp etouffee was still one of Miranda's favorites.

"Mir-randa, you're not eating. Is something wrong?"

"Not real big with fish, Remare."

"Please take a taste."

"I'd rather not."

His voice sounded patient. *"It would be considered rude if you don't at least taste it."*

Miranda silently glared at him. *"I would rather not. Fish doesn't agree with my stomach."*

"Then, pretend to at least cut it with your knife."

That she could do. And then hid the small morsel under the garnish.

The meal continued with oysters, squid, and other variations of fish. Her stomach began to sour.

"Mir-randa, please take at least one bite."

"I didn't realize vampires were such fish connoisseurs."

"Some of us are." He grinned naughtily.

"Har, har!"

Winifred turned toward her. "You're not eating. Are you not hungry?"

"I didn't know Remare and I would be dining this late, so I had an earlier dinner."

"That's quite all right." Herbert speared what looked like a sardine and took a bite.

The small fish still had its head with the round eyes. Miranda's stomach almost roiled.

"I see." Winifred exhaled.

Miranda knew she'd just committed a faux pas but wasn't sure how to alleviate the dark look Remare was giving her. *"Please don't make me eat this."*

"Do I often ask favors of you?"

Actually, not that many. *"That fish has a head on it. It has eyes!"*

"Your point being?"

Oh God, her stomach was acting up. She couldn't do it. What was worse, being impolite or vomiting at the dining room table? She glared at Remare, who was still waiting for her. She cut another tiny piece of the fish and scooped it up. *"I hate you."* She lifted the fork to her mouth and chewed. *"I can't stand it."*

"Swallow."

Her jaw tightened, so did her throat. *"I don't think I can."*

"Swallow!"

She wanted to graciously spit it out in the linen napkin but didn't think that would go over well. She looked around for her purse but had left it in the other room. Her esophagus constricting, she stared at Remare as the fish slipped down her throat. *Ugh!* Not wanting to grimace in front of the others, she quickly drank from her water glass.

"Now, that wasn't so bad, was it?"

Her face heated. *"You are* so *not getting any later."*

"We'll see." He smirked as he lifted his wine in her direction and saluted her.

After dinner, they made for the study where Remare and Herbert continued to discuss business. Winifred noticed Miranda scanning the books and said, "Would you like to see the library? We have quite an extensive collection."

"I'd love to, Winifred."

"Oh, please call me Winnie." She took Miranda's arm as they walked. "Everyone else does."

"All right."

Winnie opened the doors, and Miranda nearly gasped at the overwhelming comfort of the room. The other rooms were for entertaining, but this room was for relaxation. Oak bookcases lined the walls from floor to ceiling with books. Miranda breathed the scent deep into her lungs.

"Herbert and I have been collecting for centuries. On this side, you'll find literature and philosophy," Winnie waved her hand in the other direction, "and on that side, biographies and books on science and finance."

Miranda marveled at the collection. "Any books on art history?"

"Quite a few." She led Miranda to the far end. "Feel free to peruse them. Remare has been a friend of Herbert's and mine for centuries, so if you wish, you may borrow whatever you want. I'm going to check on our other guests, and then, I'll be back."

"Okay." Miranda managed as Winnie left. Scanning the shelves, she discovered a book on the Medicis and the artists they'd patronized. She curled up on one of the Chesterfields and thumbed through the pages.

She was unaware of how much time had passed when Remare came to collect her. "Ready to leave?"

She yawned. "I think so."

"What are you reading?"

"A book about the Medicis and the artists who worked for them."

"Ah, I met a few of them in Florence. Interesting family."

"You knew them?" Miranda shouldn't have been surprised he'd known one of the most notorious and powerful families in Italy.

"Oh, yes. Would you like to borrow the book? I'm sure Herbert wouldn't mind."

"Winnie already said I could."

Herbert joined them. "It was a pleasure meeting you, Miranda. Ah, the Medicis. Now, there was an intriguing clan if ever there was one. Remare tells me you're an art authenticator. Feel free to keep the book as long as you like." He gazed around the room. "We have so many."

"Thank you. I'll be sure to return it. It was lovely meeting you and Winnie."

"We look forward to seeing you and Remare, again."

Winnie joined them and put her arm around Herbert. "We must do tea soon."

Miranda glanced at Remare. "I'd love to."

After saying their goodbyes, they were in the car on their way back to Remare's home.

Miranda tried to stifle another yawn. "Charming couple."

"That they are. They've been together for centuries and are quite happy. Herbert's invited us to spend a few days at his country estate. Would you like that?"

"Where is it?"

"In Sussex. It's a grand home with many rooms. The gardens are some of the best in the world."

In truth, Miranda was beginning to feel overwhelmed by the city, and spending some time in the country was something to look forward to. "Sounds great."

He started grinning as he held her hand. "You've been very patient in not asking me about Auriel."

"I noticed you avoided her gaze whenever she looked your way."

"No jealousy on your part?"

"Why would there be?" She smiled back at him. "If I wanted blond hair, I'd dye it; if I wanted to be thinner, I'd stop eating chocolate." *Like that's ever going to happen!* "Besides, if my hubby was going to get an itch," she kissed him, "I'd think he'd need more than a week to get bored."

"I will *never* get bored." He caressed her hand. "Auriel is the daughter of one of Valadon's strongest allies. We've known the Harringtons for a long time. A while back, she made her interest in me known. I told her then I was already involved. With the woman of my dreams."

"You didn't say that." Miranda laughed.

"No, but I thought it. And I made it quite clear to her she held little interest for me, except for her continual loyalty to Valadon."

"I suspected as much. You didn't give off any duplicitous vibes."

"Nor will I ever. I take our marriage vows seriously."

"Hmm."

"What was that 'hmm' for?"

Miranda frowned. "We had a very strange wedding."

"Agreed, it was not the ideal, but we are married."

"I know. It's just that it doesn't feel real. It all happened so quickly. I mean, we barely dated. And I think we had the shortest engagement on record. What were we engaged for? A minute?"

He shrugged. "Maybe ten."

"I think, in a year from now, we should do it for real."

"Mir-randa, it is real."

"I know. But I want the ideal. Not one of my friends was there. Lizandra was supposed to stand up for me. I didn't even have one solitary flower. Sucks." She rubbed his hand. "We never got to have one lousy dance together. And...there was no friggin cake!"

"What are you suggesting?"

"We got married in Valadon's shadow under Valadon's colors. Someday, I'd like to do it under our colors with our choices. Not his. I'd love it if Orion sang at our wedding."

"You want a redo?" He seemed to ponder the thought. "I suppose we can, if that's what you want."

"I don't mean anytime soon. But maybe, in another year or so, it'd be kinda nice."

He kissed her temple. "We have time to decide."

Chapter Eight

Miranda made it as far as the bedroom, toed off her shoes, and nearly passed out on the bed. "I can't move I'm so exhausted."

Remare shook his head. "Are you planning on sleeping in your gown?" He unzipped her and peeled the dress off, then hung it in the closet along with his suit. "I'll join you in a moment; I'm going to take a shower."

Wearing only her thong, she slipped under the sheets and moaned at the comfort. Sleep claimed her as her head hit the pillow. Out cold, she drifted along clouds in dreamlandia. She was in the country, old earth. A beautiful woman with dark, long flowing hair was in the distance, swinging beneath a tall oak tree, her handsome companion laughing along with her as he pushed her higher. They seemed so in love; Miranda was happy for them,

The woman gazed at Miranda, her smile welcoming. Miranda didn't want to intrude on the couple, but the woman gestured for her to come closer, and she did, at once recognizing her as the mysterious, fire-dancing woman she'd previously dreamt about. Before the woman could speak, her face turned to horror, and she pointed at something in the distance.

Miranda turned to see an older, white-haired man on a horse. His face was twisted in rage and emitted hatred. Her heart hammered as his animosity clawed at her. The woman's fear combined with Miranda's, and she woke, her breathing ragged.

Next to her, Remare remained peacefully asleep. She was glad her nightmare hadn't woken him and slipped out of bed.

Spotting his shirt, she donned it and, relishing his scent, buttoned up, and then made her way to the kitchen.

After pouring some orange juice, she slumped into a chair at the table and took a few sips. A moment later, Orion, rubbing his eyes and wearing only a pair of shorts, joined her. "Another nightmare?" Not bothering with a glass, he drank from the carton then sat beside her.

Miranda massaged her arms as if she could absorb Remare's scent into her skin. "Yeah, but this one wasn't as bad as the others."

"Same lady as before? I think I caught a few glimpses of her on a swing."

She grimaced. "Yeah. I don't understand why I keep having these dreams. Or why you can share them with me. I'm so sorry you have to live through my nightmares."

Orion shrugged. "Didn't this happen the last time you did research?"

"I think so, but this time, she seemed younger, happier."

"Why didn't you wake me?" Remare entered, wearing only his pajama bottoms. Apparently, neither he nor Orion were chilled.

She was grateful for his hand on her shoulder and caressed it. "You were sleeping so serenely. I didn't want to disturb you."

Remare, somewhat bewildered, addressed Orion. "Interesting that you share her dreams when I, who was nearest to her, did not."

"We were just discussing that. I don't know why either." She grasped his hand. "I suspect you sleep in a far deeper pattern than we do. Your breath is so diminished, you surely go to a different plane of existence."

He stroked his goatee. "And yet, Valadon could sense your dreams when he is in a different wing at ValCorp."

Miranda considered that. "I think it's because of your earth element. I don't understand it, but you ground us." She peered up at her friend. "Orion is air, and I'm fire. When awake, you somehow keep us tethered to this plane."

Remare sighed. "I wish we knew more about *Elementals*; maybe, then, we'd have a deeper understanding."

So did she. "I suspect it might also have to do with our blood bond."

"How do you mean?" Remare's eyes narrowed.

"I think Valadon can sense the nightmares because you and he have shared blood over the centuries. And you and I have also on occasion."

"How does that explain Orion? He's never shared blood with us."

Orion grimaced. "That's not quite true."

Miranda and Remare turned their heads in Orion's direction.

"When Valadon made me *'Liaison to the Court'*, between Black Star Clan and House Valadon...we exchanged blood."

Miranda nodded. "When we got back from Paris, in ValCorp's garage, by your car, I saw the bite marks on your neck."

"Valadon wanted an oath of loyalty."

Remare leaned forward. "Did you swear allegiance to Valadon or to House Valadon?"

"I told him my first loyalty was to Lizandra and the Black Stars. He concurred. The agreement he proposed was that I would never betray him or the trust he had in me."

Miranda wondered if there was more involved than Orion was willing to share. Valadon could be cagey when he wanted to be. And not always forthcoming. She made eye contact with Remare, who, from his expression, was probably wondering the same thing. She yawned. "I think we should get some sleep and save this conversation for the morning."

Remare nodded. "I agree. It's very late, and soon, it'll be dawn."

After Remare and she were nestled under the blankets, Orion knocked, and she said, "Come in."

Orion sat on the edge of the bed. "I was thinking about something. I mean about the blood bond and if there's some truth to your theory."

Miranda snuggled more into Remare's arms. "What do you mean?"

"I mean, I'm your bodyguard, right? So, what if you needed me and couldn't get to your phone? If there was a blood bond between us, you could mind speak to me if you were in any danger."

Miranda exhaled. "Humans and Weres don't share blood, Orion."

"I don't think that's what he means, Mir-randa."

She gazed up at Remare, and then, it hit her. She glanced back at Orion. "You want to exchange blood with Remare?"

"It makes sense. Especially if I'm guarding you." He rubbed his neck. "You sometimes go off by yourself. And I worry. You're like a sister to me. You're family. I don't want to lose you."

Remare seemed to consider the possibilities. "There are few people I trust with Miranda's well-being. You're one of them, Orion. I know you would lay down your life for her."

Miranda gave Remare a look. Had he forgotten how much her powers had grown? "People, really? I'm not defenseless. I can handle myself, so there's no reason for either of you to be concerned about me."

"I will always worry, Mir-randa. Asking me not to is like asking the winds not to blow." Remare kissed her knuckles. "That will never happen."

"You realize, if you let Remare drink from you, he'll be able to see into your mind?"

"Well, damn, Mira, if you trust him enough to marry him, I think I can trust him enough to let him bite me and not invade my privacy."

"What about Bastien? Exchanging blood can be a very personal thing. He might not approve."

Remare sat up straight. "At one time or another, I have exchanged blood with all the Elite Torians, Bastien included. This is not a sensual matter, Mir-randa, but one of safety. I'm certain Bastien would understand."

Miranda wasn't so sure, but Remare knew more about vampires than she ever would. She turned to him. "What do you think?"

"I think that if this is something Orion wants and is comfortable with, it is a good idea. The time may never come when it is needed, but there's every chance it might. Of all our people, I plan to call upon Orion when it is not possible for me to protect you."

Miranda brushed her lips along Remare's. "I'm not helpless, you know."

"I know. But you are precious to me, and I would sleep better knowing you are protected." He kissed her more thoroughly.

"It's your choice, Orion," she said.

"I've thought about it. It's what I want."

"Then, it is settled." Remare motioned for Orion to join them on the bed. "Any preferences."

Orion's lips thinned. "Not the neck; that's Bastien's. Wrist?"

Miranda moved to the side so Orion could fit between them. She couldn't remember ever seeing Remare bite anyone; the thought of him biting any other female infuriated her. But, with Orion, she was okay with it. She understood his purpose. Transfixed, she watched as Remare's fangs, long and sharp, emerged, and he bit into Orion's flesh. Remare kept his eyes on her the entire time he drank from Orion's wrist. Her heartbeat quickened as she observed them, wondering if she could ever bite anyone should she become vampire.

When Remare was finished, he sealed the minor wounds.

"It didn't hurt." Orion smiled at her then faced Remare. "I take it that now, I drink from you?"

"Close to the heart is best." He moved to cut above his left pec, and Miranda stopped him. "Hey, that's mine."

"Forgive me, my love." Remare motioned to his right pec, and Miranda nodded. He used his thumbnail to slice a thin line. Orion hesitated for only a minute, then leaned in and sucked at the tiny opening as Remare massaged the back of Orion's neck.

It shouldn't have aroused her, but for some reason, the idea of two men intimately together did. Miranda's breathing sped up, again, her body's reaction betraying her. Remare and Orion were dangerously enticing men, and she just now realized she was in bed with the two of them while barely dressed. Few, if any people, she'd be comfortable sharing Remare with, but Orion was one of them.

The act was functional, but blood possessed properties that made it seem far more sensual, more stirring to the soul. Remare seemed to read her mind and smiled.

After swallowing a few gulps, Orion licked the wound closed, even though Remare was more than able to heal the wound on his own. Sluggishly, Orion lay down between them and, in a moment, was sound asleep.

Miranda asked, *"Your blood has narcotic effects?"*

"Apparently, in his case, it does." His eyes downcast, he exhaled. *"I did not think, on our first night in London, we'd be sharing our bed with another."*

Miranda grinned as she moved a strand of Orion's hair off his face. *"No, the thought never entered my mind, either.*

Will it bother you overmuch if he sleeps with us? This bed is huge!"

He frowned. *"Under other circumstances, most definitely. But, for tonight, I suppose no harm is done."*

"You're aware he's the closest thing I have to a brother, and he's in love with Bastien?"

"And it is because of those very reasons I chose him to be your bodyguard and will permit this. Do you think I would allow another to come between us?"

Smiling, she reached up and stroked his jaw. *"I think if Auriel had made a play for you, I would have stabbed her with my fork, so I understand where you're coming from."*

Remare sighed as he glanced down at Orion. *"He is one handsome devil, isn't he?"*

"He's a good man, Remare. He'll never betray either one of us. I so hope it works out between him and Bastien."

Remare kissed her palm. *"I hope so, too. I've seen the way they look at each other."*

"How's that?"

His eyes lit up, and a sound escaped his throat halfway between a growl and a purr. *"Like the way we look at each other when we're both thinking the same thing."*

Orion turned over onto his stomach and burrowed deeper into the blankets. His voice was muffled by the pillow. "I love you guys." And then, his breathing slowed to that of a person deep in sleep.

"We love you, too, Orion." Miranda smiled up at Remare as she bent and kissed Orion goodnight.

With one brow raised, Remare purred. "Should I be concerned about your feelings for him?"

"Not at all," she whispered. "I care deeply about him." She considered his words. "There's always going to be handsome men: Orion, Gavin, even Valadon. My body may react to them, but nothing like the way it responds to you."

He kept his voice low. "Oh, and how's that?"

"You're the flop."

"I'm the *what*?!"

She chuckled. "Attractive men may walk into the room, and my stomach may do this little flip. It's no big. It's just a reaction." She linked their fingers. "But, when *you* walk into a room, my stomach flips and then flops. No one else does that to me."

"Ah, so I'm the flop." He frowned. "I think I'd prefer it if you came up with a better analogy."

"Well, let's see. I love chocolate. Many types, but there's one above all the others: chocolate mocha. Nothing like it, orgasm-inducing. Sort of like you."

"Hmm. Chocolate." He still looked less than thrilled.

"Okay, as far as artists are concerned, you're the best of the best, my favorite, Da Vinci."

"Ah, now, that I like." He turned toward her. "And you are my Ornellaia."

"Your what?"

"Ornellaia is a red wine made in Tuscany. There are other more expensive wines, but the Ornellaia is my personal favorite. Robust, complex, and very tasty." He gave her a smoldering look. "Like you."

"I think I like it better when you call me your sorceress, but if I remind you of wine, that's good, too. All right, then." She rose from the bed and examined Orion's sleeping form. Using her power, she lifted his body from the middle of the bed and moved it to the right.

"Your powers are improving."

Nodding, she climbed on top of Remare and nestled between his legs, pulling the covers over them. "I suspect it's because you're here and him. I think we all become stronger when we're together."

He played with a strand of her hair. "I suppose."

She glanced back at Orion. "You know, Orion has always wanted to belong somewhere. He once told me he never felt comfortable growing up in the Midwest. That's why he moved to New York." She rested her palms on Remare's chest. "Even at Werehaven, he felt...detached. Surprisingly, he told me he feels more at home at Valadon House."

"Not so surprising." He shrugged. "He loves Bastien."

"He can belong to us, as well. He'd be your brother, too, if you let him."

Remare gazed over at Orion. "That remains to be seen, but perhaps, in time..."

Miranda brushed her lips over Remare's. "I love you." Then, she deepened the kiss and welcomed Remare's strong arms around her. Warmth seeped into her bones, and she snuggled closer.

He growled seductively. "We could move to one of the guest rooms."

"Damn, Remare, you are temptation personified. But nah. I need sleep." Her voice was more throaty than she'd intended. "And you only do longies." She chuckled. "In the morning, when Orion goes jogging." She slid to his side, believing the nightmares would stay at bay within Remare's embrace and with the presence of Orion so close to them. She wondered how strong the bond between them would evolve. And the possibilities thereof. The energy pulsing between them hummed softly, lulling each to sleep.

Chapter Nine

Bas and Tristan crept silently along the shadows of the Ehrlich Industries factory, manufacturers of the device that almost killed Valadon's son, Vincent. While Tristan methodically set explosives in the Research and Development area, Bas scrutinized the contents of the vault. Having seduced and scanned the brain of the lovely designer, Gita Brenner, Bas had been able to obtain her access codes, as well as copy her fingerprints. She'd been so sex-starved, he barely needed to use his allure to enthrall her.

Fucking her hadn't been a problem; she was desirable, and he gave her exactly what she craved. Coolly detached, he'd hardly worked up a sweat at all. Part of him wanted to kill her for designing such a deadly weapon harmful to vampires, but that hadn't been part of the plan. Veiling her memories had been. As a Blueblood, that ability came naturally.

He photographed all pertinent data concerning the device then destroyed the prototype and the other models. There would be no remnants of the design or the weapon after they left.

Tristan nodded that all the bombs were in place. Together, they moved stealthily down the corridor. The cameras within the complex had been disengaged, and the security officers were still out cold from the drugs Tristan had shot them with. When questioned, they would have no recollection of any break-ins or any disturbances. The problem wasn't getting in; it never was. The trick was leaving without setting off any alarms that might have been inadvertently overlooked. That rarely happened. But every now and then...

They were nearly to the exit when the sound of growling reverberated from around the corner in front of them. Bastien didn't want to kill the Dobermans, even though they were trained attack dogs, so he fired the darts that would put them to sleep. They were barely conscious when they hit the floor.

Once outside, they drove up into the Austrian countryside and watched from a distance as the explosions tore through the building and lit up the night sky.

Bas snapped some photos and smirked. "Valadon wanted to send a message to Blackmore. I think this pretty much does the trick."

Tristan nodded. "I'd say so."

"Bastards will come up with something new. They always do." Bas headed back to their car.

"And we'll deal with it. Now, we can go home."

"Not quite. I got a text from Remare." Bas read his message. "He wants us to meet him in London. Orion and Miranda are with him."

"What for? I was hoping, once this mission was over, we'd go back to New York. Did he say for how long?"

"He'll explain when he sees us. Let's get to the airfield. I've already contacted the pilot."

Once in the car, Tristan waved his hand back and forth. "Man, you need a shower. You reek of sex."

"All in a day's work. I'll rinse off on the plane." Bas spied Tristan's grimace. "Don't give me that look. I did what was necessary."

"Hey, I didn't say a word."

"You didn't have to. Your scowl says plenty." Bastien put the car in gear and drove. "Seriously, you should be better at concealing your emotions."

"I didn't realize I had to with you."

Bas shrugged. "You don't." He thought about how he'd taken Brenner. There'd been no joy in it. He'd dommed her in every way. Whenever she'd tried to take the top position, he would pin her to the mattress, taking her from behind. He told himself it was so she'd have no memory or dreams about him, but he hadn't wanted to see her face. She'd been a means to an end. Nothing more. He'd done this dozens, if not hundreds, of times, so why was it bothering him, now?

"You gonna tell Orion about her?"

"What the fuck for? He doesn't need to know. And I don't want you saying anything, either. Missions are secret for a reason."

"I won't say anything. But make sure you shampoo your hair. It smells floral-like. Not your usual."

"I will. There's the airfield, now. Ever been to London before? It's one helluva town."

"Nah. Most of my travels have been between Canada and the States."

"That's right. You're originally from Montreal."

"You were born in Paris. Ever think of going back?"

Bas rubbed his chin. "Not really." He wasn't sure how he was going to explain his relationship with Orion to certain relatives. And he knew, once he was home, the interrogations would start.

It was nothing he wanted to deal with, let alone think about. Truth was, he missed Orion. The Were challenged him in ways no one else ever had. Made him laugh and feel things he hadn't felt in a long time. He blew out a long breath. It would be good to see him, again. Bas glanced up in the night sky. The moon was almost full, and Orion would need somewhere to run in his wolf form. He could still feel the thickness of Orion's pelt under his hand. Remember the smoothness of his fur and his wonderful scent.

Maybe, this time, he'd join him during the lunar run.

***

Miranda stretched as she woke and smiled to see Remare beside her. His dark brown eyes were intoxicating, bewitching. "Now, this is a sight I don't mind waking up to."

"I rather like the view, as well." He kissed her forehead.

"You're usually gone when I wake up. It's nice waking up with you here."

He stroked her cheek with his thumb. "Yes. I look forward to many more mornings with you by my side."

"What time is it?"

He checked the clock. "Almost noon."

She turned to see the empty space Orion had occupied. "He's probably had breakfast and gone running."

"And, so, we have some private time." Remare rolled on top of her and nuzzled her neck.

She laughed. "Your goatee tickles. Some women complain beards give them skin burns. But yours is so soft it doesn't chafe." She rubbed his finely trimmed hairs, loving the way they brushed against her fingers.

"I keep it soft for you." He smiled wickedly. "Especially when I take you here." He moved down her body until his head hovered over her lower abdomen."

She laughed. "Stop. Come here, you. I just want to look at you for a little while longer."

Remare undid the buttons of his shirt she was wearing and kissed his way upward. "I enjoy watching you, too."

Miranda hadn't had time to tell him what she wanted. "You didn't ask me about meeting the other *Elementals*."

"I figured you would tell me when you were ready."

"After lunch, I'm going back to the library. I've been doing research on artists who mention people with my abilities." She waved her hand for emphasis.

"I'll come with you."

She grinned. "You'd be bored. Research is rather dull unless you're interested in the topic."

"I *am* interested. I told you, once before, I'd help you if you ever wanted to complete your PhD."

Miranda considered the possibilities. "Can you read Latin?"

"Of course. I did grow up in Rome. As Valadon's former ambassador to the European courts, I learned to read and speak many languages."

She remembered he'd once told her that, before he became Valadon's second in command, he'd been an ambassador. She recalled something else he'd told her. "You're half British, aren't you?"

He nodded. "My mother was British. My father met her when he was stationed here. After his service ended, he brought her back to Rome. Since she loved country living, he built her a magnificent villa in Tuscany."

"Is it still there?"

"I'm afraid not. The wars ravaged the countryside. However, newer structures were constructed on the site."

She knew his parents had died long ago. "Do you ever go back?"

"No. Italy hasn't been home for centuries. New York is."

"I'm glad." She stroked his jaw. "I wish you could meet some of the *Elementals*, but they believe in secrecy and don't welcome outsiders."

"I would like to make their acquaintance, as well. I'm not sure I'm comfortable with you socializing with them alone. They may share your gifts, but they're still strangers."

"I know. There's one I get mixed vibes from. Don't worry. I keep my cards close to the vest."

"I'm just saying be careful."

"I am. Sarita told me there's an elder who might meet with me. Give me some background information on us. Remare," she linked their fingers, "I've waited so long to find others of my kind. This is important to me. Since I was young,

I've always wondered why I have these abilities. I want to learn more."

He grinned. "You're still young, Mir-randa." He kissed her cheek. "Young and beautiful."

She ran her fingers along his jaw. "You make me feel that way."

Just then, her phone vibrated. "Hmm, Sarita texted Agatha will meet with me later today." She flipped the covers off. "We should get moving."

He dragged her back. "We have some time." His voice sounded sexy before he kissed her.

"Mmm. Hold the thought. Bathroom." Miranda rushed in, used the facilities, then brushed her teeth. Nothing was worse than morning breath. After splashing her face with water, she dried it on the towel, and then tossed off Remare's shirt.

Wearing only her skimpy thong, she opened the door and stood seductively in the doorframe, staring at her lover. The butterflies in her stomach raging for release. Her heart pounding with anticipation.

Remare growled. "You are truly a beautiful woman." He pitched the blankets aside and slid his hand down his groin. "Your breakfast awaits."

"I'll say. Lose the jammies." Miranda tossed her panties to the side.

With vampire speed, his pajama bottoms joined her thong on the floor. Heat simmering in his eyes, he crooked his finger at her. She lunged for the bed and kissed him soundly, inhaling his masculine scent as his cool body slid against her warmer one. She couldn't tell which of them purred more loudly. Her hand covered his heart, and she relished the rhythmic beating. "I'm so glad you're here."

"Yes, I thought it was a good idea." He positioned her on top of him so that her core was directly over his rigid cock. "But I think this is an even better one."

Since she was already wet with desire, no foreplay was needed, and she slid down the length of him, moaning at the velvety smoothness. "Oh God, you feel so good." Closing her eyes, she arched her back, letting her head drift back.

Remare's fingers dug into her hips as he rocked her to increase her rhythm. "You bring out the beast in me, Miranda. With you, I have hunger like I've never known before." He reached up to nuzzle her neck then trailed his lips to her breast and sucked her nipple into his mouth.

His teeth grazed her enough to send shards of sensations quivering to her lower belly. Miranda groaned loudly at the pleasure. "The breakfast of champions." She giggled.

"It's about to be." In a flash of movement, Remare reversed their positions, and she welcomed his partial weight on top of her. His smooth muscles flexed under her touch as she ran her fingers along his spine to his lower back. Clutching his glutes, she dug her nails into him. His growls stirred her even more, making her float higher. A fine coating of sweat covered their bodies as they moved in sacred synchronicity. Her breaths rapid, her heart pounding, she watched as Remare's eyes darkened and he reached for his climax. She knew he was as close as she was.

Her body became strung so tight, riding an impossible wave of ecstasy no surfer could ever imagine. She met him stroke for stroke, cresting so high, so intense, she howled in pleasure when he sank his fangs in her neck. Her body convulsed beneath him in a wonderful mix of exhilaration and exhaustion. After removing his fangs and sealing the tiny wounds, he thrust two more times, the muscles in his arms and neck tightening, straining, before throwing his head back and roaring his own pleasure.

Still breathing heavily, he pulled them to lie on their sides. It was moments before her heart resumed its natural rhythm. Within Remare's embrace, the world was a safe place, her haven where no nightmares existed. A place where she was free to be simply herself.

When she could finally find her voice, she uttered, "We're going to need a proper honeymoon." Still trembling from the aftershocks, she whispered, "One where we don't have to get up early for work."

"Now, that is a very good idea."

***

In one of his many store rooms, Lord Acton went through what was left of his former lover's possessions. He hadn't searched through her things in ages. She'd died long ago, but when she'd been alive, she'd been a powerful seer, an *Elemental*, whose abilities netted him many profits. Because she'd become so valuable to him, he'd allowed her many indulgences, gave her freedoms he normally didn't grant to those who served him.

And she'd betrayed him. After that, he was more scrupulous in his dealings with others. His *Elemental* thought he hadn't learned of her plans, but he had. He'd had her watched, knew of her movements and her desires. And he'd played with her. If she'd only been loyal, he would have been more successful, more powerful, and the chancellor's position would have been in grasp.

But, now, another possibility had made itself known. From what his sources were reporting, Remare's new wife, Miranda Crescent, was a powerful *Elemental* who kept her talents hidden, latent. *Does Lord Valadon not know what a valuable asset he has in his house? Why has the High Lord not demanded fealty from her? Why would one with such power not use it to benefit herself? Unless the rumors concerning her were false or exaggerated.* No matter, Lord

Acton had his people looking into it. He would learn soon enough if she was worthy of his investment.

And if she was? He smirked in gleeful anticipation. He'd make sure all preparations were in place for that occurrence. He would not make the same mistakes he'd made with Esmerelda. No, this time, he would exert the control he should have used long ago.

This time, he would not fail.

Chapter Ten

After studying texts for hours at the Herkimer Library, Miranda at the desk, Remare on the couch, she gazed up at him; he'd proven himself a worthy researcher. Man, with him as her study buddy, grad school would have been a breeze. No need for translation programs; he read Latin, French, Spanish, German, and several other languages at a speed that boggled her mind. With his keen acumen, he often volunteered helpful information about books written during the different epochs, but especially the time of the Medicis.

She was charmed by his intellect and whimsical sense of humor about past events. When he saw her staring at him, he gave her an inquisitive look.

"I wasn't sure you meant it—about doing research. I didn't think you had the patience for it."

"Long ago, I attended several universities. Valadon and I both did. And, may I remind you, I have a great deal of patience." His grin was naughty.

"I suppose I should have known better. I stand corrected." She pointed to a page in her book. "I was just reading an account in the 1490s of a Dominican priest, Giralamo Savonarola, who went up against the Medicis—one in particular, Loren."

Remare laid his head back in memory. "You mean Lorenzo the Magnificent."

"Giralamo didn't think so. He burned Loren's books, artworks, music, and anything else he dubbed hedonistic and anti-Church, *'De Ignium Festorum de Vanitatum'*."

"Yes, but history remembers it better as, 'The Bonfire of the Vanities'. He was a fool to challenge the Medicis. Within a year, he was excommunicated and executed. The Medicis had little tolerance for those who thought they had the authority to dictate their behavior."

She turned another page in her book. "Well, that's interesting."

"What is?"

"This is the second time I've come across an artist by the name of Antoine Caron. The Medicis favored his work in the mid- to late-1500s. Not only did he design festivals for them, he also worked on cathedrals. Quite an allegorist. Some of his favorite themes include magic and the occult. I came across a rendition of a painting of his titled, *The Book of Origins.* Fascinating work, but no mention of it anywhere else. I asked Mrs. Gordon, the head reference librarian, if she'd heard of it. Didn't ring any bells. She texted she's still searching for it. Have you ever come across it?"

"Alas, I never gave much consideration to artworks. I was too busy practicing détente and planning strategies in times of war. Had I known I would one day fall in love with an art historian, I would have paid better attention."

She smiled. "You may have glanced at it and not even known what it was."

"Magic and the occult would not have gone over well with the Church, at the time; it's possible they burned the original painting."

"It makes you wonder what other valuable paintings and works of literature were lost through the ages. What a shame we'll never know what great works of art were lost because of political maneuverings. Mrs. Gordon told me the library lost close to twenty-five thousand books during WWII. And still, to this day, many paintings were stolen by the Nazis and never returned." She shook her head in regret.

Remare laid his book on the coffee table and patted the cushion next to him. "Come here."

Eyes tired, she closed the book she'd been reading and joined him. With his arm around her, she snuggled against his side. "This feels good. Feels right."

"It is right." He stroked her arm and played with a strand of her hair. And, for a moment, they sat in happy solitude, content to just be together.

"There's something I have to tell you." She'd been wanting to tell him about Peralt's book for some time. As her husband, he should know who and what he married. "I found an old copy of Peralt's theories about *Elementals*. Some of his stuff is really out there. The parts about astronomy and the alignment of planets, but some of his other ideas were fascinating."

"Tell me." He continued stroking her hair. "I've wanted to learn more ever since you called Valadon "the chameleon." You never really told us what you meant."

"Peralt's theories include the four elements: fire, air, water and earth. He used a lot of Latin and Germanic terms. He believed people like me could manipulate the elements. But he also spoke of a fifth group, the chameleons—the most powerful and rare of us who have dominion over all four elements."

"And you think Valadon is a chameleon?"

"In a manner of speaking. Water covers nearly three-fourths of the earth, and his power is profound. It nearly burns my skin when he doesn't mute it."

"But vampires aren't *Elementals*. Humans are."

"If humans can be *Elementals*, why not vampires? Or, for that matter, Weres?"

Remare leaned his head back as if in memory. "I've heard stories of ancient vampires having unfathomable abilities. That they could control the elements."

"But you can't?"

He shook his head as he held her close. "I don't know any vampires who can. All myths and folktales created by fiction writers."

Miranda didn't want to tell him Montglat was an ancient who possessed some incredibly terrifying talents. But there were other things she wanted to discuss. "Some of the things Peralt mentioned were downright scary."

"Such as?"

"He mentioned transmutation. I wasn't sure what he meant by that, so I did some research."

He smirked. "Please do not ask me if we ever turned into bats or mist, Mir-randa. Solely the imagination of an Irish writer."

She laughed at his bored tone. "I wouldn't dare. However, in some ancestral writings, there's mention of people morphing into all sorts of animals. When I was studying petroglyphs in New Mexico, I learned that ancient tribes believed in such metamorphosis, as well as other cultures in the world."

"Civilizations of the world always sought reasons for phenomenon they otherwise couldn't understand. The ancient Greeks made up stories about the gods to explain common occurrences in nature like thunder and lightning. The peoples of ancient India and Asia have their myths, as well." Remare pulled her onto his lap and kept his arms loosely around her.

"Yes, I'm aware. Did you know just about every continent has its myths and references to 'night people', or 'wraiths of the night', that sound a lot like vampires? Except for Antarctica."

"We never did like the cold very much."

Miranda laughed. "I'm serious. If you check the annals of literature: poems, folktales, even art has numerous references to vampires."

"For many centuries, we tried to keep a low profile. Only revealing ourselves to those we deemed necessary for survival. When the plagues hit Europe, humans needed a reason for all the deaths. Before science explained diseases, many believed vampires were the monsters of lore. Fear only magnified their imagination."

"So I've read. But Peralt also mentioned *Elementals* as being the offspring of the angels."

"The Nephilim?"

"Not quite. There are stories about the children of angels and humans. The angels were supposed to be our guardians, to watch over us, protect us. But some had progenies with human women. They defied God's will and were banished for it. However, the descendants were seen as innocents, their powers bound. According to Peralt's theory, some of their legacies weren't completely expunged. They skipped generations. And, every now and then, someone is born with remarkable abilities. Most likely diluted through the centuries."

"And did you know science has proven humans only use a small percentage of their brains?" He kissed her knuckles. "I suspect there are humans who use more. You, my sorceress, I suspect use significantly more."

"I've read those reports. So much they don't know. Still, some of the ancient theories are fascinating, if not substantiated."

His tone was mild, but concern laced his voice. "Is it that important where your talents come from?"

"I've always been curious. At night, when I stare up at the starry sky," she shrugged, "I wonder."

"As we all do."

"And that is why it's important I meet with the other *Elementals*. Sarita's invited me to a yoga class tonight. Then,

I'll meet with Agatha, their elder." She rose from his lap. "You look less than enthused."

"I'm concerned your quest may arouse the interest of others whose purposes are less than congenial. There may be people who desire your powers, Mir-randa. Human and *Other*. I know not what happened to your race of beings, but I do know people desire that which they don't have, especially power. Promise me you'll be careful."

"I will." Just then, her stomach started growling. "Oh, look, here comes Orion. Right on time."

Her Were leaned against the doorframe. "You guys ready to head out to dinner?"

"I am. I'm starving. Research works up an appetite."

Remare rose. "I know a great restaurant you two might enjoy."

"That may have to wait. Orion and I agreed, if we went to The Flat Iron for steaks yesterday, he'd come with me for pizza tonight."

Remare scowled. "Pizza?"

"Yes, I've had a yen since we left New York."

Orion straightened. "No one makes pizza as good as they do in New York, but hey, I'm game."

Miranda shrugged. "Not so sure about that. When I was out west in New Mexico, we stopped in a place called, Kathy's Chicago Style Pizza. It was very good, tasty. Lots of peppers and onions. Mouthwatering. Reminded me of New York."

Remare sighed. "All right, then, let's head out so you can make your yoga class tonight."

***

Valadon was busy going over ValCorp's financial earnings when there was a knock on his door. "Enter."

"Is this a good time? If not, I can come back later." Eric hesitated in his doorway.

"Not at all. I always have time for Rosalyn and her family." Valadon had given the young Finnish vampire sanctuary in his territory after he'd requested it. Eric had already shown his loyalty by offering up interesting pieces of information regarding Vivienna's court and her alliances. He'd confessed it was Brandon who'd made him record the disturbing tape Valadon had received after Miranda returned from Paris. The youth had suffered miserably at Valadon's brother's hand, as well as Vivienna's, who regarded Eric as little more than a plaything.

Eric sat in the seat in front of him, but only after Valadon had gestured for him to do so.

"What brings you to ValCorp?"

"I told Rosalyn I needed to find a job, or I was going to go out of my mind. She offered me work at her club. And Jason said he would find something for me at one of his companies, but I said no to both."

"Why?"

"I don't want to be known as someone who's related to the boss. That isn't me. After I told her that, she suggested I come talk to you."

Rosalyn and Jason Morgan were two of his favorite people, both intensely loyal. "Your sister and brother-in-law are doing well, yes?"

"Oh, very well. I'm glad as hell she married the love of her life, but I don't think I can take much more of their overly sweetness. I thought I'd overdose on it if I stayed around them any longer."

Valadon chuckled. "I see. What kind of work were you considering?"

"I know my standing in Vivienna's court wasn't much more than an amusement," he exhaled, shame showing on his face, "but before that, I did attend university. I was thinking of becoming one of your Torians, but I must admit I'm not physically on that level, and I doubt I ever will be."

Valadon studied Eric's form. The handsome, red-headed vampire was of medium height and build, but he lacked the muscular physique of his Torians. "What interests you?"

"I thought about that. In all my journeys with Vivienna, I tried to hide out in the kitchens. The one place she would never look for me. I learned a great deal about food preparation."

"You wish to be a chef?"

He laughed. "Not really, but I told Roz, if she ever did any catering, I would help her out. I was hoping you would have some suggestions."

Valadon swiveled his chair. "I'll give it consideration. You said you visited the other courts with Vivienna. Have you remembered any other conversations you might deem useful to me?"

"Sure. Just ask. You'd be surprised what you can hear hanging out with household staff in a lord's kitchen."

He didn't doubt it. "Did you ever travel to London with Vivienna?" He wondered about the rumors that had reached him about her and Gideon.

"Many times. Vivienna liked personally checking on how well her designs were selling in cities like London, Milan, Venice and Rome. London was one of her favorite cities to visit. We went there many times."

Valadon brought up Gideon's picture on his monitor. "Do you recognize this man?"

"Yes, I do. Vivienna had many lovers throughout the courts, but this one, Gideon, she tried to keep secret. I know they whispered about politics, but I could never get close enough to hear exactly what they were saying."

"She was his lover?"

"I think she still is. I once overheard her say they got along well because they respected each other's ambition. She didn't elaborate any further than that."

"I see."

At that moment, Cesare, chief designer for Valadon Creations, knocked. As the door was already open, he walked in, portfolio in hand. "I brought those mark-ups you wanted to see." His eyes lit on Eric, and it was as if Cesare had been struck by lightning. "Who is this person?"

Valadon laughed as Cesare gestured for Eric to rise then walked around him scrutinizing his body.

"Eric, meet Cesare, ValCorp's head designer. Hmm. Now that I think of it, there is one position that has recently become available. Tell me, Eric, have you ever done any modeling?"

"Not professionally, no."

"You should. The bone structure of your face is perfect." Cesare smiled from ear to ear. "The camera's going to love you."

Valadon grinned. "Well, Cesare, I think you just found Jeremy's replacement."

Cesare continued studying Eric. "I think so, too. Can I have him? Please?"

"For what?" Eric looked terrified.

"Nothing ominous," Valadon placated Eric's fears. "We have recently lost our top model to another house. Would you be interested in modeling for us? Menswear and cologne. I assure you the position comes with perks and a very reasonable salary." Valadon wrote out a figure on a piece of paper and passed it to Eric.

After his eyes nearly popped out of his head, Eric asked, "When do we start?"

Chapter Eleven

Miranda felt uncomfortable leaving Orion alone in the car while she attended her yoga class. She agreed with Remare that Orion would stay in her general location. To assuage her guilty feelings, she finally convinced him to have a drink in the tavern across the street. If she were in danger, she'd contact her wolf mentally. Through their shared blood bond with Remare, they were now able to transmit thoughts with ease.

"So glad you could make it." Sarita greeted her by the yoga studio's door and handed her a mat. "We had extras in the back."

Esme approached. "Have you studied yoga before?"

"Oh, yes, back in New York. I've studied both Hatha yoga and Dyana or meditative. After work, it was much needed and appreciated."

"Good. I usually start with the basics of Anusara and Vinyasa, then I'll move on to the Kundalini and Dyana. Did your instructors use music in their classes?"

"Definitely. I've found the sounds of the ocean very relaxing."

"All right, then. We'll start in a few moments." Esme went to speak with some of her other students.

"Let's check out the jewelry." Sarita gestured to the display cases. "Esme makes the prettiest necklaces; she made the one I gave you."

Miranda was awed by the raw beauty of the crystals. She recognized the garnets and the hematite. "They're beautiful. I know a few people back home who'd love them." She quickly purchased three of the crystal necklaces.

"Give her one of the handbooks on the crystals, Jen." Esme joined them. "You should know what they're known for."

Miranda read the title, *Mysteries and Mystical Aspects of Minerals.* She nearly scoffed. *Magic rocks?*

As if reading her mind, Esme said, "For centuries, people believed minerals held metaphysical properties that aided in healing. The ancient Greeks used them for many purposes."

Sure, why not? Miranda just thought they made beautiful pieces of jewelry. "I'm sure my friends in New York will appreciate them."

Esme nodded and pointed. "You can put your purse and jacket on the shelves over there."

"All right." Having done so, Miranda joined the group of twelve who already had their positions picked out. As always, she chose a place in the back as Esme lowered the lights and lit the scented candles.

Esme's calm voice echoed through the room. "We have a guest tonight from America; please welcome Miranda."

So much for keeping a low profile. She waved at the group consisting mostly of women and a few men who smiled warmly at her.

Esme's voice took on a hypnotic quality that encouraged everyone to strive for their personal best, no competition whatsoever, during the physical movements.

Miranda centered her breathing as she'd previously been taught, slowing down her heart rate as she assumed the positions of The Cobra, Lotus, Garland and various lunges. She liked pushing herself to see how long she could hold the pose and keep her breathing modulated. It was fun and oh so relaxing. Discipline, on this level, took time and effort. Miranda was grateful she'd practiced for years and had an excellent yogi in New York.

The time flew by quicker than she thought. Some muscles were a little sore from the rigorous training, but overall, she felt good. Then, it was time for the meditative part. Clearing the mind wasn't always easy. It took much more focus than most people realized. Especially on nights when she went directly after work, when her brain was buzzing with so much work-related business. But, here and now, she was content she'd found other *Elementals*. Centering her energy seemed to come naturally for her. Body and soul were one. She was at peace.

Esme played soothing music as the air was scented with aromas found in nature. Miranda felt herself drifting as time lapsed. She wasn't a yoga master, but she wasn't a novice, either. She opened her eyes to see what appeared to be a spirit in front of her. Stunned, she blinked. It was Esme. Miranda barely whispered, "You're on the astral plane?! I thought that was only a theory."

Esme's voice was but a mere echo of a whisper. "Free your mind, Miranda. Much of what you think you know about *Elementals* is only a drop in a much larger ocean." She reached out to touch Miranda but pulled away, barely brushing her cheek.

Now, Miranda had to work overtime to steady her breathing. What had once come easily was now labored. She breathed deeply and gazed over the group. A woman of indeterminable age on the far left nodded in her direction. *"Pleased to meet you, Miranda. I'm Agatha"*

So, this was their elder. Although Agatha had a few streaks of gray, her face remained serene, and she seemed in excellent shape. She'd been here the whole time, watching. Miranda wondered if she'd passed some sort of test.

After more time spent in meditation, Esme used the small cymbals to announce the end of class. The students slowly rose and smiled. Each seemed more refreshed, revitalized—the mark of a good teacher.

Sarita approached. "Please stay and have tea with us. Agatha wishes to speak with you."

Yeah, Miranda had a few questions herself for the elder.

After the others left and the mats were put away, Miranda joined the small circle of *Elementals*.

Agatha seemed to be sizing her up. "So, you're the American. I imagine you must have a great deal of questions for us."

Miranda hated it when she couldn't get a sense for someone. Usually, her empath skills didn't fail her, but on occasion, there were people she just couldn't read; Agatha was one of them. "A few."

"They tell me you were orphaned and received no training in the *Elemental* arts. A pity. I suspect you might have become quite powerful."

"I wasn't even sure there were others like me in the world. Why did you wait to introduce yourself?"

"Like any of us, we prefer our anonymity, and I wanted to be sure before revealing myself."

"Be sure of what?"

Esme smiled. "Your aura is golden with blue and violet striations."

Esme can read auras? "Is that a good thing?"

"If it weren't, we wouldn't be having this conversation. Your colors signify you're a *Light Elemental*."

"As opposed to…"

"*Dark Elementals*. Surely, you knew there were different types of us?"

"I've read there are four basic types: Undines—water, Sylvestris—air, Gnomes—earth, and Vulcans—fire."

"Some profess there are more." Agatha gestured to Esme. "Esme has incredible talents that don't fall into any of the four categories. But her mental abilities are of the finest."

Agatha asked, "Did your research indicate there is one group, very rare with incomparable powers?"

Miranda said, "The fifth *Elemental*, the chameleons—people who have talents in all four areas. According to what I've read, they were exceedingly rare."

"Very." Agatha sipped her tea.

Miranda wondered aloud. "How would you know if someone was a *Dark Elemental?*"

Esme answered. "Your aura would be covered in black."

Miranda leaned forward. "Exactly what is the difference between the two?"

"*Light Elementals* use their powers for good: healing, assuaging the fears of others, giving guidance when necessary. That is why so many of us are in the health and education fields."

"And *Dark Elementals?*"

Agatha sneered. "The dark ones use their powers for nefarious reasons. You've heard of the seven deadly sins: envy, greed, wrath, and so forth? They give free reign to their dark desires. Often causing harm to others."

Strange, Miranda hadn't gotten that vibe from the one she'd met in the back alley behind the bar who Sarita said was a *Dark Elemental.* "And you can tell the difference by their auras?"

Esme nodded. "Of course, actions speak loudly. But there are other ways of knowing."

Miranda was very interested in learning what those other ways were, but before she could ask, Agatha spoke up. "I think that's enough for tonight. If you truly want to know more about us, about yourself, come to The Gathering."

"What's—"

"During the full moon, we meet at my home out in the country." Agatha set her tea down. "We're not Wiccans, but we pay homage to our ancestors and to nature."

Sarita said, "Mostly, we enjoy a night out with friends and good food. We sing some of the old songs and show off our powers. It's a night of celebration and sisterhood. I hope you'll join us."

"When is it?"

"The night after tomorrow."

Miranda sighed. "I'm sorry, but I've plans to stay with some of my husband's friends in the country. We leave tomorrow."

"Where in the country?"

Miranda wasn't quite sure. "I think it's somewhere in southeastern England."

"So is my home." Agatha reached inside her purse and retrieved a card. "If you can somehow manage it, we would be delighted if you joined us."

Miranda read the card. "I'll have to check with what plans my husband has made, but if at all possible, I'll be there."

Agatha nodded. "Pleasure meeting you, Miranda."

"Same." Miranda turned toward Esme and Sarita. "Thank you for inviting me tonight. It was…illuminating."

Once outside, she decided to join Orion at the tavern.

"Miranda, is everything okay? You look a little pale."

"I'm fine. Although, I'd like a beer before heading home."

After she chose a corner table, Orion returned from the bar with their beers. She gulped hers down. "Thanks, I think I needed that."

"So, what gives?"

"I just wanted a few moments to process all that I've learned."

"Such as?"

She reached across the table to grasp his hand in hers, needing their connection. "There's so much about being an *Elemental* I don't know. Each time I discover more, it just throws me for a loop."

"What'd you find out?"

Miranda took a deep breath. Then another. "You're part Cherokee, right?" She remembered his Native American grandmother helped raise him.

"Yup, on my mother's side."

"Did she ever tell you tales of spirits that visited during the night or something like dreamwalkers?"

"It's part of the lore. I grew up with a lot of stories of myths and magic. None of it was real, though."

Miranda pondered the preternatural world. "I wonder, sometimes, how much is myth and how much isn't."

"Now, you're sounding scary."

"I met someone with incredible gifts tonight. *Elementals* have powers—the four elements. But I suspect some are more powerful than others. A lot more powerful."

"And?"

"The *Elementals* I've met are real big on secrecy. They guard their powers and don't trust outsiders much. I don't think they want me discussing them too much. But I will say this. One of them has crazy-ass mental abilities."

"Telepathy?"

"I'd think so. I felt her essence, Orion. No joke, she's able to reach out on a different plane of existence. Scary stuff."

Orion leaned back in his chair and appeared to be studying her. "My grandmother used to tell stories of evil spirits who used to invade the minds of people when they slept. That they were the reason for nightmares."

"Did you believe her?"

"She scared the crap out of me. I was just a kid. I don't know what I believed. Thank God, we're leaving for the country tomorrow. It will be good to get out of the city, and with the full moon, I'll need space to run." They finished the rest of their beers.

In the car ride back, Miranda texted Remare they were on their way home. "Remare says he has a surprise for you."

Orion turned toward her. "What?"

"He didn't say. But I suspect something good." She patted his knee and smirked. "A reward for taking such good care of me."

When they arrived at the house, Miranda unlocked the door and was surprised to see Tristan sitting in one of the chairs, watching the international news on TV—something about an explosion at a munitions plant in Austria.

"Hey, Miranda. How was your yoga class?"

"It was fine. What are you doing here?"

"He, along with Bastien, are going to escort us to Herbert's house in the country." Remare entered, kissed her temple, and spoke to Orion. "Thank you for seeing to Miranda's well-being. Bastien is upstairs, taking a shower."

"Hey, Tristan." Orion waved at the Torian, who nodded back. "I think I'll go see him," he said as he mounted the stairs.

"How was your class?"

"Pretty good. Orion and I stopped off for a beer, just to unwind. Come upstairs with me. I'll tell you all about it. How does a long, soothing soak in a warm bath sound?"

"With you?" He growled deep in his throat. "Fantastic. Tristan, make sure all the doors and windows are secured before turning in."

"Will do."

Once in the bathroom, Miranda turned the lights down low, found some bath salts and filled the tub with warm water. The air immediately smelled like the ocean. She quickly undressed and submerged herself. "This is heaven."

Remare entered. "You look relaxed. Did you have a good time tonight?"

"I did." She slid deeper into the water. "Remare, there is so much I don't know. Thank you for helping me in the library. It meant a lot to me."

"I know." He began undressing.

Miranda admired his masculine body and the length of him. Strong muscles layered over with his Mediterranean skin tone. He then joined her on the other side of the massive tub that could accommodate at least four people.

He nearly flinched at the water's temperature. "I didn't realize you prefer baths with the water one degree beneath boiling."

She laughed. "It's not that hot." His cool body quickly lowered the heat level. She was tempted to use her power to reheat the water but nixed the idea. Instead, she stroked his calf with her foot and then told him about the other *Elementals.*

"Where is it that they want you to meet them?"

"I left her card in my purse. Somewhere in the country. Not sure if I want to go, not if it's important to you I visit with the Herberts."

"We'll have plenty of time to socialize. I'm curious about these new friends of yours, but I also understand their desire for privacy."

"I wish you could meet them, too. I'd like your take on them. We'll talk more tomorrow about it during the drive. That was one helluva surprise you had for Orion."

"It was, wasn't it?" He smiled. And, suddenly, all was right with the world.

Miranda joined him on his side of the tub. With his arm casually dropped over her shoulder, she nearly purred in bliss. "This is nice."

"Yes." He kissed her forehead.

"What time do we leave tomorrow?"

"Mid-morning. There's no rush. Herbert and his wife are already there. I told them we'd arrive in time for dinner."

"Mmm." She stroked his chest. "So, we can sleep late tomorrow?"

"Well, that depends on how long it will take you to pack."

"Not long at all. I didn't expect to be in England this long, so I didn't pack much."

"We'll stop in one of the towns along the way to get you more clothes, if you want."

"Sounds good. Remare?"

"Yes?"

"As important as it is to me finding out about my kind," she kissed him slowly, tenderly, "you're more important."

"Hmm. Good to know." He brushed his lips against hers. "You're my heart. Don't ever forget that."

Chapter Twelve

Safe in Remare's arms, Miranda slept soundly, deeply. She was not expecting the dream that came upon her. But, instead of the fire-dancing woman, another took her place. A spirit whispered to her. *"Miranda, wake. Come with me. Wake, now!"*

Miranda rubbed her eyes, not sure if she was still asleep or in that hazy in-between state of being half-awake and half-asleep. She shook off the last vestiges of sleep and stared at the familiar apparition. Esme. "How?"

"Shh! Come with me." The ghostly figure urged her on.

Miranda's mind drifted through all that she'd read by Peralt. Something he mentioned about spirits, one group apart from the four main *Elementals,* the *Ethereals.* Those beings who were the quintessence of life and could set free their spirits. Miranda couldn't remember if Peralt said they could transcend time and place, or place only. If so, Esme was far more powerful than she'd let on. Miranda followed the spirit down the stairs into the study and closed the door behind her.

The spirit of Esme turned and smiled back at her, then flew into the mirror over the fireplace. "I'm sorry to have startled you, but I didn't think there was any adequate way of explaining my abilities without just showing you."

Miranda spoke to the swirling figure. "You did tell me your powers were mental. You're an *Ethereal,* aren't you?"

Esme laughed and seemed to applaud her deduction. "You *have* been researching us. The old Greek philosophers called us *aithereas,* but the Swiss alchemist, Paracelsus, called us *aether* in Latin or, in his preferred German, *atherisch.*"

Miranda made a mental note to research the alchemist. She could sense no evil intent of the spirit. "Have you been sending me dreams?"

Esme hesitated before answering. "If you're asking if I'm a dreamwalker, the answer is yes. I learned at an early age I could enter the minds of others, especially during sleep. When I reached out to you in your meditative state during our yoga class, I saw that your shields are strong. You've come across others with telepathic powers."

"Possible. Do the others know?"

"Only Agatha does; I've kept my talents secret. If the extent of my abilities were known, it would be cause for concern."

Miranda nodded. "I would think so."

"One of them has darkness in her aura. We've been watching her for some time."

"Why tell me; why meet with me this way?"

"I've come to warn you." Her spirit came closer and hovered in mid-air. "You, too, have black streaks coating your aura, even though your primary color is blue, and you fight against the darkness. The others can't know; they would shun you."

That would explain a few things. "You said you came to warn me; about what?"

"My talent includes precognition. I sometimes see images of the future and the past, as well as what is current. Time is like a river, constantly flowing, constantly changing. There is no way to control it. I cannot summon the visions; they reveal themselves to me when they want."

Miranda's heart sped up. "You're a seer! What did you see in your vision?"

"A dark force has seen your ability. I fear he's already touched you once, his mark is faint, but I see it on you. He wishes to possess you. His mental talents are extraordinary, but he has a weakness—he fears the future."

Miranda was wary. "This dark force have a name, by any chance?"

Esme smiled sadly. "I cannot tell you his name, but I believe your paths will cross, again. Soon."

"When? Where?"

"I'm not sure, but I sense it will be happening soon, here in England."

Well, that's just great! "How will I know him when I meet him?"

"You must learn to use your second sight, Miranda. You keep your gifts hidden, but soon, you must use them to protect yourself. Danger surrounds you."

No kidding! "How do I invoke a second sight?"

"Stop fearing it."

"How can I fear something I don't even fully comprehend?"

"You've been living in the mansion of your mind, hiding from your talents. They are a gift, Miranda, not a curse."

Miranda believed they were both. "I don't understand. I've never had telepathic abilities before. I don't know how to summon something I've never felt before."

"Ah, but I suspect you have. Have you never felt something deep in your soul, felt what others do not, sense the essence of others?"

Miranda didn't want to know this. Didn't want to accept what Esme was telling her. "I've been having dreams. About a dark-haired woman I've never met. I think her spirit has found a way to make contact with me."

"Tell me."

"A woman who dances in fire. Deep in an underground cave. Old earth. She's surrounded by other women who seem to be singing or chanting. At first, the dreams seemed innocuous enough, but then, I had one where the flames turned black, and she died in the fire. I have no idea who she is, or why this dream keeps recurring."

"No names?"

"None. But she did call me sister. I have no idea why. Nothing about her was familiar."

"I shall think on this. I must go—my powers are fading. Be wary, Miranda. Not everyone is who they say they are."

Miranda watched as the spirit of Esme dematerialized then disappeared completely. *Can my life get any weirder?* Feeling cold, she pulled Remare's shirt tighter around her as she sank onto the couch and sat in the darkness, contemplating all that Esme had told her.

After a while, the door slowly opened, and Remare stood in the doorway, tightening the belt to his robe. "Another bad dream?"

"Not really." She rested her head on her drawn up knees. "I don't know how to explain it. I think my mind is working overtime trying to learn what I can about *Elementals.*"

"Want to talk about it?"

Miranda gazed up at him. "Do you believe in ghosts?"

He smirked. "No. I have lived for centuries, known many who have lived and died. Caused the deaths of several." He sat beside her on the couch. "Some who, if they could, would come back from the dead to harm or kill me. But no apparition has ever appeared to me."

"Peralt mentioned in his writings what he called *Ethereals.* Not quite one of the four main *Elementals,* their powers are psychic in nature: clairvoyance, telepathy, precognition and the capacity to enter dreams, the dreamwalkers."

"And you think you've been visited by one of these *Ethereals*?"

She shrugged. "If you want to divorce me on grounds of lunacy, I will not stop you."

He laughed and pulled her closer. "I have no such desire."

She clasped his hand. "You must think I'm insane. I halfway think so. How do you explain the supernatural to someone who can't see what you do?"

"I think you have yearned for answers about your kind for a very long time."

"That I have." She snuggled against him. "I'm beginning to suspect I'm not going to like the answers I've been searching for very much."

"Then, we will seek them together." He scooped her up in his arms and lifted her. "It's late, and you, my love, are in need of sleep."

She grinned. "You know I can walk."

"True, but this is much more romantic, and it's been a fantasy of mine to carry you in my arms up to bed."

"Any other fantasies?"

His eyes glinted with mischief. "One or two."

***

Gideon threw the photos on the table and murmured to himself, "If I have to look at one more picture of Remare's wife with her nose in a book I'm going to kill someone." He considered his former nemesis and frowned, "*Whatever possessed you to marry an academic?*" When she wasn't involved with doing authentications, her life seemed pretty undistinguished. Perhaps the news out of New York was grossly exaggerated about her abilities. She just didn't seem the type to go one on one with Irina and win. Now, when it came to Irina, he could understand Remare's involvement. That woman was as sexy as she was deadly. Something stirred inside Gideon, something hungry.

He contemplated the pictures of the human woman, again. Instead of relishing London's night life, she preferred to spend her time studying at libraries. History, for God's sake. How impossibly dull.

Although, when she'd gone for that leisurely stroll with her Were bodyguard along the Thames, he'd thought he'd have something to torment Remare with. But the heat between them appeared to be genuine affection only. Hell, she couldn't even be trusted to cheat on her husband properly.

And her talents as an *Elemental* seemed suppressed. According to his agent, her skills were undeveloped, at best. Lord Acton was going to be sorely disappointed, but that was his problem.

Gideon had his own agenda, and in a little while, he'd be meeting a woman far more exciting. He checked his appearance in the mirror one last time to make sure he was fashionable enough; she liked it when he dressed to please. His blond hair was styled appropriately, and his hazel eyes conveyed whatever he wanted, and tonight, his desires ran deep.

"Right, then." He donned his leather jacket and made for his Porsche. Once on the road, he thought about her. His lover was beautiful and cunning. She thought she was good at manipulating others to get what she wanted. Little did she know he excelled at the game.

After all, he'd learned from one of the best. Her ambitions ran high, he liked that about her, but so did his. He'd been Lord Acton's second for centuries and had grown restless, bored. He didn't plan on being Acton's right hand much longer. Not when other opportunities presented themselves. And what sweet prospects he had. Soon, one of them would become a reality.

He parked in front of her London mansion. Over the years, he'd been to a few of her homes throughout Europe.

Her taste in all things was impeccable. She'd amassed a fortune, but so had he. Investing well whenever he could. He rang the bell, and the butler escorted him inside. He knew she'd be waiting for him upstairs and made his way to her.

She was brushing her long raven locks and smiled at him in her mirror. "Right on time, Gideon. You never keep me waiting. I like a man who knows the value of punctuality."

He could think of no woman more beautiful or more talented in the bedroom. He admired her sensual form; it made him hard. How fortuitous that their ambitions were in synchronicity. He snorted. As long as they had mutual ambitions, they were an unbeatable team. If their desires ever ran in opposing directions, it would be a different game altogether.

But, for now, life was to be enjoyed. "Neither one of us has time to waste, Vivienna."

Chapter Thirteen

"God, can you believe how many hills England has?! I think I've seen every possible color variation of green: blue-green, yellow-green, aquamarine, and verdant. You name it. It's beautiful here." Miranda marveled at the English countryside as they passed another farm with sheep grazing in the meadow. "I'm glad we decided to get away from London for a few days."

Remare glanced Miranda's way as he drove the Bentley Bentayga, one of the world's most expensive cars and, since Remare liked speed, the fastest SUV around. He handled the car like he did everything else, with skill and confidence. "I thought the change of scenery would do us good. Wait until you see Herbert Manor. It's one of the nicest estates in England. Similar to Combe Castle."

"I'm sure I'll love it. I think Orion was disappointed he didn't get to ride in the Bentley. His eyes nearly bugged out when he saw it." She held on tighter when the road suddenly dipped and then evened out.

Senses sharp and attuned to his surroundings, Remare smoothly navigated the bends in the road. "I believe he is quite comfortable with Bas in the Range Rover behind us. I'm certain they have much to discuss."

Miranda glanced back. "I think they will with Tristan riding in Alex's car behind them."

"I wanted Tristan to get some sleep. He'll be on guard duty tonight."

Miranda didn't think they needed three cars for just the six of them, but when she saw all the luggage the guys had, she understood. Some of their gear looked like weapon cases, and the insulated cooler probably carried their bagged blood.

"I really liked meeting Herbert and Winnie. They're easygoing people."

"We've fought in many wars together. Herbert and Winnie are some of my oldest friends." He glanced at the book she was reading. "Anything interesting?"

"Esme, the yoga teacher, gave me this book on crystals." Miranda shook her head. "I can't believe people, going back to the time of the ancient Greeks, believed in minerals having magical powers."

"Old superstitions. Different civilizations around the world have believed they were gifts from the gods."

"At least, from what I've read, most of the stones supposedly have healing powers or were used in rituals to aid the convalescing. However, some of the crystals are considered toxic. Hard to fathom how such beautiful crystals can also be poisonous."

"It's not so far-fetched. Think, Miranda, certain plants have medicinal purposes—some can aid in healing while others are lethal. Certain minerals, such as cinnabar can contain mercury—very deadly—as is torbernite, which comprises uranium and emits radon."

Miranda's jaw dropped. "Now, how did you know that?"

He grinned. "I thumbed through the book while you slept late this morning. The picture of the metallic stibnite with the sword-like features interested me. Again, very lethal."

"So far, I've read about thirty-seven different types. Some are incredibly stunning, fascinating in their radiance. No wonder Esme makes such fantastic jewelry. It says here garnet, my birthstone, is used to boost energy and protect from evil. Seriously!" She laughed. "Emeralds were thought to protect people from being manipulated by telepaths. Topaz augments psychic abilities." She glanced at their rings. "As for sapphires, guess which god it was associated with?"

"Ah, that would be Apollo."

Miranda raised a brow. "Yes. It says that sapphires, along with rubies—both part of the corundum family—were used to elicit prophecies and to protect against being taken captive. Popular with soldiers, I guess." She continued reading. "Hmm, a treatment for eye disorders, fosters the immune system. Interesting. Believed to strengthen the third eye, access and transmit power." Miranda's breath caught as she considered the ancient beliefs and what Esme had said last night.

"We're coming up on the town, Rye. Did you want to stop for lunch?"

"Oh, wow! Now that is what I call picturesque! It's like stepping back in time a couple of centuries." Miranda had watched a few videos of England before the trip, so she knew Rye was a lovely town, but nothing had prepared her for the sheer beauty and magical sense as they drove down Mermaid Street."

"There's an inn up ahead we can go to."

"Right." But Miranda spotted Rye Old Books down Lion Street. "You go on ahead. I want to stop at the bookstore." She kissed his cheek. "I'll join you in a moment. Order me soup; you know the kinds I like."

"Don't take long."

"I won't, I promise." She didn't have to turn back to know he'd assigned Orion to tail her. "Guard duty, huh?"

"Yup."

She gazed down the cobblestone street lined with shops. "Isn't this town great?! I'll only be a minute." A bell tinkled as she opened the door to the old bookstore and inhaled the aroma, loving the quaintness of the shop. Then, she approached one of the salespeople and gasped. She quickly checked the older woman's badge. "By any chance are you related to Alice Gordon who works in a London Library?" The resemblance was uncanny.

The woman smiled beneficently. "Yes, Alice is my younger sister. I'm Gemma Hastings. She called to tell me a Professor Crescent from the States might be visiting. I guess she was right as we don't get that many Yanks visiting us this early in the season. Especially with such handsome companions." She nodded to Orion then turned as if she were studying Miranda's features. "Welcome to Rye. How may I help you?"

"Alice said you might have books on healers of the past."

"Ah, yes. Before modern science, healers relied on remedies that were passed down through the generations. It's this way." She led them around the corner of the aisle toward the back and reached for a volume. "This book discusses various healers."

Miranda glanced at the pages. "I'd also like a book on medicinal herbs."

"Let's see. Oh, yes, we have several," she scanned the shelf, "but I think this one is probably the best of the lot."

Miranda accepted it and scrutinized the photographs. "My mother was an herbalist. She died when I was young, so I never really got the chance to ask her much about the plants."

"I'm sorry. If you have any questions at all, I'd be happy to answer them. Alice told me you were interested in art history. May I recommend a book on artists who were absorbed with the idea of healing? Some had limited scope in their ideas, but others had incredible imaginations about people who had certain abilities. It wasn't only kings and queens who supposedly had the healing benediction."

"Sure, I'm a history buff."

Alice led them to the other side of the store and picked out an old volume. "I think you'll find this one of particular interest."

After ringing up her purchases, Miranda spotted several beautifully engraved fountain pens in the display case and bought a few. She'd planned on using her British pounds for the books, but with the added expenses, she used her credit card, instead. At times, she felt she got glimpses into the past, as if she squinted, she could see people dressed in the old fashions, so seeing the other customers on their iPhones made her feel better. The place might remind her of the past, but the computerized cash register was modern.

Alice asked, "Will you be visiting Rye long?"

"No. We're visiting friends of my husband's, but I'll try to come back if I have any questions."

"Right, then. I slipped a few of our cards inside the books. You can call, anytime. The machine will pick up if it's after hours." She smiled. "Enjoy your stay."

They had almost passed The Rye Tea Shop when Miranda pulled Orion inside. "I swear, Orion, this is the last store." Met by an older man, she asked, "Do you have any Jasmine Green tea?" Then, she remembered Remare preferred another. "And Moroccan Mint?"

"Of course, we have many different blends from various regions." He led her down an aisle with loose tea in decorative colored tins.

After making her selections, Miranda then used British pounds to pay for her teas.

The inn was cozy with its wooden floors and stone fireplace. Miranda liked the blue and white checkered curtains hanging in the windows. She spotted Remare and Bastien in a booth in the back. Bastien had ordered a sandwich for Orion, who promptly set upon devouring it. He'd always had a healthy appetite. Most Weres did. Remare had already ordered for her.

"They didn't have turkey soup, so I ordered you a vegetable chicken potage."

"Thanks." She dug in. As the soup was tepid, she used her powers to heat it.

Remare must have realized what she'd done because he smirked. "I thought you might have stopped for new clothes as you said you weren't sure you brought enough."

Miranda shrugged. "Maybe tomorrow. You think, if I ask Winnie to go shopping, she'd come with me?"

"I'm sure she will."

After lunch, they were on their way. Miranda had to sit up straight as they approached Herbert Manor. "Amazing, simply breathtaking. You're right, it does look like Combe Castle." She'd Googled the castle after he'd mentioned it. But seeing it in all its glory was something else entirely. The tan façade appeared to be made of limestone with ivy growing along the front of the structure. The many tall windows seemed modern, and the Herberts obviously took great care of their country home. She couldn't wait to go exploring inside.

The guys gathered up all their luggage. Miranda wanted to take her own, but Remare insisted on pulling it along with his. Before they made it halfway to the door, the servants came to collect them. The chateaus in France were luxurious and grandiose with all their marble, but the English estates had a welcoming ambience, an old-country sense the French didn't have. She checked Bastien's expression. His parents had one of the handsomest homes in all of France. But then again, they were aristocratic vampires.

And, unfortunately, like in France, while there were many grand homes in England, there were also others that had fallen into disrepair, due to neglect or time's ravages. They'd passed a few on the road coming here.

The Herberts greeted them in the main hall with the high-arched ceilings and dark English oak beams. Historical images flittered across her mind. She'd expected to see knights' armor and tapestries with coats of arms, but the furnishings were modern.

Herbert led them into the study, where drinks were waiting for them. While the others discussed plans for the day, going horseback riding and dinner, Miranda glanced around at the paintings and nearly stopped breathing when she saw the portrait above the fireplace. A gorgeous dark-haired woman sat smiling. It was as if she were staring directly at Miranda.

"Who is she?" she murmured aloud.

"Ah, that would be Esmerelda." Herbert stood beside her. "My brother Leland's fiancé. Or was at one time. They've both been gone for some time now."

For one brief moment, the portrait seemed to come alive. *"Hello, Miranda."*

Her heart thudding against her chest, Miranda's knees almost gave out, and Remare caught her elbow to steady her. "I think I need to sit down." She gulped down his glass of wine. "Can I have another?"

***

After, the others left to unpack—Remare and Tristan didn't like anyone else handling their luggage, especially the ones containing weapons, so they volunteered to do it. Bastien and Orion didn't seem to have a problem with the servants unpacking their belongings and decided to tour the gardens with Winnie. In truth, Miranda didn't like anyone else handling her laptop, so she was glad Remare carried it up to their room.

"This tea is perfect." She inhaled the soothing aroma from the sofa by the window.

"I'm glad you like it." Herbert sat across from her in one of his leather chairs. "Remare tells me, as an art historian, you read extensively."

"Yes, I'm so sorry for my reaction." She peered up again at the portrait. "It's just that she looks so familiar. I feel like I've met her before, even though I know that's not possible." She sipped her tea. "It just surprised me."

After studying her for a moment, he said, "I'm not quite sure when I've seen Remare this happy. I believe you're the cause of that. Though, I must admit, I was a bit put off that neither Winnie nor I were invited to the wedding."

"It came up rather suddenly. I wasn't crazy about being married in Valadon and Vivienna's shadow. If Remare and I decide to have a reaffirmation of our vows ceremony, you're at the top of the list."

He laughed. "I do believe Valadon had one of the shortest marriages that I can remember." He lifted his brandy snifter. "Here's to righting wrongs."

Yeah, like my so-called engagement! "Not a fan of Madame Lord Vivienna?"

His disapproving expression almost made her laugh. "As lords, we must maintain a certain decorum; however, she's sometimes referred to as Lady Viper by members of my household," he chuckled, "but I won't tell you which ones. Although, we do have mutual business associates. She wanted to visit us, but I told her to postpone her plans for next week."

"Does she visit often?"

"I'd say about once every few months." He shrugged. "Sometimes more, depending on corporate matters concerning her fashion industry, as I must travel to Paris concerning politics and financial interests. It's best to maintain social graces with her. She's an ambitious woman. I can see her becoming Council sometime in the near future."

Miranda was glad they wouldn't be there when Vivienna arrived. That was one person she had no desire to see, again. "Can you tell me about her?" Miranda pointed to the painting.

"Esmerelda's death hit us all very hard. She and Leland were very much in love. I dare say it was love at first sight when he saw her in the marketplace. It's been centuries, but I can still remember the look on his face when he met her."

"Was it the same for her?"

Herbert nodded and held his pipe up. "Will this bother you?"

"No, not at all. I like the smell of the smoke."

He moved around his desk and rummaged in one of the drawers for his tobacco. "All right, then." He lit the pipe then inhaled and sat behind his desk so as not to blow smoke her way. "Most of the townspeople thought she was a Castilian, but that was only because her ship had stopped in Spain. Originally, she was from Venice. Apparently, there was some sort of trouble with members of the clergy. She was a great healer, had knowledge of potions and medicinal herbs; she helped many of our villagers."

"What kind of trouble?"

"A nobleman, who had connections with the Church, became infatuated with her and wished for her to become his mistress. She refused, and one night, his wife walked in on a situation where she thought Esmerelda was seducing her husband. Rather than believe her husband would commit an indiscretion, she blamed Esmerelda and spread rumors about her to the other noblewomen of Venice. In time, she was forced to leave the city and wound up here on our shores."

Remare appeared at the door and joined her on the sofa. "You never told me she was Venetian."

Herbert's eyes widened. "You never asked."

Surprised, Miranda asked, "You knew her?!"

"Briefly. I was never as taken with her as Leland was, so I didn't pay much attention."

"Remare always had his attention tuned to battles and politics."

Miranda was certain he'd probably managed to find a lover or two but didn't feel inclined to ask. "What happened to her?"

"Now, that is a sad and unfortunate story." Herbert leaned back and closed his eyes in memory. "When she first arrived, she set up an apothecary's shop in town, selling her herbs and potions. Most of the people suffered from mild infirmaries associated with farmers. Others suffered more severe wounds. In either case, she was able to help. Word quickly spread of her curative powers. The townspeople grew to love her. And so did Leland. Theirs was a love story to last the ages."

He glanced up at the portrait. "They attended many dances together, went on picnics. He even sang to her." Herbert leaned toward Remare. "You remember what a great singing voice Leland had?"

"I do." Remare smiled. "I remember one time he even sang when we rode into battle together."

"Now, that sounds like something he would do. Anyway, while Leland was away on one of his adventures—he loved traveling almost as much as you did, Remare," he continued to puff on his pipe, "another became curious of all the stories told about the fascinating Esmerelda. And, much to my regret, he came calling."

"Who?" Remare asked.

"Another lord who'd heard of her abilities. By this time, the stories had gotten out of control about Esmerelda's talents. Some called her angel, others who were jealous—less desirable terms. When gossip circulated that she was a seer and could predict when storms would come and which battles would be won, this lord became determined to make Esmerelda his. He waited until Leland and I were away on business to start courting her. She had no interest in him, yet he persisted, lavishing attention and gifts on her, which she promptly returned. If memory serves me right, the villagers called him 'The Dark Lord'," Herbert faced Remare, "but you know him better as Lord Acton."

Agitated, Remare stood. "You never told me this."

Miranda remembered the horror stories Remare had told her of Acton's abuse. He'd suffered miserably at Acton's compound, so she understood his outrage.

Herbert shrugged. "I didn't find out until I returned from our main court just how serious things had evolved. One night, he fabricated a story of a child who'd been injured in a fall and convinced her to ride with him to his territory. I heard, much later, he'd bribed the baker, Thomas, to ride to his mansion and inform her that Leland had been killed in battle."

"Did she return to Rye?" Miranda asked.

"She did briefly, seeking information. Unknown to me, Acton procured the services of a parson who wrote misleading information about the battle. Saddened and despairing, she stayed with Acton. As far as I know, she never returned to Rye after that. When news reached Leland that she'd become Acton's mistress, he became irrational, started drinking much heavier than I'd ever seen him. I was told later that, during one of his stupors, he walked onto a field of battle. He was the first soldier killed." Herbert pointed to a painting near the corner. "That's his portrait."

Miranda gazed up at the handsome blond man. It was the same man she'd seen in her dreams. He'd been so happy pushing Esmerelda on the swing. "So, if she hadn't been manipulated, they could have had a good life together."

Herbert nodded. "I kept some of her journals if you'd like to read them. I'll have one of the servants bring them to you, if you wish."

"There you are." Winnie entered with Bastien and Orion. "I thought you would join us in the atrium for tea."

"I was just telling Remare and Miranda about Esmerelda and Leland."

Winnie stood by Herbert's side and rubbed his shoulder. "You always get forlorn when you speak of them. I prefer to remember how happy they were when they were together. It's rare that two people find each other in this world. To love, I mean." She gazed at Bastien and Orion. "They had many months together. It was quite something to see."

Miranda was eager to read the diaries, but Winnie insisted they get some fresh air before dark. Herbert agreed and convinced Remare to go riding with him.

Miranda accompanied them to the stables. "Your horses are magnificent."

Remare asked, "Do you know how to ride, Mir-randa?"

"Do the horses on the carrousel in Central Park count?"

Remare grinned. "Not in this case." He kissed her forehead. "I'll teach you, but not at this moment."

"Go on. I think you need the exercise. Spend time with your friend. I'll be fine, and Winnie said she'd give me the grand tour of the place."

"We'll be back before nightfall."

Chapter Fourteen

Miranda was almost ready to feign a headache to forego the tour of the castle, but she sensed good vibes from Winnie, who now opened a door to the billiards room. Miranda smiled. She knew there had to be at least one room in the manor that had the knight's armor, assorted swords and weapons, and a few tapestries of old. She knew her men would probably be playing here sometime tonight.

Then, Winnie led her down toward the hallway to the atrium and indoor pool. Miranda couldn't hide her glee. "My god, it's beautiful. And inviting."

"Yes, I use the pool almost daily. It's heated, so it stays warm during the cooler months. We use the outdoor pool in the summer months only. I find it soothing and helps keep me in good shape. We have extra bathing suits for our guests if you or any of the others wish to take a swim."

Miranda eyed the svelte but toned Winnie. For a woman who appeared to be in her forties, she was in excellent shape. Miranda nearly had to run to keep up with her vigorous pace.

Winnie gazed out one of the large plate windows. "He looks happy. Your Remare. I'm glad. It's been a while since I've seen him so relaxed."

"I'm glad, too." Miranda stood beside her. "You and Herbert have been together a long time."

"Yes, for centuries—some good, some bad, but mostly good."

Miranda sighed. "Most couples I've known barely make it to a decade. You're lucky."

"Luck has little to do with it."

"What does?"

"Seeing eye to eye, in most cases. But not all. Though, we are united in most concerns. It's a matter of priorities, my dear."

"I would think so. Compared to you and Herbert, Remare and I have known each other just a short time. Only about a year or so. We've only been married less than two weeks."

"And you're worried if it will last? Don't be. From the way he looks at you, I'd say you have very little to be concerned about."

"How do you keep from—"

"Getting bored?" she laughed. "Herbert is many things; boring is not one of them. As I said, we're united in most things. But there are times I'm tempted to take a pike to him. And, I suspect, at moments, he feels the same about me. When it gets to that point, we take what you Yanks call a *'time out'* and spend some time away. Separate vacations."

"I've heard some couples do that."

"It makes the coming home all that more engaging. The sex is quite good, actually, probably at its best."

Miranda was thinking *TMI*.

"Though, I hardly think that's an issue for you and Remare." A servant approached. "Would you care for more tea or some biscuits? I have a private stock of truffles you simply must taste."

"No, not right now. But, if it's alright with you, I'd like to retire to my room. It's been a hectic morning."

"Of course. If you change your mind about the tea, just call down, and we'll have some sent up to you."

Miranda grinned when she opened her door. As promised, someone had delivered Esmerelda's old diaries. They were waiting for her on the bed. She couldn't wait to read them. Maybe in a little while, she'd order some tea, but right now, she was driven to learn what she could about the dark-haired woman who haunted her dreams.

***

"Caltrone will make a terrible chancellor, if elected. You should run, Herbert. You know more about economics and politics than he does." Remare dodged a tree branch as they steered their horses along the wooded path in Herbert's forest.

"I have quite enough on my plate being Lord of London. So many events now occurring at the same time. And don't even get me started on human legislations."

"I wouldn't dare." They'd both seen troublesome events throughout their long friendship and had managed to survive even the darkest of times. "If not you, what about Harrington? He's been a member of the financial commission for some time. Surely, he'd be interested."

"Not really. Anyone who assumes the position will have to deal with Magritte. There are few who would welcome that opportunity. Cheer up, Remare, we've endured various wars and worse circumstances; we'll withstand whatever comes our way."

As they crossed the stone bridge over the running stream, Remare wondered about that. Each century, they always thought things were at their worst and couldn't imagine anything more disturbing, yet they always found ways to cope. "I'm concerned about Lord Acton and what you told us about his involvement with Esmerelda."

"That was such a long time ago. He stays in his northern territory, knows better than to challenge me. You and your new wife are perfectly safe within my borders."

"Miranda is special, Herbert." He sighed as they stopped their horses for a rest. "You don't understand."

One corner of Herbert's mouth rose. "That she's more than human?"

Remare eyed one of his oldest friends. "How did you know?"

"I've read Paracelsus. You should, too, if you haven't."

"Paracelsus?" The name rang a bell in the back of his mind.

"A Swiss alchemist who lived during the fifteen-hundreds. Among his many interests was his obsession with *Elementals*; he wrote extensively about them in his *Philosophia Magna*. Fascinating book. I have a copy if you'd like to read it."

"I would. Thank you." Remare had nearly forgotten how much Herbert had been enamored by books and learning. Philosophy had been an interest of his for centuries. Miranda would want to know all she could about her ancestry. So would Remare. He'd help her any way he could. "By any chance did you ever come across a volume called, *The Book of Origins*? Miranda discovered a painting by Antoine Caron in the Herkimer Library. She suspects one of the books in the painting might contain information on the origin of *Elementals*."

Herbert seemed to reflect. "I own some of Caron's paintings. But I don't ever recall a book by that name."

Remare exhaled as he studied the landscape. "It may very well be just a myth."

"Perhaps." Herbert laughed. "I knew Miranda was an *Elemental* the night you brought her to dinner in London. When everyone's tea had chilled, her cup was still steaming." He smirked. "And the way she stared at the painting. I suspected it was more than idle curiosity that made her so rapt and determined to know about Esmerelda. Like recognizes like. She has the same look as her. As if they can hear songs from a different dimension. See things we never will. Have knowledge we'll never possess."

"Is that why Acton took such an interest in Esmerelda?"

"It's true he was envious of Leland and Esmerelda's happiness. Many were." Herbert steered his horse near the ridge to look over his lands. "But he was never content with the High Council's decision to make me Lord of London and him Lord of the Northern Territory. London is far more lucrative than what his shipping fleet makes."

"You think he went after Esmerelda as a means of vengeance against you?"

Herbert pursed his lips, as if missing his pipe. "In part. As vengeful as Acton was, that wasn't his greatest flaw. Power was. When he heard the stories about her abilities, he simply had to have her and set out to obtain her any way he could. Destroying Leland in the process was just a bonus for him."

Remare could tell Herbert missed his brother dearly. They'd been close at one time, and Herbert had loved his younger brother greatly. Remare knew Herbert blamed himself for not being able to, somehow, circumvent Acton's malicious intentions. If Acton resented Herbert for becoming Lord of London, he hated Remare more for when he left the cruel lord's household.

Valadon had told Remare stories of some of the more powerful lords in France and what Magritte had allowed at Chateau Durand. But nothing in Remare's eyes could compare with Acton's cruelty. His fists tightened. "If Acton ever found out about Miranda's abilities…"

"Then, we'll just have to make sure he never finds out. Come, it will be dark soon, and we should get back."

***

Miranda was admiring Herbert's lands from the roof of the manor when she heard Remare's voice.

"There you are. What is this?" He held up the cane she'd bought him in London.

"A present for you, though," she took the came from him, "I'm thinking of keeping it for when I go walking in Rye; those streets are hilly. Just think, in Manhattan, we'll have a matching set. Let me show you something." She cupped her hand to the side of the top, and the crystal orb started glowing. "Pretty cool, huh?"

"Hmm. I know this type of cane." He examined it then pressed a tiny lever near the top. Immediately, a dagger shot out at the bottom end. "It's a dagger cane."

Miranda stared in amazement. "Now, that's something the sales clerk forgot to mention."

"He probably wasn't aware of its lethal nature. Please be careful with it." He retracted the blade with a twist of the crystal and lay the cane against the roof's barrier.

"I will." Miranda admired the sun's descent on the horizon. "England is truly one beautiful country." She inhaled the early evening air. "Look over those rolling hills; have you ever seen such greenery before?"

He held her from behind. "Perhaps, but I've never embraced such beauty before." He kissed her temple.

She slanted him a look. "Flatterer."

"I am, yes, but you look especially beautiful with the fading sun's rays on your face."

She covered his arms with hers, enjoying the sensation of him at her back. "How was your ride?"

"Sublime. Herbert has some of the most magnificent woods to go riding in. By the way, he knows you're an *Elemental.*"

She turned in his arms. "How?"

"In London, after dinner, you kept your tea steaming long after everyone else's had cooled. He noticed. He also recommended we read a book by Paracelsus called, *Philosophia Magna.* He said it contains information on *Elementals.*"

Paracelsus! The same one Esme had recommended. "It's written in Latin, isn't it?"

"I'll read through it and let you know what it says. I also asked him about *The Book of Origins*. Sadly, he's never heard of it, and Herbert is one of the most well-read men I know."

"Thank you for asking.

"And how did you spend your afternoon?"

"After Winnie showed me around the castle, I read some of Esmerelda's diaries. Poignant stuff. She very much loved Leland. Was heartbroken when she thought he'd died in battle. From what I read, she would never have taken up with Lord Acton had she not been lied to. She called him *'The Deceiver'.*"

"Disturbing reading material."

"Yes." She shrugged. "It just gets to me. Esmerelda and Leland were so much in love, and they were cheated out of a happy life together because of one man's cruelty."

"It was centuries ago, Mir-randa. And, as Winnie pointed out, they had several months of joy together."

"Should have been years, if not centuries. Did you know she'd heard rumors that Leland had survived the battle and went looking for him? She found him drunk in one of the local brothels with another woman. Having thought Esmerelda had cheated on him with Acton, he'd decided to drown his despair in drink and with the company of other women."

Remare exhaled. "She should have confronted him about his bad behavior. It's possible, they could have worked things out."

"Not so. By that time, she was already pregnant with Acton's child. She wrote about it in her diary. As humiliated as she felt that Leland had taken other lovers, she still wished it had been his child."

"I didn't know she'd had a child."

"By drinking Acton's blood, her powers had grown substantially. She wrote how her abilities had grown each day. Was afraid what Acton would use the child for if he knew. So, she used her talents to hide her pregnancy. When it was almost time to deliver, she told Acton she was going to London to get more of her supplies. After giving birth, she entrusted the child to a friend. How sad is that? She gave up her baby because she was so afraid of what Acton would do."

"What became of the child?"

"I don't know. But Esmerelda grew terribly despondent. The longer she lived with him, she saw his malevolence, his cruelty, and learned to fear him."

"Why didn't she just leave him?"

"She planned to. Her last diary entry said she was devising a way to disappear so that he would never find her. I think she was planning to reclaim her child and return to Venice. I guess we'll never know." She peered up at him. "She was a powerful *Elemental*, Remare. Acton thought by drinking her blood he could become more powerful, absorb her abilities."

"Did he?"

Miranda shrugged. "She didn't say. I just hate the thought of two lovers not being able to be together because of someone like Acton. Leland used to sing to her songs he'd learned in his travels. You never sang to me," she teased.

"I am a man of many talents, Mir-randa, as you know. Sadly, singing isn't one of them. And how come you've never sung to me?"

"Oh, please. They threw me out of sixth-grade chorus because my voice was so bad. The only one who would take me in was the art teacher, Mrs. Rossoff. She taught me how to draw. I fell in love with art, then. Now, as for singing, you should have heard my sister, Cassandra, sing. She had a voice that was magical."

"You rarely speak of her."

"It was a long time ago. When she died. Cassie was beautiful and good at everything she tried. I was the gawky one. Cassie had long blond hair, was tall and incredibly smart. That was about the only thing we shared: a love of books."

"What was she like?"

"She was kind. Except when I got on her nerves. She used to say, *'Mira, Mira, on the wall, who's the ugliest of them all?'*"

"She did not?! My parents would never have allowed such degradations. She would have been punished for uttering such obvious lies."

"Thanks. You know, Leland used to dance with Esmerelda. We never got to dance at our so-called wedding."

He grinned, and his eyes lit up, making his handsome face even more alluring. "If dancing is what you want, then dancing is what we shall do." Remare took her hand and swooped her into his arms.

Heart throbbing in sensual joy, she laughed at his romantic nature. "We have no music."

"Who needs music when we have the stars shining down on us?"

Miranda looked up and saw that a few had appeared. "That we do."

She remembered how they'd sword danced and what an excellent teacher he was. Remare was far more graceful in his steps than she'd ever be, but she followed where he led. As the sun slowly set behind the hills, they swayed to the music only they could hear, and Miranda smiled in the perfect serenity they shared. Her body attuned to his in sensual harmony. Their breaths, their vibrations in spiritual synchronicity. This had to be one of the most romantic nights of her life. The moon nearly full, dancing with Remare, the cool breezes washing over them, the night gleaming with stars. She couldn't remember a time when she was happier.

In the distance, a wolf howled at the moon. "That's Orion. Bas and he are loping through the woods. It's hard to tell who's chasing who."

"Ah, I wondered where they'd gone off to."

They continued dancing in the moonlight, Miranda forgetting all about the ill-fated lovers, glowing in the love she and Remare shared. It was a night of bliss. She closed her eyes for a brief moment and used her power to levitate them.

Remare looked amazed that they were actually dancing on air. "Sorceress."

She laughed. "Do you think we'll be dancing like this, years from now?"

His brow arched. "Centuries from now, if you wish."

Right there and then, under the starry sky, she made a decision. "One year, Remare. One year from now, I'll give you my answer."

"What answer will that be?"

She lowered them to the surface. "If we'll have centuries together."

He stopped dancing. "You mean…"

"I'll tell you, then, if I decide to become vampire."

Remare laughed in delight as his eyes sparkled in the evening sky, shining as brightly as the moon and stars above.

Chapter Fifteen

Having made an appointment to meet with Gemma after the bookshop closed, Miranda enjoyed the ride back to Rye with Tristan, although she felt bad that he'd pulled guard duty. "I told Remare I didn't need a bodyguard, but he insisted. Said Orion needed a break."

"I don't mind. At least I don't have to watch Bastien and Orion frolicking naked in the pool." He rolled his eyes. "Besides, Remare's got this thing about us working in pairs. No solo acts. Doesn't like any of us going out alone. Makes sense. I got worked over pretty good a while back in New York by Rogues. If Remare hadn't arrived when he did and shared his blood with me, I might not have made it."

"He's a little over-protective of me. I get it. We're not in his territory, and we're fairly close to Lord Acton's territory."

"He'll probably have guards on you when we get back to New York, as well."

Miranda scoffed. "Overkill. I can take care of myself."

"No argument from me." He grinned. "I saw what you did to Irina in the training area. What'd she do to set you off? I asked Gregori, and he nearly took my head off."

A growl rose up in her throat. "Y'know, I don't even remember her exact words." She waved her hand in the air. "Something to the effect I wasn't good enough for Remare."

"I guess you showed her. You slammed her halfway across the room. Those of us in the back could hear her bones cracking."

"Yeah, not my shining moment. Valadon read me the riot act, made me promise never to use my powers against any of his people. Unless, of course, someone attacked me first."

"I don't *ever* see that happening. Even if you weren't Remare's wife, your powers are amazing. The only one who would challenge you was Irina, because she was once Remare's lover, but she's with Gregori, now, so all's good."

Miranda gazed at her fingertips. They were still warm from making the cane's crystal glow. "I won't be longer than an hour or two, at the most. I promised Remare we'd be back in plenty of time for dinner." She still couldn't get used to midnight meals, but as vampires, they liked the late hour. "There's the bookstore, now. You don't have to wait in the car. There are a few bars in the area."

"I'll be fine." Tristan parked the car. "You have your phone with you? And my number?"

"Yes and yes." After reading Esmerelda's diaries, Miranda had a few questions for the owner and sales manager of Rye's bookshop. The sign said closed, but Gemma was there to greet and escort her to a quiet sitting room in the back where a pot of tea was brewing. Several scones were also laid out on a doily-covered plate.

"I thought I'd be hearing from you but didn't expect it to be this soon."

"I read fast." Not as quickly as Remare, who had helped by perusing and analyzing the books at an astounding pace.

After Gemma poured her a cup of tea and they were settled on the couch, all social niceties finished, she asked. "What did you want to know?"

Miranda sipped her tea. "Your sister, Alice, let me read several books in London, and I read through parts of the ones you sold me. The history of the healers fascinates me, and I wondered why you shared my interest."

"Many myths interest me. Like you, history has been more than a hobby to me." She glanced outside. "This is my land, and the people who lived here through the ages hold a special fondness in my heart."

"There were tales of one particular healer who lived in this area centuries ago. She had an apothecary shop somewhere in this area. Ever hear of her?"

"There've been several through the years, but the most famous one was Esmerelda. She arrived by ship, one day, and promptly set out to open her store. It wasn't long before she had many customers; one of which was Lord Herbert's brother, Leland. It was told they had great love for one another. She was supposed to be a stunning beauty. Helped many of the villagers with her tonics and healing touch. Then, one day, she disappeared as suddenly as she'd arrived. No one knew of her fate."

"Were stories handed down through the generations? Possibly with things not written down, stories that would seem too bizarre to be believed?"

Gemma waved her hand in the air. "Oh, there are always stories. The sailors who frequented our shores told many tales of their adventures at sea. But I think I know what you are referring to. Are you asking if Esmerelda was a witch?"

"Was she?"

"I don't believe so." She sighed. "Of all the deadly sins, envy is one of the worst. I'm sure those who were jealous of her beauty spread tall tales about her. Esmerelda used healing stones in her treatments. Did you know some massage therapists also use hot stones to aid soreness in the back and legs?"

"Yes, I've actually heard that." Another thought occurred to Miranda. "You wouldn't happen to have any drawings or paintings of Esmerelda, would you?"

"I do, but I would have to dig them out. Give me a moment." Gemma opened a closet door and rifled through some old boxes.

Miranda took the time to gaze around the sitting room, admiring the old woman's many plants while she searched. The outside lights illuminated a garden rife with colors.

"They're not here; they must be upstairs. Would you like to accompany me?"

"I didn't mean to trouble you."

"No trouble at all." Upstairs from the shop was Gemma's apartment. It was small, but tidy. And above that was the attic. "I haven't been up here in some time."

Miranda felt guilty for making the older woman climb so many steps but followed her up the pull-down ladder.

"I'm not sure why I kept so much of these for so long. I suppose I had hoped Rye would approve a museum for some of this stuff, but that never happened." She searched through more boxes then said, "Ah, here it is."

Miranda admired the portrait of Esmerelda. It was similar to the one at Herbert Manor.

"And this was Leland. Handsome devil, wasn't he? The vampires only revealed themselves about twenty years ago, but some people knew, or at least suspected, there were different ones among us for some time."

He certainly was handsome. And cheated out of a life he should have had.

"And this is Lord Acton." Gemma passed her another portrait.

From her dream, Miranda recognized the stern-looking man on the horse who Esmerelda was so frightened of. There was something inherently evil in his countenance, in the way he glowered. She could almost feel it in the canvas. "Intimidating fellow, wasn't he?"

"Oh, he's still alive, a vampire. He has his shipping company up in the north. Does quite well for himself."

"Have you ever met him?"

"Good gracious, no. He doesn't look like someone I would want to know, even though I researched him after reading some of Esmerelda's letters."

"Letters?" That perked up Miranda's interest right quick.

"Yes, after she disappeared, people rummaged through her shop for anything valuable. Some, they stored in a closet, in case a relative should come looking for them. But no one ever did. I kept them; I'm not sure why." She moved toward the back of the attic, accidentally knocking over an old photo album covered in a fine layer of dust.

Miranda bent down to retrieve the article. A few photographs slipped loose. If these were of Mrs. Hastings, she'd been a knockout when she was younger.

Gemma's voice barely registered. "Ah, here they are. I'm afraid they're quite withered, but you might still be able to read them."

As if in a trance, Miranda stood staring at one of the photos and then at Gemma Hastings. She turned the photograph toward the older woman. "You knew him?"

Gemma sighed, refusing to meet Miranda's eyes. "Yes, I did. He studied architecture one summer at Oxford. He wanted someone to show him the different buildings in the outlying towns, a tour guide, so to speak. I volunteered. I was rather smitten with him at the time."

Miranda glanced one more time at the picture and then at her hostess. "Gemma, this is a picture of my father."

Gemma stayed quiet for a moment then met Miranda's eyes. "I know. Your resemblance to him is uncanny." Her face was sad with a hint of shyness. "We should take these downstairs. The lighting is better there."

Once back in the sitting room. Miranda waited for Gemma to start.

"It was so long ago—nearly forty years, now. Please don't look at me like that. It was years before Carl met and married your mother. We were so young back then, barely twenty." She slid her finger over his likeness. "He enjoyed studying the structures of the old churches and other buildings. I knew, then, he would be a great architect. Such an eye for detail. Always with his camera, taking photos of the interiors, as well as the exteriors."

Miranda searched her memories for any mentions of her father having traveled to England. She thought she remembered something about his one semester at Oxford but couldn't be sure. "What was he like, I mean, back then?"

"Handsome. He sure knew how to turn heads. Kind. And dedicated to his studies. He loved learning, had such an appetite to discover new things and traveling to different places. At the end of summer, he decided to postpone his education in America for one semester and invited me to come with him when he toured the other countries in Europe, but I couldn't go." She waved off the idea. "My family would have forbidden it, and I had my own studies to deal with."

"Where else did he go?"

"Paris was his first choice, but he also wanted to see Spain, Portugal and other Western European countries. My parents called him *The Wanderer*. It nearly broke my heart to have to say goodbye to him when he left for Paris. We promised to stay in touch, and we did...for a while, but I knew, eventually, the letters would stop coming, and they did." She shrugged. "Still, it was one of the best summers of my life."

Miranda wasn't going to ask if they'd been lovers—she could see it on the older woman's face. Some things you just didn't want to know about your parents. Even though it had been years before he married her mom, she still felt an edge of betrayal on her mother's behalf. She supposed all kids wanted to believe there was no one else in their parents' history. But Carl and Sarah Crescent had been in their early thirties when they married. And they were entitled to whatever happy moments they had in their lives. "He's passed on. About twenty years ago, both my parents were killed in a car crash."

Gemma's eyes glazed over as she rubbed her chest. "I'm so sorry to hear that. I'd hoped he'd had a full life." She laid the picture down then opened the photo album. "I have a few more pictures. Would you like to see?"

Miranda didn't hesitate. "Yes."

"This is when we were up near Dover. He took so many photos of the cliffs. And here we are in London. He couldn't get enough of St. Paul's Cathedral, Buckingham Palace, and a few other local places."

Miranda studied the pictures of her father, and bittersweet memories surfaced. People always said she looked more like her father than her mother. They were right. In the pictures, he was so full of vitality, so much enthusiasm, it almost hurt. His life had been cut down at the age of forty-six. He, along with her mom and Cassie, should have lived much longer. Miranda gazed up at the clock and realized hours had flown by. "I have to go. It's later than I realized."

"All right. Here, take these." She handed her the bundle of Esmerelda's letters. Miranda had almost forgotten them but stored them in her messenger bag. "You need not return them. They should be with the Herberts. I think she was closer to them than anyone else here in town."

"Thank you for seeing me this late." Her voice nearly caught. "And for showing me the pictures of my father."

Gemma reached back and handed her the one loose picture of Carl. "Take this one. I have the others."

Miranda's heart ached. "Are you sure?"

Gemma nodded.

After their farewells, Miranda ran down the steps and opened the driver's side door. "Scoot over. I'm driving."

"Why?" Tristan looked confused.

"Because I want your hands free."

He immediately patted his side where his gun was concealed. "You do realize you have to drive on the left side of the road?"

"Yes, I do." Miranda needed to be behind the wheel and, wanting the fresh air, lowered the window. "Just tell me where to turn." With the moon shy only a sliver of being completely full, the sky was lit up. "I want you to text Remare for me."

"All right. Turn left at the corner, then right at the intersection. That'll take us home."

When they were out of Rye, Miranda said, "Ask Remare if he could do a full investigation on someone."

He started texting. "Name?"

"Gemma Hastings."

"Anything in particular you're looking for?"

Something wasn't sitting right about what the older woman had told her. "I want to know her whereabouts for the last forty years."

He continued texting. "Not too demanding. What's up?"

"It's personal."

"Okay. Remare said he's on it."

"Good." She took a deep breath of the evening woods. "Ask him to do one more."

"Sure, who?"

"Carl Crescent, my father."

Tristan's brow rose.

"See if there's any connection between them. Nearly forty years ago. My father may have taken a course at Oxford during that summer. Thanks." She remained silent during the rest of the drive, only once nearly forgetting to stay on the left side of the road.

Wisely, Tristan didn't ask any further questions.

Chapter Sixteen

At Herbert Manor, Miranda threw the car in park. Remare was already waiting for her near the door; she went into his arms. "I'm sorry we're late. I lost track of the time."

"Not a problem. Is everything all right?"

She wasn't sure if he was asking her or Tristan, who came up behind her, but she answered, "Everything's fine."

"Dinner is just now being served, but if you'd rather…"

"No. I could use some sustenance." She kissed Remare's cheek. "I'll tell you more later. It's really not important. Just something I'm curious about."

He took her messenger bag from her. "What do you have in here, rocks?"

"Not quite." Miranda wasn't really hungry, but when Remare opened the door, she was hit with the mouthwatering scent of roasted turkey, sweet potatoes and other delicate aromas. *"Making up for the fish?"*

He grinned. *"I thought it the least I could do, after you so graciously acquiesced to my request the last time."*

When they were all seated in the dining hall, Miranda gazed around the room at the wainscoting and decorative flower arrangements. It helped ease the tension in her stomach.

Winnie smiled at her. "How was your trip into Rye?"

"Good. The manager at the bookstore found some more items she thought would interest me. I'll read them later."

Tristan glanced at the place settings. "Orion and Bastien said they'd eat later. They're busy traversing the woods. Orion wanted to stretch his muscles."

With the full moon tomorrow, Orion would need to run long and hard to answer the lunar heat that stirred all Weres. She was glad Bas was with him and that he wasn't alone.

The soup was served first, and Miranda smiled at Remare. He knew turkey soup was one of her comfort foods. *"Thank you."*

He nodded to her. *"Anytime."*

Once dinner was served, Herbert was the first to speak. "Your husband is still one of the best swordsmen I've ever met. He nearly severed my hand while we were sparring."

Her appetite not quite right, she was able to get down a few bites. The meal was lovely, the turkey tasty and moist, the sweet potatoes delicious, but she really wanted dinner to be over, so she could spend alone time with Remare. She gave herself bonus points for being cordial and gracious with Herbert and Winnie. After a few one-word answers, Remare nudged her mentally to offer more complete sentences. She did.

Miranda forewent the dessert but relished the green tea, breathing in its warmth. As if sensing her desire to be gone from the table, Remare said, "I think we'll call it an early night. All this traveling is exhausting for Miranda, and she could do with some rest."

"Yes. I think it's catching up with me. If you'll excuse us."

They made their way upstairs to their bedroom, and Remare closed the door behind them. Her arms slowly circled him, needing to feel his strength surrounding her. "Do you realize how much I miss you when you're not around?"

"As I do you. Now, will you tell me what all this is about?"

She reached inside her bag for the photo of her father. "This is my father, Carl Crescent. The owner-slash-manager of the bookstore in Rye knew him. Intimately. She's the sister of the librarian we met in London. Doesn't this feel too coincidental to you?"

"Possibly. After our sparring match, Herbert let me use his computer to complete the investigation. I did the preliminary report on my laptop, but I wanted to be thorough. His computer network is quite extensive."

As Lord of London, it would have to be. "And?"

"Your father did spend one summer at Oxford nearly forty years ago, although his bachelor's and master's degrees were from Columbia. Mir-randa, there was nothing that stood out about his record. Everything was as it should be."

She moved to the window, wondering if she'd spot Orion and Bastien darting through the woods. She glanced back at him. "Did you investigate me when I first worked for Valadon?"

One corner of his mouth rose. "You know that I did. As I did your parents." His arms went around her waist. "There was nothing dubious in any of your records."

"Do you know how disconcerting it is to find out your father had lovers before your mom?"

He shrugged. "Your father was in his thirties when he married. If he'd not had lovers, I would have been surprised."

"There's an eww factor here you're missing. I'm gonna take a hot shower then hit the hay. I really am tired."

"Miranda, it's perfectly normal that parents have other lovers before the one they marry."

"Yes. I know that. I do." Miranda hung back from the bathroom door. "But it's another thing to come face-to-face with someone who actually has carnal knowledge of your dad. It's creepy." She closed the door behind her.

Later that night, while the others slept, Miranda tossed and turned. Haunted by images of Esmerelda, Leland, members of the coven, Gemma and her father, a pervading sense of loss invaded her mind. Miranda couldn't sleep. Childhood memories clouded her consciousness, and a tear slipped down her cheek. Before she could suppress it, a sob escaped her mouth.

Remare pulled her closer to him, his voice groggy with sleep. "It's all right, Mir-randa. I'm here."

She snuggled into his hold. Her heated face buried in his cool chest, she breathed deep of his woodsy scent. She needed him to hold her, make her forget her troubles and just let go of everything else. "Make love to me, Remare. Make it so that it's just us. Make the world disappear."

He rolled on top of her. "I cannot make the world disappear. But I can make you forget. Make you believe in me and you." He kissed her soundly and thoroughly, a supernatural world of sensation, his touch a healing balm.

Inside his magical web of spells, the world did feel like it was slipping away. Fragments of the past, glowing crystals morphed to life, then dissipated. Her arms tightened around him, and her fingers raked down the hard ridges of his back as she returned his kiss like a woman possessed. Ghostly books, pages manifested, then also dissolved into the ether. Paintings, artists, images all coalesced, then floated away. Stirred by things she didn't fully understand, she reversed their positions so that she was on top and could stare down into Remare's dark eyes.

As she straddled him, his thick-lashed eyelids lowered in arousal; the red rims around his irises seemed to pulse, intensify. The dark, decadent brown of his eyes beckoned and seduced; striations of gold and green began to glow. She saw the depth of his hunger for her. His desire and need amplified her own feelings. Her heart thundered as her lips crushed his in a burning need to prove her want of him. And he reciprocated all the passion and craving she felt.

Breath ragged, Remare buried his face in her neck, licking, biting, stirring emotions that made her tremble, not in fear, but in ecstasy. That joyous notion only lovers share when they are as one. He laced their fingers together and tightened his hold on her. Possessing her, owning her body and soul.

She returned the favor by stroking her tongue against the vein in his neck and nibbling on his ear. The growl tore from his throat instantaneously as she bit down gently on his neck, enjoying the taste of him. Drinking him in, his essence, his emotions. Him.

Together, they soared from this world to another, where no disturbing thoughts were permitted. Free, they flew higher and higher, enjoying their whirlwind of emotion. Existing in a place where no others could touch them nor comprehend who they were.

Perspiration gathered on their bodies as they danced in achingly beautiful rhythm. Her hands stroked over his pecs to his ribs. Maneuvering herself lower, she kissed first one nipple then the other, biting down oh so gently. Another growl, this one slower, more dangerous, more carnal than the first. She licked down his chest until she reached his navel, then sucked it into her mouth. He cursed her in Italian, but she only chuckled.

Her tongue traveled down that fine line of hair until, after torturing him with lingering kisses, he held her head over the tip of his erection. She licked him as if he were an ice-cream cone, from base to tip and then underneath until she found his twin globes. She nearly giggled as she remembered the book on crystals described how to cure sterility. She imagined putting the stones near his, well, stones. *Oh, yeah, that'd go over well!* And then, she did laugh.

He glared at her questioningly.

"I'm happy. You have no idea just how happy I am at this moment."

"Another man would feel intimidated by your laughter."

She continued with her ministrations, determined to rock his world as she'd never done before. Teasing, taunting him to new heights until he was ready to explode.

When he could take no more, he pulled her up, reversed their positions, and hovered over her. "You are my sorceress. You bespell me like no other. Make me forget myself." His hand traveled down the center of her chest until he reached between her legs and massaged her in slow, tantalizing circles. Each touch sending swirls of sensations through her, fueling her hunger even more. Her breath was labored now, her heart thudding in her chest, her nails clawing the sheets.

When his mouth closed over her nipple, she thought she saw stars. Her back arched, and a scream nearly broke from her mouth. "Rem!"

"Who is this Rem? Do I know him?" he teased.

Miranda laughed. "Remare, you're killing me here."

"Never. But I will make you shatter."

And he did as he sank his fangs into her breast. "Remare!" Lights flashed for a moment as she fought to breathe through the orgasm. She no sooner came down from the high, then he was inside her. Nudging deeper, probing, prodding the tight muscles to open for him. She welcomed him in wet abandon, wicked desire and the wildness that spoke to the most primal part of her.

They rocked, caressed and stroked each other until the fires burning within them grew and expanded to impossible heights, until the maelstrom burst out of control, igniting more raw and sensuous emotions. They looked at each other as if for the first time, recognizing each other, united in passion and in contentment.

A bond so powerful, so binding, nothing could break it.

Awed by the power and intensity of their lovemaking, Miranda fell into a deep sleep, safe within his arms.

***

Lord Acton walked up the stairs to the one room he hadn't visited in a long time: her room. He opened the door and examined the interior. He'd had bars installed on all the windows—for her safety, he'd told her, he smirked. But, still, the room had had every luxury a woman could want. Huge poster bed, vanity, and a closet most could only dream of, filled with more clothes than anyone would need. Jewels fit for a queen. None was ever good enough for Esmerelda.

He strode over to the wall and pulled a curtain back, revealing her portrait. The act reminded him of Robert Browning's poem, "My Last Duchess". He snorted. Yes, there were certain similarities between both women. Each had been strikingly beautiful, enchanted others with their smiles, and vexed their masters. And each had been silenced.

Few had known he'd adored Esmerelda from the first moment he met her. Captivated by her beauty. He seemed to remember even trying to please her. For a time. He'd bought her everything she wanted. He sighed. But she'd grown despondent. He'd hoped she'd forget her former lover, but despite all his attempts to eradicate that romance, her love for Herbert's brother, Leland, had endured. Had he known the drunken fool would get himself killed in battle, he may not have deceived Esmerelda prior to his death. How satisfying it was that he'd been able to destroy the brother of the man who'd become Lord of London, a position that should have rightfully been his.

He examined Esmerelda's portrait. She truly had been a magnificent woman, but that was not what had caught his attention. Her power was her most prized asset. With her by his side, he knew which battles to participate in and which to avoid. Even when it came to investments, her seer abilities had been amazing, had netted him quite a profit.

But, like other women who had come before and after her, she'd grown restless. Wanted out of their arrangement.

He would not allow that to happen. Foolish woman hadn't learned her place. She was his and should have understood that. No one walked away from him without paying a stiff penalty. Like that traitor, Remare.

He sneered. How he enjoyed tormenting his war commander. Remare had been superior to all his former lieutenants in skills and strategies. He'd won many battles with Remare's cunning. Unfortunately, his chief lieutenant had the audacity to grow a conscience. What was it that had set him off? Ah, he remembered. Some young soldier had admired Acton's sword collection and had handled one of his prize swords, something forbidden to underlings. Remare had thought highly of the lad, despite his lack of restraint. Acton had ordered him to cut off the lad's hand to teach all those about respecting the possessions of others.

Remare had refused, saying the youth was guilty only of using poor judgment and should not be punished so harshly. If he must suffer a castigation, let him be whipped, those scars, in time, would heal; a hand would never grow back. Vampire or human.

"Either he loses his hand or you lose yours. Decide!" Acton had shouted.

Knowing he would not relent, Remare had the lad bound to the table. The youth struggled, twisting and turning in his captors' hands, and begged for leniency. There would be none forthcoming.

Remare had whispered something to the youth, and to this day, Acton still knew not what. But, before Remare lifted his sword, the icy stare he gave Acton was scathing. Acton had relished such looks from men before he eventually broke them. After Remare severed the lad's hand, he thrust the sword into the ceiling beam and stormed out.

The lad hadn't passed out from losing his hand, but when Acton had cauterized the wound with a torch, the pain was so severe, the soldier dropped to the floor. No one had ever touched his prized sword collection, again, without authorization.

Remare was later whipped for his insolence. His lack of loyalty for defying Acton. Later, when Remare escaped with Valadon's help, his betrayal had cost Acton plenty. Had he known Remare and Valadon's friendship was so strong, he might have done things differently.

But, now, an opportunity presented itself. Remare's wife, or rather Valadon's mistress, if the rumors were correct, was in England. So close, so within Acton's reach. It was said she, too, had powers. He had one of his agents spying on her, learning her abilities. Like Esmerelda, Miranda was human, easily manipulated, easily controlled. He would have her here, soon, in his castle. Finally, pay back Remare for his treachery. Oh, how delicious that would be. Another *Elemental* in his territory. Once in his lands, there was little anyone could do to defy him.

Miranda Crescent didn't know it, yet, but she was soon to be his. And, if she was a seer, then he would know how to proceed with his political ambitions. He had his eye on the chancellor's seat. She would help him attain it.

For certain, Lord Valadon would want her back. Acton would make a deal with the High Lord. If Valadon wanted her back so badly, let him throw his support for Acton as chancellor, only then could he have her back. After Acton played with her for a while, of course.

He laughed. How he loved killing two birds with one stone. Once he was chancellor, no one would be able to stop him.

He pulled the drape closed over Esmerelda's portrait and strode out, confident in his plans.

Chapter Seventeen

"Use your inner thigh muscles to coax him."

Miranda was glad Remare had suggested a horseback ride this morning. Wanting a reprieve from reading old letters and books, she looked forward to a quiet, uneventful ride in the country. However, her horse was considerably taller than the pony ride she'd had as a child, and for a moment, she was disconcerted. She quickly recovered and whispered mentally to the horse how handsome he was and that they would get along fine. "This feels a little strange, but I think I've got the knack of it."

"You'll do fine." Remare adjusted the last of the straps on the saddle, making sure her legs were high enough for proper riding. "We'll go slow this morning."

Miranda admired the ease with which he mounted his horse, all skill and grace. Earlier, he'd gone over all the particulars she needed to know about handling a horse, proving, once again, how great a teacher he was. Comfortable with her position, she was eager to go exploring on the paths.

Winnie handed him a parcel, which he placed in the saddlebag. "There're refreshments inside in case you get hungry or thirsty. Have a good ride."

Remare nodded. "We will. We'll see you when we get back."

"Bye, Winnie." Miranda waved as they turned for the trail that would take them through the forest. At first a little nervous, she took to it easier than she thought possible. Once they entered the woods, she breathed in nature's invigorating scent. "I love the way the trees smell after a hard rain, so fresh, so clean. The air is still cool."

The path was wide enough that they rode side by side. "I thought we could use some alone time, and you needed a break from your studies."

Miranda couldn't agree more. All the reading she'd been doing was taking its toll, and she feared a migraine was looming. "We should do this more often."

"Not many places to horseback ride in Manhattan. Central Park, maybe."

"No," she smiled, "I mean spend more time together. Away from ValCorp, Valadon. Away from the dangerous missions, bloodshed, violence. Just us."

Pulling his eyes away from the landscape, Remare gazed at her. "We will."

Miranda hoped so. Though, she knew his career choice was precarious. As they rode peacefully together along the path, he pointed out different markers and where the lake was. "Is that an eagle there?" She pointed up in the tree they were passing.

"Yes. It's a golden eagle."

"I didn't think England had eagles."

"Oh, yes. Eagles have an almost eight-foot wingspan, one of the best birds of prey, along with the peregrine falcon and hawks." He explained the difference in birds to her as they rode, and she enjoyed listening to the soothing cadence of his voice.

"I think I just spotted an owl hiding under a branch. It looked similar to the ones I saw out west in New Mexico."

Always on guard, always scanning the terrain, he said, "I've seen a few since we've been here. England is rife with different types of owls."

Miranda relished their leisurely ride and felt more relaxed, more content, than she'd been in a long while. She hoped it was the same for Remare. "So, this is how you traveled? I mean centuries ago. Didn't you ever get sore after a long day's ride?"

"Not really. Some missions required several nights of riding; others, weeks. Our bodies adapt to what is needed."

"Not sure I could have ridden that long."

"Oh, I don't know; you're doing pretty well." He grinned as he regarded her. "You had no problem riding me last night." His eyes glinted with mischief. "I'd say your skills were impeccable."

"Stop." She laughed. "Not everything is about sex."

"No. Not everything."

She wondered if, during his time in England, he'd had any lovers. He must have; he'd lived for centuries. "Did you ever have anyone special in this area? I mean, someone besides the Herberts."

"I know what you're asking. Did I ever go riding with another female? The answer to your question is yes. With Lady Horton. She was a friend to the Vampire Nation during a time when many were not. After discovering her husband's dubious business transactions with our enemies, she volunteered to spy for us, was able to procure valuable information on those who conspired against us. And, before you ask your next question, no, we weren't lovers. She was my friend, one I had great respect for. She risked much to help us."

"What was she like?"

"Determined. Intelligent. And kind. I was happy when I heard her husband had passed, but I never pursued her. Lord Byron wrote a poem for her, 'She Walks in Beauty'." Remare recited the poem, and Miranda was enthralled with his rendition, listening to his dulcet tones as he spoke. She'd read the poem in college and appreciated it, then, but now, the poem took on new meaning.

After they'd ridden for a while, enjoying the splendid solitude of the forest, he said, "There's a stream up ahead. We can rest the horses and have something to eat."

"Sounds good."

After tying the horses to a fallen log near the water, Remare laid out a blanket under one of the trees. As was the case most of the days they'd been in England, the sun seemed to play hide and seek with the clouds. Miranda preferred the shade, anyway. After munching on turkey sandwiches and drinking some wine, they rested alongside each other with their backs against the tree trunk. Each had mirrored the other with their arms crossed over their chests and one ankle over the other.

It was beautiful here, listening to the sounds of the rambling water and the birds overhead. Away from the real world, but the fact that Remare's work entailed danger weighed heavily on her mind. "If I asked you to consider limiting the amount of assignments you take, would you?"

"It's true I've taken on more than most of the Torians. I've thrived on it and felt, as their leader, it was my obligation. And the notion that I had no one special to come home to." He clasped her hand and brushed his lips against her knuckles. "Now, I do. Would you consider working less hours, either at the museum or at the university?"

"I've been thinking about that. I really do love what I do. I can't see giving up either one, but I think I'm going to tell the university I'll only teach one class a semester, instead of two. And I'm going to give up doing home authentications. Focus more on the research and authenticate whatever Jordan assigns me in-house."

"I'm glad to hear that. Now that Aiden has proven himself completely competent as Valadon's second while I was away, I feel I can delegate more to him. And with Asanti's son,

Jacob, joining the Torians, I'm certain I can lessen the amount of hours I put in."

She kissed his temple. "I hope so. The thought of you on clandestine operations makes my stomach twitch." She knew he was skilled and strong; she'd seen him fight. And he was faster than any of the other Torians, but sometimes, all that mattered was blind luck. "I know you're intelligent and an expert with weapons, the best of the Torians, but still...I worry."

"There's no need, my love. I've managed to stay alive for nearly a thousand years. I'm sure I can continue as such."

Somehow, in this quiet moment, in this peaceful place, she felt a measure of grace and had confidence in his abilities. "Maybe the fates will smile down on us, after all."

He stroked his thumb along her cheek and smiled. "They have so far."

When Remare smiled, her stomach flipped with joy. Was it possible to fall more in love with someone when you already loved them? It seemed so. The more time they spent together, her feelings for him continued to grow. He was constantly showing her sides to him that amazed her. Made her glad they were together and realize just how powerful the connection between them was. She traced the line of his jaw with her finger. "You are one handsome and desirable man."

He placed her hand over his sternum. "And you are the reason my heart beats."

She smiled. "Part of me wants to say let's stay here. Forget the rest of the world, forget ValCorp and Valadon. Let's find our own paradise away from the horrors of the world. But that's not possible, is it?"

He tugged on a strand of her hair. "Where is this paradise you speak of, Miranda? No place on the earth is free of worries. We've had this discussion before. We're safer belonging to a House, and Valadon House is our home. I will not forsake either one."

She knew his views. "I'm not asking for that. Not really. I guess I'm a dreamer." She looked, one more time, at their tranquil surroundings. "At the very least, promise me we'll have more moments like this. Time where we can just be ourselves without having to be on guard for any dangers." Her gut clenched at the thought they might not have many moments like this one.

"We will make the time, I promise."

She brushed her lips against his. "We should probably head back. Tonight's the full moon, and I told Agatha I'd meet with her this afternoon before their party this evening."

He started gathering up their things. "I want to escort you there."

She understood his concern as she folded the blanket. In truth, she was edgy about attending their meeting. "They don't like outsiders much." She didn't want to tell him what they really didn't like was vampires. She'd find out why when she spoke with Agatha.

"Don't worry, Mir-randa. I'll keep a respectable distance. Surveillance, without detection, is something I excel at."

"All right."

They rode back together, and Miranda was amazed at the rightness of being with Remare. Years ago, if someone had told her she'd be married to a vampire, the leader of Valadon's Elite Torian Guard and second in command to the High Lord, she would have laughed. But, now, she was overcome with the feeling that this was where she was supposed to be.

And that, for this perfect, blessed moment, all was right with the world.

After they returned the horses to the stables, they continued holding hands and made their way to the front of Herbert Manor. "Were you expecting company today?"

"Not me." Remare's body tensed in alertness. "And I don't recall Herbert or Winnie saying they'd be having visitors."

Miranda gestured with her chin. "I wonder who that young man is by the door." The youth was wearing jeans and a dark gray sweater. He looked to be about seventeen or eighteen, at the most, and was holding a large manila envelope. As they drew closer, she saw his nametag, "Harry".

Herbert opened the door. "You said you had a delivery."

"Yes, for Professor Miranda Crescent. Gemma Hastings, from Rye's Old Bookstore, said she was staying out here."

"That's me. Do you need me to sign for it?"

"No. Mrs. Hastings said to make sure you received this. I feel so bad for her. She was such a bundle of nerves this morning. She wanted to close the bookstore for a couple of days, but I told her Evelyn and I could run it while she's in London."

Miranda knew Gemma's sister, Alice Gordon, lived there and wondered why she didn't mention it last night. "Why'd she go to London?"

Harry looked like he'd seen a ghost. "Not sure I'm supposed to talk about it." When he saw Remare's scowl, his face blanched. "The police showed up this morning. It was dreadful. I thought Mrs. Hastings would faint from the news."

Remare asked, "And what news would that be?"

"Oh, it's her sister. In London, they found her body. She'd been murdered. The police in London think it was a burglary. Her apartment was rifled through, but they need Mrs. Hastings there to see if anything was taken. I still can't understand why anyone would want to hurt a librarian."

Miranda's heart thudded in her chest. "How...how is Gemma doing?"

"She left as soon as the police finished asking her questions. I volunteered to drive her, but she said she wanted me here to run the store and could drive herself. I probably should have insisted, but she's my boss, and I didn't want to make her angry."

Remare focused his stare on Harry. "Are there any other details you can tell us?"

Harry scratched his head. "No. I can't think of anything else, other than her saying I had to get that package to Professor Crescent."

Miranda looked down at the postmark. "It's from London."

Remare gazed downward at the envelope and then at Herbert. He addressed Harry. "Thank you for coming out here and providing us with the information."

Miranda wasn't sure who'd intimidated the poor youth more, the vampire lord, Herbert, or Remare with his dark eyes, but after accepting a generous tip from Remare, he quickly got in his car and drove off.

"Remare."

"I know, Mir-randa. I don't trust this at all. Herbert, can you have your people look into Alice Gordon's murder?"

"Certainly. I'll notify my people immediately." Herbert led them inside the library.

Miranda went to the desk underneath the window and opened the package and laid out its contents. "There's a letter here. Alice remembered the research I was doing and found a book I was interested in misfiled in the maps division." She peered up at Remare. "Gemma evidently told her we were here. Alice sent this to me 'in care of' Gemma. She must have sent it just before…"

Herbert declared, "My people are looking into it and will report when they have answers. Now, would someone mind telling me what this is all about?"

While Remare explained what he could to Herbert, Miranda thumbed through the book, which not only contained text, but illustrations reminiscent of Raphael,

DaVinci, Botticelli, and other Renaissance artists who painted scenes of *The Annunciation.* This book was written in the seventeenth century by a monk whose order deemed him "touched in the brain" because of his wild stories of healers. In the drawings, the *Feminae Santatem,* or the *Healing Women,* were depicted as being angelic. Rays of illumination were emanating from them as they healed the afflicted.

Apparently, the monk hadn't let his obsession with the women go. If his order had seen this book, they would have labeled him a blasphemer. As far as she knew, only the Virgin Mary was ever painted as being visited by the angels with the cascading light. She pondered if the other artists had painted scenes contradictory to the church's teachings. No wonder the clerics burned the paintings of the Medicis and others.

Miranda turned to Remare. "I'm going to go upstairs and rest for a bit."

"I'll come with you." He addressed Herbert. "Let me know what you find out."

Once in their bedroom, Miranda reached for her messenger bag. "You're right, it does weigh a ton. Gemma loaned me letters that Esmerelda wrote. Between the letters and the journals, my eyes are beginning to feel fried."

"Hand me half of them. I'll read through them quicker than you can."

She handed him the pile and then dumped the contents of her handbag on the bed. "I bought a few books and pens at her bookstore." Her eyes lit when she discovered three gemstones she hadn't purchased. "That's funny. I bought three crystal necklaces at the yoga studio. I don't know how these got in my bag."

Remare examined the stones. He held a brownish red one up to the light. "Staurolite."

"Wait, let me get the volume on crystals that Esme gave me." She thumbed through the pages. "Okay, here it is. In folklore, it was believed to bring good luck. Found in Scotland and...New Mexico. Whoever possessed the stones could summon all four elements at will." *Sheesh, powerful crystal!*

"I know of this stone. During the Crusades, many soldiers wore them on their journeys. See the cross-like structure. They believed it connected them to the spiritual plane." He lifted up the second one. "Peridot."

Miranda recalled her research but turned to the page. "The Stone of Destiny. From meteorites. Supposedly helps in regeneration, improves intuition. Visions."

Remare handed her the last gemstone. "Hematite. This contains iron."

"I remembered that one, as well. Enhances psychic abilities." She read from the book. "Hmm. Aids in astral projection. Wow! That's a biggie. Wait." She peeled off a smaller stone that had stuck to the larger one. Also red, this one was clearer. "This looks a lot like carnelian." She sniffed it. "There's some iron oxide in it."

After consulting the book, she said, "Wards off psychic evil. For remembering past experiences, a grounding stone, used by earth and fire *Elementals*." She gazed up at him. "That's us. Good Lord! Why on earth would someone slip those crystals into my bag?"

"Obviously, they wanted you to have them."

"Remare, only a few people know I'm a fire *Elemental*." She had a pretty good inkling about who gave them to her. Fire had always been her strong suit; her talent with the other elements was slowly catching up. "I don't know about you, but I'd like to go to Cranbrook, now. Agatha Winslow has a cottage there. She's their elder. I have a few questions for her."

"Mir-randa. Are you sure you want to do this? Throughout the centuries, people have had various beliefs in stones, totems and other amulets of magic. Witchcraft."

"I know. This gathering is beginning to sound more and more like a witch's coven. But I don't think they are. Either way, I want answers."

"If you are determined to go, I'm coming with you." His eyes met hers as he held her shoulders. "Be vigilant."

She kissed him quickly then gathered up her things. "Always."

Chapter Eighteen

"Oh, look, there's a winery. Some place you can hang out and read while I'm with Agatha."

Remare scoffed at her comment as he drove them to Cranbrook. Miranda could tell he really wanted to drive the Bentley but settled on the Range Rover so as not to look conspicuous. Somehow, with their accents, she didn't think they could stay undetected long. Like a snake coiled tight, just waiting to attack, Remare always looked dangerous, whether he was sitting or standing still. His body language, the way he moved, and his facial expressions all hinted at a dark demeanor.

Even his expensive suits suggested a muscular body you did not want to mess with. But, once he donned the sunglasses, he appeared even more threatening. No one was going to think he was local.

"Hmm, I never thought of England as producers of wine; I just thought they were big on beer."

"If you're so interested in wineries, I will take you to Tuscany. The countryside is warmer, more beautiful, and the wines far superior."

Miranda teased, "You mean like a real honeymoon?"

He smiled at the notion. "We would need a minimum of three weeks to see it properly."

"Sounds good to me. I didn't realize England was still cool this late in May." They drove past the Cranbrook Museum. "Maybe we can check out the museum later. Gotta say, I love these small towns. They're so charming, quaint, it's like going back in time. London is great, but it's a megatropolis. Too congested. Too much to see in too little time."

"Some would say the same about New York."

"True, but big cities like London, Paris, New York, all have their neighborhoods. There are still sections in Manhattan I've never been to."

"If that is a subtle attempt to remind me I've yet to take you up to The Cloisters at Manhattan's northern edge, I haven't forgotten."

Miranda laughed. "No, it wasn't, and yes, I still want you to accompany me there." She remembered telling him she wanted to show him her world. "Are you okay with all this? My realm of museums, libraries and research can't be all that exciting for you."

Remare brought her hand to his lips. "I'm enjoying this trip. More than I thought I would. I don't mind the research, Mir-randa. In fact, I find I quite enjoy it. It's a welcome break from the work I usually do."

Miranda knew his usual work consisted of investigations of Valadon's enemies and often dangerous missions that turned bloody and violent. Something she wasn't sure she'd ever get used to. But Remare was the best of the best, and as he'd told her, he didn't survive nearly a millennium by being irresponsible. "Do you mean that?"

He caressed her hand. "Absolutely, or I wouldn't have said it."

"I'm glad, then."

"I'm just concerned where your research will lead you. What doors will be opened that you won't be able to close."

In truth, so was she. Something about this whole trip wasn't sitting right. "I'm tempted to say, you worry too much, but yeah. It feels like someone handed me this huge jigsaw puzzle, tossed all the pieces in the air, and I'm trying to figure out where all the pieces go. I don't even have a clear picture in my mind of what I'm supposed to be seeing."

"You will. I have faith in you. I'm just worried that there are others who might covet what you discover."

"Like Lord Acton."

He clicked his teeth together. "That's one possibility. There might be others. Some we don't know about as yet."

"All right, that's Agatha's place up ahead. You know you don't have to wait for me. I'll probably be a couple of hours. Go, get a room at that hotel we passed, The George, relax for a while. If you want, read up some more on the crystals or Esmerelda's letters. I'll call you if I have need. And..." she used her mental ability to connect with him, *"I can contact you this way."*

"I'll be close by. Take care of my sorceress. I only have one, and she's quite precious to me."

She kissed him. "As you are to me." *The only vampire I'll ever love.* She watched as he drove off, thinking there was no way a lethally sexy vampire in a ten-thousand-dollar suit was going to blend in. Not in a small town like this. Shameful to admit, even now, but it was his air of danger that had first attracted her. Her body shivered at the thought. With his raven hair and goatee, he radiated a degree of darkness that might cause others to retreat, never really knowing who he was or what he was capable of.

Miranda knew and loved him, regardless.

She scanned the acres of greenery. Agatha must like her privacy; the nearest home was more than a mile away. The two-story dwelling was modest in size with flower beds along the front and winding around the sides of the house. The scent of hyacinth perfumed the air. Miranda knocked on the front door and was greeted by a young woman she didn't recognize, who told her Agatha was around the back.

As Miranda rounded the corner, she spotted Agatha sitting on a wooden bench, admiring her garden. "Hello, there."

Agatha glanced up at her. "I see you found the place all right. Welcome."

"Thanks. I think your town is charming. I might stop at the museum later. It seemed to beckon to me."

"Ah, we have quite a collection of paintings by local artists. I'm sure you'd enjoy it."

Miranda sat across from her. "Thank you for seeing me."

"It's not often we discover a new *Elemental.*" She smiled enthusiastically. "We're thrilled to have you. I think you'll like our moonlight ceremony. We've been cooking since early this morning; there'll be plenty of food. You should meet others of our kind."

"I'm looking forward to it. I know it couldn't be easy letting me into your group. I appreciate your concern for secrecy."

Agatha arched a brow. "I Googled what I could about you. It's not like we take complete strangers into our circle. You've lived an interesting life."

"Not really. Academics tend to have sedate lives." Miranda shrugged, wondering just how much of her life was public record. "I was an orphan for a long period of my life. My Aunt Meg raised me. The only interesting thing was going to grad school in Paris."

"Oh, I think you've had other more intriguing adventures. But that's yours to share when you choose."

"In London, you said you would answer my questions when we met, again. I have so many I don't know where to start."

Agatha gazed out at her garden. "It's so unfortunate your parents never told you more about us."

"Yeah." *It was unfortunate they lost their lives to a drunk driver!* Miranda used to have fantasies of hunting that guy down and beating him to death for depriving her and her family of the lives they should have had. "They never had the chance to."

"What do you wish to know?"

Miranda should have written a list of all the things she wondered about. "Why is it that we have these powers? Why some people, not others?"

"Surely, with your credentials as an art authenticator, you've researched us. What books have you read?"

"The only one of any note that I've read is Peralt." Remare had told her he thought Peralt based his theories on the writings of Paracelsus, the alchemist who lived a century before Peralt. "He was pretty detailed about describing the four groups. I've read other books on the history of the Inquisition. It seems anyone who was marked *different* or had any powers they labeled as witches. Destroyed them mercilessly."

"Yes, historically speaking, there were many groups who hunted us down. Too many lives lost. That is why we keep our true natures hidden. There's talk that some of the groups are still around today." Agatha met her eyes. "Did you learn about the Brotherhood of Light?"

Miranda did. Only she knew them as the Human Order of Light. A powerful hate group who seemed to abhor vampires more than anyone else. "Yes. Originally, an offshoot of the Church, they executed those they deemed 'Demon Children'."

"Every group has their radicals. Whether or not they were actually sanctioned by the Church, or set out on their own, no one knows. But I believe they still exist today. Corrupt officials guilty of misogyny. They didn't understand our powers, so they feared us, hunted us down, in hopes of exterminating us. We've endured, nevertheless." Agatha turned to her. "How familiar are you with the Bible?"

Not very. "I know the basics."

"Do you know the seven deadly sins?"

If this was a test, Miranda was probably going to fail. There was always at least one that she forgot. "Let's see, there's greed, envy, lust, pride," she counted on her fingers, "gluttony and revenge?"

"Not quite, but close enough. Revenge is associated with wrath." Agatha seemed to be waiting. "You forgot one."

Miranda mentally counted, again, and couldn't remember the last one. "Which is?"

Agatha stared at her. "The one you are guilty of the most, my dear."

Wait a minute! While not flawless, she didn't think she was guilty of any of them. Okay, maybe lust after Remare had just finished showering and walked around their room naked. *Who wouldn't lust after him in that state?* Possibly gluttony when chocolate was involved, but really, no one was perfect. "And?"

Agatha smiled. "Sloth."

Hell to that no! "Lazy?! I don't think so! I worked my tailbone off in grad school, and even now, I work two jobs, one at the museum and the other at the university, so I think you're dead wrong there."

"Am I? Sloth does not just imply laziness. It also concerns indifference to duties or obligations. Ceasing to use your God-given talents. For good. Sharing your knowledge, strength, and insights with others of your kind."

Miranda stuttered. "I put my talents to use."

"In serving others or yourself?"

Miranda thought of how she once helped Valadon defeat the evil ancient, Mulciber, healed Asanti's son, Jacob, when he was poisoned and, not long ago, aided Valadon's son, Vincent, when he'd been shot with coils that wrapped around his neck. "Both, I protected myself and others when it was necessary."

"That's good to know. Maybe I misjudged you. I have one question, though." Agatha seemed to be studying her. "Why do you let your fears rule you?"

Miranda didn't like the question, felt like she was being put under a microscope. "What makes you think I do?"

"You wear your fears like a shield. It keeps you distant. Perhaps that will lessen, now that you are among others of your talents."

Miranda wondered what fears the older woman was seeing in her.

"Of the seven, which do you think is the worst?"

Miranda sighed. Another test. She'd probably fail this one, too. "I'm not sure, but I'd think revenge or wrath, maybe greed or jealousy." She'd seen how Valadon's enemies had been so motivated.

"All evils, yes, but only one is responsible for all the rest: Vanity, aka, pride. Those who hunted us down believed they were above everyone else. Arrogance. They were supposed to put the needs of the people before their own; instead, they became self-absorbed, seeking out anyone who they believed posed a threat to their status, their security. They refused to consider, let alone acknowledge, others had worth, as well." Agatha turned to her. "Are you a Christian?"

Miranda sighed, unsure how to answer her. "I lost my faith when my family was taken from me."

"I see. Do you know the archangels?"

Never met one! "If I remember correctly, there were Raphael, Michael—the avenging angel and...Gabriel." That was about the extent she knew.

"According to medieval Christian theologians, there's a hierarchy of the angels arranged into orders called Angelic Choirs. If you find the time, read Thomas Aquinas' *Summa Theologica.* It makes for interesting reading. Also, you might find Francesco Botticini's *The Assumption* interesting. It's hanging at the National Gallery in London. In any respect, there are four archangels that are generally venerated by many religions." She peered at Miranda. "Four, an interesting number, don't you think?"

"I suppose." Miranda wondered where she was going with this.

"The archangel you didn't mention was Uriel; he is associated with wisdom, north and the element of earth—grounds people in their time of need. His is the red ray of light."

Miranda was stunned. She'd never heard this before. "The archangels were related to elements and colors?

"Yes. Raphael was the archangel of the east and healing, the air, his is the green light, and Gabriel—the archangel of communication and messages, the water and westerly direction. White is his color."

"What about Michael?" She knew he was supposedly the most powerful.

"Ah, the fiery archangel, protects and fights against evil, the discoverer of spiritual truth, empowers people to let go of their fears." Agatha smiled as she nodded to Miranda's sapphire ring. "His color is blue."

Miranda blinked and needed a moment to process all she was hearing. Her mind was whirling with everything Agatha was saying. "Four directions, four elements, but weren't there supposed to be seven?

"It depends on which religion you follow. Some agree there were seven, others an eighth and quite possibly a ninth. Some were even suggested to be female. Uriel, for instance, may have been Ariel, and others suggest the name Raguel or Raquel was an archangel."

Miranda didn't know much about religion, but she did know some. "The Church would not be amenable to females in the hierarchy."

"Hardly. The Church has always been patriarchal. Even though there were supposedly seven or nine, the focus has always been on the four—no debate on their masculinity."

Miranda shook her head. "As fascinating as this is, what does that have to do with me?"

"Peralt wrote he believed we descended from angels. They were sent to watch over us, The Gregori—the Watchers. However, some mixed with us. There were theories that not only the good angels walked among us, but the rebellious ones, as well. That is why we have Light and Dark *Elementals.*"

And any combinations thereof. "Yin and yang, dark and light. It makes sense. Hard to have one without the other."

"You asked why some of us have talents and others do not. You should read *Genesis* from the *Old Testament* or *The Book of Enoch.* They allude to beginnings. You may find your answers there."

Miranda wondered if that might be the mysterious *Book of Origins* and made a mental note of her suggestions. "I've read how the Church burned the writings and paintings of those who they believed challenged their teachings—The Bonfire of the Vanities, among others."

"Yes. I believe the Brotherhood was behind that. Anything that pertained to the power of women, of *Others,* was eradicated."

Miranda didn't consider herself a religious person, so she didn't share Agatha's reveries. These were someone's theories, conjectures. Sure, she believed in a higher power, forces at work in the universe she couldn't begin to imagine or understand. "One last question. One of the *Elementals* I met said the word vampires like it was an anathema to us. Why?"

"During the time of the Inquisition, rather than be hunted themselves, certain vampires gave us up to the

Church officials. They had wealth, you understand. Made covenants with the leaders so they stayed secure." Her voice chilled. "Great wealth buys great protection."

"Surely, there were others who betrayed those who died?"

"Yes, I'm certain there were. But the vampires were known for guarding their own, not us, when it counted most. Something you should keep in mind."

Before she could ask any more questions, Esme neared them, carrying a tray of lemonade. "Hello, Miranda. I thought you might be thirsty."

"Yeah, I could use something to drink, thank you." Miranda gulped down the cool liquid.

"Esme, why don't you take Miranda to our crystal room? Let her see for herself."

"Sure. Feel like walking, Miranda?"

Agatha's backyard stretched back farther than she thought. Once they climbed the small hill, they descended on the other side, which had a stream running by. The air was sweet here, and Miranda wondered what wild flowers grew in the area.

"Over here." Esme moved the tall grass away from a mound of earth. "It's a cave. Wait until you see what's inside. It's truly remarkable."

Miranda was a little hesitant about entering, but when Esme handed her a candle then used her own to light the interior, she felt less anxious about exploring the dank and musty-smelling cave.

But nothing could prepare her for what lay inside.

Chapter Nineteen

As Esme led Miranda down a dark, winding path that was hauntingly familiar, fragments of a foreboding dream appeared: Esmerelda. Singing. Old earth. Cold air brushed against her senses, making her skin tingle, as the long passageway narrowed. Miranda suspected aspects of the supernatural thrived here. Mysteries she could neither comprehend nor have the answers to. The deeper they went, the more the cave seemed to be vibrating with energy. Her heart was pounding in anticipation. Yet, she followed where her guide was taking her until Esme lit the last of the torches in a large rectangular space, a room that seemed to be a living, breathing entity.

Miranda's jaw dropped, and she was struck speechless at the near blinding illumination. Every color in the spectrum was here. Dozens and dozens of iridescent crystals, artfully placed on pedestals, lined the walls of the cavernous room. She shook her head in amazement at the intensity of the natural beauty. It was a treasure trove of geological wonders.

Instinctively, she knew she was witnessing something wonderful most humans could never imagine. She stood in exhilarating awe of the brilliance of the crystals; her eyes drifted over the bedazzling shapes and sizes that seemed to be pulsating with life and beckoning to her. "It sounds as if they're humming."

"Very good, Miranda. It's the air currents that drift between them that make it sound as if they're singing."

Singing rocks?! "Where did all these come from?"

"Several were already here when we discovered this room. Others—members of our group brought from various places. We've been collecting them for a long time. Sarita's cousin in India discovered many. Agatha has traveled the world for them. Some are from Scotland and points north, and others from the Mid-East and China. And a few are even from your American Southwest."

Miranda started on the right and examined each of the displays. Some of the clusters were the size of pine cones; others exceeded her height. "I love the violet colors." She almost reached for one then thought better of it. "They're magnificent."

"It's amethyst." Esme grinned. "You can pick it up, you know. It won't break."

Miranda held the crystal in both hands and then held it up to the light. "Unbelievable. Beauty in its rawest form."

"Do you see the shape inside the crystal?"

"Yes, it looks almost like the ocean."

"It's called a phantom. Several of the quartz stones have them. Do you remember from the book I gave you what the properties were?"

Exhaling, Miranda closed her eyes in memory. "Umm. Amethyst, found in Asia, South America and the American Southwest. Known as a healing stone, supposed to enhance psychic abilities."

"You did read the book." Esme clapped. "I was afraid you didn't. Do you recognize the next one?"

Miranda carefully placed the amethyst down and lifted the nearest stone. This one was darker red, she remembered most red stones contained some degree of iron ore. "I'm not sure." Her eyes narrowed. "Carnelian, maybe."

"Yes. It's used to get a glimpse into the past. A specialty of fire *Elementals*. It guards against telepathic assaults."

Miranda shivered as a memory of a stronger force, a more powerful *Elemental*, had invaded her mind. Valadon's enemy, Stuart Blackmore, aka, The Regent. She held the stone tightly in her hand before laying it down. The next one was such a dark red it was almost black. What's this one?"

"Hematite. People like me use it for astral travel."

Miranda raised a brow. Did the *Elementals* really believe the stones bestowed such powers? But then, she fingered the amber necklace Montglat had given her. She couldn't begin to understand the metaphysical properties of the crystals.

"Only a few *Elementals* have the ability." Esme waved her hand around the room. "All these crystals you see here make great jewelry, ornaments. But *Elementals* can absorb the energy they radiate. The average person cannot. Either you are born with the ability or you're not. The stones only enhance whatever energy you already have."

"So, if an ordinary person wore a necklace with these crystals, there'd be no *otherworldly* effects?"

"Define ordinary." She laughed. "There are people, non-*Elementals,* who are more sensitive than others. They may sense something is off, but they wouldn't know what it was."

Miranda moved on to the chunk of obsidian. "Volcanic rock, black, but translucent. I like how it reflects the light."

"A protection stone. It neutralizes poisons."

"Good to know." Miranda moved down the aisle. "God, some of these almost look like diamonds."

"One comes close. That quartz there is called the Herkimer Diamond. It's a powerful amplifier to those with talents. Improves insight into visions. They call it the 'Dream Crystal'."

And, so, it went on and on: Miranda remembering most of what she'd read, and Esme reminding her of the supposed possibilities of each of the crystals. Some of the explanations were pretty far out there, but Miranda tried to have an open mind. At the end of the cave, dark crystals were behind a thick glass wall. "What's with those?"

Esme let out a breath. "They are deadly stones." She pointed to the left one. "Cinnabar, the worst of them all. Highly toxic, contains mercury, lethal. Stibnite—very poisonous. And galena—not as bad as some of the others but still harmful."

In her dream, Esmerelda had told her the crystals were poisoned, but not by whom. "I don't get it; if they're so dangerous, why have them?"

Esme faced her directly. "So, others will not. They're a reminder that, as helpful as some of the energy in this room is, there are also dangers."

"I see." Beauty may be fascinating, alluring, offering opportunities, but it could also be deceptive.

"Do you? Do you, really?"

Miranda knew people had beliefs she had no such faith in, but she wasn't about to insult someone who radiated kindness. "I believe some people are born with gifts others will never have." Orion was blessed with a voice that could make the angels jealous. No matter how much someone like her practiced, she'd never be able to hold a tune. "But you have to admit, some of this stuff is pretty much out there."

"Yes, to an outsider, who cannot see or understand, this would all seem like nonsense. One would have to experience the energy firsthand to know its possibilities."

"Experience?"

Esme's mouth quirked up in one corner. "Are you ready, Miranda? To open your third eye? To see what others cannot?"

Miranda was skeptical of anything she couldn't analyze, prove, or authenticate. Her work was based on science, not superstition. "My job requires me to evaluate chemicals in paints. I believe in chemistry. Facts, not fiction." She sighed. "I believe there are forces at work we'll never understand. But this..." She gazed around the room and shook her head.

"You need to see for yourself." Esme started gathering a few of the crystals. "Haven't you ever wondered how you can conjure fire when others cannot? How some can command the winds, how others have extraordinary talents that defy all that is commonly believed?"

Miranda wasn't sure she wanted answers as much as she once did. She gazed down at her hand. How was it that she could hold fire without it burning her? How could she erect walls of blue flames? "I've wondered about a great many things."

"Then, let me show you." Esme gestured for Miranda to follow her to another section of the cave where the vibrations whirred around them. Esme lit two more torches then sat in the middle of the room and started placing the crystals in a circle in front of her.

Curious, Miranda sat across from her. When Esme completed the circle, the crystals seemed to glow, and it was as if they were pulsating.

Esme pointed. "Amethyst enhances intuition, moonstone improves meditation, and lastly, staurolite—to strengthen control over the elements. I'm glad you wear a sapphire ring. Do you know what it's used for?"

Miranda ran her finger over the ring Remare had given her on their wedding day. "It's supposed to help open the 'third eye'."

"A very powerful stone." She leaned her head to the side. "You wear a necklace of amber."

"Yes. It was a gift from a friend."

"Amber is a protection stone, even though it's not really a stone, the ancient Greeks believed it was an energy magnifier."

Esme crossed her legs in the Lotus position Miranda had seen her use in the yoga studio when they meditated.

"Close your eyes and shut out everything else, Miranda. Free your mind of all negative thoughts. Breathe deep."

Miranda did as requested. She was used to this yoga routine. It was relaxing and liberating. The darkness of the cave helped alleviate other considerations and ideas. Soon, her breath had slowed remarkably, her body at peace.

"Can you feel it?"

"What exactly?"

"The earth's vibration. We're sitting on top of an earth energy line."

Miranda opened one eye. "That sounds suspiciously like ley lines."

Esme snorted. "Not at all. Ley lines go in straight directions, energy lines weave across the earth. There's scientific research on this. The earth has a magnetic field that protects it from the sun. Within the field are planetary waves. They drift across the planet in the oceans and in the air and in the ground. Rest your hand on the ground, see if you sense it."

Miranda had to admit she'd felt vibrations in the earth, had many times. "It could be an underground river."

"Could be but isn't. Now, concentrate. Let the vibrations pass through you."

Miranda closed her eyes and exhaled long and slowly. She'd heard of bio-magnetic energy and wondered if it was somehow connected.

"These energy waves move westward. Do you know what direction the earth rotates?"

Miranda thought that was something she should have known. "East?"

"Correct. The opposing forces create friction or energy. The planet has so much to offer, so many mysteries we'll never know. Can you feel the magnetic pull?"

Miranda felt a tingling in her fingers. She'd always been sensitive to vibrations, but she attributed it to the constant movement of commuters in the city. Out here in the country, where everything was still, it was easier to sense the environment around her. "I feel...something."

"Good. You don't have to explain it. Just experience. Remember to breathe. Slowly, deeply. Keep your mind open. Go to that quiet place of peace in your mind. Just relax. Let the energy come to you."

Miranda did. She'd learned, long ago, how to shut out noise, distractions, to keep herself focused. She believed, in relaxation, there was rejuvenation. Energy fields? Planetary waves? Magnetic pulls? There were forces she didn't understand completely, but she knew they existed. Something in her kept her in tune with the earth. How was it she could tell when the sun was rising or setting when she was underground at Werehaven or at Valadon House? She didn't know; she just did.

She opened her eyes to see Esme smiling over her. But it wasn't Esme's body. It was her spirit. The same one that had visited Miranda in London. Her breath caught. "How?"

Esme laughed. "Still don't believe in the power of the crystals?"

"I'm not sure what I believe in, anymore."

"That's good; it means your mind is open. Would you like to travel on the astral plane?"

"I can't. I'm not an *Ethereal* like you."

"You don't have to be. Take my hand. I'll show you how."

Miranda wasn't sure about that. She'd seen forces she didn't understand, wasn't certain she could comprehend or if she even needed firsthand knowledge.

"No reason to be afraid. We'll stay local. Our bodies stay here; it's only our auras that travel on the astral plane."

It wasn't so much the leaving that concerned Miranda; it was the returning. "How do we get back?"

"The same way we left. Don't worry. The stones help to ground us. We'll be perfectly fine."

Miranda's heart was beating hard against her chest. She'd never attempted anything like this. Wasn't sure it was even possible, but every instinct she had suggested that Esme meant her no harm. She raised her hand slightly then dropped it. "Could we just stay in the cave?"

Esme sighed. "If you want. Though it won't be very interesting. The fun is in the traveling."

Miranda shook her head. Indecision clawed at her. Finally, her hand seemed to raise of its own volition. "The cave only."

"All right."

Miranda took a deep breath and then another. She clasped Esme's hand, and a jolt of energy transpired between them. She felt her essence begin to leave her body and had to suppress a moment of panic. "This is scary."

"All new things are, until you learn to master them."

Disoriented, Miranda gazed at her sitting form. "I don't understand how this is possible."

"Is the how really all that important? Or the wonderful possibilities you're afraid of?"

Miranda wasn't fearful; she was cautious. "How many times have you done this?"

"Many. It gets easier each time. Would you like to see what's outside? See the world from a different perspective?"

Part of her wanted to, badly. Curiosity was so much of who she was, but she'd learned to be careful. "What's the kickback? Power like this always exacts a cost."

"There are no residual effects, Miranda. If you're afraid, we don't have to go."

"Will our bodies be safe here?"

"Yes, all normal biological functions continue." Esme's voice was soothing. "Only a part of our essence leaves; the rest operate, as usual. No one will harm us."

Leap of faith, Miranda kept repeating in her mind. Of all things to take with a leap of faith. She steadied her breathing. "Okay, I'm ready."

"Good."

Miranda no sooner said the words when she realized Esme and she were floating out of the cave into the open air. Exuberance mixed with awe and shock. Fascination transcended fear. To believe in the unimaginable, the unbelievable. She thought her heart was beating out a staccato, but when she looked down, her essence was translucent. "We're out of our physical forms, but it still feels like my heart is banging against my ribs, and my breaths are ragged."

"It's the shadow of a memory. It will fade as you learn control."

"Can anyone see us like this?"

"Only if you want them to. Where would you like to go?"

Nearly overwhelmed, Miranda felt strangely liberated, exhilarated by this new foreign, yet impossibly familiar, power. "I'd like to see what Cranbrook looks like from above."

As they flew over the town, Miranda wondered if she should check on Remare, but if he decided to rest at the hotel, she didn't want to disturb him. Confidence in her abilities was growing.

"It's a small town, but there are some nice spots." Esme pointed out where the church, museum, and hotel were. When they landed on the roof of the museum, Miranda was giddy with joy. "I can't believe we did that. We were flying!"

Esme laughed with her. "Yes, we were. There's so much more to this life, Miranda, than most people will ever know."

She gazed out over the town and then at Miranda. "We're the lucky ones."

They certainly were. "Why me?"

"I chose you because I believe you're gifted in many areas. Remember, the crystals only enhance whatever abilities you already have. The others don't possess what you do."

Miranda wondered if they would be jealous if they knew.

"We should get back. There's still a lot to do before the gathering tonight, and you don't want to exhaust yourself."

Miranda wasn't tired at all. Empowered by this beguiling feeling of being, of becoming who she was meant to be, destined to be, part of her wanted to fly across the hills and valleys, to go exploring. But Esme was right. *First, we walk; then, we run.* "Okay."

They made their way back to the cave. Once inside, Miranda floated easily back into her body. The snap of bio-magnetic energy wasn't as loud or unnerving as it had been before. She looked down at her arms and legs, and the feeling was normal. She missed the euphoric sensation of flying but knew she'd be doing something similar soon enough.

Esme's body seemed to absorb her aura back into place with a fluidity that suggested mastery. But, before her transition was complete, she seemed to take on the form of an owl.

Miranda stood in shock. "Oh my God! How?"

"Haven't you ever heard of spirit animals?" Esme shimmered back into human form. "Transmogrification is a rare talent only a few possess. It takes much time and practice to master."

Miranda shook her head at what she'd just seen. Peralt had mentioned transmutations, but she hadn't been sure what he meant. Now, she was. Exiting the cave, Miranda felt somehow reborn, revitalized with energies she'd not known before. She looked up at the sky, feeling somewhat enhanced, as if something inside her had fundamentally altered, evolved. As if her veil of destiny had been pulled back, and she could see the world clearer than she ever had before. She said, "Thank you. You didn't have to share that particular talent with me."

"I wanted to." Esme spoke in that soft, soothing voice she always used with Miranda, as if she were reassuring a child. "Wait until tonight, then you'll see some truly amazing things."

Miranda breathed deep the fresh air of the outdoors. She wasn't sure how traveling on the astral plane had changed her, but she felt as if a door had opened that had previously been hidden. She'd somehow unlocked a new and strange power that had always been a part of her. Primal, dormant, waiting. "I'm looking forward to it," she said as they climbed the hill back to Agatha's place.

After their goodbyes, Miranda texted Remare, who immediately called her back as a tawny owl flew overhead. Strange, she thought owls only came out at night.

His voice was music to her ears. "Mir-randa, Tristan is closer to you. He'll pick you up shortly. I'm at the George Hotel."

"Tristan's here?"

"Yes, he arrived shortly after us. We have a policy of no solo missions, so he volunteered to shadow us."

Miranda didn't see how a drive in the country constituted being on a mission, but she shrugged it off. "Okay, then, I'll see you in a few."

Chapter Twenty

Within minutes, Tristan pulled up on a motorcycle. She hadn't been expecting that but, then remembered someone had mentioned to her that Tristan had a prized Bugatti back in New York.

Removing his helmet, Tristan said, "Hey, gorgeous, someone mentioned you might be needing a lift?" He grinned as he handed her a helmet. With his handsome features and winsome smile, Tristan was a looker.

"Oh, and would that someone be Remare? Where on earth did you find the wheels?"

"One of Herbert's men lent it to me. Rides pretty well. Hop on."

"Do I really have to wear a helmet? We're so close to the hotel."

"Yes! It's the law, and Remare would kill me if you got hurt. Put it on."

She did. After flying around the town, riding on the back of a motorcycle shouldn't have been a problem, but still, Miranda hesitated. She didn't like being that close to another male, especially when she had to put her hands around his waist to hold on. The gun tucked in the back of his pants didn't help. Even with his jacket on, she could still feel it.

Tristan dropped her off at the front of the hotel and went to park the bike.

Upstairs, Miranda knocked twice then used the key Tristan had given her and entered Remare's room. He was lying on the bed and just finished his call. Still exhilarated from the flight and motorcycle ride, she jumped on top of him and straddled his hips. Her body seemed to be emitting energy. She was vibrating with it. "I missed you." She kissed him soundly, and he returned her fervor. A sexy growl that sounded more like a purr slowly crept up his throat.

His hand wound around her hair. "And I missed you. Did you have a nice visit with your friends?"

"As a matter of fact, I did. I can't wait for later tonight." Glowing with joy, she sat up. "Remare, they're an intriguing group. Fascinating. There's one; her name is Esme. She's a remarkable person. All good vibes. I like her."

He seemed genuinely happy for her. "I'm glad you had a good time."

The connection between them strong as ever, she kissed him, again, barely aware of Tristan entering the room. "Don't mind me. I'd say get a room, but..."

She smiled up at him. "Hey, anyone figure out where we're going for dinner? I'm starved."

"I'm good with the restaurant downstairs, but Remare wants to go to Campo Vecchio's."

"Mmm, I'm always in the mood for something Italian." Grinning, she nipped Remare's lower lip.

"It's a little early for dinner, but if you're hungry, then that's where we'll go."

Remare was right, it was more like a late lunch than an early dinner, but she didn't care. They dined at the lovely Italian place. Remare and Tristan had a veal dish, but Miranda was in the mood for angel-hair pasta with shrimp in a light cream sauce. *Heavenly!*

Since they had time, Miranda wanted to visit the Cranbrook Museum. Although it was not as huge as New York's or London's museums, she loved the quaintness of the smaller building with the wildflowers out front. While Tristan studied the old weapons display, Miranda and Remare strolled through the art exhibits, enjoying the paintings. She overheard one of the attendants explaining some of the works of art were done by local artists.

Miranda was fascinated by the portraits. It felt almost as if, if she could touch the paintings, she'd somehow develop an insight into the person whose portrait it was. Remare commented on the ones he favored, as well. When they turned a corner, Miranda's breath caught. Hanging on the wall in front of them was a stunning portrait. "Oh my God, do you see who it is?"

"Hmm, I do." Remare crossed his arms over his chest and stood examining the painting.

"How on earth did a painting of Esmerelda wind up here?"

"Oh, you found Tom Hawkins' painting. She's one of our treasures. Painted by a contemporary artist," said the attendant, Benjamin Woods.

Miranda's eyes widened. "How could that be? This woman lived centuries ago."

"That's correct." Woods nodded. "Old Tommy's great-grandfather had been infatuated with her. He was a sea captain, you understand. I think he drew several drawings of her. Not very good, but Tom—now, he had talent. I think he's in his nineties, by now, but still keeps active. Somewhat of an eccentric. He lives in that old castle just outside Cranbrook. Comes into town, every now and then, for supplies."

"Who's the woman next to her?" Remare asked.

Miranda hadn't even noticed the stern-looking woman until Remare mentioned her.

"That's Aurora Draxton. Lived nearly two centuries ago. Married Dr. Thaddeus Draxton and lived here mostly during the summers. Originally from up north, Leeds, I believe."

Remare seemed to be considering the portrait's countenance. "Leeds, hmm."

Miranda wondered if he was related to Thomas Draxton, one of the authors Peralt had mentioned. Since centuries separated them, she dismissed the thought. "I'd like to speak with Hawkins." Miranda showed Benjamin her work ID. "I authenticate works of art. Do you think he would talk with me? About his artwork."

Woods shrugged. "I don't see why not. He's a bit of a recluse. But he's given some art lessons to a few of the schoolchildren. I can call him, if you'd like."

"Yes, I'd like that very much. Thank you."

Remare waited until the attendant left. "Mir-randa, do you think this wise?"

"We still have time. It's not that far. Don't you like meeting new people?"

"Not ones I haven't thoroughly checked out."

"So, check him out. Don't worry," she teased. "I'll protect you if he comes at you with one of his paint brushes."

Remare gave her a look she was becoming accustomed to. "He probably won't want strangers imposing on him, anyway."

The attendant returned. "I spoke with Tom. He said, if you bring pastries, he'll welcome you for afternoon tea."

Miranda said, "Let's go to the bake shop."

***

During the drive to the Hawkins estate, Miranda pointed outside the car's window. "Is it my imagination or does it seem like a mist is rolling in?"

Perusing the place, Remare drove up to the front section of the castle. "It comes in off the water to the east."

"Good Lord! Now that it's becoming dark out, this place looks a lot creepier than when we first passed it. Kinda eerie." Miranda grimaced. Some of England's castles were works of beauty that had withstood the ages. Not so much with this one. "It's a ruin. The larger part of the castle must have decayed over time." Decomposing stones outlined what once must have been a magnificent structure. "No one maintained it."

"The funds necessary for upkeep can be staggering." Remare gestured to Tristan, who got out of the car and scoped out the place. "There are many castles here and in other parts of Europe that were abandoned, either due to the wars, financial downturns, or simply because the owners wished to live elsewhere."

Once Tristan nodded to them it was okay, they exited the car and walked to the door. They were met by an old man with a cane. Age and arthritis had the man stooped over a bit. But, for a man in his nineties, his eyes were alight with good humor. "I should have warned you the fog rolls in at this time nearly every night. Did you happen to remember the scones?"

Miranda held up the bakery box. "Apricot and raspberry, is that good?"

"Yes, and I thank you for getting them. I'd invite you in for dinner, but we old folks like to dine early. I do have several teas you may like."

"That's all right. We dined early, as well. This is my wife, Professor Miranda Crescent, my associate, Tristan, and my name is Remare."

"Thomas Hawkins. Come in, come in." He gestured for them to enter his modest kitchen. "Benjamin, at the museum, said you wanted to ask about my painting." He poured water into a kettle and then put it on his stove.

Remare sat at the seat facing the door, a practice she'd seen him do on a consistent basis. He'd already sized up the nearest entrances and exits. Tristan remained standing, as if still on guard duty.

"Let's see. I have Earl Grey, English Breakfast, orange pekoe and spearmint."

Miranda said, "Orange," as Remare gestured to the spearmint.

Tom signaled for Tristan to help with setting the plate of pastries on the table. "I'm sorry you didn't get a chance to see this house when it was in its glory. Over the centuries, many of the stones gave way, and only this small section still stands. It's enough for me, though." He poured them their teas and joined them at the table.

"You live out here all by yourself?" Miranda felt sad for the old man. He must have gotten lonely from time to time. She knew she would have.

"I have Jonas to keep me company. Here, boy."

A Great Dane came charging into the kitchen, his tail wagging rapidly in enthusiasm. All Miranda could think was how much he reminded her of Marmaduke. Her eyes widened in near horror as he made a beeline for her. Just when she thought he would tackle her down to the ground with slobbering licks, Remare snapped his fingers and pointed to the floor. "Heel!"

The dog immediately slumped down and whimpered until Remare pet him behind the ears.

Tom tossed the dog a treat that he swallowed in one bite and licked his jowls. Tail still going a mile a minute, he looked like he was waiting for another. "He gets excited when people come to visit."

An old woman came bustling in afterward. "And my housekeeper, Maddie, takes good care of me."

"Well, someone has to. You'd forget to eat if I didn't remind you. Jonas got into the vegetable garden, again. Made a mess of the cabbage and carrots. But all's well, now." She wiped her hands on a small towel. "Hello there, I'm Mrs. Wilkins, but everyone calls me Maddie. Some of the younger folk in town call me Mad Maddie because I yell at them when they try to sneak on the grounds for a quick shag."

With her frenetic movements and wide-eyed expression, Miranda wondered if Mad Maddie might be a bit touched.

"Pleasure to meet you." Remare was polite and gracious.

Maddie whispered to Tom, "You didn't tell me you were having visitors."

He shrugged. "I didn't know until a little while ago. They were admiring my painting in the museum. Benjy asked if I wanted company."

Maddie retrieved napkins and cutlery from the cupboards. "Oh," she sighed. "Must be Esmerelda. It's one of Tom's masterpieces."

Miranda leaned forward. "From my research, Esmerelda lived nearly two centuries ago. How were you able to make a painting of her?"

"Now, that's a long story." Tom sipped his tea then took a bite of his apricot scone. "Caitlyn makes the best scones."

When he seemed to forget she'd asked him a question, Remare reminded him, "Esmerelda?"

"Oh, yes." He wiped his mouth on the napkin. "When I was younger, I found several drawings of this stunning woman in my grandpapa's trunk. He told me his father, my great-grandfather, Samuel, met her in London. She wanted passage on his merchant ship, said she needed to get back to Italy, even though his boat was only going as far as Marseilles. She was in a rush to leave but wouldn't say why. Just that it was urgent. He was the captain, but she didn't have the necessary funds, so she tried to bargain with him and said she would cook and clean to barter passage."

"Did he?" Miranda asked.

"That's the thing. I dare say, he fell in love with the lass the moment he laid eyes on her. He made a deal that she could help with the cooking, but that his men did the cleaning. In his eyes, she was too fine a young thing to stoop to cleaning up after his men."

"What happened?"

"Hmm." He paused as if the memory was just out of reach. "Well, that's the mystery. They had dinner together at one of the local inns, enjoyed each other's company. He'd been enchanted by her. In the morning the boat was ready to sail. Esmerelda never showed. Samuel delayed the ship for as long as he could, but they were on a schedule. My grandpapa said he was heartbroken. That some emergency must have come up."

"Poor thing was so desperate to get away." Maddie added. "I've heard the stories so many times, I could repeat them. Tell them about the child, Tom."

"I was getting there, Maddie."

"Just as the ship was about to depart. The innkeeper where they were staying comes running up the deck with an infant in his hands and gives a note to Samuel. Apparently, Esmerelda was needed elsewhere, and she asked that Samuel watch over her child until she returned."

Miranda shook her head. "Sheesh, they must have had one incredible night together if she trusted him with her child."

Tom nodded. "Must have been, indeed. Anyhow, Samuel didn't know what to do with the child and asked the innkeeper to take care of the child until his return, but the innkeeper refused, so Samuel, not knowing what else to do, took the child with him. When he returned, he asked all over for Esmerelda. But no one knew where she'd gone off to. A long-time bachelor, he had no female friends to ask for advice, so he kept the little girl, hoping one day, she'd return."

"Little angel." Maddie sighed. "At least your great-grandfather took good care of the child. When he returned to Cranbrook, everyone assumed the infant was his. He even named the girl, Lilybeth."

Remare cleared his throat. "So, no one in your family ever heard from or saw Esmerelda, again?"

Tom shook his head. "No one ever did. And it's not for a lack of trying. Samuel had been infatuated with her. Did several drawings of her, passed them around. But it was as if she'd vanished."

Miranda thought the tale terribly depressing. She wondered if Esmerelda had fled from Lord Acton and he, somehow, had discovered her whereabouts and prevented her from leaving. "Do you still have the drawings Samuel made of Esmerelda?"

Tom turned toward Maddie, who said, "I'll get them. If we still have them, they'd be in the trunk upstairs."

Remare asked, "What became of the child?"

"Like so many young ones, she wanted to go to London. When she was of age, Samuel granted her request to visit the city. She became a governess to a fine family." Tom nodded in approval. "Married a good man and had children. Samuel made sure they were all provided for."

Miranda asked, "Did Lilybeth ever return to visit him or your grandfather?"

"Yes, she and her family would spend summers here. They bought a summer cottage not far from town. Since Samuel never legally adopted her, we considered her family cousins. Even though most people thought Joseph, my grandpapa, was her step-brother."

"Well, I'm not sure what happened to the others. We had so many at one time. Samuel really took a shine to Esmerelda. But these are the ones I was able to find." Maddie handed the old drawings to Miranda.

There were three that Miranda perused. The first one showed Esmerelda deep in thought, almost a scowl on her face. The next was of her glancing out a window, probably from a room at the inn, but the last one captivated Miranda. Esmerelda was smiling as if she'd just won the lottery.

"That one's my favorite," Maddie said. "Looks like she swallowed a canary, doesn't it?"

Remare agreed. "Yes, it does. Would you be willing to part with one of these? I'd be willing to pay you handsomely."

"I've kept these for so long. No one has ever inquired about them. They're just drawings. Samuel was more a seaman than an artist." Tom glanced at Maddie, who just shrugged. "I suppose so."

Remare took out his wallet and laid three one-hundred British Sterling pound notes down.

Tom looked stunned and put a hand over his heart. "That's too much! They're only drawings."

"But they are beautiful drawings, and my wife seems enamored of the one." Remare winked at her.

"Thank you." Miranda turned toward Mr. Hawkins. "I'll take good care of your drawing. I find it captivating."

"I'm sure you will. It's a pity Lilybeth's grandchildren never found the stories of Esmerelda all that interesting."

"Her grandchildren?" Miranda asked.

"Most died during the wars, but one granddaughter, Dolores, died...let me think, oh some years ago, but her daughter, Esmerelda's last living descendant, lives in London during the week; she comes here, sometimes, on the weekends."

Miranda narrowed her eyes as a thought took shape in her mind. "By any chance, would her name be Esme?"

"No, not at all. She was named for her grandmother."

Miranda sighed. "Thank you for your time, Mr. Hawkins. And I must say the painting you did in the museum is stunning. You have an eye for detail."

He shrugged nonchalantly. "Well, I used to, anyway."

"One last thing. The portrait of the woman next to her. I think Mr. Woods said her name was Aurora Draxton. Did either of your grandparents know her?

Maddie scoffed, shook her head, and started cleaning up their plates. "Why they hung those two portraits so close together in the museum is beyond me."

Miranda asked, "What do you mean?"

"Well, according to *my* grandmother, after Dr. Draxton died, Aurora got a little lonely, so she decided to turn her home into an inn. Hired poor women who lost their husbands in the wars to do the cooking and cleaning." She snorted. "At least that was the story told in town."

"But you heard otherwise?" Remare prompted.

Hawkins sat back in his chair. "Now, Maddie, you know as well as me those were only rumors."

"Rumors, my begonias!" She gave Tom a look. "What the history books never reported is that some of those women were destitute and desperate for funds. The poor unfortunates. So, old Aurora gets the idea of offering 'companionship' to the soldiers returning from wars on the continent. A way of procuring money for the girls."

"Innkeeper? Like the one in the story?" Miranda asked.

"Some inn! My grandmother swore it was a brothel. In order to maintain a modicum of decency, Aurora would tell the girls, 'Get more wood for the fire.'" She whispered, "That was code that a gentleman was waiting for them in one of the back rooms."

Hawkins snickered. "Well, they had to keep the fires going, somehow."

Maddie looked like she was ready to slap Hawkins on the side of his head.

Miranda wondered aloud. "Did she know Esmerelda?"

Maddie grumbled. "Knew her! She was jealous of her. Wanted Esmerelda to become one of her girls. When

Esmerelda refused, she denied her a room at her inn. That's probably why no one ever heard of her."

Miranda shook her head at all that they'd learned. "So, Esmerelda did come to Cranbrook?"

Maddie shrugged. "My gran thought so. Said no one from these parts had her beauty. She gave my gran some herbs to mix in her tea to help with her arthritis. I always thought she came looking for her child, but she disappeared as suddenly as she arrived. Completely vanished." She gestured with her hands. "Poof."

Tom grinned. "Through the years, some of the locals used to tell stories of a ghostly figure out near the cemetery. But they only surfaced around Halloween."

Maddie nodded. "My gran swore she thought she once saw a spirit, but that might have been because of too much whiskey."

Miranda didn't know what to make of these stories. "Thank you for seeing us on such short notice." She turned to Remare once they were by the car. "What do you think?"

"Not sure I trust the memories of two so old. Over time, rumors become embellished with falsehoods, elaborations designed to delight."

Miranda looked back at the ruins of the castle and wondered if jealousy had played a part in Esmerelda's disappearance.

And eventual death.

Chapter Twenty-One

One of them had to die. It was as simple as that.

Gideon walked along the Thames River, relishing the cool breezes off the water. After his meeting with Vivienna, he'd wanted a cigarette. He hadn't smoked in years, and even then, he'd hardly lit up. But, tonight, he wanted to breathe in the calming smoke. Decisions needed to be made. Either Caltrone or Acton had to be eliminated in order for their plan to work.

Vivienna was centuries older than him and twice as cunning. Or so she thought. Like him, whenever she set her sights on something, she was sure to attain it. And what she wanted more than anything else was a seat on the High Council. The only way that would happen was if Caltrone suddenly died, or...he was named chancellor. As chancellor, he would have to give up his seat on the council.

What Gideon had waited centuries for was to be named lord of a territory. The only way for that to be possible was if Acton was dead or elected chancellor. He could then claim the territory as his own. Decisions, decisions. He *could* help Vivienna attain her goals. She could see to it, then, that he was named lord of some territory. But did he trust her? He scoffed. *Never in a million years!* She'd made promises to others and then reneged. Remare came to mind. The fool had actually fallen in love with the raven-tressed temptress, and he'd been played.

That was not going to happen with Gideon. He'd kill the bitch before he let that transpire. Unlike Remare, he didn't love Vivienna. But, together, they made quite a team. The possibilities were endless if their union could somehow last. Only time would be able to reveal the future.

Memories of another dark-haired beauty came to mind. One who he'd had genuine feelings for. One who never asked him for anything. Even when she needed him most. Esmerelda had been a seer. She could tell the future. He wished she was there with him, now. She'd been Acton's pet, but Gideon had allowed himself to care for her, allowed some part of his heart to love her. Even though he knew she'd never feel the same about him.

Acton had played with her. Let her think there was hope of escape. Made promises, gave reassurances. He'd played her worse than Vivienna and Caltrone had played Remare. Remare! Gideon shook his head in regret. It wasn't until long after Remare had left Acton's service that Gideon had learned half the arguments he'd had with his adversary were instigated by Acton. His lord loved watching them fight, watching them bleed. They'd been an amusement for him, neither one knowing how they'd been set up. Esmerelda could see the past as well as the future. She'd warned Gideon, told him about past encounters. She'd been right all along.

Her death haunted him. Before he could stop it, he'd learned Acton had paid one of the members of the coven to poison her. His way of proving his superior cunning. Acton had once told him, "Revenge must be worthy of your opponent. Complete and final. Others must not see you render leniency. They will think you weak for it." Acton had let her think she'd escaped him, let her think she was safe. She wasn't, but there'd been no way to warn her, no way to prevent her destruction.

Given time, Gideon wondered if she'd have fallen in love with him. If, somehow, he could have secreted her to someplace safe. He'd never gotten the chance. But he did get her justice. Unknown to Acton, he'd hunted down the one who had poisoned Esmerelda and killed her. Without mercy, without hesitation. "Complete and final."

Gideon gazed out over the river. The time was nearing when he would have to act. He smiled as a thought formed in his mind. Perhaps there was a way for both, Vivienna and he, to get what they wanted most. It would be tricky. It would require patience and planning, but if he could do this, if he could see it through to its delicious end, there would be no mercy for one. And hell to pay for the other. He smirked. Remare would not see it that way. Would probably kill Gideon if he found out.

Well, Gideon would have to make certain he never did.

***

Miranda made her way to Agatha's backyard. She knew Remare and Tristan would remain somewhere close by, no matter how much she tried to convince them to go back to the hotel. She did warn them it could be hours, but Remare had only smiled and blew her a kiss. *Stubborn vampire!*

She heard the music and dancing of the *Elementals* before she even turned the corner. Their voices were spirited and endearing. One voice, above the rest, was high and sounded almost like an angel—unbelievably crystal clear and inspiring. It made Miranda shiver with its mystical beauty. The other voices joined in, and a choir, unlike any she'd ever heard before, sang in exquisite harmony.

Miranda stood in the shadows, feeling the vibrations along her skin. There was definitely strength in numbers by the intensity of the energy the *Elementals* were emitting. One circle of dancers moved in graceful steps while the inner circle swayed in the opposite direction. Each of the dancers held a candle shielded from the wind in their glass holders. All of them exuded profound ecstasy; it nearly brought tears to Miranda's eyes. *Do I belong here?*

Would she ever give up her life in New York to be with others of her kind? Could one of them ever replace the friendship she had with Lizandra? Forsake everyone and everything she knew to simply belong? Her heart ached, the old soul-destroying feeling of not belonging haunted her, but still, she didn't know the answers to her questions. But, if it was a possibility, why did she hover in the shadows? Why didn't she join in where she would be most welcomed?

At Werehaven, Liz and the other Weres had adopted her into the clan. They saw her as one of their own, treated her as such. Even the vampires at House Valadon seemed to have accepted her. And that was before she'd even married Remare. And yet, she was neither Were nor vampire. Miranda didn't know where she belonged. She felt as if she was being pulled by mysterious hands in a direction she was unsure of.

She stepped forward. *Am I home?* The magical backyard was filled with thousands of tiny lights strung between the trees. Everyone was either dancing, singing, or partaking of food and drink, obviously in a celebratory mood. The fire *Elementals* in the back were using whips of green, red and yellow fires to draw pictures in the night sky: Portraits, pictures of animals, nature scenes. Miranda searched, but there was no trace of the *Dark Elemental* she met who painted with violet fire.

The water and air *Elementals* seemed to be having a contest between them, forcing fountains of multi-colored water to sprout high up from the stream. The earth *Elementals* were summoning the ground to form statues of people in striking detail. Miranda thought it was a scene out of Giuseppe Pietro Bagetti's painting, *The Tree at Benevento— The Gathering.*

"Glad you could make it." Agatha enthusiastically accepted the box of pastries Miranda remembered to purchase when she'd bought Tom's scones.

"It looks to be a fun night." Miranda gazed up at the full moon and the bright stars illuminating the dark sky.

"The party's just getting started. Help yourself to something to drink and eat. We have enough to feed a small army." Agatha gestured to several picnic tables loaded with various types of food.

Miranda wasn't particularly hungry after her dinner and then dessert with Mr. Hawkins, but she did make her way to the bonfire in the middle of the yard where Sarita and several of the *Elementals* she'd met previously sat. She savored the fire's warmth kept in the circle by the placement of the stones and crystals. The mist that had rolled in earlier brought cold, damp air, and Miranda pulled her sweater tighter around her. She found an empty chair closest to one of the trees where a handsome, young man played guitar. She was happy to see there were a few male *Elementals* present, as well.

Agatha sat beside her. "We do this when the moon is full to celebrate our gifts." She peered up into the night sky. "Wherever our talents come from, we give thanks."

Since everyone raised their drinks and saluted the firmament, so did Miranda.

Vicky waved. "We're glad to see you, Miranda. We weren't sure you'd make it."

"Yeah, I decided to take a few extra days off from work. England's countryside fascinates me; the towns are so beautiful, so historic. I feel like I've lived here in another life."

"Maybe you have." Vicky smiled in a way that made the hairs on Miranda's arm stand up.

Agatha sipped her drink. "So, what do you think of our little gathering?"

"It's great. Where does everyone come from?" There looked to be anywhere from two to three dozen people present.

"Some are local." Agatha shrugged. "Others from the outlying areas."

Esme, munching on one of the apricot scones, joined them. "It's a remarkable night. Too bad you won't be here next month when we have the summer solstice. Then, you'd see some truly amazing sights."

"Such as?" Miranda knew, as soon as she'd said it, it was probably one of the things she shouldn't have.

Sarita, the water *Elemental*, finished pouring her bottle of water into her cup then spread her arms equal distances apart and had the water return in an arc high in the sky back into the bottle.

"Now, that's impressive." Miranda grinned, amazed at Sarita's talent. She'd once made the waves in the Hudson River back home in New York submit to her command, but she wasn't about to share that bit of information.

"If you want to see something truly impressive, watch this." Rose held her hand out to the side. An earth *Elemental*, she made the ground tremble so much the tables holding the food nearly toppled over. Miranda could feel the vibrations in the ground beneath her.

"Save the entertainment for another time," Agatha chided. "Miranda had her first glimpse of the crystal cave today."

Loren, the other earth *Elemental,* sat up. "What did you think of them, pretty awesome, huh?"

Miranda agreed. "I'd say so. I never saw so many all in one spot. Even in the Natural History Museum. Some of the stones are so incandescent. They're mesmerizing."

"Any favorites?" Loren's brow rose.

Miranda sat back and gave it some thought. "They're all so beautiful. I don't know if I could have a favorite." Odd, she thought. Even though Rose pulled back her talent, she could sense the heightened energy in the group. She wondered if so many *Elementals* in one place at the same time augmented each of their talents. It certainly felt that way.

Loren leaned forward. "Wasn't there one that seemed to call to you, above all the rest?"

Miranda felt like she was being tested but didn't know how. Somehow, she didn't want to fail their line of questioning but wasn't sure how to respond. "I can't remember any particular one, but then, I did quickly scan them, wanting to see each and every one."

Sarita said, "The stones call to us. Each of us has talents that become enhanced with the power imbued in the crystals."

"The crystals vibrate with the earth's energy; they're powerful amplifiers." Loren nodded in Esme's direction. "She told you what each one is capable of?"

"Ah, yes she did." Miranda warmed her hands by the fire. "It's quite a lot to take in."

"Our collection is pretty good, but I've also heard tales of other covens in the world having superior collections. There are over a thousand different types of crystals." Agatha sighed. "I doubt one coven can ever possess half that amount."

Miranda glanced upward. She knew some of the crystals came from meteors, others pushed up through the earth's crust, and still others from volcanic activity. "So, what's so special about the summer solstice?"

Agatha answered, "The gravitational pull is stronger. During the winter and summer solstices, our powers get a boost, much stronger than just the full moon."

"A non-believer," the others chided good-naturedly when they heard Miranda's sigh.

"I didn't say that. I've read up on the earth's energy lines. I get that there are places with more energy than others, the vibrations more pronounced, but I don't completely understand the influence of the cosmos."

Rose asked, "You've heard of sun flares?"

Miranda nodded.

"There's energy in our planet's core, the oceans and the air. Earth, air, water and fire," Agatha reminded her. "Of course, there's energy in the cosmos. And, when the planets configure, our talents are increased. Haven't you ever felt a stirring either at sunrise or sunset?"

Miranda had. She rubbed the palm of one hand. Could the vibrations she'd picked up on that woke her as the sun rose be due to increased energy fields? "I'm afraid I haven't studied much on astronomy."

"You should." Rose said, "You'd be surprised what the universe has to offer."

Miranda nodded. She'd make it a point to learn more about it.

When some of the others got up to dance and sing, Miranda was content to sit back and observe, but they tried to pull her up to join them. "Thanks, but no. I've already been horseback riding and sightseeing today. I'm a little tired."

"C'mon, it would be fun." Loren encouraged, "Enjoy the feeling of being free."

Miranda waved her off. "I'm good."

"Let her rest. Our American visitor isn't used to British air or walking as much as we do," Agatha teased.

"They're quite remarkable." Miranda smiled as the women danced, each so incredibly content and happy as they swirled and moved in a circular manner.

"Yes. I call them my 'children of the light'."

Miranda wondered aloud. "Have you known them long?"

"Long enough. Like calls to like. In one way or another, we recognize our own kind. It didn't take Sarita long at all to make you."

"No, she's very observant. You're lucky to have found each other." Miranda marveled at the thought of all these wonderful women, united with their talents, able to find one another. She wondered if there were more *Elementals* in New York. If there were, they'd never revealed themselves to her. A pang of aloneness hit her harder than she thought it would. All her life, she'd felt like an outsider, a freak among humans, and wondered for so long if there were others of her kind.

"We take care of each other." Agatha sipped her drink. "It was foolish of you to use your powers in public. You not only endanger yourself, but others as well. I don't have to tell you what the Brotherhood would do if they ever captured one of us."

Or government types. "I know. I slipped up." Miranda shook her head at her own stupidity. "I've rarely used my powers. It was instinct more than anything else."

"Remember what I told you. There are others out there who would not understand our powers. You recall what was done in the past to women who could command the elements?"

"Yes."

"Then, I won't have to worry about you when you leave here. Miranda, there are so many wonderful gifts we've been given. You have potential. Don't waste it."

Miranda wondered if the older woman was being protective or offering a rebuke for Miranda's chosen profession when so many of the *Elementals* were in the health field. "I won't. In my own way, I use it properly."

"Do you, now? Then, that's very good to hear."

The others joined them in the large circle as Miranda yawned. "I should be getting back, soon. It's been a long day."

"But you've only been here a short while. Stay a bit longer. You haven't seen what I can do." Vicky smiled roguishly and leaned forward. "As a fire *Elemental,* you should find this particularly interesting."

Vicky waved her hand, and the fire grew larger. Sensitive to this element, Miranda's skin began to itch. She suspected

Vicky's talent was stronger than she'd let on. The heat beginning to be too much, Miranda moved her chair back a little. She gazed at Vicky, sensing a shadow hovering around her aura. She wondered at all the things she could not see then stared deeper into the flames, as if the fire called to her, was somehow beckoning her. It was mesmerizing, the flames appearing to take on shapes of animals and humans.

Miranda shook her head and blinked, trying to see better. The fire became a living entity, turning different colors, the prominent one red—Vicky's color. Flames swayed and danced to the music in the background. Everything else seemed to fade away. The fire was summoning Miranda to come closer, but she held back, not trusting the strange sensations.

The flames slowly turned golden as the crystals pulsed with energy. Miranda had seen this before in her dreams, but never this color, never quite like this. The fire became a form, nearly blinding in its intensity. The gold, an absolute purity, unearthly. Its brilliance not something she'd ever seen before. The preternatural shape had wings. Beautiful, powerful wings of gold. Each feather startling in its radiance.

When she looked up at the head, she expected to see a bird. It wasn't. The entity turned in her direction, frightening in its magnificence. It looked almost human but couldn't be. A cosmic being, perfection in every possible way, came to life. The eyes opened and stared at Miranda.

In that moment, time stopped. Life as she knew it ceased to exist. This was power in its rawest form. Primal. Ancient. Energy pulsed, not of this world but of many worlds. Past, present, and future commingled in the phantasmagoria. Her heart almost exploded from the rapture. Miranda saw events in history from hundreds—no, thousands—of years ago. Colors swirled then swam in many directions at one time, a kaleidoscope offering fleeting glimpses of worlds she'd never known, never imagined. People she'd never met, languages she'd never spoken. Inconceivable comprehensions. Undeniable freedom from mortal constraints. A prisoner of the impossible, the unimaginable. It was terrifying and exhilarating. It was power in its most glorious form. Miranda reached out, desiring to know the unknowable.

Just one touch.

Miranda shrieked as a blinding light, like a thousand rays of the sun, hit her eyes. The fire must have crackled, and a piece of ember flew at her face. Both eyes felt like they'd been seared, the scorching pain unbearable. Agony like she'd never known. Heart beating impossibly fast, her body vibrating in uncontrollable waves, she screamed, *"Remare!"* Clutching her eyes, she fell to her knees. *"Remare!"*

He was at her side, a second later, gathering her in his arms. "What's wrong, Mir-randa? Tell me what happened!"

She could barely detect the people frantically scattering in all directions. Whispers of "vampire" sounded through the women, their aversion to vampires a palpable thing. She could hear Tristan questioning those closest to him.

Her breaths were ragged. "Something hit my eyes, Remare." She tried to bury her face in his chest. "I can't see anything. Everything's black."

"Let me see, Mir-randa. Put down your hands."

"I can't; the pain is too much." Trembling, she kept her eyes covered with one hand and held on to him with the other as if he were her lifeline.

Agatha's voice boomed in the darkness. "Who the hell are you?"

His arm holding her protectively, Remare growled at Agatha. His voice was a scathing rebuke. "I'm her husband. What happened here?"

Gasps and hisses rent the air. More whispers of shock and fear floated toward her.

Rose's voice rang in her ears. "Let me look at her."

"No." Miranda shook her head. "No one else, Remare."

Rose insisted, "She needs medical attention. Let me see."

"Who are you?" Remare's voice thundered. "What the hell happened here?"

"I'm a doctor. Let me examine her. I need to see her eyes. Miranda, I have my bag here. If you were injured by the ashes, I may have medicine for you."

Miranda was shivering, her body racked with chills. If she was blinded, life as she knew it was over. She needed her eyes to live her life. Still in Remare's arms, she turned toward Rose's voice and lowered her hand.

"It looks like her eyelids suffered a burn. Her eyelashes are seared off."

Miranda cried and sank farther into Remare's embrace.

Rose's voice was compassionate. "Miranda, I need you to open your eyes. I need to see if there's any damage."

She refused. "No bright lights! Remare, take me away from here. Please. Now!"

"Wait." Miranda heard rustling noises, and then, Rose said, "This is an ointment for the burn. Spread it over the eyelids and in the corners of her eyes. It will help. She should go to the hospital."

She felt Remare's thumbs gently sliding the medicine over her eyes. The slightest touch augmenting the pain.

"We're leaving." He gathered her up in his arms as Tristan joined them. Once by the car, Remare said. "We'll take you to the hospital."

Her knees were shaking. "Not here, Remare. Please! Take me back to Herbert's place. I don't want to be here any longer."

"You need medical attention, Mir-randa."

Knowing shock was beginning to set in, she said, "It can wait until we get to Herbert's."

Remare placed her in the backseat of the car and joined her. "Tristan, drive. We'll send someone to retrieve the motorcycle in the morning."

"I questioned the women." Tristan's voice. "Most said they didn't see anything but thought an ember crackled then spewed from the fire and hit Miranda."

She continued trembling, horrified at what had just happened.

"Mir-randa. Let me see." Remare tenderly pushed her hands away. "Both eyelids look like they were scalded. Can you open them?"

Miranda shook her head. "It hurts too much."

"I'm contacting Herbert. I'll have him have one of his medical staff there."

She couldn't stop shaking as Remare continued stroking her back and whispering tender words of support. She thought she felt a few drops of his blood fall on her eyelids and then the slightest of touches. All Miranda could think was that her career was over. So many injuries she could endure—she'd survived a terrible car crash when a child—but to lose her sight, she couldn't imagine how she would cope.

She must have passed out, because the next thing she heard was Tristan's voice. "We're coming up on Herbert Manor."

Chapter Twenty-Two

Wanting to know how Eric was making out with his fashion line, Valadon walked into Cesare's suite at Valadon Creations and smirked. The sight waiting for him amused and gratified him. "I see you've been to the hairdressers, as well as the tailors."

"They darkened my hair and cut it, then gave me highlights. Said it would photograph better this way." Eric shrugged as he stood in his elegant suit and turned in a circle. "So, what do you think?

Valadon crossed his arms and admired Eric's new look with the darker shade of red hair. "I think you're going to work out just fine."

"We haven't even started with the makeup, yet." Cesare stood alongside Valadon. "When he's completely finished, you'll hardly recognize him."

One of the assistants, Paolo, stuck his head in and said, "Cesare, you're needed outside. Omigen added something to the design I think you should see before we start cutting."

"Omigen!" Cesare grunted. "She's always trying to be more creative than necessary. If you'll excuse me, I'll be right back."

Valadon scrutinized his newest model. "How are you getting along with everyone in the department?"

"They've been great. I never realized what hard work modeling really is." Eric looked chagrined that he'd spoken aloud. "But I'm not complaining. It just takes a little getting used to."

"It does. I was wondering if you remembered anything more about Vivienna and Gideon. He was once an adversary of my second, Remare, so any other information you may have would be most welcome. They're both in England, now. Remare and Miranda."

Eric rubbed his neck. "I can't think of anything. Other than the fact that Vivienna knew Miranda was an *Elemental.*"

Valadon sighed. He remembered Miranda's blast mark on the wall when she'd tussled with the Madame Lord. "Yes, after the wedding, Miranda used her powers when your sister, Rosalyn, fought with Vivienna. I believe she did it to protect Rosalyn."

"She did?" He shook his head as if confused. "Wait, that's not what I meant. I mean back when she came to Chateau Vivienna. Vivi spied on her. She locked me in a room with Miranda, hoping to film us in a compromising position; she was going to show you the tape. But Miranda made it clear she wanted no part of me. When she fell asleep, she looked so peaceful. I was just watching over her."

Eric's body tensed with nerves. "Really, I wasn't going to do anything, but Miranda woke and thought I was making advances. She nearly strangled me with her power, blasted me against the bedpost. She didn't even have to touch me. Vivienna saw it on the tape. Asked me about it." Eric shrugged. "I didn't know what to say, so I just said she had really good reflexes."

Narrowing his eyes, Valadon recalled Miranda went to Paris on his bidding almost a year past. "Vivienna knew, even then?"

"Yeah, I overheard her discussing it with Magritte and Lord Acton."

"Acton knows?" *It's bad enough Magritte knows, but Acton, as well?* And, if he knew, it was more than likely his second, Gideon, also knew.

Eric nodded. "Did I just say something wrong?"

"No. Not at all, but I think this is something my second needs to know. If you'll excuse me." He turned back to Eric.

"We don't discuss Miranda's abilities with anyone. Everything you learn here at ValCorp is confidential. Is that clear?"

Eric's eyes rounded. "Absolutely. I won't ever talk about it with anyone else. I swear."

Confident in his new employee's loyalty, and grateful Remare was with Miranda in England, Valadon made for his office.

***

The doctor was waiting when Remare and Miranda arrived at Herbert Manor. Remare guided her into the library and had her sit on one of the couches. She could hear Herbert and Winnie's voices of concern. Miranda did not want anyone examining her. "I can't do this. Not right now." No matter how hard she tried, she couldn't stop her hands from trembling.

"Mir-randa, at least let him look at you." Remare rubbed her hands between his and then kissed them.

She knew he was right, but her emotions were irrepressible. "Promise me no bright lights. Promise me, Remare." Her voice sounded haunted, even to her ears.

"All right. I'll be by your side the entire time."

Herbert introduced them. "This is Dr. Roberts."

Miranda heard whispers but couldn't make out what they were saying, her mind too clouded with horrible images.

"What happened?" Dr. Roberts asked her. The snap of latex gloves sounded.

"I'm not sure. I was sitting by a fire. Something hit my eyes. Please, Doctor, do not shine anything bright in my eyes."

He lifted her chin as she removed her hand from her eyes.

"Something burned your skin. Did you feel it in your eyes or just on your eyelids?

Miranda tried to steady her breaths. "I don't know. I never saw it. It just happened."

Roberts tried to lift her eyelid by pushing her eyebrow up, but the slightest touch inflamed her, made it feel as if her skin were on fire, and Miranda's scream reached a gut-wrenching crescendo. "Don't! The pain is too much!"

"Did you put ointment on it?"

She could hear Remare's exhale, then the movement of his arm. "The doctor at the outing gave me this to use."

"Right. It should help with the healing. She should be seen by an ophthalmologist. If not tonight, tomorrow the latest. I know someone in London who specializes in eye trauma. I can make a call."

"Do so." Remare and Herbert's voices combined.

"Please, Remare, take me upstairs. I'm exhausted and just want to sleep."

The doctor's voice was calm. "I want to bandage your eyes first."

She reached for his hand. "Remare."

"I'll do it. Miranda is stressed from her ordeal. I've bandaged soldiers in the field. I know how."

"All right, then. Here's more medicine for her eyes."

Miranda didn't want to be around anyone. Exhaustion—physical and emotional—was pulling at her. She heard more whispering, words of encouragement, but tuned it out.

Remare's arm came around her shoulders as they left the room. She should turn and thank them, it would be the right thing to do, but she just couldn't. At the stairs, Remare scooped her up and carried her the rest of the way to their room.

Once there, he sat her down on the bed. She could hear something unwrapping. Probably the bandages. He had her hold two pads over her eyes, then wound the gauze around them. She hated having her head wrapped. It reminded her too much of the car crash that killed her parents and her sister, Cassandra. And had her laid up in the hospital for weeks.

"You should try to get some sleep. It's late."

But Miranda couldn't sleep. She was too wired. "Stupid. It was so stupid. I never saw it." Anger was overtaking her fear. She got up and paced a few steps toward where she remembered the window seat was located. The sense of helplessness was overwhelming. The not knowing if she'd ever see, again, frayed her, and her fate as an invalid grated. "I hate this! I fucking hate this!" She screamed then used every curse word she'd ever heard.

"I was wondering when you were going to vent. You were holding up remarkably well. Under the circumstances."

She bristled at the direction of his voice, needing someone to aim her animosity at. "What if I'm blind, Remare? My life will never be the same. I won't be able to function."

"You don't know that." His voice was calm, sympathetic. "The specialist will be here in the morning. Do not start imagining worst-case scenarios."

How could she not? Her fear and anger combined to create a firestorm within her. "I have to. I have to know what to do. Can you imagine me wandering aimlessly around the corridors in Valadon House? What a fucking spectacle I'd make."

Self-disgust and loathing gnawed at her stomach. "My whole life I spent in studying. Seven fucking years of intense studying. For what? For fucking what? I'll never be able to validate another painting." Another scream of torment tore from her throat.

"Oh, so you're an eye specialist, now." Sarcasm laced his voice. "You know this to be fact?"

Remare's words chafed. She wanted to hate him. To throw something at him. She reached out with her hands and couldn't even find anything. Just empty air until she banged into the wall. "You didn't plan on having a blind wife. I'll be a burden to you. Useless."

He grasped her arms. "Stop this, now! You're imagining the worst! You don't know the extent of the damage. If you should require surgery to repair your eyes, you will have it."

"Oh God, Remare. It felt like my retinas got fried." She sniffled into his shoulder. "I can't do this. What if the damage is so severe I'm blinded for life?"

"It's not. I don't believe it is. You're stronger than this, Mir-randa. Trust in me to see to your welfare. I will hire the best doctors in the field. If it should come to it, and I don't believe it will, there are donor programs. You will see, again. I promise you that."

Her emotions finally drained, and she clutched her stomach. "I feel so empty inside."

He held her to him. "You're not empty, Mir-randa. I'm there with you."

She moaned in silent gratitude. His warmth, his faith calmed her. But she shuddered at all the possible outcomes. "I was burned at the stake, shot, stabbed. Remember when Mulciber slashed my face? You healed me, but if you couldn't, if I was disfigured, I could have lived with it. My legs got scarred, I hated it, but I survived it. This?" Another sob. "I'm not sure I can."

"You will. My blood helped heal your burns then, it will, again. Your legs would have been worse if I hadn't."

"What do you mean?" Confused, she leaned away from him. When her legs had been injured, she was with Gabriel. "When did you give me your blood?"

"After the fight with Mulciber, when you lay half-dead on the cave floor. I had to choose between going after Brandon or seeing to you. I chose you. Then, when you were in the infirmary, I waited until everyone left and snuck in to give you more blood. You were too precious to me to let you suffer."

Precious?! She remembered someone whispering that word. She'd thought, at the time, it was Gabriel. It had been Remare all along. She lay her forehead against his chest. "Thank you."

"My blood is yours whenever you need it." He kissed her forehead. "You're strong, Mir-randa." He gently shook her. "So, stop with the mental torture. It will not do you any good. You need your rest."

"Rest?" She huffed as she pulled away from him. "I can't rest. I hate this."

"I hate that this happened, as well, and that I wasn't there to protect you."

Miranda slid both of her hands around the back of her neck. It was slowly beginning to dawn on her that Remare was being incredibly patient with her. It wasn't just she who had been injured tonight. When she suffered, so did he. When he'd been hurt, part of her felt the pain, as well. She shouldn't have forgotten that. "You protect me from everything else. You're the strong one." She exhaled slowly. "You can't protect me from myself. It was a simple gathering. Nothing like this should have happened. I don't even understand how it did."

"Tristan said the women thought a piece of the wood crackled in the fire and flew in your direction. There was no warning."

"I don't remember that." She paced a few steps away. "Remare, I was staring at the fire. I don't remember anything flying in my direction."

"If it happened as fast as they say, you might not have seen it."

"Something's off here." She placed her hands on her hips. "I don't know what it is. But I feel like I should be remembering something."

"Something...or someone?"

Images started flying in her mind, too fast to comprehend. "I don't know." She continued pacing. "It feels like it's right in front of me, but I can't grasp it." She growled in frustration. "Something happened tonight. Something I saw or heard, but I can't remember what." She beat her fists against her thighs. More images from the research books, the monk who'd been healed by an *Elemental,* the painting of Esmerelda, the crystals, the man playing the guitar, flying on the astral plane with Esme, everything was fighting for clarification in her mind, but she couldn't get a handle on it.

"I don't know why, but I feel like I've been played."

Remare's voice turned icy. "How?"

She shook her head. "I don't know. But, ever since Orion and I landed in London, something's been off. The forgery. Meeting the other *Elementals*, the research at the library, Alice, Gemma, everything. I just can't figure it out." She exhaled. "If I asked you, could you run background checks on some of the women there tonight?"

"Before you left to join your friends, I'd already instructed Tristan to copy down license plate numbers. He took down many. He was working on it earlier tonight and should have a full report in the morning."

Miranda thought she should be angry with him for invading her privacy, but in this case, she agreed with him. "Why didn't you tell me?"

She pictured him shrugging. "I didn't think you'd approve."

She rubbed her shoulders.

"You've suffered trauma. Please lie down, Mir-randa. You're stressed. Sleep. Maybe then you'll remember what you've forgotten."

She reached out for his hand then wrapped her body around his, breathing in his wonderful scent. "I won't sleep much."

"Then, you'll rest." He sat her down on the bed and began to undress her.

She covered his wrists with her hands. "Let me sleep in one of your shirts, okay?"

"Yes. It's more than okay."

When they were situated under the covers, he pulled her against him. "Sleep, Miranda."

She thought he was using his voice with the vampiric power of suggestion to lull her. She wanted to remind him they'd discussed him never using his powers on her, again, after he'd searched her memories once before. But she was too emotionally drained.

Something had happened at the party tonight. Damned if she could remember what, but it was something significant. Did one of the *Elementals* use her gifts against Miranda? If so, who and why? She started replaying the events of the night through her mind, but nothing was clicking. Bits of conversations with Alice Gordon, Agatha, Esme, the dream with Esmerelda were all there in her mind, like pieces of a puzzle, but she couldn't see what the images were trying to tell her.

Frustration, fear, the not knowing the extent of the damage done to her eyes exhausted her. She wanted to be strong for Remare. The last thing he needed was an over-emotional wife or, worse, an invalid. He wouldn't leave her; he was honor bound. His life would be marred with guilt for not protecting her. *As if he could.* No, she'd have to leave him. She would not be a burden to him. She'd learn to live her life alone without him. Give him the freedom he deserved.

The thought of it made a single tear creep down her cheek. A sob broke free. Remare held her closer. She covered his hand with hers. His whispered words of support were bittersweet in the night. A darkness that might last forever. When another wave of weepiness threatened, she fought it back, pulling Remare's arm tighter around her.

Sometime during the night, she reached for him. Held her palm to his cheek, feeling the familiar curve of his jawline. She reached up to run her fingers through the waves of his hair. Remare was truly the handsomest man she'd ever met. But he was oh so much more to her. Need to feel, need to forget, need to just be clawed at her.

As if sensing her hunger, Remare kissed her palm and rolled on top of her. Her lips met his in mutual desire. As if in a dream, he moved ever so slowly. No need to rush, they had all the time they needed. Remare could be vigorous when it came to their lovemaking, a Roman warrior claiming what was his, powerful and strong.

But he could also be incredibly tender, gentle even, when the mood suited, as it did now. Butterfly kisses on her jaw and throat, a slight nip at her ear, followed by his tongue sliding down the side of her neck to her shoulder.

Her body responded by arching slightly off the bed, her hands gliding down the smooth, slick skin of his back. She enjoyed the rippling effect of his muscles under her touch, like a wave slowly approaching the shore. His mouth found hers, a kiss so tender it seared her to her core. Remare was hers. His touch had branded her long ago. How could she even think about leaving when they were together like this?

She reached up and traced his brow. She couldn't see his face, didn't need to. It'd been imprinted on her brain. She knew every curve, every angle. How he looked when he was angered and when he was amused. The exact shape and texture of his goatee. Her fingers traced his lips. He was smiling down on her then sucked one of her fingers in his mouth and gently bit down. After he released it, one word left his lips. "Mine."

Miranda shuddered as he rubbed against her, the friction creating heat where there'd only been cold earlier tonight. She traced her hands over his shoulders and down his sides, loving the cool, silky sensation of his skin. When her hands reached his butt, she dug in with her nails, raking him slightly so that a moan escaped his throat.

He positioned himself on top of her and then entered her, slowly, almost delicately. Miranda hungered for this, for him. The undeniable feeling of being one with him. Together, they were bound in need and in love. She was humbled by the intensity of their emotions and how loving someone could make them this vulnerable, this precious. Miranda would need decades, if not centuries, to understand the depth of all she was feeling. Emotions she didn't fully comprehend and was just beginning to realize.

Together, they moved in a warm embrace. As the water caressed the sands, he caressed not only her body but a part of her soul. And she him. Rarely did he smile as he did in moments like this, but knowing that one perfect smile made her heart ache. As the pressure built, as they soared higher, Miranda knew truths she hadn't known before. Magic, this pure, came from only one place—the heart. And hers beat for this man, this vampire who had dove into her and showed no mercy in claiming her. Nor had she'd shown any less for him.

They came together in a blissful sheen of stardust. Two hearts beating as one in the mystical, moist night air. Neither one let go of the other for some time after. The feeling of rightness, of sacredness, too beautiful. Sleep soon claimed them, offering comfort and a respite from the waking world. Miranda felt at peace, serene. Grateful to the powers that be that there were moments like this.

Sometime before dawn, during the darkest part of the night, a howl in the distance sounded. Orion. It was the full moon. He'd be out loping through the woods with Bastien. She wondered if he ever felt as content with Bas as she was with Remare. Experienced what she felt with her mate. She hoped he did. Orion deserved the happiness she knew. Miranda's breaths quieted.

Until a gunshot exploded in the night, and the howl turned into an excruciating yelp of pain animals only make when severely injured. She bolted upright.

"Oh, no! Someone shot Orion."

Chapter Twenty-Three

Remare was up and dressed before Miranda took her next breath. "Stay here. I'll see what's happened."

Miranda was pretty sure she heard the sound of a gun being checked and the magazine being slapped in. She hated guns, but if whoever out there had one, she wanted Remare as fully armed as possible. "Don't get killed."

"Not going to." His voice sent chills through her.

And, then, he was gone. Instinct screamed that she go with him, but in her current state, that was an impossibility.

Unless... She cocked her head. Her physical eyes were useless, but...her third eye wasn't. Esme had shown her how to travel on the astral plane. She'd only done it once, but she could see perfectly projecting her spirit. Could she do it, again? Without Esme? She didn't know. But Orion was out there, wounded.

She rolled out of bed and gingerly walked toward the window seat. As she opened the window, she was met with a blast of cool air. She inhaled deeply. Even though she couldn't see it, she knew the full moon shone brightly in the sky. She searched with her hands for her messenger bag. Remare had placed it on the window seat so she wouldn't trip over it. But what she found first was the cane. She kept it by her side and pulled her bag closer. Reaching inside, she pulled free her crystals and laid them out in front of her the way Esme had done.

Not knowing if this would work, she breathed deep, relaxing her heart rate until she was in a state of deep meditation. The crystals began to glow; she could feel the heat in her fingers. She whispered to her inner self, *Find Orion.*

She no sooner said the words, then her spirit floated up, and she opened her third eye. Miranda could see the room and the outdoors perfectly. She sent her spirit out into the night sky, past the fields and into the woods. The connection between Orion's air element and her fire one was strong. She could sense him and the pain he was enduring. Hear the voices of the men searching the grounds. The others were far away, wouldn't reach him in time. Miranda flew past branches and downed trees to get to Orion.

She found him alone, in human form, bleeding on the forest floor. His naked skin reflected the light of the moon. She bent over his semi-conscious form. "It's me, Orion. I'll heal what I can."

His head turned toward her, but his eyes were unfocused. She found the bullet hole on his upper thigh, near his hip. If only flesh and muscle had been damaged, it would make her job easier. If bone was shattered, that would take more energy than what she was used to. She peered around the back of his leg to see if there was an exit wound. There wasn't. Somewhere inside him, a bullet was lodged. Miranda held her hand over his leg and concentrated. She could feel the vibration of the metal bullet through his skin.

"This is going to hurt. I'm sorry, Orion, but there's no other way. The bullet has to come out." Miranda used her power to pull the bullet that had been embedded in bone through his flesh and skin to create an exit wound. Orion groaned loudly. She was sure the others in the forest must have heard him. She felt badly for Orion, but the quicker she did this, the faster he would heal.

Once the bullet was emitted, she searched the vibrations for fragments of the metal and bone. She had nothing to cleanse the entry and exit wounds with, so she tried to stem the bleeding as much as she could. She dared not close the wounds completely until they were cleaned. When she heard the others approaching, she kissed Orion's forehead and flew above.

Bastien was the first to arrive. "I hated leaving him, but when I tried to lift him, he was in more pain."

Doctor Roberts, who had gone out with the men, examined the leg. "The bleeding's almost stopped." He checked the wounds and found the bullet on the ground, which he handed to Remare, then poured some liquid over the lesions. Orion howled. Miranda knew, as a Were, Orion could heal most wounds faster than a human, but it still took time.

Mother Nature not only had a wealth of medicinal herbs, but also deadly poisons, and she had no idea if Orion's open wound had come into contact with any of them—better to let the doctor clean it.

Remare growled. "I don't like this. Herbert, you're sure your soldiers are vigilant?"

"Yes, of course, they woke as soon as we did and are patrolling the perimeters."

"Miranda is vulnerable in her current condition."

Bas, who'd been out when they came home, asked, "What happened to Miranda?"

"We'll tell you when we get back." Remare contacted her, *"Miranda, are you all right?"*

"I'm fine." She nearly laughed when Remare peered upward. Apparently, their mental bond was strong when her spirit was close.

"I've bandaged the wound. Get ready. When I say three, we lift him."

The men carried Orion to the manor. Miranda flew back faster through the air. When her spirit entered her body, she shuddered as the familiar bio-electrical connection snapped.

Disconcerted from seeing to non-seeing, Miranda stubbed her toe on a leg of furniture and cursed. She could search for her socks, but that would take time. This way, she could tell when she was on carpet or flooring. She tried using the cane as she'd seen blind people use theirs and made her way out of the room and down the hall.

The stairs were going to be tricky. Miranda figured, if she held on to the bannister, she'd have no problem. And, for the first few steps, she was right. Unfortunately, halfway down, she stumbled and went tumbling down. "Oh fuck!"

Remare was going to rip her a new one when he saw the bruises on her forehead and arm. She didn't want to know how her back looked. But, from the pain, she was sure she bruised a few ribs. She made her way to the bench in the hall and waited for the men to return.

Miranda stood when she heard them bringing Orion in.

"Let's put him in the library, he'll be more comfortable there," Herbert's voice rang out.

She sensed Remare, smelled his wonderful sylvan scent, before he clutched her arms. "What the hell are you doing here? You were supposed to stay in the bedroom."

"I got tired of waiting. How's Orion?"

He took her hand and led her to the study. "I suppose you got those bruises from falling?"

Miranda nodded. "They probably look worse than what they are. Yell at me later."

Remare growled.

Once in the study, the doctor said, "I don't feel any broken bones, but from the angle of the gun wound, I'd have thought there would be."

Miranda smiled then felt Remare's hand tighten on hers. Oh, yes, they'd be having a serious discussion later.

"I can have x-rays taken to be sure."

Orion moaned. "Take one of my head. Someone hit me with something. I think they knocked me unconscious."

She sensed Bastien was by his side. "Did you see who shot you?"

"It was dark." Orion moaned. "I thought they were Herbert's sentinels, but when they saw me, they lifted their rifles. There were two of them. If there were more, I didn't see them."

Dr. Roberts said, "He may have a concussion."

She imagined him shining the light in Orion's eyes.

"Thank God, Miranda showed up. My leg was bleeding so much; I think I was going into shock."

"I'm here, Orion." Holding Remare's hand, she moved toward Orion and knelt beside him. "I'm sorry you got shot."

He must have just noticed her bandages. "Holy hell, what happened to you?"

"Some embers flew into my eyes. The specialist is coming in the morning to check me out." She managed a smile and shrugged.

"But I saw you in the woods. I heard your voice."

She hated to lie, but for now, felt it was necessary. "I've been in the manor since we heard the gunshot and your howl." Which was technically true, since her body had been in stasis.

Orion yawned. "I must have hit my head harder than I thought."

Tristan entered. "We checked the area. There's no sign of them; however, we were able to find two separate tracks leading to the back road. That's it. I'm gonna do another perimeter search when the sun comes up. See if we find anything else."

"Well, at least there's that." Herbert exhaled.

"It's almost dawn. I think it best we all get some rest." Remare pulled Miranda toward him. They left Orion in the care of Bastien and the doctor.

Once in the room, Remare sat her down on the bed. She wondered if he spotted her crystals by the open window. She'd forgotten to bundle them up in her haste to get downstairs.

"In the future, if you're going to be meeting with associates of mine, especially men, would you please consider wearing underwear?"

Oops! "Sorry. With all that happened, I forgot." Wearing only Remare's shirt, which came halfway down her thighs, she pulled the covers over her naked legs. She wondered if the vampires and Orion could smell the remnants of sex on her. They probably could.

"Something you wish to tell me?" Remare's tone spoke volumes.

"Yes, quite a bit actually, but can it wait until later? I really am exhausted."

He exhaled, and Miranda could imagine him standing there with his arms crossed. Finally, he relented. "I suppose it will have to."

***

The next morning, after a breakfast of fruits and cheeses, it was time to meet with the eye specialist who had arrived from London. Remare led her back to the library and sat beside her on the couch Orion had previously vacated.

"Hello, Miranda, I'm Dr. Leewan Akimboto. Lord Herbert tells me you may have suffered an eye injury."

"Yes. I was at an outdoor party, not far from a fire. I really don't know what happened, but embers must have broken free from the flames and hit my eyes. It was very painful, but Dr. Roberts gave me some ointment to put on them."

She heard rustling noises and imagined Remare handing the doctor the tube of medicine.

"All right, then. Let's have a look." Dr. Akimboto undid the bandages then removed the two gauze pads over her eyes.

"It does look like some kind of burn. Can you open your eyelids?"

Miranda tried. There was still pain, but nothing like yesterday. "I can't. I think they're stuck."

"Yes, I can see that." She used a cloth to wipe at the corners of Miranda's eyes. "You have congealed residue. It looks like blood."

Miranda wasn't sure if she should tell the doctor it was probably Remare's blood. Turned out she didn't have to.

"When I saw the damage and the pain Miranda was in, I let fall a few drops of my blood on her eyelids."

"I wiped away most of the gel. You need to wash them. I have a solution I want you to use. Have you ever used an eye cup before?"

"Yes. When I was younger." Dinner out with friends, someone had cracked open a lobster, and she'd gotten spritzed with the juice.

"I'm filling the cup, now. Bend down and hold it, then lean your head back a little and try to blink at least three to five times. Can you do that for me?"

Miranda nodded.

"Then, let the liquid fall in the pan I have here." She placed it on Miranda's lap.

Miranda applied the solution. But try as she might, she couldn't open her eyelids. She tried the next eye. "I don't know what's wrong. I can't open them."

Dr. Akimboto's breath brushed against her cheek. "I'm going to lift one brow." She did. "Well, that's interesting. It appears your eyelids are welded shut."

Miranda gasped and clutched Remare's hand.

"Can you undo it?" Remare's voice was authoritative.

"Fascinating. You have the exact same injury on the left lid as the right. Nearly the same amount of eyelashes missing from both. You say you didn't see what hit you?"

Miranda was still stuck on the "welded shut" phrase. "Yes, I mean, no, I didn't see what it was."

"Try the solution, again."

Miranda did. With each eye. She still couldn't open them.

"Did you feel sensation when I wiped them with the gauze?"

"Yes." Miranda's heart was racing. "Do you think I suffered nerve damage?"

"Not quite. If you had, you wouldn't have felt the gauze. In any respect. You're going to need surgery to separate the lids. I can do this. I've worked with burn victims in the past. I have the equipment. I'm sorry, but you have to be awake during the procedure."

"Can you please explain what's entailed?"

"Yes. I need to make a small incision to separate the lids."

"With what?" Miranda started shaking.

Dr. Akimboto hesitated then said, "I can use a scalpel. I have done similar operations with good results, Miranda. There's no need to be fearful."

Hell to that fucking no! "I don't think so. The only one who's coming close to me with a scalpel in his hands is Remare."

"Mir-randa, the doctor is a specialist. I think you should let her do it."

"Can I have a minute alone with my husband?"

"Of course."

Miranda heard the Herberts' voices whispering with Dr. Akimboto's as they left.

When they were alone, she rested her forehead on Remare's chest. "You've done something like this before. Remember, when Vivienna pierced my nipples. You used a knife on them then healed me."

"Yes, but we're talking about your eyes. It's dangerous, Mir-randa." He rubbed her shoulders. "I've never cut anyone there before."

"Remare, I can't have anyone else with a scalpel come near my eyes." She shook her head. "I just can't. I'll flinch. You're the only one I trust to do it. Please. Do this for me." She took his hands in hers and brushed her thumb over his knuckles, a gesture she learned from him. "Please, Remare."

At that point she heard Orion and Bastien's voices. Orion limped in and asked, "How's it going?"

"Miranda needs surgery to open her eyelids. She doesn't want the doctor to do it." Remare continued holding her hands.

She heard the scraping of chairs, and then, another chair pulled up close. Orion sat in front of her. "I'd do it, Miranda, but the doctor is the expert."

"It won't work, Orion. Could you deal with someone coming at your eyes with a scalpel?"

"If it was necessary, yeah." Orion massaged her knee.

"I can't. I want Remare to do it."

There was a moment of silence, then Orion asked, "Can you do it?"

Remare sighed. "I would prefer not to, but if Mir-randa isn't comfortable with the doctor," he exhaled, "then I will."

Miranda clasped both his hands. "Thank you." She brushed her lips across his.

The door opened, and Herbert walked in with others. "Has a decision been reached?"

"I'm going to do the surgery."

Dr. Akimboto's voice. "Have you any experience doing surgery?"

"When I led armies into battle, I was often called upon to remove shrapnel from my wounded soldiers. Some were injured in rather intimate places. My hand has never slipped."

The doctor exhaled. "Very well, then. You will follow my instructions to the letter, yes?"

"Yes."

"All right, let's get you sterilized. I have the instruments."

Miranda heard rustling sounds. Then, someone pulled one of the end tables closer. She stood. "I should face you. I need to be sitting in a chair when you do this. Orion, I'm going to need you to restrain my head, and Bastien, my arms. Can you guys do that for me? Otherwise, I might flinch."

"Sure thing," they both said.

"One moment." She leaned forward and kissed Remare. "I love you. And I trust you with my life and my eyes."

"I love you, too, Miranda."

"And, if you fuck this up, I will hate you forever," she smirked, "but no pressure."

"Right." Remare scoffed. "No pressure at all."

Bas restrained her arms. "Is this too much?"

"No, not at all. I need you to hold on to me tightly, so I don't shift."

Orion kissed her temple. "I've got you, Mira. I won't let you flinch." He held her head back against his abdomen. His grip was strong.

"Thanks. Okay, I'm ready."

Dr. Akimboto said, "Good. I think it best you start from the outer corner and work your way in. The incision should be no deeper than one-sixteenth of an inch."

Remare agreed. "Yes, that's what I thought, as well."

Miranda heard him maneuvering himself forward. He rested one hand on the side of her face. "Do you remember the first time we met?"

She knew what he was doing. He could hear her heart going a mile a minute and was trying to get her to concentrate on something else, besides him with a scalpel cutting her eyelids. "Yes, Remare. That would be the time you tried to kill me when you thought I was an assassin."

"You couldn't blame me. You did have a weapon in your hand at the time."

She felt either a tear or blood begin to drip down her cheek. The instinct to jerk away was strong, but Orion held her firmly. "It was the dart aimed at Valadon. It hit me in the hip; I was removing it. You didn't even wait for an explanation."

Remare kissed her cheek, licked the droplet and then her eyelid. *"You're very brave, my sorceress."*

"I have to be; look who I'm married to."

Miranda's feet started tapping on the floor. She could feel him moving to the other eye.

"Ah, but do you remember the first time we were together, alone, intimately?"

Miranda smiled. *"Yeah. Upstairs at Nightworld. It was one of the best nights of my life."*

"Mine, too."

"You're almost done." He reached over and licked where he'd cut.

Bastien and Orion released their hold on her. Each sighed loudly.

Dr. Akimboto said, "I want you to wash out your eyes, now."

Miranda repeated the steps she'd done previously. But, this time, she could open her eyelids. *Thank the lords of the universe and anyone else who helped!*

Dr. Akimboto handed her a towel. She dried her face.

"Moment of truth, huh?" Miranda slowly opened her eyes. "It's blurry, but I can make out shapes. She could see the dark colors of Remare's hair and goatee. "Everything looks like shades of gray, dark and light."

"Your eyes are adjusting to the light. Blink a few times. I have some drops I want to give you. Please lean your head back."

Miranda followed her orders completely. Once the drops were in, she blinked repeatedly.

"It takes a few minutes for the medicine to take effect. Keep blinking."

She did. Then, she opened her eyes. "It looks like I'm underwater, but now, I see colors. Faded, but colors."

"Good. Follow my finger. Keep your head still, just move your eyes."

She did.

"Wonderful. I suspect your focus will improve shortly."

Everyone let out a collective sigh.

"They told me you don't like bright lights. But I need to use one to see inside your eyes."

Miranda didn't want her to. She'd seen enough of bright lights. One had blinded her. "Is it absolutely necessary?"

"I'm afraid so. It won't take but a minute."

Remare slipped his hand in hers. "Courage, my love."

"All right."

"Your eyelashes will grow back in time. From what I can see the cornea wasn't damaged. Now, let's see about the retinas." Dr. Akimboto shined the light in, and true to her word, she was fast but efficient. "I see no impairment, but..." She shook her head.

"What is it?" Remare and Miranda asked simultaneously.

"There's a tiny starburst in the back of your right eye. Common enough in diabetics or those who strain their eyes from too much reading. Yours seems to resemble...an eagle. Other than that, you're perfectly fine."

Miranda sprung out of the chair and hugged Remare. "Thank God. Thank you, Remare. And thank you, Dr. Akimboto."

"Not at all. I'm just glad you can see, again." She packed up her stuff. "You should see your doctor in another week for a checkup."

Gabriel. "I will."

There were hugs all around when Dr. Akimboto left.

Miranda sighed. "I think the adrenaline is finally crashing. I didn't get much sleep last night with everything that happened, so I'm going to try to get some rest."

"That's a good idea," Remare said as he took her hand. "Bastien, coordinate with Tristan. If anything pertinent comes up, notify me immediately; otherwise, I'll be upstairs in my room."

"Sure thing." Bas nodded.

Chapter Twenty-Four

Miranda didn't wait long when they were in their room to push Remare against the door and kiss him thoroughly. Relief and gratitude at not being blind rolled through her. Being in his arms made the butterflies in her stomach dance and her toes curl. She wondered how long they'd have to be together for the sensations to wear off. Probably never.

He stroked her face with his thumb. "You look exhausted, Mir-randa. How are you feeling?"

"Like I could sleep for a week." Before she could say anything else, there was a knock at the door.

"Sorry to disturb you." Tristan glanced at her, then Remare. "I can come back later, but I have intel on those people at the gathering last night. There's something I think you should see."

Remare stepped aside so Tristan could enter. He sat in front of the corner desk and set up his laptop. "Herbert's people in London were good at sharing information with us. They got right on it after he made the request. This is what we came up with after I supplied them with the license plate numbers on some of the women at the party." Images and bios lit up the screen.

"First one up is Esmene Athena Komanos. Teaches yoga at a London studio. Makes and sells jewelry. Her parents are second-generation immigrants from Greece. They own and operate a restaurant in London."

"Esmene?! Athena, the Greek goddess of wisdom." Miranda remembered the goddess's favorite animal was the owl. "I thought for sure she'd be Esmerelda's descendant."

"Not her." Tristan arched a brow. "Someone else. It took a bit of digging. The old man at the ruins said Esmerelda's descendant was named for her grandmother, but he didn't specify which one." He punched in some keys. "Dolores was the name of the paternal grandmother. However, her maternal one had a different name. Married Jonathan Winslow when she was younger. Kept his name after he passed away from a boating accident." Several pictures surfaced. "Agatha Hawkins Winslow, descendant of Esmerelda and Lord Acton."

"Agatha?" Miranda fell into the chair next to Tristan's. "Even younger, she looks nothing like Esmerelda."

"Several generations separate them, Mir-randa. Not all relatives share similar features."

"I guess not." Miranda gazed at the images. No wonder she knew so much about the history of *Elementals* going back to biblical references. "The other *Elementals* consider her their leader. Who else did you find?"

"Several others. Nothing interesting on any of them. They pretty much are who they claim to be. However, there was one who stood out prominently." He hit some keys. "When I questioned the women, one gave off a bad vibe. I didn't like it much, so I kept digging. This is what I found." Images danced across the screen. "Victoria Needham. Vicky to her friends. She owns and operates a salon in London. Likes to go clubbing." Tristan gazed up at Remare. "Check out who her dance partner is."

Miranda didn't recognize the man, but Remare sure did. More expletives than she was used to erupted from his mouth.

"Gideon. Lord Acton's second," he sneered. "I should have known he'd be involved."

"Friend of yours?" she asked sarcastically.

"Hardly. More like an adversary. He does Acton's bidding. We had an altercation the last time I was in London." Remare stroked his goatee. "If he's hanging around Victoria, he has a purpose."

"That's not all," Tristan said. "I dug deeper. She's not from London, originally. Wanna take a guess from where?"

Remare growled. "Leeds."

Tristan nodded. "Northern England, Lord Acton's territory. She grew up there. When she came of age, she moved to London. Set up shop. I figure she's some sort of spy for Acton or Gideon."

"But that doesn't sound right." Miranda shook her head trying to make sense of this. "Agatha told me the *Elementals* don't trust vampires. Avoid them at all costs."

"Not in this case. I checked her financials. Guess who gave her the money to buy the salon and a swanky town house in an affluent section of London?"

Remare groused. "Acton."

Tristan nodded.

"None of the other *Elementals* knows Agatha's ancestry." Miranda tapped her fingers on the desk as ideas swirled in her mind. "She keeps her cards close to the vest. Secrecy is a huge deal with them. I bet you anything Lord Acton's been searching for his offspring, if he had, in fact, found out Esmerelda was pregnant when she left him. Makes me wonder who else he has on his payroll."

"I've read up on how Acton used Esmerelda's talents to further his ambitions." Remare sighed. "Through the centuries, he always seemed to have knowledge before others. His network of spies must be impressive."

A chill ran up Miranda's back. "How long has Acton known about the coven?"

"Not sure. But I think we should question Ms. Needham." Tristan swiveled his chair around.

"Not yet. You've hardly gotten any sleep, Tristan. Let Bastien handle the rest. I want a full investigation into Lord

Acton's affairs; tell Bastien to email me his results. I'm sure Herbert is aware of plenty; see what else we can find."

"Okay, I can use a few hours' sleep. I'll let Bastien know and then join him later." Tristan was halfway to the door when he turned back. "One other thing. The police in London believe it was an intruder bent on burglary who killed Alice Gordon. There'd been other burglaries in the neighborhood, especially now with the school term over. Drugs may have played a factor. However, when I spoke to a senior officer, he said it seemed like the place was trussed up to make it appear like a burglary, but twenty years on the force tells him otherwise. There was money frozen under the ice trays. Any competent burglar would have found it."

"Any news on Gemma Hastings?" Miranda liked the bookstore owner.

"The police cleared her. She's on her way back with her sister's body for burial in a local cemetery. That's all the information I have at this time."

Remare accompanied him to the door. "Thank you. Get some sleep, now."

"Will do."

Miranda sighed after Tristan left. "You think it could have been a burglary?"

"I'm not sure." He cocked his head. "It's possible. With the end of the school term and other robberies in the area." Concern marred his face. "Or it might not be."

Miranda didn't want to consider the possibilities. "I'm exhausted. I need to rest. Will you stay with me for a little while?"

He ran his knuckles down her cheek. "Of course."

She cuddled up against him, hoping not to dream. But her mind was racing with all that had happened in the last few days. She couldn't make sense of it. There was so much she wanted to say to Remare but wasn't sure where to start.

He had to know about her growing *Elemental* powers. How was she ever going to explain astral projection? Or even transmutation? She wanted to tell him about Esme's ability to change form, but she'd be breaking coven rules.

Sleep soon overtook her.

Miranda was back in the cave. Cold, old earth, musty smelling. The planet's vibration strong here. The dream felt real. Too real. She held a blue fireball in her hand to light her way.

Esmerelda's spirit was in front, imploring her to follow deeper into the darkness. In her hand was a glowing crystal. *"This way, come. It's not far."*

Miranda wasn't sure this was a good idea, but the spirit seemed intent on showing her something.

"You must see; you must see."

What must she see? What was so important? *"Why, Esmerelda, why?"*

"So, you can know. You need to know!" The path opened up into a cavernous room with stalactites and stalagmites. Somewhere in the distance, water was dripping. Here, the rock face was lighter. Esmerelda's crystal hummed then lit up the room in brilliant illumination.

Drawings covered one wall. It looked like a village with people farming, doing chores. Children played with what looked like a ball. Down further, an injured man lay on a bed, his leg in bandages. A sunrise over him with dozens of streaks of sunlight over him.

"A sunrise," Miranda murmured.

"No. Look closer."

Miranda did as requested. *"Not rays of the sun?"*

"No. My rays. My energy."

Miranda could feel the vibrations when she placed her hand over the drawing. *"The earth's energy. Healing energy."*

"Yes. Yours, as well. You must complete the task, now. Succeed where I failed."

Her heart thumped against her chest. *"What task?"*

"Hurry, he comes. Beware the dark man. He's loathsome. He will use you for his own purposes. He will kill you as he killed me."

"Who? What are you talking about?"

"I must go. Before it's too late. See what has not been seen. Do what must be done, that which is righteous. You must not fail!" Esmerelda's form began dissipating.

"Wait!" But it was too late. She was gone. Why had Esmerelda sought her out? What was it she wanted her to do? Who was the dark man? Miranda wandered down the cave, her blue flames lighting the way. She tried to make out the next drawing, but it had faded with time. It looked to be several men with a strange symbol on their clothing. She moved in closer when she heard the noise. She was not alone. A susurration, as if something near was breathing. Something not of this world. The sound grew louder. Angry, vengeful.

The cave was alive, it was breathing, and Miranda had been swallowed whole.

She woke panting, her face covered in sweat, even though she felt iced to the bone.

"Are you all right?" Remare stroked her arm.

"Strange dream. Esmerelda has got to find someone else to haunt."

"Tell me."

She knew she had to. From the beginning, Remare had always had her back. Even when he'd wanted to kill her, she snorted. But that was long ago. Now, he loved her. And she loved him. "I have so much to tell you."

She cupped his face. "When I was a student and on my own, I yearned for a family. I'd sit up on my rooftop garden and look up at the moon. I felt so alone, cut off from the rest of the world. And I wondered why my family was taken from me. I cursed the gods, the fates and even myself for not being what I should have been."

"What was that, Mir-randa?"

"Good enough. Strong enough to have saved them." She bowed her head. "I know I was only a child when they died, but I felt like heaven had rejected me, and I didn't know why. Later, I met Lizandra, and she made things better for me. So did Gavin. But they weren't my family. Even though I pretended that they were."

She took his palm and held it against her face. "You're my family. What we have together is real, precious."

"You're my family, too, Mir-randa. My heart, my sorceress. I've waited centuries for you." He kissed her forehead.

"I lied to myself. I thought myself strong. Physically, I worked out with Liz and with Cyra, when she was alive. But I never really used all of my strength."

"What do you mean?"

"Agatha called me a coward. Because I've refused to use my powers. But I have, helping Jacob and Vincent. Also, when we fought those who would harm us: Rogue vampires, drugged up humans, feral Weres. But I never really tapped into certain parts of me."

"You're the least cowardly person I know, Mir-randa. You've shown bravery where others would not. No one who truly knows you could ever call you a coward."

"That's what I thought. I used to think you knew me better than anyone else. That I showed you more rooms in the mansion of my mind than any other. Hell, you took me by the hand and showed me parts of myself I didn't even know I possessed." She exhaled. "But there were rooms I kept hidden from myself. Buried deep inside. An oubliette I was too afraid to stare into." She gazed downward. "I think I looked into it."

"What did you see?"

"Remare, *Elementals* have more powers than just controlling the elements. We pull energy from the earth others cannot. Peralt got most of it right, but there were a few things he left out."

He wiped the tear from her cheek. "Does it frighten you?"

"I'm being pulled in a direction I have no knowledge of. I'm learning more and more." She shook her head. "Some things I can't tell you. Secrets that belong to the other *Elementals*. But I want you to know me. Know the side of me I've kept hidden for so long."

He stroked her face. "I know you're an *Elemental*, Mir-randa. I've seen you fight, control the elements. And I've seen you heal people."

"Oh, Remare. There's *so* much more." She breathed deep and peered up at him. "I know how to travel on the astral plane."

Startled, he sat up. "Explain it to me."

"I can't. I barely understand it myself. Another of the *Elementals* can, too. She said she recognized the power within me. She showed me how to use it. It takes a great deal of concentration, almost like an altered state of consciousness, to be able to free the spirit. But I can. I've done it twice, now."

He nodded. "Ah. So, that's what Orion meant when he said he saw you in the forest. Mir-randa, are you sure you know what you're doing when you use your gifts?"

"Like a bird learning to fly, you only learn by doing it. There's more. Peralt mentioned transmogrifications in his writings. I wasn't sure what he meant, but I think I do, now. I saw someone change form who wasn't a Were. An *Elemental* who could transmute into an owl. It was mesmerizing to watch. I don't have that power. Yet. But I think, someday, I might."

"Mir-randa. Listen to me. These powers you speak of are fantastical, may have far-reaching consequences, and I suspect are very dangerous. If others knew what you could do, I hate to think of the lengths they would go to. Vampire lords would kill to possess you."

"I know. The thought has occurred to me. That's why I've kept them hidden. Not only vampire lords, but the brotherhood, as well."

Remare cocked his head.

"Peralt wrote of the *'Ordo Lucis'*. The order of light, as in The Human Order of Light, the HOL. I think Esmerelda was trying to warn me about them."

"How?"

"In dreams. In the cave. She showed me pictures, cave drawings. The men wore a strange symbol on their clothing; it looked like a triangle with a cross in the middle. She told me to beware of a dark man. I have no idea what she meant." Miranda curled a strand of his hair around her finger. "I know lots of dark-haired men who are good. You, Orion, and even Tristan all have black hair."

"She didn't happen to give you a name, now did she?"

"Nope. Not that forthcoming. But something scared her. I think she wanted to tell me more, but she fled. Then, I woke up."

Remare narrowed his eyes, as if studying her.

"Yes. You have a lunatic for a wife. If you want to divorce me, I get it. I'm not entirely sure I'm completely sane, either."

"There will be no divorce. Ever." He lay beside her. "I'm going to finish reading the books and papers we have. See if we can learn anything more."

"I'll help you."

Chapter Twenty-Five

"We've been at it for hours. I think we need a break." After munching on assorted fruits and vegetables, Miranda thought they were due for a rest from all their research.

"A little bit more."

She watched as Remare speed read through biblical references to the angels. Miranda downloaded what she could of *The Book of Enoch*, and sections of *Genesis*. Some of the information was difficult to interpret, but what she could decipher only opened up new avenues of questions.

"I'm still curious as to why Alice sent me this book." Miranda held up the monk's diary. "Basically, he just recounts his final years as a wine merchant traveling from town to town. He states, *'It is my everlasting regret that I ever mentioned the healing woman to my order. Their laughter and disparagement were nothing compared to what I learned years later.'*"

She turned the page. *"'It is with a heavy heart I recount the disservice I did to the village and 'The Shining Woman'. While returning a book to our monastery's library, I happened upon and listened in on a conversation amongst others of my order. They were discussing Richard, a monk whose ambitions far exceeded my own, and his ties to the Holy Roman Church. Apparently, my account of the spiritual sister resonated with him, and he made sure the news reached Rome. A group was dispatched to find and eliminate 'the threat' to their beliefs.'"*

Remare put down his book. "Does he say what beliefs?"

Miranda continued reading. *"'The people of the village were kindhearted and only meant to help me when I'd been injured. I repaid their kindness with bloodshed and death. I know, now, I am responsible for what happened afterward. In fear for my life, I acted the inebriated fool. The faction within the church was far more widespread and powerful than I thought possible. It was my own brethren who hunted down the healing woman and killed her. Believing there might be others with similar powers, they diligently searched for them. Anyone they thought possessing powers was branded a heretic and brutally tortured until death ensued.'"*

"Witchcraft."

"Yeah, I think so. Remare, this journal goes back to the seventeenth century. I wanted to find the origins of *Elementals*, but I think I just found the origins of the HOL."

"Possible. But I think it might even go back further. The Church has a strict patriarchal hierarchy. The only ones who could read and write were either the nobles or the clergy. If the son of a poor farmer did not wish to spend his life in backbreaking labor, he would enter the monastery. Not only would he be provided with shelter and food, but access to education not readily available elsewhere. I've been told that if a low-ranking member of the clergy wished for advancement, he often did favors for the ruling upper members. Sometimes, that included dirty work."

"Such as murder?"

Remare nodded. "Be aware that any order with a substantial amount of wealth attracts all types. Some more ambitious than others."

"It would be nice to believe all men who entered the order did it for love of God and religion. It's hard to imagine people living such cloistered lives if not for their passions."

"Some did. But passion has many faces. You have to remember options were not readily available back then as they are today. Men of ambition were severely marginalized in their choices. For some, the Church was the only viable choice they had."

Miranda shook her head. "It's hard for me to imagine how powerful the Church, or the faction within, had become. How they were able to amass the fortune they did."

"Not difficult. People have fears. Once learned, they become easy enough to manipulate and control. Men who do not have the love of a woman, learn to love other things. Power is just one of them."

"But why women?" Miranda ran her hands over the monk's diary. "Why did they fear women so much?"

"If it were common knowledge women possessed gifts, such as yours, it would bring about questions about faith the Church could not risk. It would shake the very foundation. Remember, we're only talking about a small percentage. Our sources within the organization have nothing but complete respect for many of their officials."

"Every bushel has its bad apple. But from somewhere within the hierarchy came the order to eliminate these women."

"Yes. As did the order to eradicate vampires and Weres. The Vampire Nation has fought long and hard throughout the centuries to discover the members of the HOL. But, every time we think we've neutralized a threat, another takes its place."

Miranda sighed. "The world just got darker."

"The world has always been dark. And light."

Miranda ran her fingers along the back of the leather journal. "Remare? Does the back of this book feel thicker than the front?" She handed him the book.

He opened the book and slid his hand down the front and back covers. "Yes, the back has more filling." He started peeling the inside material.

Miranda gasped at the damage he was doing to the rare book.

Remare's brow rose. "Do you want to find out what's embedded back here or not?"

If she wasn't certain something was hidden in the back binding, she wouldn't consider damaging such a work of art. She nodded.

Remare pulled back the rear interior to reveal several layers of folded papers. Miranda examined them. "It's in Latin."

He unfolded the parchment. And smiled. "The monk lists names of those he thought were violators of the faith. He calls them, '*Ones Tenebris*'—The Dark Ones."

Miranda examined the other sheets. "He drew their acts of terror. In this picture, the woman is surrounded by a corona—her aura. In this one, she's being killed by her attackers." Miranda sneered. "See the symbol on their cloaks? It's the symbol I saw in my dream with Esmerelda. The triangle enclosing the cross." She was sick to her stomach.

"Had the monk tried to stop them, raised suspicion among his own, they would have murdered him."

"No wonder he hid the parchment in the back." Miranda blinked. "Do you think this could be the cause of Alice Gordon's death?"

Remare squinted. "The timing is questionable. The HOL would have had to have known about these papers. Or this journal. It's a stretch. But it's possible."

Miranda closed her eyes. She didn't want to believe she was the cause of Mrs. Gordon's death. But how would Alice or anyone else know what was secreted in the back, unless they themselves planted it there. "I guess we'll never know."

A knock at the door. Orion entered, followed by Bastien. "The Herberts have invited us on the terrace for drinks."

Miranda cracked her neck. "I certainly could use one." Then, she blinked, remembering she was in a house of vampires. "They meant alcohol, right?"

Remare laughed as Bastien grinned. "Yes, my love."

Once outside, Miranda relished the cool, crisp air. The gardens were meticulously manicured, and she could smell a hint of hyacinth in the air, among other floral scents as the breezes blew through the trees. "This feels good."

"How are you feeling, Miranda?" Winnie asked as she patted the chaise lounge next to her.

"Better. Thank you. I needed the rest." She reclined near her hostess.

Remare accepted the wine Herbert handed him. "We've been doing some research on Esmerelda and Cranbrook's and Rye's pasts. Miranda has a fondness for history."

"Well, we certainly have a ton of books. We've donated many to libraries over the years," Winnie said.

"What would you like to drink, Miranda?" Herbert asked.

Not in the mood for her usual cranberry and vodka, she asked for a beer, as did Bastien and Orion. "You have lovely grounds here. Remare and I enjoyed the horseback ride through your lands yesterday very much."

"Yes. The weather's been mild, but I fear rain will be coming soon. Storm coming off the sea later tonight." Herbert lit his pipe.

Miranda sank further back into her lounge chair and gazed over their gardens and outdoor pool. Another time, she'd be tempted to go for a swim. But not tonight. Presently, she was content to enjoy the company of friends. The Herberts were good people who radiated warmth and affection. She was glad Remare had known them through the centuries. When she glanced at Orion and Bastien, she was happy their bond seemed to be growing. The two looked good together. They were even beginning to dress alike.

Orion said, "Hey, where's Tristan? We should invite him to join us, as well."

"He may be sleeping." Remare said, "We've had him on assignment late into the night and early this morning."

The servant arrived with a tray of several canapes and offered them to Miranda. She hadn't realized how hungry she was until she breathed in their delectable scent. She washed down the meat encrusted pastries with her beer. She nearly groaned in pleasure at the savory taste.

"I'm going into town in the morning to pick up a few things." Winnie asked as she rose, "Would you like to come with me?"

She peered up at Remare to check if they had plans. He gestured for her to go. "Yes, I'd like that very much. I think I could use some new clothes."

"The next time you visit us, we'll have to take you out on the boat. Give you the tour of the English Channel and the coastline." Herbert smiled. "The sight is something to see."

"And, next time, plan to stay longer. At least three weeks. There's so much I want to show you." Winnie adjusted the sound system until she found a song she liked.

Miranda smiled at Remare, grateful his friends seemed to like her and wanted to include her in their activities. When Adele's "Rolling in the Deep" song came on, Winnie grabbed Herbert to dance. Warmth bloomed in Miranda's stomach for the couple. Herbert appeared genuinely happy to be dancing and twirling Winnie around. They could move all right, but Miranda remembered how seductively the Weres danced.

When it came to pure sensuality and grace, no one beat the Weres, especially Lizandra and Gavin. Liz had a style of her own, moved in such fluid motion, she was heaven to watch. Her body arched like no other, as if she absorbed the music into the very fiber of her being. Miranda missed her best friend.

She glanced at Remare and wondered if they'd still be dancing after being together for centuries the way Winnie and Herbert were. Remare smiled and tilted his head as if asking her to dance. Miranda shook her head. She was exhausted, and they'd already danced in the moonlight. She wondered if Bastien and Orion would ever dance together. Orion already swirling to the beat, singing along with Adele. Miranda was glad he was in a jovial mood, especially after having been shot.

Since it was such a mild night and the air scented with blossoms, they dined alfresco. She didn't participate much in the conversation, content to observe and listen. Once upstairs, Miranda gazed out the window.

"Are you all right, Mir-randa? You hardly ate anything at dinner." Remare stood beside her.

"I was thinking about Brandon."

"That traitor. Valadon told me Montglat would keep him imprisoned in a very dark and cold place." Remare stroked her face. "He can't hurt you, anymore."

"I know." She had every faith in Blu's ability to make good on his promises. "That's not what I was thinking about. More about his relationship with Valadon. God, Brandon is his brother. How could he have betrayed him so? I mean, I just don't understand that level of jealousy."

"What's not to understand? People desire what others have."

"Not always. My sister, Cassandra, was tall, thin and gorgeous. You would have been enchanted. She was smarter than me, always got straight A's and was great at athletics. I was never jealous of her. I was happy and proud for her. She worked hard for her accomplishments."

"You're a beautiful woman, Mir-randa. I'm sure I've mentioned that many times."

She laughed. "I'm not fishing for compliments. I know I shine up good when I want to. But Cassie was a natural beauty. Her features were softer. In school, when teachers did the roll call and regarded me, they would say, 'Oh, *you're* Cassie's sister?' They would have that look on their faces. All younger sisters and brothers know *that look* of not quite measuring up. After the third or fourth time, I just accepted it. It wasn't an ego thing. I used to dress more tomboyish. I just wasn't the frilly type and never tried to be."

"Frilly is not a word I would ever use to describe you. But you earned advanced degrees in grad school with your stellar mind. I'm sure you were just as astute as Cassie."

"Not really." Miranda thought about it. "She was more analytical; I was more intuitive. I was lucky. Some subjects came ridiculously easy for me. I didn't even have to study too hard. I'd read a book and seek out all the important parts. And just know. Absorb it. I think it infuriated her. Cassie would pour over the books for hours—very systematic. I didn't get that way until college."

Remare stroked her arm. "You also keep yourself fit. I suspect Lizandra was influential in that regard."

"Cassie was good at almost every sport she played. Because she was tall, she was good at basketball. With me, you could place me at one spot at an angle to the net, and I could hit the basket every time. Move me five inches away, and I couldn't." She shrugged. "No big. The one sport I shone in was gymnastics. I was naturally flexible, and you should have seen my moves."

"I know well your flexibility." His eyes glinted with mischievous desire. "I believe we've tested that many times, now."

"Har, har!"

"I'm sure, when you were young, you excelled in areas she did not."

It certainly wasn't in singing. "Yes, I did. In art. My drawings and paintings were better than hers. I even won a blue ribbon in a contest. She was so happy for me, rushed home to show my parents the certificate and everything." She tilted her head. "Why wasn't Brandon proud of Valadon?"

Remare crossed his arms and leaned against the wall. "I suppose, early on, he might have been. But, after years of seeing Valadon receive the accolades he did not, it must have grated on him."

"I watched Cassie bring home trophies and awards; it never grated."

"That's because your heart was full of affection. Brandon's was not."

"I suspect, in the beginning, it was. What made him turn bad?"

"Something lacking in his personality. Humility, I think. I watched over the years how he seethed underneath whenever Valadon closed a prosperous business deal. It festered in him. Until, one day, he decided to move against Valadon."

Miranda considered Remare's words. "Agatha says of all the seven deadly sins, vanity is the worst. You think Brandon's ego played a part? That he couldn't match Valadon's financial acumen, so he chose a different path, a deadly one?"

Remare nodded. "I think so."

"But you and Valadon were close for centuries, did you ever feel jealous of him?"

"I admired him. Was I ever jealous? I don't think so. We were too busy celebrating our victories together. He with his economics, and I with battle strategies and tactics. We shone in our respective fields."

"And you never wanted a territory of your own?"

"I could have had one. I chose not to. I did not, then or now, wish for the responsibilities and restrictions inherent in a lord's position."

She tilted her head. "How come?"

"Because I relished the freedom men of position cannot. I travelled more, enjoyed myself, and took certain liberties not available to lords. It was a conscious decision on my part, one that I've never regretted. And...I appreciated working with Valadon. He is quite something to see in action. I've known many lords, Mir-randa. None do I respect and cherish as much as Valadon. He is the brother I never had."

"And Herbert?"

"Hmm, a beloved cousin."

"Liz is like a sister to me. I respect her, too, but I would never want to be a Were queen. Too many disputes to deal with, too much détente needed, and I don't have that level of patience."

"So, we are content in who we are and the choices we've made. Each of us shining where we wanted to be."

"I don't know about shining. But, yeah, content in who we are."

"I think you do shine. I think your eyes are brighter than before."

"That's because I'm looking at you." That was part of it. She knew she was harboring powers she hadn't possessed before. Could feel it glowing inside her. She gazed lovingly at Remare's eyes. Eyes the color of the most decadent, delicious chocolate. Eyes that glittered with amusement—sometimes sarcastic, sometimes poignant. But always with truth. She needed to share certain truths with him, now. "There's a reason I was thinking of Brandon and jealousy. I started remembering things from last night. I think one of the *Elementals* threw something in the fire to blind me."

His voice was a controlled fury. "Which one?"

Chapter Twenty-Six

"Remare, there's something you have to understand. I'm not normal." Miranda thinned her lips. "At least not as far as humans go. I'm different."

"I know. You're an *Elemental* with some vampire blood in your ancestry."

"I'm beginning to suspect there might be more."

His eyes narrowed.

How the hell did she even begin to make him understand things she was just barely discovering herself? "Bear with me here. What happened at the fire stunned me. Damned near traumatized me. I suppose I was in shock for a while. Couldn't think, couldn't process what I'd seen."

Remare crossed his arms over his chest. "Go on."

She paced a few steps away from him. "It's all so surreal, like a dream. I was sitting there at the gathering, chatting with the others, enjoying myself. The thing is I'm very good at observing things." She faced him. "In my line of work, that's imperative and makes me a fine authenticator. Jordan says I'm exceptional because I notice details others don't. The human eye sees only a limited amount of the shades of any given color. Computers detect dozens more. I see better than the average human."

"Yes, I've often thought you very perceptive. That's how you were able to figure out who was behind Valadon's attempted assassination."

"True, but that had more to do with scent than seeing. Last night, when I turned the corner to enter the backyard, it was as if it was a tableau in front of me. When I analyze a painting, I break it down into quadrants and decipher it from there. Shades—light and dark contrasts, color variations, depth of paint, angle of strokes. I perceive it all."

"What did you see?"

She closed her eyes in memory. "Upper left quadrant: gardens, tables laden with various foods, meats, vegetables. Lower quadrant: desserts, bottles of wine and beer. Upper right: more gardens, statuary, people dancing, some in long skirts, some in jeans. Tiny lights strung up all over, bright, colorful. Lower right: man sitting under a tree playing a guitar. He wore a hat and sunglasses. I couldn't see his face too well. People sitting in a circle by the fire, the *Elementals* I met at the bar. All was good."

Remare's voice was patient. "What happened next?"

"I sat near Agatha. Pleasantries exchanged all around. *Elementals* like to give innocuous displays of their power. Simple things really, like making water flow upward in an arc instead of downward. Making the ground tremble underneath."

"That doesn't sound harmless."

"It was a little shiver, meant to amuse, nothing more, really. No malicious intent. Then, one of the women wanted to impress me with her ability. The other fire *Elemental*. Her fire burns red, like Esmerelda's. Mine is blue. She made a figure dance in the fire. Simple enough. But I remember staring into the fire and looking past the dancer. This is where it gets scary. You might want to sit down for the rest."

"I'm comfortable standing."

"I saw something. Something that terrified me. At first, it appeared to be a large bird. Golden. Each feather more stunning in its brilliance, intricate in design. Shimmering in its iridescence. I'd never seen anything like it before, and I've studied art covering many centuries. The luminescence was nearly blinding. I remember thinking this was absolute perfection. The color of the gold so pure, so intense, it caused tears to fall. Truth, not meant to be seen, let alone comprehended. I saw things I can't even begin to describe. It was as if the bird held me in thrall. Something was urging me to turn away, not to look, but I couldn't. I ignored the warning, the voice within, to behold such exquisite beauty."

Remare held her against him. "What did you see?"

"It wasn't a bird. When I gazed upward, I expected to see its beak and eyes. I didn't. I saw the face of a man. But he wasn't a man. The power he emitted was incomprehensible. Not of this earth." She started shaking as Remare rubbed her arms. "I think he spoke to me, but I couldn't make out the words. My eyes felt like they were bleeding. I felt like I was being seared from the inside out. I saw time. I saw ages I've never lived in, places I've never visited. It scared the hell out of me. Then, in an instant," she snapped her fingers, "everything went black." She bowed her head to his chest. "That's when I called out for you."

Remare exhaled as he massaged her back in a comforting gesture. They held each other for a few moments. "Who is the woman you think threw something in the fire?"

She gazed up at him. "Victoria."

"Acton's spy. It's more than possible she tossed chemicals in the fire to make you hallucinate."

"That's what I thought. Initially. Remare, I don't think so. There's more." She stepped away from him. "Agatha told me she believes *Elementals* are the descendants of angels. I'm beginning to wonder if she might be right. All that we've read in *The Book of Enoch*, Esmerelda's letters, and the monk's drawings suggest the unbelievable."

The look Remare was giving her was a combination of sadness and wonder.

"Yup, that's why I wouldn't tell you, wouldn't tell myself. I have powers, Remare, ordinary humans don't have. I can do things that should be impossible. And what's worse, they're growing. I can feel it here." She rubbed her stomach near the solar plexus.

"How?"

"Through meditation. Deep contemplation. In yoga, they refer to it as the chakra. I can make myself go to a place inside my head that's hard to imagine, but it's possible." She huffed. "It's funny I've always thought there were two angels inside me. My Dark Angel and my Angel of Light—my sources of deliberation when I have tough choices to make. Now, I think I might have been right all along."

"Descendants of angels." He shook his head. "You give me pause to consider the possibilities."

"Something I should have told you earlier. Yesterday, after I came back from learning to travel on the astral plane, I felt the power pulsing beneath my skin. It changed me. I'm not sure how, but I know I vibrate at a sharper pitch. I'm stronger. I'm evolving."

The sadness was back in his eyes. She couldn't tell if he pitied her flights of fancy or the implications if what she was saying was true.

Remare sighed. "There's something I should tell you, as well."

"What?"

He lifted her chin. "Vampires have red rims around their irises. You now have golden ones. It's faint, but there. I doubt anyone else can notice it, unless they get as close to you as I do."

Miranda strode to the mirror on the wall and exhaled. "Well, life just keeps getting more interesting."

He chuckled. "Understatement. Let's not try to figure out everything tonight. When we get back to New York, we have a sage we can confer with. He's a learned man. He may have answers we do not."

"You mean you're not going to have me committed somewhere? I was having nightmares about that."

He scoffed. "No, my sorceress." He held her face between his palms. "You are many things. Insane is not one of them."

"Thank God for that. I gotta tell you, I wasn't sure about that for a few moments." She held his wrists and asked sarcastically, "Do you think they have drugs that can cure me?"

He gave her that look. He was about to kiss her when there was a knock at the door. "Enter."

It was Bastien. "We got problems. Tristan's missing. We can't find him anywhere."

"Did you check his room? He's been working long shifts; he may be resting."

"First place we looked. When I questioned Herbert's guards, they said he got a call from one of the sentries and went to check the perimeter. When I asked who made the call, none of them acknowledged it."

Remare took out his phone and pressed the button for Tristan. "No answer." He'd no sooner ended the call when his phone rang. Checking the ID, he said, "Tristan, good, we were worried about you."

"As you should be. It's not safe to wander alone in the woods." The voice on the other end of the call was loud and clear enough for Bastien and her to hear.

"Gideon! You fuck! What did you do with my man?"

"He's safe. For tonight, anyway. Acton wants to see you. Meet me at our usual place in London. We have things to discuss."

"I'm warning you," Remare snarled, "if any harm comes to Tristan, I will personally remove your head from your neck."

Gideon chuckled. "You can try. Tomorrow. Noon. Don't be late. I'd say come alone, but we both already know you won't. Neither will I. Ta."

Remare was seething in rage when Herbert entered. "My men told me you were having trouble locating Tristan."

"Gideon has him. I have to go to London to meet with him."

"I'll come with you," Herbert said.

"You can't. After meeting with Gideon, I'm going to Acton's stronghold in Leeds. More than likely that's where they're holding him."

"Bloody hell! Don't tell me what I can and cannot do!" Herbert was livid. "This is my fucking territory!"

Remare turned to him. "You can't enter another lord's lands fully armed. It will seem like an invasion. The High Court will reprimand you. They could seize your properties."

Herbert seemed to consider Remare's words. "At least let me accompany you to London. It's my kingdom, I know it better than anyone."

"No." Remare put his hand on his friend's shoulder. "This is between Gideon and me. You're safer here, and I won't endanger you."

"You're not endangering me. I'm volunteering. You and your people are invited guests. They're under my protection. If Gideon took Tristan, he has me to answer to."

"Gideon knows this. That's why I know Tristan is already in Leeds or soon will be."

Miranda volunteered, "This smells like a trap, and you know it."

"Of course it is. That's why I'm leaving, now, to scope out the place." He turned toward Bastien. "Arm up. You're coming with me."

Bastien nodded. "Sure thing. Orion?"

Remare shook his head. "He's still healing. And I want him here with Miranda."

Bastien left to gather his stuff.

Herbert insisted, "You'll take a dozen of my guards with you. And many more will be waiting for your orders in London."

Remare grinned. "Seems like old times."

"Meet me down in the communications room before you go."

After they left, Remare retrieved his luggage from the closet and undid the false bottom. An array of guns and knives gleamed in the light. *How in hell's name did he get all that through customs?*

"I don't like this. I want to come with you." Her body was vibrating with quiet rage. She remembered the stories he'd told her of Acton's abuse when he'd served the cruel lord.

"No." He unbuttoned his shirtsleeves to fasten the knife sheathes to his arms, A gun went in one of his boots. Inside his suit jacket, he hid several throwing stars and more knives. "The last thing I want is for Gideon or Acton to meet you. They would only hurt you to get to me. Stay here."

"I have powers, Remare. I can help you."

"New powers you're only beginning to learn. I won't endanger my wife." He held her arms. "Trust me to know what I'm doing. I've planned tactics and strategies for centuries."

"In someone else's territory?"

"Yes. Many times. I'll be all right."

"Acton wants you. He took Tristan so you'd follow. He doesn't know what my powers are. I can help you," she pleaded.

"He may at that. While you slept, Valadon texted me that Eric informed him Vivienna knew of your powers. She spied on you when you were in Paris. She's Gideon's lover. More than likely, Acton and Gideon are aware of your powers."

Miranda groaned. She thought she felt eyes on her when she'd been alone with Eric.

He ran his knuckles down her face. "You have no idea what he would do to you if he captured you. I do. I assure you it's not pretty. He would do unspeakably ugly things I simply cannot permit to happen."

"Mulciber had me for a day imprisoned in his cell. Do you think that was pretty?"

"And you suffered because of it. Not this time."

As Remare finished arming himself, Bastien must have informed Orion he wasn't going either because they heard the argument erupting next door.

Miranda accompanied Remare to Herbert's library and the door at the far end of the room, and to the staircase that led below. The huge underground bunker resembled NASA's control center with dozens of computers and several large screens. It reminded her of Valadon's tech-heavy communications room. So, this was where Herbert kept an eye on his empire and his army of soldiers. On the massive overhead screen was a map of London. A red dot hung over the destination point. Other smaller dots lined outlying areas.

Herbert pointed to the red markers. "This is where my personal army is located. I keep them in several areas as London is so spread out. I've already sent to your phone the contact information, should you need it. Winnie will accompany you to London and points north, but not enter Lord Acton's territory. That is non-negotiable."

Winnie grinned at Remare. "Things have been quiet for too long; I was wondering when they'd pick up."

From the bulges under her jacket, Miranda knew she was also well-armed.

Remare nodded to her.

"These are the most current photos we have of Castle Acton." Winnie gestured to the screen. "Note the various entrances and exits. His receiving room is located on the main floor, but he likes to entertain his guests in his dining room on the second floor. Acton always had a taste for weapons, and this room is decked out with antiques and modern-day armaments."

Remare studied the board as if memorizing it, then checked his phone as Bastien entered with a frustrated Were behind him. When it looked like Orion was going to protest, Remare held up a hand. "Not this time. Stay here and guard Miranda. You wish to be a Torian, someday? Learn to accept orders without question." He turned toward her. *"I'll return to you with Tristan. Don't let Orion do something stupid."*

"I wasn't planning to."

He kissed her quickly then exited with Bastien. Miranda could feel the anger radiating from Orion.

After they were gone, Herbert invited her into the library as Orion accompanied them to the cars.

Herbert joined her by the window. She asked, "Will they be safe?"

"Remare and I led many expeditions into enemy territories during wartime. He knows what he's doing. If he weren't so damned loyal to Lord Valadon, I would have had him as my second."

"Why does Lord Acton want Remare so badly?"

"He hates him. Remare humiliated him long ago. Some vampires harbor old grudges for centuries."

"All this because Remare left his territory without permission?! Excuse me, but it seems ludicrous. You'd think he'd get over it by now."

After Remare and the others drove off, Herbert sat at his desk. "It was a bit more entailed than simply leaving."

Miranda turned toward Herbert as he lit his pipe. "How so?"

"You have to remember it was the ancient Romans who once conquered England. Remare's father, Remel, was one of the commanders who subjugated the English people. As with all wars, there was much fighting and bloodshed. The fact that Remel also protected them against northern invaders didn't seem to register. He was a foreigner who reported to Rome. Many Englishmen resented him and the presence of the Roman forces and the money they extorted from the citizens. Not only was there much loss of life, but loss of finance."

Miranda processed what Herbert was telling her. "Remel married an Englishwoman, Remare's mom."

"Unfortunately, Remare takes after his father with his Mediterranean looks. The fact that he is half English didn't seem to matter."

"They can hardly attribute any atrocities committed by the father against Remare."

"To a point, you are right. But there is more." Herbert exhaled smoke from his pipe. "Centuries ago, when the former lord of London died and a new lord was to be appointed, there were several choices to consider. But it came down to Acton and myself. Acton was older, so he, as well as others, thought he should be so named."

"Not to be."

"Not quite." Herbert's grin took on an edge. "Acton may have been older with certain allies on the High Court, but *I* had something more valuable."

"Such as?"

"Commerce." He puffed on his pipe. "The revenue I was able to generate with trade with the European countries, as well as other places, impressed the members of the High Court more. They still continue to receive a substantial amount from me. That, along with Remare's testimony of abuse in Acton's court, put the vote in my favor. Acton has never forgiven him. Or me, for that matter."

"And you're okay with Winnie accompanying Remare knowing this."

He laughed. "Don't let Winnie's slender physique mislead you. She's as deadly as Remare when needs be."

Miranda had trouble imagining Winnie in warrior mode, but she supposed it was possible. "I'm feeling a little tired. Would you mind if I lay down for a while?"

"Of course. I promise I'll let you know when I hear back from them."

"Thank you."

Chapter Twenty-Seven

Miranda was on her way to Orion's room when she spotted the tawny owl on her window sill. As she entered her room, the owl morphed into human form.

"Esme!" She secured the door behind her. "What are you doing here? Now is not a real good time."

"Your eyes are healed. I knew they would be. I've come to say goodbye. Agatha was incensed that you didn't tell her you were married to a vampire. She's forbidden any of us to have any further dealings with you."

Oh, really! "I'll have words for her when I see her next."

"She's moving all the crystals to another location. You're no longer welcome among the coven. I tried to reason with her, but she wouldn't hear it."

"Esme. I need to ask you a question, and I want an honest answer."

"I've always been truthful. What is it?"

"Did you see how I was blinded?"

"You were near the fire, an ember broke loose and flew into your eyes."

"Yeah, I'm beginning to wonder about that. Did you see anyone leaning toward the fire? Maybe see someone throw something into the flames to make it ignite that way?"

"What are you saying?"

"The wounds on each eye," she gestured to them, "were identical. I don't believe it was accidental. I think one of the other *Elementals* did something to the fire."

"No. That's impossible! No one would do that."

"Think not? Did you know Vicky was friends with Lord Acton in Northern England? He sponsored her in London.

Helped pay for her flat and her salon. Want to tell me, again, no one would hurt me?"

Esme gasped. "Are you certain?" She shook her head in amazement. "This can't be."

"It is, *sistah!* Get a clue."

"What are you going to do about it?"

"Right now, I'm on my way to London." Miranda stared at Esme. "But, first, I need your help with something."

"What?"

"Show me how to transmogrify."

"I can't, Miranda. It takes years of practice and intense concentration. You're not nearly ready enough for that."

"Try me. And, before you say no, know this. I've already done it once before."

Her intake of breath was almost comical. "How? When?"

"Don't ask. A long time ago. When I was studying petroglyphs out in New Mexico. Someone used black stones and chants to change me. I flew as an eagle. My memory is a little hazy, thought I dreamt it or had too much to drink. Now, I'm sure that wasn't the case."

"Only another *Elemental* could do that to you."

"Yeah, I'm beginning to think so. A *Dark Elemental.* Black hair, black feathers." *William.* She went to get a fresh shirt out of her closet, discarding the worn one.

Esme pointed at her. "Miranda! My God, you've got an eagle tattooed on your back. He marked you!"

"Yeah, I woke up with it. He had one the width of his back. I thought nothing of it at the time. Only that it looked so incredibly real."

"So does yours. The eyes are eerie. Golden."

Miranda finished buttoning her shirt. "Shall we get started?"

"There are risks involved, Miranda. I may not be able to complete the process. You could wind up stuck in bird form."

Her lids lowered. "I'll risk it. My husband is meeting with some very nasty people. He's putting his life on the line to protect one of his own. I can do the same for him."

Esme rubbed her head as if conflicted. "If I do this, I only do it once. And you can't blame me if something goes wrong."

"I won't." Miranda wasn't sure where her sense of confidence was coming from. She only knew she had to be with Remare.

"Do you still have the crystals I gave you?'

"You mean the ones that magically appeared in my bag?" Miranda raised an eyebrow as she retrieved her bag and gathered up the crystals.

"They were a gift."

"Thanks. Let's get started."

***

Miranda knocked on Orion's door and then entered. He was shirtless, working out with some dumbbells. Sweat was pouring off his skin. The frustration and anger that were etched in his face was now replaced with surprise and confusion.

"What did you do to your hair?"

"I thought I'd try a change." Fact was, when she attempted the transformation, pretty much all that had been altered was the color of her hair. *Some Elemental!* She'd been arrogant in thinking she could do what others took years to learn. She now had black hair with two golden streaks down the front. "How's the leg?"

"It's fucking fine. I tried to tell Bastien I was completely healed, but he wouldn't listen to me. How's your vision?"

"Pretty good." Actually, it was better than before she was blinded. She leaned against the doorframe. "I don't know about you, but I don't dance in anyone's shadow."

One corner of his mouth rose in conspiratorial solidarity. "Yeah, I don't sing backup in anyone's opera either."

"Did you get a good look at Herbert's map of London?"

"Yeah, I did."

"Feel like a little reconnaissance?"

"When do we leave?"

"Now."

"Remare's going to be pissed."

"Let him. If he wanted someone to follow his orders, he should have married someone else. Besides, I'm not one of his Torians."

"Apparently, neither am I."

When they left the mansion, Miranda quickly donned her sunshades, her eyes more irritated than usual by the sun. They looked both ways to see if any of Herbert's guards would stop them from leaving. Herbert met them himself. "Where are you off to?"

"I wanted to show Orion the stables. We could both use the fresh air."

Herbert scrutinized her hair. "Will you be riding today?"

Orion answered. "No, we're just going for a walk."

"All right, then. If you change your minds, ask Milton to assist you with the saddles." Before he turned and entered the castle, she thought a smile crossed his face.

They turned the corner toward the stables. "Ah, Miranda, the cars are all gone."

"Not a problem. Our ride is over that hill." She pointed.

Esme was waiting with her car. Her jaw dropped when she saw Orion.

She made the introductions. "Orion, Esme."

"Mind if I drive?" Orion asked.

"No. Not at all." Esme handed Orion her key fob with the owl.

"Next stop, London."

***

From the comfort of his Bentley, Remare scrutinized Gideon's choice of meeting place. It had been decades since he'd visited The Black Horse Tavern. Unfortunately, the last time he'd been here, one of his men had been killed in a fight. Except for a few renovations, the place hadn't changed much. The sign over the door swung as the original had, but this one included the image of a black stallion, as well as the bar's name. "Send Kyle and Bruce to scout out the interior."

"Done." Bastien texted each with Remare's orders. "Can Gideon be trusted?"

"Not usually, no. But I want to hear what he has to say before I slit his throat."

"What about Tristan?"

"He's still alive. Lord Acton does enjoy his games. Right now, he's probably toasting himself believing we're imagining the worst possible torture for Tristan."

"Would he be right?"

"Whatever hurts he has visited on Tristan, I will inflict ten times as much on him."

"Bruce texted he believes a man sitting in the back booth is Gideon."

"How many are inside?"

"Including the bartender, twelve."

"I knew he wouldn't wait until noon. Stay here." Remare made his way to the tavern. Once inside the bar, he stood near Gideon's booth.

Gideon smirked. "I'd say good to see you, again, Remare, but we both know it would be a lie."

Remare sat across from him. "Likewise. Why did you want to see me?"

"I was hoping to meet your pretty wife. I hear she's quite extraordinary. The rumors concerning her abilities have been reaching our shores for some time now."

Remare stifled a growl and wondered just how much the Madame Lord of Paris knew of Miranda's gifts. "My wife is of no concern to you. Leave her out of this."

"She's of little consideration to me." Gideon drank his beer. "However, Acton's taken quite an interest in her after hearing reports from Magritte herself."

"Continue."

"Magritte was offended that Vivienna wasn't able to snare Valadon as a husband. Our reigning queen has long wanted ValCorp." He swallowed more of his beer. "My money was always on Valadon."

"Tell me something I don't know, Gideon, or I'm walking."

"Impatience? That's not like you, Remare. You always had that icy control about you."

"I still do, but I bore easier, now." When a server approached them, Remare waved her off.

"Then, I won't waste either of our time. Acton has long desired another *Elemental*. He had one years ago until she, one day, disappeared."

"Esmerelda. I heard he had her killed because she left him."

Gideon sat up straight. "What did you know of Esmerelda?"

"That she was Leland's lover, and once he was away at sea, Acton insinuated himself in her life. Seduced her with lies and deceptions about Leland's supposed death. I've read her diaries. She grew to hate the monster, her life with him, and planned to leave him."

Gideon's eyes were downcast. "Esmerelda was like no other woman I've ever known. She was good of heart. Far too good for Acton. When I saw he was draining her dry, I knew he would kill her. He fed too often and too much."

"Did you order her execution?"

"Me? No! Never. I was fond of the woman." His fists tightened. "I wanted her free of him. I'm the one who helped her escape."

"Why, because she was pregnant with Acton's child?"

"Pregnant?! That's impossible. Acton's sterile. She couldn't possibly be..."

Remare sat back in his seat, realization hitting home. "You were her lover. Did Acton find out? Is that why he had her killed?"

"How would you know if she was pregnant?"

"As I said, I've read her diaries. And a few of her letters. She was supposed to be Herbert's sister-in-law. Leland damned near drank himself to death when he found out she'd taken up with Acton."

"I knew she'd been heartbroken when I met her. She was easy prey for a predator like Acton. I loved Esmerelda. Even though I knew she did not feel the same about me, I loved her anyway. That's why I helped her escape to London. I gave her the finances she would need for the trip. She wanted to return home to Venice. At least that's what she told me. She was not going to last long with Acton."

"From what I read, I believe she was murdered. I'm not sure where or by whom."

"Did she make it to Venice?"

Remare shook his head. He was not going to discuss Miranda's dreams and her beliefs how Esmerelda had died. "The details are sketchy. But I don't think she ever made it back there. Now, tell me why I'm really here."

Gideon blew out a breath. "Acton wants your woman. He wants another *Elemental.*"

Remare's eyes iced over as he contemplated all the ways he would kill Acton. "He'll never get his hands on Miranda."

"Don't be too sure of that. Acton has a way of getting what he wants. And what he wants most is to be chancellor."

"Chancellor?! He thinks to challenge Caltrone?! He's a fool; Caltrone has the majority of the High Council in his pocket."

"Don't underestimate him. He's been sleeping on and off with Magritte for years and wooing members of the High Council. Can you imagine the state of the Vampire Nation if he was appointed?"

"What's your stake in all this? If Acton became chancellor, you would become his chief advisor. Power and glory. A rather large step for someone of your background, wouldn't you say?"

"If I were that ambitious." He leaned forward and grinned. "I have a proposal for you. Something we can all benefit from."

"I'm listening."

***

After following Remare and Bastien to London, Miranda and Orion sat silently in the car, observing. She turned to Orion. "Can you pick up his scent from here?"

"I would know it blindfolded. Oh, you mean Remare? Yeah, his, too."

"How much further to Castle Acton?" she asked Esme.

"Usually, it takes three or three and a half hours, but the way Orion drives, I think we can make it to Leeds in three."

Miranda pointed. "Look, they're leaving, now. Give them a head start then follow."

They continued on for hours until they were within sight of Leeds. "Orion, change form. See if you can track them." Miranda moved into the driver's seat.

"All right. Let me strip down in the back."

Esme quickly slipped into the front passenger seat. Neither one wanted to watch as Orion removed his clothes before morphing into a wolf, but Orion's body was nearly perfect. Sleek skin over solid muscle. It was hard not to notice. Nearly impossible. For either of them.

Esme exhaled as they watched him lope to the castle. "He certainly is handsome."

Miranda smirked knowingly. "In wolf form or human?"

"Both. I love his music."

"Yeah, so do I. He hopes one day to play at Albert Hall. Seriously, Esme, you don't have to do any more. You already took a great risk in getting us here."

"Are you kidding? This is the most fun I've had in...ever."

"Listen to me. Some of my husband's associates are...murderous. I won't ask you to get any more involved."

"Understood. What do you need me to do?"

"Use extreme caution. But can you transmute to owl form and take a gander inside the windows of the castle. Let me know what's going on?"

"I can, and I will. Unlike Weres, *Elementals* don't have to strip down. Our clothes morph with us."

Good to know! Esme's body shimmered into an owl and flew out the car window toward the castle. Miranda tapped her fingers on the steering wheel and hoped she knew what she was doing. Waiting was always the hard part; something that was growing increasingly difficult to do.

Turned out she didn't have to wait long when a vampire pressed a revolver to her window. "Get out."

Chapter Twenty-Eight

If waiting had been arduous, keeping her emotions contained was even more challenging as she was marched into Lord Acton's home. Miranda could feel her power simmering just beneath her skin, pulsating with vibrancy. But she breathed deep, focused her concentration, and buried her rising energy within her oubliette. Now that she knew the key to unlocking her psychic abilities, she'd call upon it if the situation warranted it. No need to let Acton and his minions become aware of what she was harboring.

Lord Acton's castle was as grim as she'd imagined it. The vampire lord liked his weapons and showcased them throughout. The interior was as gray and uninviting as the exterior. Dark English oak paneled the walls with banners bearing crests of lions. Black cast iron chandeliers and sconces hung in the foyer. She tried to examine the paintings hanging on the walls as Acton's men escorted her upstairs to the main dining room.

The formidable Lord Acton sat at the head of a table long enough for twenty people. Guards lined the walls on either side of him. His long, wavy white hair framed a face reminiscent of a skull. His dark, deeply set gray eyes were the same color of his suit. No warmth radiated from his form, only icy cold that could freeze the Sahara. But it was his arrogant sneer that defined him. Vanity to the ninth degree. In that one expression, she saw evil. A thing that had worshipped power so much, for so long, anything remotely resembling humanity was now devoid in his being.

In the recesses of her mind, she remembered the chilling tales Remare had told her of the abuses he suffered at the monster's hands. Disgust and a desire for vengeance burned within her. The darkness within stirred. She held it at bay.

Another memory surfaced of a different monster. Mulciber had had a similar look, but the ancient had become deranged over his long years, and his actions were chaotic and unbalanced. Not so with Acton. He lauded himself with his control, his ability to manipulate people. He thrived on it. As if people were his private puppets to do his bidding when and how he wished.

She'd come to understand fear was his weapon of choice. He wielded it wherever and whenever it suited his purpose, held those close to him in check with it, fed on it. With his penetrating gaze, he learned his adversaries' weaknesses, their darkest fears, and used it against them. And destroyed anyone who might challenge his sovereignty.

Like he had with Esmerelda and Leland. Miranda could feel Esmerelda's tears falling as she wept for all that had been lost. So much pain and sorrow because of one man's vanity. A true monster.

Miranda tilted her head in a birdlike manner. Somewhere in the castle, she sensed Remare's presence. Through their blood bond, she could hear him cursing Gideon for betraying him. He was engaged in battle with Acton's men, swords clashing, bodies falling to the ground. Blood was being spilt.

Miranda's eyes flew to Tristan who was seated on Acton's right. His face was a study in pain. He was shirtless to show where Acton had tortured him with silver shards embedded in his chest and arms. Bloody streaks covered his body. The bastard had even implanted shards in Tristan's handsome face. A trickle of sweat rolled down his brow, not only from the searing agony of the implants, but from the device Acton had rigged on the back of his neck. Should Tristan tire and lean forward the sharp edges would slash his spine, killing him instantly.

Miranda wanted to feel pity and sympathy for Tristan. What was once human in her screamed internally at the injustice. But, strangely enough, she was calm, numbed by all she was seeing. Her heart had turned to stone, swallowed by the darkness that lived within and was creeping its way to her vanguard.

Aware her movements resembled that of an eagle, she amended her stance. She needed to be cold for what she was planning. She wished she could speak to Tristan mentally, but they'd never shared blood. She'd reassure him this would all be over soon. Instead, she systematically loosened the silver chains that bound him to the chair in slight degrees so as not to arouse the suspicion of the others.

Something primal had awoken within her, demanding release. Something dangerous. She knew people had dark places in their psyches, but Miranda thought hers went deeper than most. That well of unforgiving light where she buried her power was brewing. Her oubliette offering her daunting, unimaginable possibilities.

The thing at the end of the table that called himself lord spoke as someone pushed her into the chair at the other end of the table so she could face the monster responsible for so much hell.

She scanned the room. Behind him, Caron's painting hung on the wall, *The Book of Origins*. Even at this distance, with her improved sight, she could make out the title of one of the books in the painting: Draxton. She exhaled slowly. Above the huge stone fireplace with the twin carved lions was the forged Vermeer painting she'd been called to the London museum to validate. She snorted. The fiend had played her from the very beginning. It had all been a ruse to get her here. Acton never had any intention of selling it. He smirked as recognition flickered across her face.

"Professor Crescent. Remare's wife." He played with a bolt from the miniature crossbow on the table. "Welcome to Castle Acton. Ever since I heard Remare had married, I wondered what type of woman he would take as a wife. Imagine my surprise to hear you were human."

Miranda didn't respond to the creature. The darkness was quickly spreading through her. Her body open in willing acceptance. She used to get nosebleeds from trying too hard to harness the energy within. Now, she knew how to let it flow freely through her system. Inwardly smiling, she no longer feared the primal being of power; she welcomed it.

Acton continued, "But you're not quite human, are you? *Elemental.*"

Miranda gestured with her chin to the painting in the corner as she silently and stealthily unwound the device behind Tristan's neck.

"Esmerelda. A fine woman. An *Elemental* like you. Her blood was the purest I've ever tasted. Her power incredible. She served me well until she decided she wanted to leave. I would never allow that to happen. You see, she belonged to me. I let her think she could escape me. Let her taste the freedom she so thoroughly desired." His smile resembled a viper. "It wasn't difficult at all to bribe one of the coven to pollute the crystals she drew power from. She died screaming for her transgression."

Miranda felt the slightest of touches on her mind as if he were trying to clutch something that didn't belong to him. She'd already constructed walls of reinforced steel to block any psychic invasions. She didn't even need the crystals to accomplish that feat. Her mentor, Blu, had shown her how. Acton was a fool. He thought by staring into her eyes, he could capture her, possess her as he had others. He didn't know she was reflecting his own darkness back at him.

Acton yearned for her blood, hungered for it. He thought by drinking Esmerelda's blood, he would become more powerful. It hadn't worked that way. Right now, he was imagining sinking his fangs into Miranda's neck and drawing her life's essence into himself. She was envisioning wrapping coils of fire around him and watching him die the way Esmerelda had: Deceived, defeated, and destroyed.

A tawny owl flew to the window sill and perched. Esme, her other mentor and friend. Her gentleness and wisdom emanated from every fiber of her being.

Acton smiled and, in a depraved act of selfish indulgence, fired the bolt in the crossbow at Esme. Her screech of terror tore through the air as her body fell downward.

Miranda closed her eyes at the loss but didn't feel anything at the death of her friend. Why couldn't she feel? In her oubliette of shadows, emotion didn't exist. Instinct did. Logic and cool calculation dominated. Esme, of all the *Elementals*, had been closest to her, offered encouragement and enlightenment. Had opened doors to things Miranda thought impossible. Now, she was gone.

Miranda breathed deep. The darkness had enveloped her. Had she been a vampire, her fangs would have emitted. She could feel her eyes slowly turning black. Out in the hall, sounds of sword fighting grew louder. Remare and Acton's second, Gideon, were engaged in battle. Heated words were exchanged. Growls rent the air, and she knew Orion and Bastien weren't far behind.

Acton signaled for half of his men to deal with the noise. "Your lover is quite an accomplished sword master. But his talent won't be quite enough for my guards."

You're wrong there, buddy. She'd seen Remare fight nearly a dozen Rogues in a dark alley. He was unstoppable.

"Still so silent?" He took one of the bolts and slammed it through Tristan's hand. The young Torian grimaced in torment, his jaw straining, but he remained unmoving. "What will it take to hear your voice?"

A miracle. In a deadly calm voice that was not her own, Miranda said, "You wanted me here, Lord Acton." She allowed herself a slight grin. "Here I am." She'd heard that voice before. In the Catacombs in Paris, when she'd encountered Bastien's sister, Isabelle, and then later, when Remare's former lover, Irina, had tangled with her. "People should be more careful in what they wish for." Laughter erupted from her mouth. It should have scared her. It didn't. She'd been victorious in both battles. She would be, again. She waved one hand and sent her power streaming in Acton's direction. "Now, let me show you *exactly* what you wished for."

His hands froze to the table. He tried desperately to free himself; hatred, piercing and bright, appeared on his face, defiant of one more powerful than he. His well-honed pride faltered as realization hit. "Your eyes. They're black!" Fear, an uncommon emotion for Acton, grasped him, and he looked to his guards for support. Miranda raised her arm and slammed them high against the wall with a blink of her power where they remained bound by her energy.

She exhaled a tendril of black vapor and coiled it around Acton's neck. She wanted to see the blood pour out of him, watch as he realized there was no escape, watch as he screamed in terror as Esmerelda had. But, before Miranda could finish the evil lord off, something caught her eye.

A bird perched in the window. A large, black and golden eagle with the face and winged arms of a man. In his hands was a crossbow. He shot two bolts in quick succession at Acton's throat. The first one pinned his head to the chair, the second one went through his throat to sever his spinal cord, effectively killing him.

Miranda blinked and the eagle/man winked at her as he pursed his lips together in a kiss she could feel against her skin. Heart pounding, Miranda knew that face. In London, the alley outside the tavern, The Wanderer, again at the gathering of *Elementals* in Cranbrook. He was the guitar-playing man. But what had her heart beating faster were the beads he wore in his hair. Like her guide in New Mexico. *William!*

Another blink, and he was gone. Disappearing as suddenly as he'd arrived. Miranda ran to the window and gazed down to search for Esme's body, but there was nothing, only a solitary black feather with a golden filament.

"Halt!" someone yelled. Gideon. "The lord of Castle Acton is dead. Put down your weapons." The last of Acton's men lowered their arms.

Panting, Remare and Bastien rushed to free Tristan while Orion, still in wolf form, ran to her.

Miranda flew to Tristan and pulled the device from his neck and threw it against the wall as Remare carefully removed the bolt from Tristan's injured hand.

Remare stared at her black and gold hair. "We've been fighting for our lives, and you found time to go to the hairdressers?!"

She smiled. "A girl's gotta do what a girl's gotta do." She and Remare quickly removed the silver shards from Tristan's body.

Remare slit his wrist for Tristan to feed then glanced at her eyes. "Your eyes."

"Yeah, I know, black.

"No. They're gold and black. Like your hair."

Miranda exhaled, not knowing how to respond.

Remare bristled. "You were supposed to keep Orion from doing anything stupid."

Before she could reply, Tristan pulled away, grabbed Remare's sword and swung it at Acton's neck, completely decapitating the evil lord. His head flew into the fireplace.

Amidst their shock at his sudden action, Tristan then shoved the sword through Acton's heart. Miranda didn't want to imagine the hells Acton had visited on Tristan to make him react that way.

But she knew it must have been brutal.

"Well, now, he's truly gone and dead." Gideon snorted. "A bit of overkill, if you ask me, but more than likely deservedly so, I'd say." He studied his men hanging on the wall. "Bloody hell." He then turned to her. "Would you mind?"

Miranda closed her fist, and the men crashed to the floor.

Glancing at Tristan, who remained resolutely silent, Remare retrieved his sword and wiped the blood away on Acton's dead body.

"Understand this," she said to Remare, "I won't stand behind you. But I will stand beside you. Orion pretty much feels the same way about Bastien. Either we're partners...or we're not."

His eyes narrowed as he growled, then he grinned and grabbed the back of her neck with one hand and kissed her enthusiastically.

"Beautiful." Gideon clapped his hands then heaved Acton's body up and tossed it in the fire.

Miranda waved her hand, and the flames grew higher. When Gideon observed her, she made blue flames appear in her eyes and then smiled. His look of perturbation was worth it. As Acton's body burned in the fire, she thought she heard the song, "The Lion Sleeps Tonight," playing in the back of her mind.

Gideon nodded to Remare. "As the new Lord of Northern England, I invite you to leave my castle. I have much work to do and paperwork to file with the Council."

Miranda asked Remare, "Friend or foe?"

"Both," Remare said.

Once they were outside the castle, Miranda hunted for the fallen owl. "Can you have your men search for an injured owl? She's a friend of mine."

Remare nodded. "We can't linger long. The truce between Gideon and me may not hold. For now, he's gotten what he wanted. Time will only tell if we replaced one monster with another."

Orion nudged her leg with his snout and took off running. With his advanced sense of smell, he'd find Esme before anyone else. He knew her scent from being in the car with her.

After he'd been gone a while, Orion returned and shook his head. Miranda hoped Esme was able to heal herself, but Acton had been vicious with his aim. "What about her car? Should we leave it here or return it to Cranbrook?"

Remare signaled his men to return. "I'll have one of Herbert's men retrieve it."

Miranda looked around one more time for the owl and the eagle. Neither were to be found. "Okay." They made their way back to Herbert Manor.

***

"This will only take a moment." Miranda promised Remare when they reached Cranbrook. But she had to see Agatha one last time.

"I don't wait in cars...for my partner." He smiled— Cheshire cat style.

"You may have to, this time. *Elementals* don't like vampires. They fear you."

He seemed to consider her words. "I'll be close by."

Miranda walked around the side of Agatha's house. She had hoped she'd found her people among the *Elementals*. A bond she could share with others of her kind that she hadn't been able to do with the Weres or the vampires. Orion had felt left out, never truly belonging at his family home in the

Midwest or at Werehaven with the Weres. Now, he seemed to have found his tribe hanging with the vampires. They were his family. He belonged. She was happy for him.

Miranda sighed. She'd wondered, for so long, if others of her kind had existed. Now that she found them, she knew she didn't belong with them. As she turned the corner, she spotted Agatha by the fire pit where she'd been blinded.

"Ah, the chameleon returns."

Takes one to know one! Agatha knew. She'd always known. No wonder the others considered her their leader. Miranda hadn't known. She'd refused to see. Until Esme taught her how to open her third eye. She wouldn't make the same mistake, again.

"You survived. I'm glad."

"Are you? You set me up. You knew what I was. You needed someone to defeat Vicky. You wanted me to kill her so you wouldn't have to." The bitch didn't want it coming back on her. Killing one of their own kind wouldn't go over well with the others.

"She was a traitor."

No shit! "You knew who I was married to. You used us to defeat Lord Acton."

She smiled without the slightest bit of guilt. "Is that so wrong?"

"You fucking blinded me! You threw galena in the fire and used your power so that it flew into my eyes."

Agatha's voice turned harsh. "You refused to use your talents. Gifts so rarely given. You wouldn't invoke your third eye until you were blind to all else. Instead of being insolent, you should be thanking me."

Miranda wanted to strangle the older woman. "You thought Acton would eventually learn who you were. You accused me of living with fear when you, yourself, lived in fear of discovery."

"Esmerelda was my ancestor. She died because of that vicious vampire. He bribed one of the others with false promises to neutralize the crystals. She died in agony. I've heard her screams in my dreams for years."

Miranda believed Esmerelda feared for Agatha, her last surviving descendant, so she sought out another *Elemental*, a chameleon with vampire blood who could best Acton. She chose Miranda. As a seer, she must have known Miranda wouldn't fail.

Agatha's body was vibrating with anger. "Vicky's body was fished out of the Thames. Her throat had been torn open, her body depleted of blood. Fire *Elementals* don't do well in water."

Peralt had written that Elementals could die in elements other than their own.

Agatha continued, "She thought Acton would bestow riches upon her."

The Deceiver. "She was Acton's spy. You knew that and didn't stop her. You fed her what you wanted her to know."

"Vampires are evil creatures, Miranda. You know that, yet you bound yourself to one." Agatha seemed to be studying her. "You're going to let him turn you, aren't you? Pollute your God-given blood with his."

"If I do, that's my business. Speaking of blood, you need not have worried so much about Acton. He wasn't your long-lost great-grandfather. He wasn't searching for you."

"What do you mean?"

"Gideon told Remare Acton was sterile. He couldn't father children. Gideon took a shine to Esmerelda. Apparently, they had a relationship. An intimate one. Remare believes Gideon will now become Lord of Northern England. As far as I know, he knows nothing about you or your ancestry."

Agatha looked beguiled. "All these years, I believed Acton was my progenitor. Everything I read on her. She feared Acton. She thought he would corrupt her child."

"She must have surmised it would go worse for her if he ever found out she'd been sleeping with his second."

Agatha's face paled.

"There's one more thing. Esme's missing. She accompanied me to Leeds. We can't find her. Acton shot her with a crossbow while she was in owl form. Have you heard from her?"

She shook her head. "Our coven will suffer greatly if she is gone." Agatha stared up at Miranda. "You could join us. You're stronger than any of the other *Elementals*. I won't live for much longer. They could use your guidance, your leadership."

Miranda scoffed at the idea. She may have wanted a group to belong to, people she could call her own; these weren't them. "Not a chance. I came to say goodbye. I'm leaving to return home. My life, my career are back in New York."

"With him." She gestured to Remare, who was now standing at the edge of the lawn. "I would have thought you'd want to be with others of your kind. You were destined to be with family. Destined to be a great *Elemental.*"

"You're not my family." She turned to leave. "And I choose my own destiny."

"Wait. There's something else. Esme wanted you to see it."

"What?"

Chapter Twenty-Nine

Remare joined her outside the entrance to the cave. "I can go back to the car and retrieve a flashlight."

Miranda shook her head. "We won't need it."

Orion appeared beside them. "I thought you might need back-up."

"All right. Let's go in. Agatha said I'd know it when I saw it." Miranda led them inside, using her power to light the torches on the cave walls as they went. She took them to the crystal room, now devoid of the precious stones. "This is where they housed the crystals. It looked like a museum. There were specimens from around the world. Each more beautiful than the other in their radiance. Wondrous stones."

Orion asked, "And these crystals gave you power?"

"No. They only augment what someone is born with." As she examined an empty pedestal, Orion went off to explore the other sections of the cave.

"Are you sad, Mir-randa, to be leaving behind people of your kind?" Remare asked.

"Not really." She gazed around the empty chamber. "It's just that I wonder how much more I could have learned. I feel like I scratched the surface, that there was more knowledge to uncover."

He stroked her chin. "This is but one coven. There must be others. You'll find them or they'll find you." He smiled. "It's not the end."

"I know." She returned his smile.

"Hey, you guys should come take a look at this. I think I found something."

They followed Orion down a narrow corridor that felt eerily familiar. Flashes of Esmerelda's dreams began to echo in her mind. They entered the singing chamber where Esmerelda danced. "This is where she died. Esmerelda. She thought she'd escaped Acton, but he persuaded one of the other *Elementals* to betray her. The other *Elemental* switched the stones. She never saw it coming. The fire engulfed her and some of the others."

Miranda rubbed her arms as if she, too, had been consumed by the flames. *Be at peace, Esmerelda. Acton is dead. He cannot hurt you, anymore. Or your progeny.*

Orion said, "There was a police report that a woman's body was found near the bank of the Thames."

"I know. Victoria, a fire *Elemental*. According to Agatha, Acton bribed her with promises of great wealth if she spied on the coven, reported to him of those with superior powers."

Remare said, "Acton was one to learn the flaws of his prey early on. He'd use those weaknesses against them to his own advantage. He often discarded those who didn't please him or those whose usefulness he used up."

"Come, it's this way." Holding a torch, Orion led them around the grotto to another room with a large rock partially blocking the entrance.

Her skin turning cold, Miranda felt a slight tremor, "I don't think you should move the boulder, Orion. Someone put that there for a reason."

"Too late. I already crept on top and peeked in." He then moved the boulder away. "I think someone was living here."

As they entered the small room containing a makeshift bed, a table and chair and some old books, the decaying scent of mold and dust assaulted them. More images of Esmerelda reading, sewing, and singing appeared in her mind. "This is where Esmerelda hid after the innkeeper in town refused her. She thought she was safe here." Miranda examined what looked like had been an old jewelry box. The wood had rotted away from age and mildew.

"Hey, who's this guy, Thomas Draxton? She must have been reading him. Smells old." Orion lifted the cover before Miranda could stop him.

"No! Don't open it!" She screamed as the pages, rotten from the dank air, disintegrated as the air hit them. She dropped to her knees in frustration. The remnants of the book no more than scattered ashes.

Remare read the title engraved in the leather binding. "*The Book of Origins.* I'm sorry, Miranda." He lifted her up. "If there's one copy, then there's another. We'll find it."

Orion hugged her. "I'm so sorry, Miranda. I didn't know. It fell apart before I could close it."

"It's okay, Orion." Part of her didn't blame him. He hadn't known what he discovered or the value thereof. Another darker part of her was furious. She buried that part. Miranda glanced around. No wonder Esmerelda never claimed her child. This would have been no life for her. "We should go. There's nothing else here."

Orion held the torch up higher near the ceiling. "What are these?"

"Cave drawings." Miranda leaned in closer to the pictures. "Men in villages. Hunters. Women sewing some sort of material."

Remare nodded. "That looks like leather."

"And here." Orion pointed the torch at more drawings.

"Esmerelda, among her many talents, was an artist, as well. I think she drew what she read in Draxton's book." She gestured to the closest picture. "A man lying on a bed. Above him a burst of radiant sunlight. And, above that, an angel with wings flared."

Miranda counted the winged creatures. "There are four of them. In most of the Christian religions, they recounted stories of four archangels: Gabriel—the messenger; he supposedly represented the West and the element, water. His primary color was white. And here. Raphael—the healer, East, the air element and green for his color."

"How was she able to make these colors?" asked Orion. "It almost looks like they're glistening."

Miranda neared the drawings. "Look closer. I'm not sure they're painted." Her hand hovered over the image. "It's crushed crystals. She used the crystals to make the drawings."

"Who's the next one?" Orion asked.

"Uriel—wisdom. His color was red. North and the earth element."

Orion was mesmerized by the drawings. "How do you know all this?"

Remare answered. "While you were cavorting with Bastien, Miranda and I were immersed in studying old texts."

Miranda grinned when she heard Orion mumble, "I wasn't cavorting."

"Agatha told me stories. She believed the *Elementals* were the descendants of the angels, the dark ones as well as the light. Antediluvian times. Supposedly, they came down to watch over humans. Some commingled, produced offspring with incredible talents in weaponry, jewelry making and...sorcery. Through the centuries, the powers weakened with each succeeding generation. Kinda makes you wonder just how powerful the early *Elementals* were."

"And who's the last one? He's twice the size of the others." Orion asked.

Miranda was spellbound by the figure's glory and gazed at Remare. He answered for her. "That would be Michael, the Avenging Angel. See the sword in his hands. The most powerful of them all."

Miranda added. "The protector. He fought against evil in the angelic wars. Supposedly, instilled courage in others, taught them to let go of their fears. His direction was South, and his element was...fire. Blue was the color most associated with him."

She glanced down at her hand. Esme had told her that her aura was primarily blue with gold and violet striations. As well as some black ones.

"And you're supposedly a descendant from one of these?"

Miranda couldn't face Orion. "I don't know. They're only one person's theories."

Orion persisted. "I've seen your fire. It's blue. And you have more courage than any other female I know."

"Thanks, but I also have my fears. I've seen enough. We should leave."

Remare asked, "Which one do you believe might have been your progenitor?"

If she had to pick, she preferred to think of Raphael, the healer. Her hand helped heal people. But she was beginning to realize it may be another. And that scared her even more. "It doesn't matter. It's just a theory."

Orion pushed the boulder back into place after they exited the room.

As they started walking, the walls of the cave started violently shaking. Heart pounding, Miranda shouted, "My god, the cave is imploding!" The noise was thunderous as stalactites fell and shattered all around them. They ran for the exit as crevasses opened up and rocks started pouring down on them. Orion was swift on his feet and ran ahead, clearing their path.

Remare scooped her up and threw her over his shoulder as they made their way past the grotto. She thought she saw the spirit of Esmerelda smiling as she waved goodbye. Miranda raised her hand to return the gesture, but the ground split open, and Remare jumped high and far to cross the chasm. More debris of the cave rained down on them, and Miranda used her power to keep the deadly projectiles at bay.

They passed the narrow passage, but when they neared the opening, the cave floor crashed downward. Frantically, she searched for an alternate exit. There was none. They were trapped inside, until suddenly, a burst of air shot them across the wide divide, and they flew out the exit just as the cave collapsed.

Once outside, Miranda coughed up some of the dirt that had gotten in her throat. "Being thrown over a shoulder like a sack of potatoes is not the romantic gesture it's cracked up to be."

Remare cocked his head. "I'm sorry, what were you planning on doing? Conjuring a broom and flying out?

Miranda's Dark Angel asked, *"Did he just call you a witch?!"* Her Light Angel giggled. *"At least he didn't call you the B word."*

She narrowed her eyes at Remare and calmly flipped him the bird.

Remare's sarcastic expression quickly turned to one of surprise. His brow rose then he scoffed; he turned and made for the car.

Her Dark Angel started chuckling as Orion rolled on his back and joined in the laughter. "Shit, Miranda, I think you're the only person on the planet who can do that and get away with it with all your appendages intact."

"Just because I can conjure fire, doesn't mean I'm a witch. I'm not."

Orion looked suspiciously at her.

"I'm not!"

He shrugged and raised his hands in a gesture of surrender.

When they reached the lawn, Agatha was nowhere to be found. She was gone. Making good on her promise to move the coven where no vampires would find them.

Chapter Thirty

Remare filled Lord Herbert in on the details of what went down at Castle Acton. At her request, Remare didn't bring up Cranbrook. Herbert raised a brow at their disheveled appearance but didn't ask any questions. When they were about to leave, Herbert requested she stay for a few minutes. He handed her a box. "After you left, I went through some of Leland's things we had packed up long ago. This is a necklace he bought in one of his travels. He had wanted to give it to Esmerelda. But he never got the chance. I'd like you to have it."

Miranda admired the old-fashioned designs of swirling gold with a ruby at its center. It was exquisite. Leland had wanted Esmerelda to know she held his heart. "He wanted Esmerelda to have it."

"Yes, but since that is impossible, I think you should have it. She would have wanted you to wear it."

Miranda knew better than to deny her host this offering. But, still, it felt wrong to accept such an exquisite piece of jewelry.

At her hesitation, Herbert added, "Consider it my wedding present to you."

Miranda smiled. "I'd be honored." She now had four different necklaces given to her by prominent men. Blu had given her blood amber, Valadon, black diamonds, and Remare had given her sapphires and diamonds. No contest which one was her favorite. "Thank you."

Once upstairs, she jumped in the shower, eager to wash off the dust from the cave-in. The shower had six heads, and the hot water felt like heaven. Apparently, Remare thought she needed help in finding every molecule of dirt and joined her in the shower.

He kept her facing forward as he massaged shampoo into her scalp, and Miranda shivered. Not from his touch, which was always exciting, but to turn her hair back to its regular chestnut color. Feeling his hands weave through her hair as he rinsed the shampoo away was relaxing. She leaned her back against his chest. "I can get used to this."

"I should be upset with you for following me to Acton's castle." His voice was melodic and sexy. "But, mostly, I'm relieved you are unharmed." He kissed her neck, and Miranda felt a jolt of heat rush through her. Her breaths escalated.

"I couldn't stay away. You're just going to have to resolve yourself to the idea I'm not a damsel in distress. I can take care of myself."

His fingers traveled down her spine to caress her butt.

"I know this." He poured liquid soap into his palms and started washing her arms and back. Every stroke of his hands made her quiver. "But there are certain lines that delineate what constitutes your work and what is mine."

"Don't ask me to sit by if I think you're in danger. I won't do it."

"Then, we shall have to work out the parameters in how you will assist." His fingers slid around her waist to cup her breasts then pinch her nipples. She was pretty sure no dust was there, but she wasn't about to stop him.

"Parameter away, baby." She turned and kissed him. If they were going to be partners, there were a few things he was going to have to get used to. Her hand fell to his groin and massaged his cock. "I think you'll find I'm pretty good at assisting."

A low growl escaped his throat.

"Is this a parameter?" She bent down and licked him from navel to groin. She knew how her tongue drove him crazy. "If it is, I must warn you." A long swirl of her tongue. "I have every intention of crossing it."

His hands tightened on her hair as she took him deep into her mouth while her fingers gently massaged his balls. When he could take no more, he raised her up by the shoulders and shoved her against the tile. Remare lifted her hips until he was pressed against her core. Within seconds he was sheathed by her velvety warmth.

"I'm not sure," she teased, "but I think you just breached one of my lines."

His voice was throaty, hungry with need. The red rims around his irises pulsed with pleasure. "This is mine, Mirranda. All mine."

"Then, by rights, this is mine." She squeezed him with her inner muscles.

"It is. But, if you don't let go, I won't be able to move inside you."

Her legs locked behind him, she slid down the length of him. "Heaven." She buried her face in his neck and licked his throat then sucked on his vein. She heard him cursing in Italian while trying to maintain his rhythm.

His thrusts quickened as raw need rode them hard. Their hearts beat as one as she stared into his eyes and saw the truths of their relationship. So much passion, so much shared intimacy. He was truly hers as much as she was his. She could imagine no other doing to her what he so easily did. He called her his sorceress, but he didn't know he was her spell caster, weaving wave after wave of pleasure through her. Her head was swimming with it.

Remare liked to take her to new heights and let her crest. He wanted her to enjoy their lovemaking as much as he did and kept the passion building until they were both drunk on sensation. Miranda thought she would burst from the sheer joy of it. Just once she wanted to see him come before she did.

Both were straining in a battle of wills not to come until the other did. Miranda didn't think she could last much longer. Her heart was hammering against her ribs and her body trembling with so much built up energy. Damn! This was one contest she could never win. Her vampire had too much expertise, too much damned patience and skill. He seemed to know her thoughts and chuckled.

She screamed out his name as a current of ecstasy rolled through her, draining the last of her vitality. She went limp in his arms as he thrust once more, then twice and growled out her name. "Sorceress." His breath was ragged. "No other woman has ever done to me what you do."

She was afraid both of them would sink to the tile floor, but his arms, steadfast as ever, held her up. A moment later, he shut off the water and carried her to the seat in front of the vanity. "Bastien knocks. Let me see what he wants." He grabbed a towel and swung it around his hips. She'd been so enthralled in the moment, she never heard the knocking. She could hear their voices through the door.

"It's Tristan. It may be nothing, but I thought you should know. He burned his clothes in the fireplace. He's been in the shower for forty-five minutes. He never takes that long."

Remare sighed. "Did he say anything?"

"No, but when I went in to check on him, his back was swollen with welts. Like he'd been whipped."

Miranda's gut clenched. Remare had told her what a sadistic bastard Acton had been in the past. Evidently, he hadn't changed through the centuries. Her heart ached for Tristan. He was the youngest of the Torians, the most vulnerable. His physical scars would heal. It was the internal ones that lingered.

Remare's voice was subdued. "I'll speak with him later."
She heard the door close and went to him. "Tristan."

"Yeah. I suspected he'd suffered some horror with the
way he decapitated Acton. He has a quiet fury raging inside
him. It will take time to subside."

There was no need for words. Miranda and he knew
Tristan had suffered miserably at the hands of Acton. "I'll be
ready in a few minutes. It doesn't take me long to pack."

"Good. The sooner we leave, the better."

***

After they said their goodbyes to the Herberts, they were
on their way back to London. Remare had already contacted
his pilot to be ready with their flight plans. Bastien, Orion
and Tristan rode in the Range Rover, Remare and she in the
Bentley. Miranda pointed to the bake shop in Rye. "Can we
stop for a moment? I want to get some scones for the trip
back."

"Certainly. I'll contact Bastien to go on ahead. We'll meet
them at the airport."

While at the bake shop, she saw the funeral procession
pass by and wondered if that was Alice Gordon's hearse. She
asked the girl behind the register, who confirmed it. "Where's
the cemetery?"

"Not far. Two blocks down and one over. It's behind the
old church."

Miranda signaled to Remare, who was waiting in the car.
He joined her. "I want to say goodbye to Mrs. Hastings. She
was kind to me with my research. I feel bad that she lost her
sister."

"The authorities closed the case. They could not find
evidence that it was pre-meditated murder, so they are
labeling it an unsolved burglary with unintentional death."

Miranda didn't buy it, but either way, the woman was
still dead. Remare accompanied her up the hill to the

cemetery. The sky was growing darker, and the mist was thick in the air. She would not go any closer because the ceremony looked to be family members only.

Harry, the delivery boy, noticed them and moved in their direction. He had a black eye and his arm was in a sling.

"Good Lord, Harry, were you in a car crash?" she asked.

"No. A couple of days ago, when Gemma was in London, someone broke into the bookstore." He shrugged. "Nothing was taken from what we could see, but her papers were rifled through. I must have surprised the burglar when I went back to make sure I locked up, and he punched me in the eye. I broke my arm when I fell down the outside stairs. He ran off."

"Can you describe him?" Remare's voice was coldly analytical.

"It was pretty dark out. Medium height and build. Dark hair. That's about all I can remember. I didn't get a real good look at him."

Miranda thought she heard Remare grinding his molars.

"However, I did find this at the base of the stairs." He handed Miranda a lapel pin—a triangle with a cross in the center. Soldiers of the HOL wore that insignia.

She handed it to Remare, who tightened his fingers around it. "Thank you for telling us. May I keep this?"

"Sure thing. I have no use for it. We filed a police report, but since nothing was taken, there wasn't much they could do. They said the pin could have been dropped by anyone."

Remare gazed around. "Have there been any other break-ins in the neighborhood?"

"No. That's the weird part. No one else reported any other disturbances. Rye is a pretty small town. We usually don't get strife like in the bigger cities. Will you join us after the ceremony?"

Miranda answered. "No, I'm afraid not, Harry. We're on our way back to London."

"All right, then. It was a pleasure meeting you."

They watched as Harry made his way back to the small circle of friends. Clouds began to gather and she could feel rain coming soon. "That's the emblem of the HOL."

"I know. They were searching for something. Either they found it or realized she no longer had it."

"The book her sister sent to me in care of Gemma."

"I think so."

Miranda was giving the tome to Valadon as soon as they got back to New York. No way was she holding on to something so dangerous. He could keep it in his archives or in his vault. She was about to turn away when something caught her eye.

A man who held Gemma's arm escorted her under the canopy from the fore coming rain. His eyes met hers for a moment, and he smiled graciously.

Miranda's breath caught. She couldn't speak. She shook her head of the cobwebs; surely, she'd been imagining it.

"Mir-randa? Is everything all right?"

The words stuck in her throat as she held onto his arm for support. She tried not to stare but couldn't help it. "See the man with Gemma. Her son, I heard them say." She swallowed audibly. "He looks exactly like my father."

Remare exhaled. "Your father was friends with Gemma."

"Over forty years ago, now. They took undergrad courses at Oxford. They were together for the summer."

Miranda remembered the picture of her father they'd found in Gemma's attic. Now, she wondered if it was her father or his son. "My God, I have a half-brother."

He studied the man. "Maybe."

"Remare. He has my father's smile. The way he walks. The way he runs his hand through his hair." Tears began to form in her eyes. She looked at his wife and his two female children. One had beautiful long blond hair and appeared to be around thirteen. The younger daughter with the dark hair couldn't stop fidgeting and seemed to be ten or eleven. Standing still was not her strong point. They reminded Miranda of Cassandra and herself when they'd been that age.

Part of her wanted to reach out and touch the younger girl's wavy hair. She knew it would be soft. She could hear the girl's voice; it was not unlike her own when she'd been that age.

"Do you want to talk to them?"

Miranda eyed Gemma, who looked solemn as she met Miranda's gaze. She clasped her hands together and raised two index fingers to her lips as if silently asking Miranda to refrain from saying anything, resist revealing the truth. Miranda wanted to meet them; the hollow part of her heart who yearned for a family demanded she walk over to them. All her adult life, she'd been an orphan, and now, only yards away were people who were her blood, her kin. All those years of feeling so desperately alone, cut off from others, came crashing into her.

But how could she invite them into her world? She thought of Esme, her friend who had tried to help her and died because of a cruel vampire lord. And a young blond Were, Dane, who'd given his life for her—murdered by the HOL. So much suffering, so much darkness. She would not endanger any of them.

She searched the area around them, wondering if any members of the HOL lurked nearby. Nothing seemed amiss. She gazed at the children, and a tear rolled down her cheek. Not only for the danger she had thrust on them, but for the undeniable knowledge she'd never see them, again. Never hear their laughter nor share in their joy. It would be too dangerous. She wouldn't risk it. Even if it tore her apart inside. She bowed to Gemma, who smiled graciously in her direction.

"We need to leave here," she said to Remare.

"Are you sure?"

"Yes." Her voice nearly hitched. "These people are innocent. I would destroy a family. They look happy together. More than likely, Gemma never told him of his real father. He may be better off not knowing." Though she was dying inside, she said, "I won't disrupt their harmony. They're safer this way."

Remare squeezed her hand. "It's your choice. Either way, I'll support your decision."

She glanced, one last time, at Gemma's family and the young girl with the chestnut hair. Her heart ached as if it were seared by a flaming arrow. The fates had been unusually cruel to have showed Miranda what she could never have. They were so close, within her grasp. She could practically smell the child's strawberry shampoo. But she wouldn't bring any more danger to them. They'd already lost their aunt. She would not be the cause of more suffering.

Resolved, she said, "Take me home."

Chapter Thirty-One

The ride down in the elevator to Valadon House was quiet. Remare had told Miranda Valadon and the Torians wanted to throw them a party, but being that they were all tired from jet lag, Remare suggested another time.

Miranda glanced at Tristan, who stood off to the corner. He still wasn't speaking much, and that concerned her. Remare said to give him time. She would. So would the others.

On the flight home, Tristan had sacked out on Remare's pull out bed in the back of his jet. When Orion, who had once been brutally attacked, saw how he curled in on himself, he switched to wolf form and put his paw over Tristan's arm. Tristan hadn't said anything, just petted his head. So, Orion jumped on the bed and lay beside him. That's what Weres did whenever a pack member was ill or had been injured. They offered comfort. She guessed Orion thought Tristan was pack.

Soon after, Bastien joined them on the bed and fell asleep as the others had. Miranda regarded the three handsome men as they slept. Each appeared young to her, brave and devoted to one another. Bound in loyalty, trust, and affection.

Remare had seen her studying the three while he sent Valadon his report of the previous events. After he closed his laptop, he held her from behind, holding his wrist loosely in one hand. Miranda had melted into his embrace. "They're wonderful men. I hope they all find the happiness we have."

He'd replied, "I think they already have." He kissed her temple. "If not, I have every faith they soon will."

Miranda had smiled. "They ate all the scones. I guess they were hungry." She'd forgotten how much Orion could eat and still not put on an ounce. At least he'd left her the apricot one. She'd shared it with Remare.

When the elevator dinged and the doors opened, House Valadon's reigning patriarch was there to greet them. His strength and love for them was a palpable thing.

"Welcome home." Valadon's soothing voice as melodic as always. But, as she met his emerald gaze, something made her hesitate. Valadon had never officially invited her to become a member of his house. Was she destined to always be an outsider?

She had wanted to stop in London at The Wanderer to say goodbye to the *Elementals*, but what would be the point? As far as they were concerned, she was outcast. No good would come from that. She considered looking for the *Dark Elemental* she'd met in the back alleyway. Let her know she wasn't the only one who was uninvited, alone. But the men were tired and had wanted to board the plane and go home. And so had she. Perhaps, sometime in the future, she would search out the *Dark Elemental*. Perhaps not.

Miranda went into Valadon's embrace, as did Remare, and breathed deep his oceanic and masculine scent. She realized, now, what had first attracted her to the vampire lord; he was the closest thing she had to a father figure. And his acceptance of her was important. "It's good to be home."

She'd thought she'd find something like home with the *Elementals*. She wasn't sure what she'd hoped for. A commonality, a sense of belonging. And, for a while, she'd found some sort of camaraderie. The feeling of being alone in the universe had abated. Somewhat.

Agatha had wanted her to join them to replace Vicky, the fire *Elemental* they'd lost, and mitigate Esme's loss, as well. It was a destiny denied. As much as Miranda had hoped for a tribe of her own, they weren't family and never would be.

The Weres and Lizandra had adopted her into their pack. She loved them dearly. But she wasn't a Were and had always felt like a distant cousin. Welcomed but not quite one of them. Orion was a Were, but he hadn't belonged, either. Seeing him with Bastien, she realized he'd found his home. And the other Torians had welcomed him into their fold. Happiness swelled in her heart for him. She hadn't realized just how raw and deep the need to belong was.

Until now.

Glancing up at Valadon's warm smile and linking her fingers with Remare's, she realized this was where she belonged. The vampires of House Valadon were her pack. And Remare was her mate.

"Go, get some rest. Your report was thorough. Any questions I have can wait until tomorrow." Valadon gestured for them to go to their rooms, then he hugged Bastien and Orion.

Katya embraced Tristan, the genuine affection between them obvious. Miranda hoped he found solace in her arms.

She heard words of comfort between Valadon and the others. They were home.

Remare held her hand as they made their way to his rooms. Once there, Remare closed the door behind them and kissed her so thoroughly it had her toes curling. "I have a surprise for you."

She grinned. "When did you have time to get me anything?"

"Before you left, actually. Come." He pulled her toward a door she hadn't seen before in his side wall."

"I don't remember this door being here before."

"It wasn't." He opened the door that connected one apartment to the other and flicked on the lights. "This is yours."

Miranda was speechless as she scrutinized the feminine touches. The apartment seemed to be a mirror copy of Remare's. But without the masculine black and blue décor or the Oriental flare. This apartment was lighter with shades of peach and deep tan. The carpeting was rust, similar to the floors she'd seen in New Mexico and had liked. The sofa and matching recliner were tan leather. "Why?"

"I don't like you living at your old house. I know you need time to adjust to being married. But I also know you need private space to get your work done, as do I. See the large bookcases along the wall? They're for all your art books." He pointed to a corner. "And that is your workspace, complete with computer. Both of us appreciate privacy when we work; now, neither one of us has to fear encroaching on the other's space."

Miranda liked the light color of the washed oak bookcases, desk and the leather chair. She couldn't hide her grin. The entertainment center was huge with a wide screen TV. "I can't wait to show Lizandra. You know we do movie night once a week. I'd love for her to come and watch. Orion, too."

He mocked being aghast. "Am I not invited?"

"Always." She moved farther into the room and up the two stairs to her bedroom. The bed had a tall canopy with four posters that held back gauzy drapes of dark peach. The duvet matched the drapes. "I love it."

"I'm glad." He stood beside her. "But I have one more surprise." He moved to the wall and pulled a sheet from a painting. "My wedding present to you."

Miranda's intake of breath was audible. "But how?"

"When we attended the underground auction, while searching for Brandon, I saw your reaction to this painting. I knew you wanted it but would never ask me for something you considered too expensive. I wanted you to have it, so I purchased it for you."

A while back, they had attended an affair upstate where they thought one of Valadon's missing paintings was going up for auction. It turned out Valadon had taken his own painting to give as a gift to the Madame Lord of Montreal. Miranda had been captivated by the painting now hanging before her. It was a scene of a party in a mansion from centuries ago. The colors, the figures were all outstanding, but what had caught her eye was the visage of Blu, aka Guy Montglat, and Felicity—her mentors and friends. "It's breathtaking. I don't know what to say. Do you recognize any of them?"

"Maybe one or two." He shrugged.

She pointed to Blu. "Montglat." She knew Remare hadn't trusted her great-grandfather, hadn't liked the idea of the vampire realm's leading spy being her relative.

He frowned. "So it is. I should have noticed sooner. He really is quite clever when it comes to disguises."

Miranda studied the scene more until she found another face she hadn't spotted when she first saw the painting. She hadn't met him until she'd been out in New Mexico. William. Like Blu, he was good at changing his face. In New Mexico, he had long black hair; in London, he had dark blond hair. In this painting, his hair was brown. *My, but you do get around!*

"You can change whatever furnishings you don't like. Move in any of your furniture from your house here or at my town house. The choice is yours."

She turned toward him. "You, sir, are a seducer."

He grinned. "And I don't even have to try very hard." He pointed to the lights over the door. "If you want privacy in which to work, leave on the red light, I'll know you're working. If you desire company, click on the green light."

"You are incredible." She circled her hands around his waist and kissed him. "Any more surprises?"

"Just one." He stood in the doorway between their suites and bent down on one knee. "For you." He opened a small black velvet jewelry box. "I know we never had the chance to be properly engaged. Now, we can be."

She thought he looked silly bending down on his knee. Remare didn't bow down to anyone. Except when Valadon had been made High Lord. She kneeled down near him and gawked at the ring. "It's a blue diamond. It's beautiful."

He slipped the ring on her finger. "I thought about what you said about us being married in Valadon's shadow. I agree." He pushed her hair back from her face. "If you wish, we'll have a new ceremony commemorating our vows."

"Oh, I wish, all right." She threw her arms around him and kissed him. "This time, I get to pick out the dress. Not sure what color I'll choose. Whatever I select, you'll like it. Something in the blue family, most likely."

His lips brushed over hers. "I'm sure I will."

"I want Orion to sing for us. And, this time, several of the Weres will be there."

"As it should be. Most people get engaged before the wedding. We're doing things a bit backward."

"I've never been a traditionalist."

His smile radiated warmth. "Neither have I. Together, we'll make our own traditions."

"Sounds good to me."

"So, where would you like to sleep tonight?" He gestured first to her room then his. "Your new room or in our other room?"

Before she'd left for London, she told him she wasn't ready to move in with him full time. To adjust, she'd stay a few days with him at his place and a few days at her own. She liked doing things in stages. To move in so suddenly without ever planning for it had grated.

Now, she was beginning to think otherwise.

She still couldn't let go of her parents' home. She wasn't ready for that, but maybe she'd only spend one day a week at her house. Or maybe once a month, until she moved in completely. And she would. Her future was written in his eyes. Remare was the destiny she'd chosen, and she was amazed at the rightness of her decision. They may not always get along, they'd have their differences of opinion, but at the end of the day, this is where she belonged.

She glanced back at the painting and then the room. "I'll need time to make it really mine. Let's sleep in your room."

"*Our* rooms, Mir-randa." He scooped her up and stood over the threshold. "I believe this is a human tradition."

She laughed. "It is. I never really understood why since the female has two good legs as well as the male. But it feels kinda nice." She massaged his nape then licked the vein that led from shoulder to head.

He growled seductively. "It's about to feel a good deal nicer."

***

In Sardinia, William Ryder Montglat walked down to the study and opened the doors to see his father behind his desk. "How's Mother doing?"

Guy de Montglat peered up from his laptop. "She's fine. Taking a stroll down by the water with Robert."

"And the fiend who hurt her?"

Montglat smirked. "I should think he will be suffering from excruciating migraines for some time to come."

Ryder thought Brandon deserved far worse for his mistreatment of Felicity and Miranda, but since Montglat had assured Lord Valadon he would keep his brother alive, he accepted his father's judgment. "May his torment be ever painful."

"It will be. Welcome home. Your trip?"

"Successful." Ryder poured himself a drink then sat in the chair facing his father. "Without competition from Acton for chancellor, it's a certainty Caltrone will be elevated."

Montglat smiled. "Or so he thinks."

"You were right about Miranda. Her powers have grown exponentially. In time, she will become a force to be reckoned with."

"As I had hoped she would." Montglat sat back in his chair and gazed outward at the blue waters of the Mediterranean. "She's opened one door, now. Life will become interesting when she opens the second one."

"And when will that be?"

"Soon. In the meantime, I want you in New York; keep an eye on Miranda and ValCorp while I conduct business from here. Is that amenable?"

Ryder grinned. "Yes, it is. I've grown fond of her." And a certain dark-haired spy Valadon had sent to Switzerland. There was something about Carla that had beckoned to Ryder. A Blueblood, for certain, but still…something else that warranted further looking into.

Oh, yes, he was planning on enjoying his sojourn in New York very much.

Epilogue

One week later

"I can't find it." The *Elemental* sighed as she searched the grounds of Agatha Winslow's Cranbrook home. "It has to be here somewhere."

"We've been searching for hours; it's not here." The vampire blew out a breath. "We waited too long. The others cleaned out everything before we got here."

"Keep looking."

"Seriously?!" The vampire exhaled. "You're never going to find it."

"Listen, Madame Lord, you owe me."

"Sure, that, again. I knew it was only a matter of time."

"It was your car that ran my parents' car off the road that killed them."

"I've told you repeatedly, *I* wasn't the one driving. It was a member of my entourage. He was punished for his recklessness. Severely. And, lest you forget, it was me who pulled you from the burning car. I would have rescued your parents, but the car burst into flames. There simply was no time."

"And my sister?" *The Elemental* sighed as she closed her eyes as if in painful memory.

"We searched for her, but by the time you woke and told us of her, the humans had already found her and taken her to the hospital."

"She was never supposed to be a part of this. Now, she knows. She has knowledge she shouldn't have."

"It's much too late for regrets."

"The planets are aligning. We won't see another confluence of energy like this for another century. Her powers will waken with a surge she may not be able to control. She'll be in danger."

"Relax, she's married to one of the world's most powerful vampires. He'll protect her. He's incredibly gifted and talented. Both now belong to House Valadon."

"A vampire. How the hell did that happen?"

"Don't be so stagy. There are vampires who also have *Elemental* gifts. You're looking at one of them, right now."

"You fed on me for years."

"That's not it, and you know it. At least I introduced you to others of your kind. Another would have drained you dry."

"Small mercies. He's going to try to turn her, isn't he?"

"I should think Remare won't wait long. They won't want her vulnerable. She'll be stronger as a vampire."

"I won't let that happen, Vivienna."

"I don't see how you can possibly stop it, Cassandra."

***

Miranda was in that quasi half-sleep consciousness when she felt Remare's fingers brush upward on her spine. They'd made love for hours in her new room's bed. The sheets were just as silky as those on his bed, but the peach ones seemed warmer. So did the hand that was tracing circles around her eagle tattoo. She could almost feel the feathers rustling where he touched it. She smiled at the caress. There were certainly benefits of being married to an amorous man. He made her feel things no one else could.

His hand drifted along her ribs to her ass, which he stroked then cupped.

Something was off. She knew Remare's scent, his touch. This felt different. Not threatening, but not him. Something strangely familiar. In the recesses of her mind, she tried to remember, tried to form a picture. She shook off the last vestiges of sleep and turned to the eagle/man over her. Shock and wonder had her screaming. *"William!"*

Laughter echoed in her mind. Whimsical, masculine, metaphysical. He'd sent his spirit out to her. Not to harm, not to alarm. But to remember.

She shrieked, *"No more dream walking!"* until the spirit dissipated.

Remare turned to her. "Who's William?"

Author's Note: If you enjoyed this story, please consider leaving a review at the vendor of your choice.

Thank You,
Diana

Coming Soon

Veil of Orion—Fall, 2019

Orion is one lucky werewolf. He's handsome, sexy, and his fame is soaring. He has more financial security than he's ever known traveling the world performing his music. He loves the stage and his fans adore him. Life is good. He should be ecstatic. But he's not. Loneliness grates. The one thing he doesn't have is the acceptance of the love of his life, his best friend, Bastien, who he just might have to give up his career to be with.

Sebastien de Rosemont is an Elite vampire operative who thrives on the adventurous and dangerous life of a Torian. That is until he realizes the charming and seductive werewolf, Orion, makes him feel more alive than any mission he's ever completed. Long ago he gave up his title and status as a vampire aristocrat to serve High Lord Valadon in New York. There was only one stipulation: He has to produce an heir. Now he must choose where his loyalty truly lies: With his lineage or with the one he loves.

Coming Soon

Veil of Honor—Fall, 2019

When his former mentor, Lord Huay lays dying, Remare is summoned back to Japan. When there, Huay exacts a risky promise from his protégé: See to it that his final wishes for his successor are carried out, a task Remare will find more complex than he could have imagined and extend his stay in Japan indefinitely. Huay's two sons will fight to the death for the chance to rule their empire, even if that means challenging Remare to a competition he can't possibly win.

Meanwhile, Miranda grows restless waiting for Remare to return. It's been weeks since he left for the funeral of a friend. How many ceremonies and formal banquets must he attend? Learning Huay's court is rife with dangerous politics and former allies who can't be trusted, she suspects Remare is being held against his will and requests the help of Lord Valadon to get Remare back. Valadon agrees, but at a cost. A high one as the honor of both houses is now at stake.

Diana Marik is the author of the Seven Deadly Veils Vampire Series. She grew up in New York City and has her MA in English Literature from Hofstra University. Before becoming an author, Diana worked as an educator, mental health therapist, yoga instructor and camp counselor.

Among Diana's passions, traveling is her favorite. One of her favorite places to visit is the American Southwest and her home away from home, New Orleans. When not writing, Diana loves discovering museums. In her leisure time, she enjoys going to the movies and hanging out with her friends.

Diana is currently at work on her latest novel in the Veilverse and would love to hear from her fans. She can be contacted at www.dianamark.com